Text copyright © 2019 by Amberley Faith
All rights reserved.

ISBN: 9781540567178

Published by Kindle Direct Publishing.

Cover design by Germancreative

# CONTENTS

This book is dedicated to the real-life small town (which shall remain nameless) that inspired Stusa. Thanks for letting me, albeit unknowingly, exaggerate your flaws and minimize your kindnesses.

Rural American struggles are real. I hope this book will shed some light on some of the most overlooked places in America. Stay strong, small towns!

# PROLOGUE

Nestled in a thickly wooded area, far away from the dirt roads, animal paths, and prying eyes that crisscrossed the area, the remnants of an old homestead rested amidst the undergrowth. A small fire burned in the crumbled remains of a chimney, its home long since decayed and vanished. A tiny, cast iron cauldron sat directly on the flames, wedged in between fallen bricks and chunks of deteriorating mortar.

Two girls wearing dark-colored, hooded cloaks tended the fire's hungry flames, feeding them small branches, dried leaves, and pinecones. A third girl, also wearing a hooded cloak - although hers was a violent shade of fuchsia - sat on a nearby log looking at her crystal-covered magenta cell phone.

"There is no service out here! I can't even send a text!" She groaned and looked up to see if anyone had heard her.

A fourth girl, keeping her face covered from view with her black hooded cloak, foraged through the undergrowth, moving in and out of the shadows while gathering bits and pieces of plants. She moved quickly and silently, so quietly that she liked to think of herself as nothing more than a shadow. She imagined herself floating along unnoticed, flickering in and out of view as the setting sun peeked its feeble rays through the dense leaves above.

*The Shadow* paused her search and responded, "We already discussed this! All of those modern conveniences you love so much interfere with the ritual." *The Shadow* turned to look at her. "So, turn off your cell phone *now* unless you want me to throw it in the fire."

While *The Shadow's* words were strong, her tone was

3

cool and even. The fire-tenders glanced at each other, silently communicating after years of practice, and wondered if the phone would indeed be tossed into the fire. The cell phone junkie openly regarded *The Shadow* for a moment and made her decision. She sighed loudly as she turned off her phone and stuffed the sparkly, pink device into her neon-pink backpack.

A fifth figure, obediently dressed in a dark cloak, watched the exchange from the edge of the clearing. She had already gathered what flowers and roots she needed but didn't want to take her place around the cauldron. The fire-tenders' ability to communicate silently unnerved her; she always got the feeling they were talking about her. She knew they didn't like her. She almost hadn't come when she found out they were. Her desperation, however, drove her to make her appearance at the last minute. It was weird, spooky even, showing up wearing nothing but the prescribed, hooded cloak at dusk.

As the two fire-tenders returned to their flames, *The Shadow* dropped to her knees to unearth one last root. Of the five, she was the only who understood the many native plants, herbs, and berries growing among the brambles and briars deep within the woods of rural America – plants that would serve her purpose, like the purple petals of the bee balm, or the pungent roots of the sassafras tree. She gathered the plant parts using her cloak as a basket and approached the cauldron.

"It is time."

The two fire-tenders and the cell phone junkie stood and formed a circle around the gently bubbling cauldron. The shy figure made her way cautiously to the circle and nudged herself in between the fire-tenders. She thought severing their physical connection might also break their mental one.

*The Shadow* handed each girl a different plant part; the first fire-tender received the flower-covered stalk of a fairy wand along with the white, tufted top of a thimble weed. The shy figure took out her twigs of cedar. *The Shadow* nodded approvingly and handed her a bit of sassafras root. The second fire-tender received a few white berries with black dots that marked them as doll's eyes along with the cone-shaped floral cluster of a scarlet-red Cherokee bean. The cell phone junkie was given a toothed, narrow leaf of horse mint and the distinctive palmate leaf of a green dragon.

As for *The Shadow*, she held the roots of three different plants – anise root, Indian cucumber root, and snake root. Each girl held the vegetation in her right hand as she touched both wrists to those of the girls on either side. Slowly, carefully, they rotated their circle counterclockwise around the crumbling chimney and cauldron. In unison, they recited.

> *Firm roots of power*
> *Strong stalks of love*
> *Burning flames below*
> *Fading sunlight above.*
> *Fine petals of beauty*
> *Sturdy leaves of wealth*
> *Harvested at half-moon's dawning*
> *Prepared in nature's stealth.*
> *Reveal to us your secrets*
> *Bestow your grace and charm*
> *Grant us what we humbly ask*
> *For we shall do no harm*
> *We shall do no harm*
> *We shall do no harm*

The first fire-tender tiptoed to the cauldron while the others repeated the last line again and again in quiet voices. As she approached, she stumbled over her cloak and almost dropped her flowers. She gasped but managed to right herself and regain her composure. She could not resist, however, taking a quick glance at *The Shadow's* face to check her reaction.

*The Shadow's* face was impassive, so the fire-tender swallowed and placed her stalks in the bubbling pot. She bellowed one loud, clear word, "Grace!" She had chosen her word carefully, deciding against ones like charm and elegance. *Grace* captured the poise she so desperately craved. She giggled and looked around at her twin expectantly.

The second fire-tender made it to the cauldron without mishap. She smirked at her sister who promptly returned a sneer. Satisfied that she had annoyed her sister, the second fire-tender took a deep breath and dropped her petals one by one into the mixture. As they fell, she shrieked, "Beauty!" She stared at the petals until they had disappeared into the frothing mixture and turned to give a nod to the shy one.

The shy one walked to the cauldron with surprising confidence and dropped in her twigs and roots. She inhaled and said, "Love!" She gave a slight nod to the cell phone junkie and returned to the circle.

The cell phone junkie strode to the cauldron without hesitation. She wadded her leaves into a small clump and threw it into the bracken-colored soup. When the ball of leaves hit the water, she screeched, "Money!" She looked over at her audience. Suddenly, laughter erupted from the four girls as they collapsed into a cackling heap, exhilarated by what they had just done.

*The Shadow*, ignoring them, stepped over the quartet of laughing bodies and squatted next to the simmering concoction. She placed her roots into the mixture one by one and whispered something, something that the giggling girls would try to remember afterwards to relive the melodramatic moment - something that sounded an awful lot like "Power."

When *The Shadow* finished, she pulled up the pile of laughing girls and made them circle up again and chant as the brew boiled. This time, they lifted their arms in the air and twirled as they rotated, cloaks flying and hoods falling back to reveal faces. The happy mood from the laughing pileup remained as they spun and swirled. The four girls let loose with the occasional whoop of glee. They felt the freedom of release and a wicked joy at being naughty, the liberating feeling of having broken the rules.

Amidst their celebration, the sun continued to sink lower and lower, the clearing lighted only by the orange fire that burned under the kettle. As the girls continued to spin, *The Shadow* stepped away from the group to the edge of the clearing. She thought she sensed a presence, but was it an animal or something more dangerous? She tilted her head and peered into the darkness.

"Everyone, stop! I need to hear!" She called out to the group of cloaked girls.

"Oh! She needs to *hear*. Let's all quiet down, then." The second fire-tender managed to call out in between bouts of laughter.

"Yeah, I'm sure there's a lot to listen to out here in the middle of the woods, miles away from civilization." The cell phone junkie added, rolling her eyes.

The shy one stopped abruptly, however, wondering what *The Shadow* was listening for. She shielded her eyes from the light of the fire and stared into the woods. She saw a glint of light at the exact same moment *The Shadow* yelled, "Run!"

The girls stopped dancing and looked over to see what was happening. *The Shadow* had already crossed the clearing and headed into the opposite side of the forest. She was running at full speed and seemed to melt into the forest. By the time the other girls saw the figure of a man, they were in full panic mode, screaming and tearing into the forest as fast as their bare legs could carry them.

The cell phone junkie realized she was an easy target, dressed as she was in vivid pink. She kicked up her speed and ran faster than she ever thought possible. She passed the other three girls and reached the cover of the forest. She didn't look back. She ran as deep into the woods as she could and hid behind a giant water oak when she ran out of breath.

Both twins, even the clumsy one, managed to pass the shy one and sprinted through the forest together. They had instinctively grabbed hands as they took off running so as not to be separated, and they ran into the forest, heading for what they hoped was the dirt road where they'd left their car.

The shy one, realizing she was last and the most likely to get caught, put on an extra burst of speed and threw herself into the forest in another direction from the twins, hoping that her pursuer would choose to follow them instead. Was she being chased? She didn't take time to look back. She thought she recognized the jacket the figure wore; one of her uncle's hunting jackets. She couldn't let him find her like this. He most certainly would *not* find it amusing. Being the holy roller he was, he'd probably think she had joined some cult.

The terror of him finding her half-dressed and chanting around a kettle in the dark sent her into another burst of panic-driven speed. She struggled through the dense undergrowth as roots and limbs grabbed at her, trying to prevent her escape. She pushed through, fighting to maintain her pace.

A large limb caught her cloak. She didn't take time to get untangled, and as she continued at her frantic pace, her cloak ripped off and fell to the ground. She wriggled clear of it without breaking her stride, crouching protectively as she ran. She couldn't let anyone see her now, stark naked except for her shoes and tearing through the forest as if her life depended on it.

She saw a spot in the forest that was darker than the rest. It seemed to suck up all the light. A hole, a cave. She dove in headfirst without hesitation, images of crash landing into a bear's den or a nest of snakes flashing through her mind. She gritted her teeth and prepared to land. She knew without a doubt that facing whatever animals inside would be easier than facing her uncle if he found her.

"They believed, in short, that they held in their steady hands the candle that would light the world. We have inherited this belief, and it has helped and hurt us."

- ARTHUR MILLER, FROM "AN OVERTURE," ACT ONE, THE CRUCIBLE

# CHAPTER ONE

*PURSUING PARADISE*

Ellie Pelletier sat on the front porch in her swing, laptop resting on her thighs, sipping a tall glass of her homemade lavender lemonade, fanning away gnats. She'd just finished planting her very first garden. It was small and only contained a few herbs: lavender, basil, anise, and her favorite – mint. She adored fresh mint leaves; there was nothing as refreshing on a hot day than a cool drink with a sprig of mint, and it was plenty hot here. Ellie added mint leaves to anything and everything - tea, water, lemonade, soft drinks, and on a difficult day - vodka.

For such a tiny garden, Ellie was surprised at the amount of work it took to prepare the soil, plant the seedlings, and water the tender plants. In the heat of summer, she had arisen early to work during the coolest part of the day. Although the plot was small, she was proud of her accomplishment.

She vowed to care for the little garden, watering and weeding it daily, in order to realize her longtime dream of preparing her own herbal creations from scratch. She knew exactly where she would start - with her signature lavender lemonade. She wasn't sure if she could grow lemons in this new climate, but she was confident that she could grow her own culinary-grade lavender for her favorite handcrafted drink.

After ten years in the big city, Ellie and her husband had decided to move their two kids and two dogs to the country.

Méline was their nine-year-old daughter, shy and sweet. Méline had long, honey-colored hair; it was in between brown and blonde. It blended beautifully with her light-brown skin. Her golden eyelashes, light brown eyes, and sun-streaked hair gave her the warm look of a sun-kissed summer's day. Ellie wanted Méline to break out of her shyness; she hoped moving to a small town would ease Méline into her pre-teen years and further.

Bibianne, on the other hand, was about as shy as their bounding, playful Labrador puppy, Dédé. Bibianne and Dédé went everywhere together, and neither of them ever met a stranger. Bibianne's complexion was darker than her sister's. If Méline was *café au lait*, Bibianne was caramel macchiato - not quite mocha, but a dark French roast - as Ellie liked to tease. Bibianne's hair was a rich chestnut color with a fair amount of red in it. Ellie supposed that came from her side of the family, along with the sprinkling of tiny freckles scattered across Bibianne's nose and cheeks. Bibianne was playful, mischievous, and charming. She would have no problem making friends in their new hometown.

When Ellie and Julien decided that they wanted more room, less crime, and less rush, they sold their city home and moved to a rural area in a state further south than either one had ever traveled. They purchased an old farmhouse, twenty miles outside the nearest town, and began job-searching. Ellie had found another teaching job on the same day that she submitted her application.

Julien quit his corporate job, cashed in his stock options, and purchased an old building in the quaint downtown area where he planned to pursue his true passion – photography. Once the building was renovated, his workshop would be the first professional photography studio in their new community of Stusa.

Ellie looked forward to finishing the refurbishment of the farmhouse. Besides being tired of living with half-finished projects, she was eager to start planning French lessons for her new students. She hoped to inspire them, as she had in her big city school, with her near-native French abilities.

Ellie had always loved the French language; it was her whole world. The food, the culture, the music, the people, and the language itself had inspired her not only to enroll in French classes in high school, but to spend her college years as an exchange student on the French half of the Caribbean Island of St. Martin. That decision had changed the course of her life; while studying there, she met the man of her dreams – Julien Pelletier.

Julien had been the bartender at *Le Chemise*, her favorite island beach bar overlooking the western coast. It had open air seating and large, colorful swaths of fabric shading its patrons from the afternoon sun. It was the perfect place to unwind after a day of studies and to watch the beautiful island sunsets. On one particularly memorable visit, Julien had given Ellie one of the bar's specialty drinks, homemade mint-infused rum. She had been absolutely bewitched, and not just by the drink.

In fact, one of the next things Ellie planned to try, after her homegrown lavender lemonade, was to recreate the mint-infused rum. It would be a romantic surprise for Julien on the night of his studio opening. She knew it would remind him of their time on the island and the first time they realized they were more than just friends. The circumstances were quite memorable.

College-aged Ellie had gone to the bar by herself that night. While she told herself that she mainly went to watch the sunset, some part of her had to admit that she also loved to watch the bartender whom she had mentally nicknamed Caribbean Crush. She hadn't yet worked up the nerve to say anything to him more than meaningless chatter. She planned to work up the courage to engage him in real conversation.

Ellie was enjoying her time on the island and knew that her French was good; she had been mistaken for a local on three separate occasions and was feeling cocky. She sat at the bar and asked for the traditional *chiquetaille de morue* on a bed of *avocat féroce* and a water. She didn't think the fruitiness of famous *Le Planteur*, or guava berry drink, would go very well with her meal, plus it made her look like a tourist, and she wanted Caribbean Crush to think of her as a long-term visitor, not just another tourist.

Ellie knew a little about him. Julien was working his way through college, studying at the American University of the Caribbean on the Dutch side of the island and bartending at *Le Chemise* on the French side. He had asked her about her work; it had been difficult for her to get a position due to the limited number of schools on the island. Ellie, too, was working her way through college. In addition to her scholarship, she assisted the English professor at a small private *école*, and took classes most evenings, working on a double major in foreign language and education.

As Ellie was taking her first bite of the creole-style dish, a glimpse of someone standing just behind her right shoulder startled her. Ellie hadn't heard anyone approach; she merely caught a flash of color in her peripheral vision. Ellie turned and recognized her at once. Madame Margaux had appeared out of nowhere.

Madame Margaux smelled of jasmine and patchouli and was quite the local celebrity. She was a dark-haired, heavy-set woman dressed in a skirt made entirely of scarves. The sheer pieces of fabric were blowing in the wind, and her olive-toned skin was smooth and beautiful except for the corners of her mouth and eyes, where deep lines marked her many years. She was widely rumored to be a descendent of the heir to Château Margaux, the famous winery in the Bordeaux Region of France.

Startled to find Madame Margaux hovering at her side, Ellie sputtered her drink and jumped. Ignoring Ellie's shock, Madame grabbed Ellie's hands, stretched out her palms, and examined them briefly. Then, with Julien watching, she kissed Ellie on both cheeks and whispered something to Ellie in French. What Ellie understood Madame to say in her throaty, unfamiliar French dialect must have been some type of riddle.

When she kissed Ellie's right cheek, Madame Margaux intoned that Ellie would marry Caribbean Crush and have two children. Crazy enough, because they were not even dating, but when Madame kissed Ellie's left cheek, her voice became about an octave lower -- deep, gravely, gruff. Ellie was never sure if she'd understood Madame's words clearly because they held no meaning for her.

Ellie heard Madame garble, *"quand les gens bourdonnent comme des moucherons, ne perdez pas la foi, vous allez survivre le creuset"* which Ellie roughly translated as "When the people buzz like insects, don't lose faith; you will survive the crucible."

After the strange pronouncement, Ellie felt slightly dazed. For a moment Ellie just stared at Madame. A whirlwind of thoughts flew through Ellie's mind at once, scrambling her brain and preventing her from thinking clearly. Ellie was shocked at Madame Margaux's boldness in approaching her. Wasn't she supposed to entertain tourists who wanted a glimpse of the island's colorful superstitions? Ellie had not asked for a palm reading or ever expressed any interest in fortune-telling. In fact, it had always frightened her.

Why, then, did Madame approach Ellie? Ellie hoped she didn't look like the stereotypical tourist. The day before, a tourist had asked Ellie for directions in his patchy French, and Ellie had been thrilled to be mistaken for a local.

Ellie wondered if Madame was trying to scare Ellie and make her see that she would never fit into Madame's people, her culture, her island. Ellie, however, thought that tactic wouldn't help Madame Margaux earn her living. Madame wouldn't be endearing her clientele if she continued scaring customers. After all, Madame's livelihood depended upon the tourists' wallets.

Nevertheless, seconds after the initial shock wore off, Ellie decided she would help fund Madame's odd lifestyle; poor old lady was probably lonely. Ellie looked down to get a few coins from her bag. She would be a good sport.

When Ellie looked up to hand over the coins, Madame was gone. It spooked Ellie. That was the second time in five minutes that Madame had snuck in and out of Ellie's proximity. How could she do that with all the tinkling earrings, beads, and bangles she wore?

Ellie's face must have revealed her shock because Caribbean Crush brought her a shot of mint-infused rum, on the house, and told her to sip it slowly. After she had finished, Julien asked if she felt better. Ellie gave a nervous chuckle, "How did you know mint's my favorite?"

He flashed a white-toothed smile that dazzled against his dark skin and said, "Well, you looked like you needed to clear your mind, and mint is known for helping with that. My *grand-mère* taught me about it when I was little."

"Does it work?" Ellie asked.

"My *grand-mère* was originally from Barbados and a bit eccentric to put it nicely." He said with a wink. Was Caribbean Crush flirting with her? His French was just as beautiful as he was. She inhaled, breathing in the scent of him mixed with the smell of the mint infusion.

"Well, I do feel better," Ellie responded with her head down, still gazing into the shot glass, "and I happen to love studying various uses of herbs, so your *grand-mère* seems like a very wise woman to me." She didn't move her head but raised her eyes to look at him from underneath her lashes. She was horrified to feel a heavy blush creeping up her neck, rapidly heading for her ears and face.

"Hey, it's okay." He reached over and gave her forearm a slight squeeze. "You don't have to be embarrassed."

*Oh, God. He noticed me blushing.* She focused all her might on trying to push the blush back down under her shirt where he couldn't see it.

"Madame Margaux can be somewhat *glauque*, but she really is harmless." He cocked his head to one side as he started wiping the bar. "What did she say to you, anyway?"

Her blush deepened. Ellie couldn't tell him what Madame had said to her since it was about *him*, so she simply replied, "Umm -- my overactive imagination was probably getting the best of me. Again. I thought she said something about buzzing insects and surviving a crucible."

But Ellie hadn't imagined it. Madame's warm, breathy whisper had tickled Ellie's ear. Her voice still echoed in Ellie's head. Caribbean Crush looked at her with a slight frown. He seemed to know Ellie was lying. Ellie knew she still looked scared and was trying to rearrange her face to seem braver than she felt.

Caribbean Crush stopped wiping the bar and stared into her eyes for a moment. Then he took her hand and said, "Well, if she frightened you, I'd be glad to walk you home. My shift ends in a half hour. Would you allow me to escort you?"

Ellie's heart fluttered, and her stomach flipped. She thought for a minute. She didn't want to seem like a coward, but if he was offering, how could she resist?

"I'd like that very much, if you're sure it's not too much trouble. And I think I'd like another one of these, please." She handed him her empty shot glass.

That walk turned out to be the best walk of her life. Along the way, Ellie confessed part of what Madame had said in her gravelly voice.

"It was really strange. Madame said that when the people 'buzzed like insects' for me not to lose faith, that I would 'survive the crucible.' But," Ellie added, "I have no idea what that means. I was unnerved by the whole incident."

And then, laughing, Caribbean Crush scooped Ellie up in his caramel-brown arms and told her that he'd protect her from all the scary fortune tellers on the island and leaned in to kiss her. Ellie may have been a little off kilter from fear and rum, but she allowed herself the luxury of believing him.

# CHAPTER TWO

## INTERNET INSTALLED

Before Ellie realized it, nearly the entire summer had passed since *the big move*. She and Julien had been so busy painting, sanding, and installing that they hadn't had time to miss their iPhones. It was a good thing, too, since there was barely any cell phone service in Stusa. Who knew there were still places in America rural enough to avoid cell phone service?

Ellie chuckled to herself as she posted her first blog entry since the move. Her teacher blog enjoyed a small following of fellow French faculty, but they would be flabbergasted when they read this week's post. Most readers knew of her relocation, but they never imagined a place so remote that internet was only available through satellite. Although the Pelletiers had managed to get the farmhouse set up with satellite internet access two days prior, a series of thunderstorms had blocked the signal completely, and Ellie had not been able to update her blog. She was eager to get back to her readers.

Despite the weather-dependent internet connection, living the sweet life outside of Stusa thrilled Ellie. She couldn't wait to tell her readers about the locals who came by every few days to invite her to church. No matter how many times she explained they were happy members of a Catholic church miles away, locals insisted on trying to convince her to "give their church a try."

Especially Lydia Bennett and Luella Baxter - twin sisters who had both married preachers. Mr. Bennett was the minister of the local Methodist church, and Mr. Baxter was the preacher of the Church of God Assembly. Lydia and Louella seemed to have a running rivalry to see who could convert Ellie's family first.

Most of the visitors shared local gossip. Lydia explained why Stusa had such spotty cellular coverage. Landowners were fighting over where the lucrative tower would be built. Louella painted a less-than-flattering portrait of the school superintendent, who also doubled as the pastor of the First Baptist Church of Stusa.

Apart from the interfering church ladies and the lack of cell service, Ellie was enjoying their new home. She chose to look at both issues as quaint advantages - reliance on people rather than on technology. She had always been a fan of Thoreau and his *Walden Pond* experiment. She felt that this was her chance to live the modern version of his foray into *simplifying*. It was all part of her new outlook on life: less traffic, less rush, less crime, less worries, and now - less cell phones.

As she blogged about her new home place, Ellie couldn't work up any jealousy of her tech-savvy readers. She was blogging from her laptop sitting on the front porch swing. The girls were playing in the front yard. Ellie was sipping another freshly made glass of lavender lemonade. Julien was taking photographs to document the renovation.

Fanning away a few gnats that persisted despite her ceiling fan, Ellie returned to her blog, informing her readers that the superintendent had called her that morning to welcome her to his school district. They'd chit-chatted for a few moments until he finally talked himself right up to the point of the call; he asked Ellie to take the proficiency exam for English Language Arts. If Ellie passed the exam, he explained, the school would reimburse her for the cost of the test, and she would be certified to teach English and French. He said that the school needed to assign Ellie one English class in addition to her five French classes.

Ellie wasn't sure what teaching English would be like, but she couldn't turn down the superintendent. He was, after all, the preacher of the local church. Ellie thought she had probably scared him a little when she told him they were Catholic. She'd better start proving that she could fit in. She agreed to his proposal and prepared to take the exam the following week.

Anyway, she loved reading and blogging, so how hard could teaching one English class be?

# CHAPTER THREE

## *PREPLANNING PICKLE*

As summer vacation drew to a close, Ellie and her family settled into their mostly renovated farmhouse. School started early in Stusa. August first meant two things: the return of lesson-planning, and temperatures well into the nineties by nine o'clock in the morning. Since Ellie and the girls didn't have much vacation time left, and the blistering temperature severely limited outdoor activities, they were all three looking forward to getting back to school. Ellie was eager to meet her new students and to bring some *joie de vivre* into their French lessons.

Ellie was curious to hear how her students would address her; since arriving in Stusa, Ellie had been called everything from Mrs. Peleteer (as in Musketeer) to Mrs. Payluhtay (as hooray) instead of the proper French pronunciation "Peh leh tee ay". Ellie was sure her *nom de famille* had never had quite so many variations. It was endearing.

She wondered if Julien (Zhoo lee ehn) would become plain old Julian, although he could use his nickname - Jules. That ought to be easy for the locals. And their girls Méline and Bibianne. Perhaps they would go by their nicknames, too – Mel and Bibi – even though their names weren't too unusual.

As the last days of July progressed in afternoons of running under the sprinkler and playing board games under the porch fans, Ellie prepared for her new job. Julien took a break from renovations to keep the girls entertained for the week of

Ellie's preplanning. Ellie loaded her SUV with all the teacher materials she'd brought from her previous position.

Ellie awoke energized and enthusiastic on the first day of teacher planning. She added a dash of vanilla to her cinnamon-sprinkled cappuccino and drank it on the front porch watching the sunrise. After she was dressed and ready, she grabbed her keys, dipped her middle finger in the *benetier* by the door, crossed herself, and said a quick prayer as she headed off to her new job.

She arrived early, got her key and room assignment, and went straight to her classroom. As she placed the key in the lock, she read the door tag.

Mrs. Pelletier – Room 9

Miffed at the misprint, she had specifically requested *Madame* Pelletier, she decided not to let it bother her. She was the new kid on the block, after all. She couldn't go around demanding every wish be granted.

Ellie continued unloading her car until she had arranged her classroom. Her lamps and scarves created the perfect ambiance for learning French. Ellie's classroom ended up looking a lot like the café on St. Martin. Well, except for the gnats. *Le Chemise* never had a problem with gnats like Stusa did. That ocean breeze managed to blow away anything uncomfortable, from gnats to nightmares.

Later, there was a long faculty meeting with the Reverintendent, Ellie's private nickname for the shifty-looking superintendent who was also a pastor. The meeting was filled with prayers, prayer lists, and prayer requests. In between names, Ellie sensed an oncoming attack by the determined-looking group of ladies approaching her, so she rashly inserted herself between Lydia and Louella, who were also co-presidents of the PTA. With frown lines creasing their caked-on makeup, the group swept past her and onto their next victim.

Instead of starting with school business, the Reverintendent opened the faculty meeting with prayer. Ellie started to squirm, but no one else reacted. Separation of church and state did not exist in Stusa. Pondering the fine line the super-intendent/pastor must have to walk, Ellie didn't bow her head in prayer. Noticing, Lydia put her hand on Ellie's shoulder.

"Well, sweetie, *I* will pray for you." Oh well. She'd take all the prayers she could get.

At the close of the meeting, the secretary distributed schedules and rosters. When Ellie looked down, she was thunderstruck to see that she was listed as the new *English* teacher. All her classes were English classes with *no French classes*! Her right hand made the sign of the cross before she registered the stares.

*No wonder they didn't put Madame Pelletier on my door!* She huffed as she rushed to the office to find out what had happened. Principal Danvers told Ellie that the current French teacher hadn't retired as planned. They needed Ellie to fill in as an English teacher since she passed the English certification exam.

"Don't worry," Principal Danvers said. "You'll get to teach French classes again as soon as Frenchie retires. Ever'body here starts out as an English teacher until the spot they really want opens up." Ellie was too overwrought to respond, so he continued.

"In the meantime, though, do your best with these American Literature classes. Each student you're teaching has several standardized tests to be eligible for graduation. There's the HSWT, the HSGT, and the EOC. Most of these kids are juniors, too, so they'll also be taking the SAT and the ACT at some point during the year, and I'm sure you know how important these high stakes tests are. You need to make sure all your students do well so that our school doesn't do poorly in our AYP report. Don't look so worried." He clapped Ellie on the shoulder. "You'll be fine." As he started towards his office, he left her with his favorite advice, "Just do what ya' gotta do!"

Ellie stood in place for a moment, speechless. English all

day? Sure, Ellie loved to read, write and blog, but what about all those tests? She didn't even know what the acronyms he'd hurled at her meant. Apart from a final exam, she'd always done pretty much as she pleased in her French classes.

*What am I going to do?* She asked herself. *Classes start Friday – four days from now. And I have no idea what I've gotten myself into.*

# CHAPTER FOUR

## *THE SHADOW*

As she snapped the leaves off the dandelion stalks and placed them in a sieve, *The Shadow* wondered for the dozenth time if her groupies would be adequate for the task. Had she at last found the necessary participants? Even though the near discovery in the woods a few months ago had scattered and scared her flock, the ritual was complete. The fire-tenders had performed tolerably, if not elegantly. The cell phone junkie was a bit of a concern; she was biddable, though, and *The Shadow* thought that quality alone made up for her annoying flair for drama.

As for the shy one, *The Shadow* had doubled back and followed her to find out if her suspicions were correct. *The Shadow* discovered that the shy one, too, must have suspected her uncle of being the unwelcome intruder. Why else would she have spent the night holed up in that dank, dark cave? *The Shadow* had waited patiently, and just before dawn, when it was still too dark for anyone to see her stark nakedness, she saw the shy one leave the cave and make her way back to her uncle's house.

The shy one's stealth impressed *The Shadow*; she'd underestimated the shy one's ability to sneak around. *The Shadow* watched as the shy one crawled in through her bedroom window, threw on a nightshirt, and crawled into bed. About five minutes later, the shy one's uncle opened the door, studied his niece's supposedly sleeping face, and then announced that breakfast was ready.

*The Shadow* crept through the home's boxwood hedge until she had a view of the kitchen table. The reverend had laid out a breakfast spread that made *The Shadow's* empty stomach growl. There were scrambled eggs, cheese grits, biscuits, and white gravy with sausage crumbles. *The Shadow* watched and waited while the shy one tore into her breakfast with a decidedly unfeminine gusto. She, too, must have been starving.

When the shy one had drained her glass of milk, the reverend launched his sly attack. He cleared his throat, *hnh hmm*. "Where were you last night, niece? I checked your room before I went out hunting, and it was empty."

"Oh," she wiped her mouth with her napkin and finished chewing, stalling. "I was out with a few friends. We went looking for leaf specimens for botany. Mrs. Sarka wants us to bring in original samples for extra credit on our exam today." The shy one rolled her eyes in feigned exasperation. She continued.

"Somebody had the brilliant idea of going to this old abandoned home site where we'd find the best samples." The shy one continued spinning her tale. "I didn't really care if the leaves were the best. I just wanted to get my homework done, and I didn't want to go by myself." She was gaining momentum. The shy one was enjoying the story she was improvising.

*The Shadow* studied the reverend's reaction to the shy one's carefully crafted lie. He closed his eyes briefly and swept a hand through his hair. The look of relief that crossed his face was followed by a quick wrinkling of his brow.

"Well, that explains it. I think I..." He cleared his throat again. He stood up and walked toward the window, so *The Shadow* hugged the side of the house to avoid notice. "I think maybe I...*hhn hmm*, walked up on your group last night and scared everyone. Girls took off running and screaming before I could explain who I was."

"Oh my God! That was you?" The shy one deftly changed

the focus of the conversation. She put her hand to her chest, breathing hard, cleavage heaving. "We were terrified thinking it was the boogey man or some escaped convict or worse. Good God, you nearly scared us to death!" Her country twang was more pronounced with each heave of her bosom.

*The Shadow's* respect grew as the shy one manipulated the conversation, putting the focus and blame on her uncle rather than on her group. The reverend interrupted.

"Do not use the Lord's name in vain in my house, missy!" He turned from the window to face his niece. "Do you think I wasn't shocked at what I saw? I never expected to find a group of girls dancing around a fire in the moonlight! I..." He hesitated. "*Hnh Hmm.*" He took a deep breath and looked right into his niece's eyes. "I thought I saw someone naked." He paused. "I found this lying on the ground." He lifted a brown-hooded cloak with a tear along the side.

His niece blinked in rapid succession. "No one was naked, uncle. I don't know what you saw, but it wasn't anyone running around undressed. Why would anybody take off their clothes in the middle of the woods?"

"What about the fire and the dancing, then?" Her uncle began to pace. "I did see that through the trees. The firelight is what got my attention in the first place." Her uncle stopped pacing, narrowing his eyes at her.

"Well, okay!" She pushed her chair back from the table. "If you must know, we were scared out in the middle of nowhere. The twins built a fire, and we started singing and laughing. We got caught up in the moment and ended up dancing around the fire. Truth be told, we were glad not to be in the dark anymore!" She spat this at him as if it were none of his business and turned her head away from him.

He sat down again across the table from her. "Look at me." She looked up at him again, arms crossed across her chest.

"Was there any alcohol at your little party?" Her uncle asked. "Was anyone smoking dope? I see no other reason to carry on in the cover of darkness so far away from town."

"How dare you!" Her eyes narrowed. "No one was drinking or smoking!"

Her uncle put his elbows on the table and rested his forehead in his hands. When he looked back up at her he said, "You do know there is a faction against me, right? If they got word of this, they would force me out of town by the end of the week. I cannot afford even the suggestion of impropriety! Now, I ask you again. Were there drugs or alcohol?"

"No, uncle. Your name is still good." She grimaced. "I haven't done anything to tarnish your sterling reputation. You're the only one who has accused me of anything!"

"Do you blame me for asking?" He sighed. "Do you think I don't understand temptation? That my position protects me from it?" He looked at her quizzically and changed tactics.

"I have given you all the freedom a pastor can give a teenager. I have housed, clothed, and fed you these last five years since both your mother and my wife died in that horrible accident." He stopped walking and turned to her. "And this is how you repay me? By inviting scandal into my house? By going out into the woods with your friends and acting like heathen?"

She immediately turned on him. "Do you begrudge me the room and board? Is that what this is about? Or are you tired of raising a teenager? It's obvious you don't know what you're doing. No wonder you and my aunt never had children!"

This was too much for the reverend. He jumped up from the table and looked as if he would hit her. At that moment, *The Shadow* decided to intervene. She ran to the door and pounded on it.

When the reverend opened it, his face was mostly composed. He had neatly rearranged his features into an early morning half-smile. Perhaps the ability to deceive ran in the family.

"Yes, dear? What brings you here so early? Is there some emergency?" He asked.

"I wanted to give your niece these." *The Shadow* handed

over a basket of leaves. She clasped her hands behind her back, twisting at the waist, swinging back and forth and said, "She forgot them in the woods last night, and I knew she'd need them. We get extra credit for each specimen we turn in with our final exam."

She stopped her girlish swaying and continued before he could reply. "Okay, well, have a good morning." She added quickly. "Sorry to bother you so early!" She winked at the shy one and ran off before either of them could lift their jaws from the ground.

*The Shadow* finished rinsing some wild berries. Nearly two months had passed since that night in the forest. Now that school was starting again, she considered her plan. Of all the girls in Stusa, she had chosen the four whose desires best matched her own. Her groupies were driven to succeed at any cost, as was *The Shadow*.

After adding the berries to her granola, she tasted it. She added some crumbled bacon and continued thinking, planning her next move. After all, her own mother had spent years trying to find it without any luck. *The Shadow* felt it was her turn to try. She would succeed where her mom failed.

Although *The Shadow* had never gotten an honest answer about who her father was, she did manage to scrape together the story of the missing family heirloom. Her mother rarely talked about it which made *The Shadow* more eager to discover it her for herself. *The Shadow* surmised early on that her mother wanted all the glory for herself and was unwilling to turn the quest over to her daughter.

From what *The Shadow* could piece together, their family had been searching for it for centuries. *The Shadow* remembered her grandmother, Grandma Abby or Gabby, who had lived with them until she died. Gabby had reminisced aloud about the missing heirloom and the riches it would bestow on their family when discovered.

The memories were seared into *The Shadow's* heart as if they had been branded there. Gabby's death was what prompted *The Shadow* to strike out on her own. Her grandmother had been the only good part of her childhood. She cherished the memory of her grandmother sitting by the constant fire, working on pieces of fine, delicate lace and telling stories. When she was very young, *The Shadow* had only thought of Gabby's stories as fairy tales. But as she grew older, she began to wonder if Gabby had been deliberately guiding her.

Gabby's most enticing stories always revolved around the heirloom. Gabby spoke of her travels with Lia, *The Shadow's* mother, and the bitterness of disappointment that consumed Lia after so many years of failing to find the heirloom. It seemed that her family had always traveled around the country looking for it. Legend said it had been stolen from a slave by a relative in the 1600s, and then hidden away; the family had been searching for it ever since.

At the age of sixteen, *The Shadow's* mother died in a farming accident, and *The Shadow* used the opportunity to disappear from public records. She took the cash her mother kept hidden under the floorboards of their old home and headed south. She went by a new last name and found that it wasn't hard to live off the grid. After her family's nearly four hundred years of searching, *The Shadow* was determined to find the heirloom. It would be hers and hers alone.

Eventually, *The Shadow* landed in Stusa. Even after only a few months there, she grew sick of the small town and all its stereotypical residents, but a few clues led her to believe she was closer than ever to locating the missing family heirloom. And if that weren't incentive enough, a new family moved into the community, a family with a disturbing aura. As *The Shadow* enjoyed her salty-sweet granola, she wondered if that aura would be as easy to manipulate as her groupies were.

*Well*, she thought, *there was only one way to find out.* A few pointed suggestions placed among the right people ought to do the trick. She would also need to silence her groupies. She couldn't risk them blabbing about the ritual they had performed months earlier.

The shy one would be easy to control after that scene with her uncle. The twins and the cell phone junkie, however, might need a little reminder of why they were nervous around *The Shadow* in the first place. As her thoughts raced, she bit into a berry that wasn't quite ripe; it was startlingly sour, yet sweetly satisfying at the same time. Just like her plans for Stusa.

# CHAPTER FIVE

## CLASSES COMMENCE

Ellie's pre-planning flew by in a flurry of activity, and before she knew it, the first day of school had arrived. Ellie crossed herself with holy water as stepped out of the front door and onto the front porch where an unwelcome scene greeted her. Her garden had withered in the August heat. The lavender stalks had dropped nearly all their fragrant blossoms, and brown, crispy mint leaves looked as if they'd been set on fire. Her shoulders sagged.

This was no time for negativity, however. She straightened her shoulders. The first day of school was about making a good impression, and she would be all smiles and silver linings even if it made her cheeks ache and teeth dry out. Her little garden might be floundering, but she would flourish. She aimed a well-practiced, welcome-to-my-class smile at her garden plants and told them, "I know it's been a tough, hot, summer, but we can thrive here!" She blew the plants a kiss. "I'll give you some attention when I get home."

An hour later found Ellie in the middle of introducing herself to her first period students, giving her spiel about expectations and procedures. She was mid-sentence when a muscular student sauntered up to the front of the classroom.

Ellie stopped speaking mid-sentence, shocked and distracted by his arrogance. He stood directly in front of her, blocking her view of most of the class and blurted out something unintelligible. Ellie's face reflected her shock. She hesitated for half a second.

"I beg your pardon?" It was all that occurred to her.

"I kygo see coh," Muscles repeated. Ellie furrowed her brow, curiosity replacing the shock she'd felt. She asked him to repeat himself.

"I kygo see coh." Muscles repeated.

Ellie begged his pardon, again. Muscles was repeating himself for a third time when it began to dawn on Ellie that he was saying he "could go see coach." Ellie repeated the statement aloud and then looked to the class for help with the translation. They stared back at her, waiting.

Clearly, this was some sort of new-teacher test. Well, she would show them she could handle it. The first challenge to her authority, and it wasn't even second period yet. Ellie knew to tread carefully. She needed to show Muscles that she was in charge without backing him into a corner.

Ellie decided on honesty. She cleared her throat and said, "I don't understand. Are you *asking* me to leave class, or are you *telling* me you're leaving without permission?"

Muscles wrinkled his brow and lifted one corner of his upper lip. He looked at her like she was from Mars, and they stood there for what felt like an eternity staring blankly at each other. Just as Ellie realized that the stare-down was not going to end well for her, the door to her room opened, and Principal Danvers stepped in.

"Mornin', students. Jus' checkin' on yore new teacher. Y'all er lucky to have Miss Payluhtay. She's gone help you sail rot through those standardized tests."

At this point, Muscles stepped over to the principal. "Coach, I kin tawk to you."

*Ha! Finally!* She awaited "coach's" reaction. The principal, however, did not share Ellie's confusion and told Muscles to stop by and see him at break.

Ding! Ding! Comprehension knocked – Ellie was beginning to understand. Muscles thought he'd asked her a *question*. When he stated he could "see coach," he meant "Can I go see coach?" Whew! Mystery solved!

Now that she knew what was happening, Ellie could fix the problem. Relieved, she said, "Students, when we ask a question, we switch the subject and the verb. *I can go see coach* is a statement. If you flip the subject and verb you end up with *Can I go see coach.* In the future, asking questions this way will make your intentions clear." She smiled.

She thought to herself that she was not even going to broach the difference between *can* and *may*. She was just going to keep it simple. While she was congratulating herself for *meeting the students where they were* just like the school's vision statement demanded, Muscles gave her a strange look and shook his head.

"You is duh only one what ain't un'stood me," he muttered, one finger making little circles by his temple as he strutted back to his seat.

Ellie was floored for the second time in ten minutes. He thought *she* was crazy? Was he kidding?

What would happen on Monday when she started trying to teach American Literature? She felt her bright, snappy mood slip and her smile falter as she realized that she was sailing into uncharted water. And from the looks of it, her vessel did not come with life vests aboard.

# CHAPTER SIX

## *CRUSHING COMPREHENSION*

Over the next few days, Ellie learned more about her students, their lifestyles, and their home situations. She began to see them in a new light, and it wasn't a bright, sunny one. The murky, burdensome weight of generational poverty hung around the neck of almost every student she taught. She realized that students in Stusa felt forgotten, overlooked, ignored by the rest of the world.

They watched TV and thought that the "American Dream" was only for rich people, celebrities, people who had parents, people who didn't watch their guardians selling drugs, people who were *different* from them somehow. The despair and apathy were tangible. They saw no hope for a better future.

One day when Ellie asked a young girl with loads of potential to stay after class to work on her writing, the student refused. She shrugged her shoulders and said, "My grandma is on welfare. My mom is on welfare. I'll live on welfare. There's no point in improving my writing."

This response dampened Ellie's spirit. The idea that having an education could improve their lives was completely foreign to most of her students. It was an abstract concept that meant nothing to them.

Malachi, a smart young man who had fallen into a bad crowd, groaned to his group one morning that he just "had to find his class ring!" For the few who could afford such a luxury, the rings were an important symbol of success. Ellie tried to help him.

"What does it look like? Did you lose it here at school? Have you checked in lost and found?" She rattled off a few questions. He described the ring in detail.

"Where is the last place you remember having it?" Ellie asked.

He responded in his country drawl. "I had it own before ah went to bed. When ah stretched, it fell awff and ah heard it hit the floor." He stretched his long arms out in demonstration.

"Oh -- that's easy!" Ellie responded, "Have you looked under your bed?"

"Pff" he grunted. "I ain't getting' under mah bed." He shook his head. "I shore aint getting' under mah bed."

Ellie stared at him for a minute. She had no words, no advice, no framework to understand his lack of effort.

With each new background story, Ellie sank deeper into her own sense of despair. She knew her students needed inspiration, so she searched for some success stories to motivate them. She felt a profoundly awesome, but at the same time *heavy*, responsibility to change their perception of reality and to motivate them to live their lives to the fullest.

She regained a glimmer of hope when she found out about a writing competition. Each year, the local farmers sponsored a competition. They held a contest for the best 500-word-essay on topics that affected the area such as *How to use Technology to Improve Local Farming*, or this year's topic *Realistic Ways our Community Can Conserve Energy*. It was a tricounty competition, and three finalists would be chosen – one from each county.

The finalists would attend an interview with a panel of judges. There were small prizes for second and third place, but the winner would receive an all-expenses-paid trip to Washington, D.C. to meet with legislators and tour the capital city with other winners from across the nation. In short, it was a fabulous opportunity, and Ellie was thrilled to present the idea.

Ellie couldn't wait to introduce the idea. This year, the farmer's guild had put together a snazzy video showcasing previous winners having fun in D.C. She played the video, barely able to contain her excitement.

"What a wonderful opportunity," Ellie started. "It's a chance to travel outside of Stusa, fly on an airplane, stay in a hotel, see fabulous museums and monuments, meet teenagers from around the nation." She was relieved to see a few girls talking about the cute boys in the video. Maybe that would move them to enter the contest.

Rejuvenated, Ellie focused on writing skills over the next several days. On the day of the deadline, she requested their entries. Blank stares and sideways glances answered. No entries. Whatsoever. Not even *one* attempt to win the contest.

"You do realize that if you turned in an essay to me by the end of the day, you would *have* to be chosen as the finalist since you would be the *only* entry from our school." She tried to guilt someone into it. "Why would you refuse to try? This is such a fabulous opportunity!"

No one responded. Next, she tried shaming them. "C'mon! Don't you want to travel and see the world? Don't you want to know what life is like outside of Stusa?" Ellie was not a very persuasive speaker.

By three o'clock that day, Ellie realized no one was going to enter the contest. Her administrators were angry, mostly because they were embarrassed to be caught empty-handed by the community leaders. Ellie was embarrassed, too, for the students. If a free trip to the capitol couldn't motivate them, what chance did she stand? The only "prize" she could offer was a good grade and the future rewards of being a deep thinker. She didn't have anything tangible.

What could she possibly say to them to encourage them to try? Life is not a spectator sport? You have to get dirty to get diamonds? Trying and failing is better than never trying at all? She didn't know which cliché would motivate them.

Ellie dove into the problem, determined to find a solution. The next day she started a new unit. They discussed various famous people with "rags-to-riches" stories, and each student was assigned a successful figure to research. Ellie wanted them to see that *effort* could make a difference. If money was to be their only motivator, then she would discuss money-makers. She started with Benjamin Franklin and moved up through history.

Ellie included one of her personal favorites -- Oprah. She showed video clips of Oprah talking about her life growing up in a poor community. They examined several celebrities over the next few days. They read about Bill Gates, Condaleeza Rice, Steve Jobs, Barack Obama, and Walt Disney. Finally, Ellie asked students to write a poem or a rap about what they had learned from the unit.

Ellie's surprise was genuine and bitter when most of the poems were about the Illuminati and how the professionals they'd studied had "sold their souls to the devil" to get where they were. It horrified Ellie to discover that her students could not believe the celebrities had *earned* their success. Rather than recognizing hard work, her students explained their success by *supernatural* contracts with demons!

*Really*, she thought, *where am I?* She was so disturbed that she spent her entire planning period venting, writing her own rap on what she'd learned from the unit. In her disgust, she was tempted to post it on her blog, but the bell rang for lunch, and Ellie decided to leave it on her desk and think about it before posting anything rash.

*School is wack.*
*Students are slack*
*Give them love - they attack*
*Stab each other in the back*
*No ambition, no hope*
*Everybody's smoking dope*

Amberley Faith

*Hung by their own rope*
*Looking for a way to cope*
*Teachers don't care*
*Act like it's not their*
*Responsibility to share*
*Or help the students prepare*
*For the trials that they'll face*
*Just living in this place*
*Constant worries, too much strife*
*Bullet, drug deal, or a knife.*
*Inspiring kids' dreams*
*It's harder than it seems*
*With no money, no means*
*Trying to help today's teens*
*So before you criticize*
*Just know I won't apologize*
*For tryin' to solve the situation*
*Facing youth and education.*

# CHAPTER SEVEN

## *THE SHADOW*

*The Shadow* slipped into Ellie's classroom during lunch. She had stolen a master-key weeks ago. No one realized it was missing, so the theft had not been reported. Now, she needed to search Ellie's classroom and get a copy of Ellie's key to Julien's studio, a building that locals simply referred to as *The Jewel*.

It would be easy enough to break into the old building, but for her plan to be most effective, *The Shadow* needed to search it without anyone knowing. She approached Ellie's desk and started rummaging. Sure enough, there were Ellie's keys in the top drawer. Predictable.

*The Shadow* pocketed the keys and straightened the papers she'd ruffled. She stopped when she saw the poem Ellie had left lying on top of her desk. What was this? She picked it up skimmed it.

It was a rap. Was Ellie ridiculing the community? Probably not, she realized as she got to the end, but *The Shadow* could easily make it seem that way if it were taken out of context. And if she deleted the ending.

This was just too easy. What would Principal Danvers do if he knew what his shiny, happy teacher thought about the school and its students? *The Shadow* paused for a moment. If she hurried, she could return Ellie's keys before the end of the day, and Ellie would never know they'd been missing in the first place. But what about the rap?

Would Ellie notice its absence? Although it might be fun to watch Ellie panic. That sickly-sweet mask Ellie wore needed to be torn off for the school to see what lay beneath. *The Shadow* knew that no one could be that optimistic, that naive.

*The Shadow* took the rap and left the room in delight, imagining all the mayhem she could create. She'd bide her time and use the poem at exactly the right moment -- the moment when she would discredit Ellie and set the gears in motion for her downfall.

# CHAPTER EIGHT

### *DREAM DEFERRED*

Over the next few days, Ellie didn't have time to ponder Stusa's limited resources. She was invested in helping her students explore pre-colonial literature and discover the imagery in Johnathan Edwards' fiery sermon "Sinners in the Hands of an Angry God." She put her frustration behind her, choosing to believe that she could make a difference.

As it turned out, she did find some success with her students as they studied the early era of American literature. The students got involved in Edwards' sermon; having grown up in a religious community, it was something they could relate to. Ellie didn't have to spend any class time at all building background. Every student there could relate to the idea of a preacher calling out sinners and scaring them into submission.

To help them connect the centuries-old sermon to modern times, Ellie had the students make posters advertising Edwards as a guest speaker at a local church revival. After all, what could be better in this conservative town than promoting biblical obedience? The students impressed Ellie with their work; she felt a moment's reprieve from her role charading as an English teacher. It was clear, after all, that the students had read the sermon because the scenes they depicted were spot-on.

Their advertisements were intense; they included Edwards' images of broken dams, deluges, arrows aiming at sinners' hearts, and insects dangling over the gaping maw of hell. Each poster included textual evidence to support the accompanying artwork. One student, JaQuandis, sketched a scene of Edwards' listeners running out of church screaming in terror as the reverend calmly berated his congregation, showing them their worthlessness in contrast to God's Divine Mercy.

Ellie was pleased. *JaQuandis must have read the historical background to have drawn that scene.* Ellie was so proud of their artistic renditions that she created a hall display. She wanted everyone to see what her students could produce. Some of the artwork was flat-out amazing.

Students made a banner to place above the advertisements. *Renowned Reverend holds Revival.* They placed their artwork underneath and stepped back to survey their work. Ellie took a picture to remind herself of what could be accomplished when students were interested and engaged. She took a group photo of her class, as well. She printed it and placed it beside the display.

She and her students had just returned to the classroom when Principal Danvers stuck his head in, a look of bewilderment on his face and asked, "Just whut are you doin' Miz Paylaytay?"

"Teaching American Literature," Ellie smiled. "Specifically, the sermon *Sinners in the Hands of an Angry God.* By Jonathan Edwards." She added, in case he was unfamiliar with the piece.

"Well, tear down these posters in the hall before some kid sez teachers're tellin' 'em they're goin' to hell." He gave her a stern look and shut the door a little more forcefully than was necessary.

Ellie's smile froze. *It's okay for us to pray at faculty meetings, but it's scandalous to portray religious imagery from required literature?*

The class was silent. They were waiting to see Ellie's reaction. There were a few grunts of indignation at the principal's assessment of their work, but Ellie knew it was up to her to smooth things over. She needed a way to show them that while she would follow her boss's rule, she would also stand up for her students.

Hephzibah, nicknamed Zibby, recovered first and asked in a small voice, "Could we display the posters in the classroom instead of trashing them?"

"Perhaps," Ellie responded. She was still in shock that Principal Danvers didn't like the project and that he wanted to get rid of such beautiful evidence of learning. He, apparently, had never read Edwards' persuasive sermon. He missed the point entirely.

Another student, Tulina, gave a little gasp and said, "You is, like, the best English teacher. You talk real good like uh English teacher should. Hey, y'all, I made a rhyme – who's hot? Whoop, whoop!" A few students laughed, but most were awaiting Ellie's decision about their artwork.

Ellie smiled outwardly at Tulina's awkward bit of praise, but inwardly she crumbled into a wad of existential crisis. *They think I'm an English teacher because I used the word* perhaps? *I have never been such an awful imposter!*

The class was still waiting for Ellie to answer Zibby's question. The dismissal bell would ring in ten minutes. Did they have time?

"Yes," Ellie swallowed, making her decision. "That's a wonderful idea, Zibby. Let's move the entire display to the classroom. Do you think we can work together and get it done in ten minutes?"

The entire class responded by getting up and going to the hall to fetch their work. Ellie ripped down her classroom bulletin board display to make room for the new one. When an entire class cooperated without complaint or hesitation, it was a minor miracle and had to be savored. They managed to get the last staple in place as the dismissal bell sounded, and Ellie heaved a sigh of relief as her students filed out of the classroom. She knew she had made the right decision, but would Principal Danvers agree?

Later that night, when Ellie recounted the story and confessed her feelings of inadequacy to Julien, he reassured her by pointing out her strengths. He stressed her love of reading and writing and reminded her how she'd loved linguistics and literature her whole life long - just in French - so making the jump to English would be natural.

Ellie felt momentarily placated, but self-doubt reared its head and whispered that Julien had always been her biggest fan. He was looking at her through rose-colored glasses. The simple fact was that Ellie was misleading her students, breaking their trust by pretending to be someone she was not.

Ellie fell asleep that night feeling uncomfortable. She tossed and turned for a while. When sleep finally arrived, it wasn't restful.

*Ellie found herself seated in the cockpit of a plane. As the plane flew through bumpy clouds, the pilot collapsed. He fell forward onto the control panel with his face turned sideways towards Ellie. His eyes were closed, and it was obvious that something was terribly wrong.*

*The plane began to nosedive as his weight shifted the controls, and Ellie realized in stark panic that she would have to take over and fly the plane. As she fumbled with the knobs and dials in front of her, Ellie yelled at the pilot in terror trying to rouse him. Suddenly, he opened his eyes and started laughing at her.*

*"What is wrong with you? Stop laughing and give me a little help here!" Ellie shouted.*

*"You're doing it" he said, still slouched over onto the flight control panel but looking at Ellie. "You're doing it - you're flying the plane."*

*Startled at his proclamation that she was indeed flying the plane, Ellie glanced around the cockpit and then yelled back at him, "Well, maybe I am! But I'm not happy about it!"*

*The pilot continued to laugh at Ellie, cajoling her, mocking her, infuriating her; she wanted to reach over and smack him. She couldn't lash out at him physically, though, because in the dream it was vital to keep her hands on the flight controls. As he continued to laugh at Ellie, and she continued to doubt herself, he began to change shape. He morphed into a dark-haired woman covered entirely in colorful beads and shawls – Madame Margaux.*

Ellie woke up drenched in sweat. The stress of flying the plane left her shaky and pensive, pondering its cause. Part of the dream was easy to interpret. She was feeling stressed about her job - *flying the plane*. What her dream-self said made perfect sense; Ellie was unhappy about flying the plane. But was what the pilot said also true? Was she flying the plane, without crashing?

Further sleep eluded her in her heart-pounding state, so Ellie climbed out of bed and made her way downstairs. She made a cappuccino and sipped it while sitting in the swing. Although dawn hadn't arrived, there was a full moon, bright enough to shine down on her small garden. In the moonlight, the herbs looked shriveled, irretrievable. She walked over to check. She knelt and touched the leaves of her favorite – mint. It was still dry and crumbly despite her attention.

Her head dropped. Every resource she'd consulted touted mint's indestructibility, the easiest of herbs to grow. In fact, they warned her to plant the tiny herbs in a container to prevent them from taking over her entire garden and choking out everything else.

She knelt there for a moment, despair slipping in. Things were not turning out like she had imagined. This "sweet life" was a lot harder than she'd envisioned. If she didn't watch herself, she knew she would dry out and crumble like her garden.

As she walked back inside to get ready for school, she could feel the edge of bitterness creeping in. It wasn't a feeling she enjoyed. Ellie sighed again. She and her herb garden both needed some nourishment – and soon.

# CHAPTER NINE

## *MADAME MERETRICIOUS*

The hot, humid month of August slogged on while Ellie trudged through what she was beginning to think of as *The Great Deception* -- pretending to be the world's best English teacher. She wondered from time to time if she were secretly being filmed as part of some ridiculous reality show, "Teacher Trouble" or "Classroom Conundrum." She couldn't imagine anyone paying to watch her flounder in her newfound profession, but she couldn't think of any other way to explain the strangeness of everything unfolding around her.

During one of their pieces of American literature, a student named Blaize decided to put Ellie on the spot in front of his classmates. He was small and insecure, always looking for ways to make himself seem macho to the bigger guys. Ellie felt sorry for him.

Blaize raised his hand halfway through their poem by Elizabeth Brown and asked Ellie, "Miz Pehlehteeair, why is yore classroom all frenchified... cuz this is Amuricuh and we is spos'd to be learnin' Amuricuhn stuff." He looked around at his classmates seeking approval for this small challenge to authority.

Ellie gave him her best you-asked-the-perfect-question-smile. She hadn't redecorated her room from pre-planning; she'd had neither the time nor the energy. Her room still resembled the island café *Le Chemise*. Without missing a beat, she responded.

"I've been waiting for someone to ask that very question! We, dear students, are studying English from an outsider's perspective. We will study basic English skills as if we were all French citizens studying English for a visit to the States. No one need be embarrassed to ask for help since we're all English language learners, and we can look at American Literature, grammar, and writing more objectively, from the perspective of non-Americans."

She waited for the class's reaction as they processed the load of crap she'd hurled at them. There was a moment of silence, representing what Ellie assumed to be deep thought, while Ellie awaited their jeers. Then, to her surprise, a few girls squealed.

"Can we wear them French bahrays to class?" and "What're French boys like?"

Ellie breathed a sigh of relief. She couldn't believe that hokey answer had popped out of her mouth! They liked it, so she liked it. Maybe it would work after all.

*Bring it on Mr. Smarty Pants!* She thought. *I am the teacher! I have all the answers! I am invincible! I am . . . a complete and total fraud.*

# CHAPTER TEN

## THE SHADOW

*The Shadow's* initial concerns about her groupies blabbing had proved pointless; she'd scared them into submission. When rumors had started circulating about their foray into the forest months earlier, she pulled them into the girls' restroom, threatening them to silence. When she confronted them about the stories of their wooded adventure, the twins immediately pointed fingers at Jelly Sarka, who was a teacher's kid and a cell phone junkie.

"She's been talking! She caves under pressure. She's got about as much backbone as an earthworm." Eve taunted.

"Yeah." Eden added. "That's probably how the reverend found out about our little meeting in the woods to begin with! It wasn't us, and it couldn't have been *you*." She gave a pointed look at the shy one, then faced *The Shadow* again. "We all know his niece here is so scared of him that she wouldn't dare let anything slip about our ceremony."

*The Shadow* and the shy one exchanged a quick glance. The twins still had no idea that the man who had stumbled upon them in the woods that night was, in fact, Reverend Peters. *The Shadow* thought it was best to keep them ignorant. She could use the information to control both the shy one and Jelly.

"Well, you better hope that he doesn't find out anything else about it!" *The Shadow* rounded on Jelly, pretending to believe the twins' accusation. "So far he only knows about the dancing, and we are going to make sure it stays that way."

"But, but...he saw someone naked!" Jelly stammered. "He thinks we were partying and doing drugs! We cannot let him think that about us, girls! I mean, even if we weren't using that night, if he gets the police involved and they dig deeper... Isn't it better to come clean now rather than risk worse later?" She looked from one girl to another but kept her eyes downcast as she faced *The Shadow*. "You'll go to jail." She added in a breathless whisper.

"Oh, we'll *all* go to jail," *The Shadow* threatened.

"But I have never taken drugs! You can't prove I have!" Jelly protested.

"Listen to me very carefully, sluts." *The Shadow's* tiny, quiet voice was more menacing than if she had yelled at them in fury. "Nothing happened that night. We danced, we sang – and nothing more. We were collecting leaves for our botany final, and that is it!" She surveyed the group looking in turn at each girl for a second.

"I know where each of you lives. If you breathe one word about this, I will hunt you down and make you sorry. Don't forget that I saw my own mother die right in front of my eyes, and I have no qualms about making you pay the same gruesome price if you defy me!"

The four girls shuddered and went completely silent. All thoughts of complaining vanished instantly. The image of her hunting them down and hurting them was a frightening one indeed. Her bullying tactics terrified them.

*The Shadow* left them in stunned silence. She laughed to herself. The twins' eyes had bulged at her pronouncement. They had been expecting her to threaten them with the secrets she knew about their drug use and other illicit activities, but an outright threat of physical violence? She had surprised them. They would say nothing. And if they did, she knew exactly how to make them sorry.

# CHAPTER ELEVEN

## *DISTURBING DISCOVERIES*

Throughout the following week of school, Ellie's peppy attitude slipped more than she admitted. She was pushed to her limit by having to teach all new classes all day long. The preparations, lesson plans, department meetings, faculty meetings, parent meetings, and grading drained her. The burden felt heavier than teaching in the city where everything had been convenient, if not easy. It was all part of the tremendous upheaval her family had undertaken.

The move had been Julien's idea to begin with, but Ellie couldn't place the blame entirely on his shoulders; she had gotten caught up in his vision of living a simple country life. And, to be fair, the house and the land were beautiful. She was enjoying living in a restored farmhouse. She loved tending to her little herb garden. Everything had been wonderful, in fact, until school started.

On top of her difficulties at work, for the first time in her life Ellie had no social outlet – no friends to entertain with her only slightly-exaggerated stories of school in Stusa. Despite her colleagues, her students, her farmhouse, her herb garden, and her beautiful family, Ellie was lonely. She turned to her blog followers for comfort, but they were no replacement for flesh and blood friends.

It wasn't that people in Stusa weren't friendly. They seemed genuinely interested in Ellie, but only during work hours. After that, they tended to their own families. Everyone had comfortable, easy groups of friends they'd known since birth, families that had been there since before the Civil War. Their social calendars were full of small-town life: family birthday parties, Sunday lunches, pee wee football. There was no room for a newcomer like Ellie.

Since making friends had been much more difficult than she'd imagined, Ellie decided to make a little more headway with the one person in Stusa who seemed willing to extend the hand of friendship. Zyla, the red-haired, fresh-faced history teacher, had an avid interest in seeing the old building Ellie and Julien had purchased and were renovating for Julien's studio. Now that they had finished up at the farmhouse, she and Julien spent time working on the studio. They had made good progress. Having no social life had that benefit.

When Zyla introduced herself to Ellie during pre-planning, she'd mentioned her interest in old buildings and that she'd never been inside Julien's studio, known locally as *The Jewel*. Ellie invited her over for tea and a tour. As they explored the old building, they talked. Ellie summoned up her courage and confided in her newfound acquaintance.

She confessed, "You know, Zyla, I'm having a hard time getting to know people here, and I haven't adjusted to the feeling of being a stranger."

Zyla put her hand on Ellie's forearm. She stopped walking and said, "Don't worry, Ellie. It takes time to crack the social scene here, such as it is. You have to understand that people here have known each other since *before* they were born, and they're not as open to new ideas as you are."

Zyla turned to face Ellie, "Give them a chance. You'll get to know us all too well – and probably sooner than you'd like. Before you know it, you'll be telling me how students and parents alike are over-sharing."

Zyla gave Ellie's arm a friendly squeeze, and they continued to navigate around the scraps of building materials. Ellie saw evidence of the progress Julien and his newly hired assistant, Taiteja Jenssen, were making. One of the freshly painted rooms held boxes of cameras, lenses, and equipment. Ellie could see Zyla eyeing the box marked *Tai*.

"Julien invited his new assistant, Tai, to help get the studio ready." Ellie explained. "Sometimes she watches the girls for us, too."

Tai was of Swedish descent – blonde, buxom and beautiful – an exceedingly attractive combination. A lesser woman might worry about her husband's choice of assistants, and sometimes Ellie felt pricks of panic, but she was determined to keep an open mind if only because Tai was a walking contradiction.

Tai looked the part of a flaming floozy but claimed to be more of a vestal virgin. Her only hobby was photography. Tai dreamed of leaving Stusa in search of a bigger future. She'd be good for the studio; at the very least, she ought to bring in a bit of male clientele. She attracted attention but seemed to be embarrassed by it; there was hardly a boy in school who could keep his eyes off her.

Tai rarely dated. She was cautious, confused about how to handle the boys that followed her around like little puppies. Ellie overheard Tai talking to a friend, lamenting her curvy figure and the unwanted attention it brought. Tai complained about people judging her and jumping to wanton conclusions. If she weren't so attractive, Ellie probably would have felt sorry for her.

Zyla accepted Ellie's explanation with a silent nod and began filling Ellie in on some of the local history as they walked around the old building. They were discussing the fire that had destroyed much of the structure years earlier when suddenly Zyla stopped and looked at Ellie with a mischievous twinkle in her eye.

"You know, Ellie, there are some strange stories that accompany this old building. It has quite the checkered past. When I was a child, my great grandmother used to tell me the stories at bedtime as a morality tale; I was kind of a handful growing up. Anyway, would you like to hear them, or would it change your perception of the place? Are you superstitious at all?"

Ellie laughed in response. "Superstitious? Me? If I were the superstitious type, I would never have married into a Caribbean family. They have quite the reputation for Vodou, Santería, and Espiritismo. If all that can't scare me away, I doubt your *bedtime* stories can. So, spill already! What's up with this old place?"

"Yeah," Zyla chuckled to herself as she replied. "You and your family are pretty exotic for this little town. Give us time, Ellie. Give us time." She smiled again, then shook her head and continued.

"Well, the story goes like this. In the early 1600s, settlers from up North grew tired of battling the harsh, cold winters and headed south in search of rich farmland and milder temperatures. They loaded their wagons and wound up here in Stusa. Our small community was formed.

"Per custom, the settlers built their church first, they were Puritans by and large, and then began working on homesteads. The local American Indian tribes were friendly enough, and some even married into the largely European community. Fast forward to the end of that century, and Stusa had a railway stop, several churches, a small schoolhouse, a tavern and inn, and some wealthy landowners. The farmers prospered from the land and the climate, and their descendants built large Georgian-style plantation homes. You can still see a few of them today. Have you ever been to Farrington Farms?"

"No" Ellie replied. "I'd love to see it! But what does all this have to do with our studio?" Ellie was beginning to get the feeling that she wasn't going to like Zyla's answer.

"Patience my dear," Zyla replied. "You've got to know the background to get the feel for the stories." Zyla paused, took a breath and continued her theatrical delivery. "Imagine a time of horses and carriages, ladies in floor-length dresses, petticoats and bustles, wealthy farmers, debutante balls, and, sadly, slaves."

Ellie gave a small sigh. "It's the same in the Caribbean – anything beautiful has the stain of slavery on it!" Ellie turned back to face Zyla as a horrible idea took hold. "Zyla, please, please, please tell me that this building did *not* have anything to do with slavery! If you tell me there were slave auctions here, I'll burn the place down to the ground myself!"

Zyla looked at Ellie again and paused before saying carefully, "Before I answer you, Ellie, remember this - when one studies history, one learns to accept the good with the bad. We live in an imperfect world, and most beautiful things are indeed tainted with some type of blood and savagery. Think about the ancient ruins of Rome."

She hesitated and then continued gently. "Or what about that diamond on your hand? Who mined it? Do you think it was a young, white businessman in South Africa? What about the pearls I've seen you wear to school? Who do you think had to risk his life to free-dive down to retrieve the oysters? The owner of DeBeers? Tom Shane himself?

Ellie looked away, not from Zyla, but from the awful realization. Ellie had never considered her jewelry to be part of anything nefarious.

"Yes," Zyla continued. "Slavery is an awful blight on our history, on the history of the world. But should we discard jewels and burn historical buildings?"

"Okay, Zyla. I see your point, but what does it have to do with *The Jewel*?"

"Ellie," Zyla said calmly. "You and I aren't responsible *for* what happened. You and I are responsible *to* it - to make sure it never happens again."

Ellie paused. "Well said. Can I quote you on that?" Ellie ran her hands through her hair. "But I still don't want to hear that our studio was in associated with slavery. Tell me the truth. Now. I have to know."

"Oh, your conscience can rest easy on that mark. The studio never had anything to do with slavery. The story starts with a settler who moved here from Salem with his daughter and his niece. He had lost his home during the ravages of the witch trials, and like so many others, wanted a fresh start.

"His niece, Beah, had a bloody background. Her mother and father were murdered by American Indians as she slept between them. When Beah awoke to the sounds of struggle, the attackers saw she was just a child and let her live. Beah was taken in by her uncle. They stayed in Salem throughout the Witch Trials, when the uncle decided they'd had enough. They ended up in Stusa. The moved here to find peace. Based on what we know about the Witch Trials, they must have arrived in Stusa sometime after 1692, around the start of the 1700s.

"After the move, Beah grew into a beautiful young woman. One of the scouts of a nearby tribe noticed her and began following her each day as she gathered herbs from the forest boundary between his tribe and her town. One day, Beah returned home from collecting dandelion leaves and claimed the young scout had attacked and raped her.

"Townspeople were not too keen to get involved in another conflict between settlers and natives. Most people looked the other way, although there were some aggressive rabble-rousers of the town who were ready to lynch the young American Indian solely on Beah's accusations. Sure enough, a few months later Beah's belly began to swell, and it became obvious that she had been involved with *someone*.

"Beah's uncle wasn't convinced of her story of rape. She had come to him with somewhat of a blighted past. Besides having seen her parents murdered, she had been a participant in the witch trials and apparently had given testimony against several townswomen - but only those who happened to have handsome, young husbands."

"Wow," Ellie interrupted with titled head and pinched eyebrows. "*The Jewel* has ties to the Salem Witch Trials, too." Ellie mumbled.

"Sort of," Zyla responded. "The story says that Beah gave testimony at the trials. Anyway, Beah's uncle suspected that she was having a dalliance with Bo, the town gambler, a handsome rogue who owned this very building. He was part American Indian himself and had his ancestor's weakness for firewater. He held monthly poker games here, even though they were expressly forbidden by the church and community.

"With rumors still running rampant, nine months passed, and Beah gave birth to a brown-skinned, dark-haired little girl. The church, her adoptive family, and the town didn't know what to do with Beah or her baby. No one wanted to get into a skirmish with the American Indians, with whom they'd enjoyed lukewarm relationships, but it was obvious that the baby was of mixed heritage.

"By this time, Beah's uncle had kicked her out of the house, and she had moved in with Bo out of desperation. She waited tables for him and assisted during his weekly poker games in return for room and board for herself and her daughter, Abea. She was shunned by many, pitied by all. A woman scorned and judged without a trial, and without a hope in the world.

"A few years passed. Abea grew to be a young beauty like her mother. One night when Abea was around ten years old, the young scout accused of rape - now a full-grown man - came to the poker hall seeking a quick way to make money for his ailing father. Since the tribe's local shaman had not been able to cure him, the scout was trying to earn money to pay the town's doctor for western medicine.

"When Beah saw the scout, she turned as pale as milk. She didn't say anything, but she refused to approach his table. When Bo realized who the scout was, he insisted that Beah serve the man a whisky, on the house, to bury the bad feelings once and for all. Beah obediently went to the bar to get the drink, still silent and pale. Once behind the bar, she leaned down to get a glass...and came up shooting.

"She shot Bo, the scout, and every man seated at the poker table. The only person to escape her gunfire was the jailer who happened to be passing by and heard the commotion. He rushed in to find Beah with a smoking gun in her hand just as she was shouting for Abea to grab their things and run. The jailer was so surprised to see the carnage around him that he stood there, mouth agape, while Beah and her daughter fled the scene, never to be seen again."

She paused and looked at Ellie expectantly. "Pretty dramatic, huh?"

Ellie's own face paled as she heard the tale. "You mean to tell me," Ellie stammered, "that at least four men were murdered *right here in this very room*?"

Zyla cocked her head and studied Ellie. "Was I right to tell you, Ellie? You said you wanted to know. You are not responsible for what happened here. Remember, we just agreed that every item of beauty has its stain of sin."

Ellie swallowed hard. She'd have to look at it through the lens of history. After all, it must have happened almost three hundred years ago.

"Well," Ellie said, shakily at first and then with more confidence. "I'm sure the fire purged any remains of the living or dead. No wonder the former owner didn't give us details about its past. He didn't want to spook me."

Comprehension dawned. "And only outsiders like my husband and me would be ignorant of the story. Now I see why he gave us such a great price. Wow. I feel kind of duped."

"It's his loss," Zyla responded. "You and Julien are taking a distant tragedy and turning it into a modern success! Your work will breathe life into this town. This place will become beautiful once more. You will erase the sins of her past."

"You think so?" Ellie asked. When Zyla nodded, Ellie added, "But whose sins? There seem to be many guilty players in that convoluted story of yours. A girl sees her parents murdered, is raised by her uncle, testifies in court at the Salem Witch Trials, moves to the middle of nowhere, gets raped by a young man who probably reminds her of her mother's murderer, shacks up with the town's saloon owner, and winds up killing a group of poker players? And how, pray tell, was your grandmother using that tale to keep you in line?"

"Well," said Zyla. "The story says that when the scout's father heard what happened to his son, his dying wish was for the shaman to curse Beah and her daughter. The shaman complied, and the curse maintained that Beah and Abea would be doomed to roam the earth, never truly belonging to any community; they would constantly seek power and affection, but neither they nor their descendants would ever find their hearts' desire.

"And this kept you in line how?" Ellie asked.

"Well, my gran-gran used to say that if I wasn't obedient, I would end up like Beah – husbandless, with a child, roaming the earth looking for comfort and a place to belong."

"God – that's an awful thing to say to a child." Ellie whispered.

"Awful but effective. No girl in our family has gotten pregnant out of wedlock since gran-gran's time. We were all terrified of the curse." She laughed. "Can you imagine telling that tale to your girls?"

"Not really," Ellie replied. "I mean, there are worse things in the world than having a child out of wedlock."

"Not in this small town, honey. Not here." Zyla stood. "You've still got a lot to learn, Ellie. But I'll give you this – you're a breath of fresh air! Thanks for the tour. I've gotta run. See you at school. Promise me we can have tea again and that you'll tell me how you ended up here." Zyla waggled her eyebrows conspiratorially.

Ellie gave her a bashful smile and nodded in agreement. As Zyla gathered her purse and keys, Ellie pondered the tragedy that had occurred in *The Jewel*. She had mental snapshots of what it all must have looked like – the clothes they were wearing, the hair styles, the mustaches, Beah's gun.

Ellie had a strange feeling. It was as if she'd sensed what Zyla was going to say just before she said it – like some old memory, half-buried, incomplete, and blurred around the edges. Ellie drove home contemplating the past and its effect on the present.

Men were *murdered* in the building they owned. Would she be able to live with it? Would Julien? Should she tell him right away or wait until the renovations were complete?

She couldn't make up her mind, so Ellie blogged about it. Zyla had left her with more questions than answers. She was not sure she'd be able to get any sleep that night. As she got into bed, she wondered if buildings maintained an emotional imprint of the past, or if her feelings were just a human attempt to find meaning in past blunders.

# CHAPTER TWELVE

## FARMHOUSE FRIEND

The next few weeks of school left little time for Ellie to ponder the topic of emotional imprints left on old buildings like The Jewel. She admired Zyla's passion for the past, though. When Zyla explained history, she painted a vivid portrait. It was as if she were there. Zyla observed things that others missed.

Along that line of thinking, Ellie asked Zyla to help her with historical connections between Zyla's U.S. history classes and Ellie's U.S. literature classes. Zyla was also curious about the Pelletier's restored farmhouse, so Ellie invited her over to work on some cross-curricular lessons. When Zyla arrived, they moved to the front porch. Somehow working there didn't feel like work.

Unfortunately, the gnats and the heat overpowered Ellie's porch fans. The tiny bugs left them no peace. They buzzed around their faces, their ears, and even their mouths. Ellie didn't want to complain about her new hometown, so she bit her tongue until Zyla finally spoke up.

"These gnats are unbearable little pests! Would you mind if we went inside?" Zyla asked.

"Oh, thank goodness! I was trying not to say anything. I didn't want you thinking I'm a city snob." Ellie responded.

"You don't have to be a city snob to hate these little buggers. Country folk hate them, too! They are worse than usual this year." Zyla replied.

"Let's work inside at the kitchen table." Ellie offered. "We can cool down with a tall glass of my homemade specialty - lavender lemonade."

As they headed to the kitchen Zyla asked, "What smells so wonderf-," she stopped mid-word to look around as they entered the kitchen. "Oh, I see. The lavender smells lovely."

"Thanks!" Ellie replied. "I love the fragrance, too. It's just what I imagined it would smell like when we were considering moving to the country. I've got my own little herbal experiment going on here in my country kitchen."

"Well, besides the nice fragrance, what do you do with all this lavender?" Zyla asked.

"Oh," Ellie blushed. "It's always been a little fantasy of mine to grow and prepare herbal concoctions. Not just sachets - but facial scrubs, herbal teas, and soaps. You know, stuff like that. I've been interested in them since childhood. I spent my teenage summers concocting natural body scrubs and skin remedies."

Ellie hesitated and then decided to bare her soul, "I have a dream of running a little shop called *Tea and Tomes* where I sell cupcakes, homegrown herbal teas, and used books. It would only be open during my summer breaks from teaching. Of course," Ellie continued bashfully, "I know it's unrealistic and would never make enough money during the summer to justify the overhead, but I daydream about how I'd decorate the place - a small, bright kitchen area in the back with an old-fashioned counter and barstools. Up front, there would be a few tables for tea and cupcakes, then lots of cozy nooks and corners for reading."

Ellie blossomed as she described her dream shop. "I can even hear the soft music that would play - something old and French. And you know how Mexican restaurants always serve complimentary chips and salsa? Well, I would serve each customer a sample of my signature lavender-lemonade along with a mini-cupcake with cream-cheese-lavender frosting." Ellie sighed. "It's just one of my heavenly little daydreams. It keeps me going when I have a bad day." She paused. "Speaking of lemonade, do you like it?" Ellie asked.

Zyla stalled by taking another sip. "It's different. The more I taste it, the more I like it. It's unexpected yet... refreshing. What if you tinted it a pale-purple color? That would add to its appeal, I think. Your imaginary customers already love it," Zyla winked.

Ellie laughed, a little embarrassed at having shared something so intimate with a colleague she was just getting to know.

"But why just dream about it, Ellie?" Zyla interrupted Ellie's blush. "Julien is opening his photo studio downtown. Why not just section off a room or two of *The Jewel*, work on your little dream shop throughout the school year, and then open for business next summer?"

Ellie chuckled. "It's still just a dream because I have no experience. This is the first chance I've had to try my hand at growing something fresh from the garden."

"Ok, then." Zyla conceded. "Enough dreaming. What lesson did you need help with?"

"Well," Ellie began. "When you started talking about Beah and her connection to the Salem Witch Trials, it reminded me of my own fuzzy connection."

"Ha! I knew it!" Zyla interrupted. "You had that look on your face as soon as I mentioned them."

"Yes, well," Ellie cleared her throat. "It's just a family tale. There's no proof." She swallowed. "Supposedly, I'm descended from Elizabeth Proctor. She's hard to trace after the trials, but family legend has it that all the girls on my mother's side have been given names that have the initials EP for generations. Even when we girls marry, we seem to choose spouses with surnames that start with P. I don't know if it's a subconscious attempt to make the legend true, or if fate has intervened – but funnily enough - I fit the pattern. My maiden name was Pendleton, and obviously, I married Julien *Pelletier* although I can assure you that his name starting with a *P* had nothing to do with it."

Zyla's eyes widened. She stared at Ellie. "You mean *the* Elizabeth Proctor? Wife of John Proctor? Accused in Salem of witchcraft and imprisoned while pregnant?"

Ellie nodded.

"Oh. My. Gosh." Zyla gave her head a little shake. "That is amazing!" She finally squealed. "Has anyone ever researched the family tree or done DNA testing to see if it's true?"

"No," Ellie replied. "I don't know if it has been for lack of motivation, or if no one wanted to be proven wrong – but no one has ever done any serious testing or research." She was a little surprised at Zyla's immediate interest in tracing her roots. Only Julien had ever met her news with that suggestion.

"Honestly, what does it matter?" Ellie continued. "I'm either related or not. It doesn't change anything either way. It's just a claim to fame, that's all."

Zyla sighed. "I guess you're right. And to do DNA testing, they'd have to find and unearth Elizabeth Proctor's body from the grave. The History Channel would be all over it. You'd probably become a reality star or something while they traced the DNA. And then if it came back without a match..."

"I'd be the laughingstock of Stusa and the Internet." Ellie finished. "It's not that important to me. I didn't even name my daughters with her initials. I'm kind of tired of it, really. It was my crazy family's way of pretending to be special, I guess." She shrugged. "I only think of it when something like your story about Beah and *The Jewel* comes up, or," Ellie's eyes twinkled, "when I see Arthur Miller's, *The Crucible*, in our American literature textbook. That's why I invited you over. I want to perform the play. Will you help?"

# CHAPTER THIRTEEN

## *MILLER'S MAGIC*

Ellie was anxious to sink her teeth into a compelling, multi-layered story, and she had an inkling that performing a play would be a great way to engage her students and get them invested in the characters. After all, the small-town setting of Miller's play was breathtakingly like Stusa, so her students would be able to relate. Ellie began working on lesson plans – newly energized and hopeful.

When Ellie introduced the idea of the play to her students, she dangled a carrot - if they did a good job reading and researching, they could perform the play for Zyla's U.S. history class. As Ellie had hoped, most of the students seemed enthusiastic about the idea of a performance.

The artistic students began planning backdrops and supplies they'd need. The drama queens read lines from the roles they coveted. The crafters discussed costumes and props. The tech kids talked about lighting, music clips, and the possibility of filming and editing.

And with that, Ellie and her students dove headfirst into a Puritan theocracy of the 1600s where religion ruled, conformity maintained a person's safety, and vengeance-disguised-as-righteousness killed dozens of innocents

As their work on the play progressed, Ellie regained some of her optimism. She asked students the significance of

the title. What exactly was a *crucible*? It was a new word for every student except one; most had only ever heard it used as the title of something all eleventh graders had to read.

One student, however, volunteered that she knew the meaning of the word. Gale Guillaume, known as GG, was a small-framed student; Ellie called her quiet but powerful. Her writing was superb, yet she never shared aloud in class.

GG hadn't really warmed up to Ellie; she appeared to be sizing Ellie up each time their eyes met. At any rate, Ellie was thrilled to have a topic that would ease GG into participating in class, so Ellie asked her to explain the meaning of the word *crucible*.

GG locked eyes with Ellie, lifted her chin, and explained, "A *crucible* is literally a melting pot used to liquefy metals. You know, like in the days when blacksmiths melted down metal for weapons or horseshoes."

"Yes, you are correct." Ellie responded. "That is the literal meaning of the word, and since you pointed out the *literal* definition, GG, will you explain its *figurative* meaning as well?"

GG replied. "Yeah. People also use the word *crucible* to mean a trial, or some type of test." She paused, then added, "For example, this play is a *crucible* we'd rather not experience."

Ellie raised one eyebrow. A few of GG's friends stifled their giggles as they awaited Ellie's reaction.

"Ouch!" Ellie feigned injury. "Pun intended. Nice one, GG!" Ellie addressed the class at large. "The language of the play can be difficult at first," Ellie explained, "but once we get into the story line, you all will be able to relate to the plot. After all, Salem Village was a small farming community, much like Stusa. It will be interesting to see your reaction to each character's choices. In fact, I think you'll be able to identify people in your own lives that correspond to characters in the play."

At that remark, GG lifted her head and in a quiet voice muttered, "Oh, you're right about that, Madame. More than you can even imagine."

    With an inward groan, Ellie guessed that GG had already read the play. Well, it wouldn't hurt her to read it again. Perhaps since she already knew what would happen in the play, GG could spend more time correlating life in Salem Village to life in modern day Stusa.

    It shouldn't be too hard of a task. After all, Stusa still revered religious leaders, whether they deserved it or not. Arthur Miller may have written an allegory to compare the witch hunts of the 1600s to McCarthyism of the 1950s, but his description of human nature and its motivators were still relevant half a century later.

    As the play progressed, Ellie found herself making headway with her students. She enjoyed finding new ways to challenge them. She had finally stumbled upon something that got the students' attention, and now that she had connected with them, she was determined not to let anything spoil it. Let Principal Danvers try to take this out of the curriculum!

# CHAPTER FOURTEEN

### *PREORDAINED PROBE*

The end of the week found Ellie seated in a chair outside Principal Danvers's office. He'd summoned her during her planning period. As she waited outside his office, she fluctuated between wondering what he wanted and trying to control her fidgeting. She hated getting called to the office; it automatically made her feel guilty. She didn't think she'd done anything wrong, but the principal hadn't sound very pleased when he called her.

The summons embarrassed Ellie. She approached via the back door and waited in the tiny chair outside his office door. She scooched as close as possible to a large Fichus tree, shielding herself from view. His door was cracked, and she could hear voices coming from inside his office.

"Good morning. *Hnh Hmm*. I have some important news."

*Oh no! Not the Reverintendent!* Ellie squirmed as she overheard the conversation coming from inside the principal's office. She couldn't imagine what kind of trouble she must be in if Principal Danvers had asked the superintendent to come to the meeting. She moved her hands to her lap and closed her eyes, dreading the summons she knew was coming.

The Reverintendent continued, "I'd like to introduce Mr. Remuel Hardy, retired pastor, former DEA agent, and newly appointed school resource officer. Remmy, these are Lydia Bennett and Louella Baxter, co-presidents of the PTA.

This is the school counselor, Mabel Jackson. And this is Principal Danvers whom you will be assisting. Let's get to the root of these rumors and accusations and put an end to them once and for all!"

Silence. Ellie wondered if he had forgotten she was out here waiting. She heard a shuffling of feet and murmurs. Then Louella Baxter spoke.

"It's nice to meet you, Remmy. Your fine reputation precedes you. I've heard nothing but good reports about you and your service - both to God and Country. Most say you use a common-sense approach. I sure hope you'll leave some of that common sense here."

Mr. Hardy responded, "Thank you, Mrs. Baxter. I don't know that I'm anything special, but I have found that common sense is what's needed is most of these situations. I'm happy to lend my experience to the team."

Principal Danvers asked, "Am I the only member of the *team* that didn't know you were coming?"

Lydia Bennett joined in, "No, you most certainly are *not*. We I should have been consulted before any additional *team* members were brought in. Is this even legal, Louella?"

"Now, now – there's no need to get in a tizzy." The Reverintendent cut her off before Louella could answer. "A special dispensation allows the superintendent to appoint a lead investigator in emergencies, and I think our school being accused as a hotbed of drugs is quite an emergency. Decree 15E under section 13 – Emergencies and Dispensations."

Another awkward silence. Principal Danvers had definitely forgotten about Ellie.

"Well," Mr. Hardy broke the quiet. "My arrival seems to have further divided us. I must warn you that I will not work with you unless there is *full* cooperation. If we are going to be a team, then everyone needs to get on board. Otherwise, I am wasting my time and your money."

*Way to take charge, Remmy!* Ellie found herself rooting for Mr. Hardy. She liked the idea of an impartial outsider exposing whatever was going on in Stusa. She had never been able to put her finger on it, but she, too, had felt the undercurrent of the town pulling at her, trying to drag her down into its murky bottom.

"We need to make this official, folks." Remmy continued. "I formally ask you now to decide. Will you accept my findings, even if I discover that respected community members are involved, or if it turns out there is no illicit activity after all?" A silence followed the sound of shuffling feet. "Believe me, I've seen it go either way. So, I ask you again. Will you work with me as a team, and will you accept what we discover based on evidence rather than hearsay?"

This time, the Reverintendent was the first to answer. "Well, I heartily accept. You'll find no illegal activities in my household, but you are welcome to look."

Ellie pictured the Reverintendent. Like a child shaking a Magic 8 Ball, the Reverintendent would be shaking Remmy Hardy's hand long enough to check if Hardy believed him.

Ellie exhaled. The Reverintendent had been trying so hard, for so long, to project *sincerity* that he had convinced himself of his own sense of moral superiority. He probably believed his own hot air.

Louella Baxter accepted the terms, and so did her sister Lydia. The school counselor gave her consent. That only left Principal Danvers.

When he spoke, he addressed the entire group, "Listen, prying into each other's private lives, dredging up rumors and accusations – it bodes well for no one. You do realize that this investigation is *voluntary*? No one has been charged with any crime, and there is not one shred of evidence to support the accusations."

Ellie heard another silence, then a rustling of movement. It sounded like someone was approaching the door. Ellie wondered if she should leave when she saw an arm rest against the door frame.

"If we carry this out, we are just encouraging more gossip. We will be giving credence to the rumors." Principal Danvers sighed. "Seeking out trouble is dangerous. I don't like it, but I consent. I will pray for God's hand to guide you."

The Reverintendent roared, "I hope you're not implying that it's *Satan's* hand guiding us now!" Ellie had never come across a more sensitive, offendable man. Of course, she had never met people who used religion as weaponry before, either.

As Ellie stitched together the swatches she'd overheard, Ellie realized the Reverintendent had orchestrated the investigation without anyone's knowledge. So, had the Reverintendent hand-picked Remuel Hardy? Did he have an unknown motive? Would the investigation reward the rumor-starters?

Mr. Hardy interrupted Ellie's thoughts. "Well, now that we have assent among those present, let's get to the bottom of this. How did you first hear of the activities involving drugs?"

The Reverintendent cleared his throat and replied, "It all started a few months ago with my niece and a back woods party that I stumbled upon. A group of teenagers were dancing around a fire after sunset. It was a remote location, even by our standards. I only came across them because I was hunting. What drew my suspicion was their erratic behavior." *Hnh hmm.* "I believe I saw someone naked. When they realized I was there, they all started screaming and running away. Why would they run if it was innocent fun?"

Mr. Hardy answered with another question, "Did you question your niece?"

"Of course. I can hardly be expected to control a school system if I can't control my own house! She said that they were just collect—"

"No," Mr. Hardy cut him off mid-sentence. "Don't tell me. I want to hear her answers for myself. Please call her to your office."

A few minutes later, Ellie heard Tai's voice, "Yes, uncle? You summoned me?" Ellie was shocked. She hadn't realized that Tai was the Reverintendent's niece.

"Taiteja," her uncle said, "this is Mr. Hardy. He has a few questions for you. We are trying to get to the bottom of Bettina's claims that she was drugged."

"And how would I know anything about that?" Tai huffed. "Shouldn't you be taking a urine sample? The little tramp lies all the time." Ellie could almost hear Tai's eyes roll.

"Well, young lady," replied Mr. Hardy, "that is none of your concern. But for your information, she has already been tested. The results were inconclusive." He paused, and his voice changed direction.

"For those in the room unfamiliar with the science," he continued, "THC drops below detection limits after three to twelve hours in non-habitual users. But if you're so eager for testing, Miss Jensen, we could easily take a sample from *you*. Regular users can test positive for THC for up to a month."

"Well, if anyone should know about *that*, it's Gale Guillaume," Tai deflected. "She is the one who is into herbs and gardening crap. Besides, it was her idea for us to go out there in the first place. Why don't you call her up and ask her if she slipped anything in those granola bars we ate beforehand? She said they would keep us *grounded* and *fearless*. And you know what? Not one of us was too scared to sneak out and party with her in the dark in the middle of nowhere. Maybe there's a reason why." Her defiant tone would have been more impressive if it hadn't been punctuated by the smacking of her bubble gum.

"Niece, this is not the same account you gave me." The Reverintendent interjected. "I will not have calumny in my own house! Get your story straight, or it will come back to haunt *you* – not me."

"I'm telling you I am innocent!" Tai responded loudly. "Bring GG here and ask *her* what was going on! I have nothing more to add." Tai proclaimed.

The next thing Ellie heard was Mr. Remuel Hardy's voice on the intercom calling Gale Guillaume to the office. Gale came in through the back entrance and passed right by Ellie.

She acknowledged Ellie with a nod of the head. Ellie had a sudden urge to explain her presence.

"I'm here waiting for a meeting with Principal Danvers and the superintendent," she blurted. Gale nodded again but said nothing as she entered the principal's office.

Remuel Hardy began questioning GG right away. "Miss Guillaume, we have reason to believe that you initiated some type of party in the woods on the night of the twenty-third of May. We also have reason to believe that some of the attendees may have consumed illegal substances at your hands. We would like you to explain what happened in your own words."

GG replied quickly and quietly. "This is all one big misunderstanding." She sounded controlled but exasperated. "Yes, we went out to collect leaves the night before our botany final. Yes, we were out past curfew. Yes, we built a fire to keep warm and to light the darkness. Yes, we danced. But there is no need to get your knickers in a knot. The dancing was just a bit of excitement in this dull town. There was nothing illicit going on."

"We will be the ones to determine that, Miss Guillaume." Mr. Hardy interjected. "Now, who was at the party? I need the names of all participants."

If Ellie thought that GG would refuse to name names, she was mistaken. GG began her list almost before Mr. Hardy finished asking. "The twins Eve and Eden Mathews were there along with Tai. Then there was Angelica - Jelly Sarka." A pause. "Oh," she added. "Bettina Roberts was supposed to go, too, but she chickened out at the last minute and went running back to her house before we'd walked more than thirty yards."

*Ah. There's the missing piece of the puzzle.* If the girls teased Bettina for being a coward, Bettina could retaliate by saying they'd given her drug-laced granola bars. Ellie knew from experience that high school girls could be cruel. Times might have changed since Ellie was a teen. Mean-girl tactics had not.

Ellie suddenly realized she was eavesdropping. Principal Danvers had forgotten about her meeting. If he wanted her, he would call for her over the intercom. He was too busy to notice her absence, so Ellie decided to use the rest of her planning period to get some work done. She stood up to return to her classroom.

Just then, Principal Danvers stormed out of his office. He blinked at her for a moment, then shoved something into her hand. She looked down to see a crumpled piece of paper. With his back to her as he walked away, he said, "Watch what you leave lying around the school Miss P."

Ellie un-wadded the paper and found her rap from the previous week, the one she had written before they'd started the play. The torn paper had her name written in red ink. Some words had been crossed out and re-written by hand. It looked like a work in progress.

School is whack.
Students are slack
Give them love? They attack
Stab *their teachers* in the back
No ambition, no hope
Everybody's smoking dope
Hung by their own rope
*All they do is mope*
Teachers don't care
Act like it's not their
Responsibility to share
Or help the students prepare
For the trials that they'll face
*In this God-forsaken* place
Constant worries, too much strife
Bullet, drug deal, or a knife.
*Is how this all will end*
*Why bother to pretend?*
*-Ellie Pelletier*

As Ellie's stomach dropped, she wondered who had altered her words. How had she been so careless? And how much trouble was she in now?

# CHAPTER FIFTEEN

## *FABULOUS FIND*

That weekend, Ellie pushed her conflicted feelings aside and tackled a project of another kind. Ellie went to *The Jewel* to battle her angst in the form of plaster that needed removing. She left a plate of fruit and bacon for the girls and a ready-filled espresso machine for Julien. She scribbled a quick note.

Meet me at The Jewel
I wanted to get an early start!
Love, Ellie

Ellie grabbed her bag - packed with a headscarf, a face mask, and a water bottle - and crossed herself with holy water as she left. It was barely six o'clock in the morning, but Ellie itched to get started. Chipping away the plaster was a tedious job, but it would chip off some frustration, too.

While a construction team did the heavy work, she and Julien decided to remove the plaster covering the original brick walls themselves. They'd been covered in white dust after only a few minutes work. She and Julien looked like bakers covered in powdered sugar, except for their face respirators. They had to stop every few minutes and wipe their goggles. They'd had to hose themselves down before they could get in the car to drive home.

As dirty a job as it was, however, Ellie found it satisfying. She loved chiseling off the layers of plaster, revealing the original surface. No two exposed bricks were alike. They must have been hand-made. The resulting brick surface was uneven and added to its charm.

She enjoyed working in solitude for a few hours before Julien and the girls arrived. It gave her time to think and to process everything that was wrong in her classroom, her garden, and her head. Something would have to change, and she wasn't sure what it would be.

As she struck down pieces of plaster, she felt a sense of accomplishment. Maybe she couldn't strike down her own problems as easily, but seeing immediate results of her hard work was addictive. Unlike teaching school, it provided instant gratification; it was exactly what she needed.

The rhythmic tap-tapping of her hammer against the chisel lulled her into a trance. She reached a place where workers had removed a room partition. This patch of brick had been covered by an interior wall to divide the space into separate rooms.

In a foot-wide section, Ellie saw the imprint left behind from the wooden support beams. This part would be easy to clean since most of the plaster had already fallen away as a result of removing the partition. As she hammered, tapped, and wiped, Ellie noticed that the mortar in one section was a different color from the rest.

*Hmm...will that be ugly or charming? Well, we can always cover it with a painting or a shelf.*

One of the bricks in the discolored section moved slightly when Ellie tapped at the plaster. She wiggled the brick a bit to test the sturdiness. The brick moved too freely; it would have to be replaced. Ellie used her chisel as a lever to tug it out of the wall, making a mental note to ask if it could be repaired.

As Ellie continued working, another brick came loose, then another, and before long Ellie had removed several bricks, revealing a little hollowed-out space. She couldn't see inside, so she stuck her gloved hand in and felt around. In the process, a few more bricks came loose to reveal a niche in the wall.

*Why would someone cover up such a lovely little niche?* As she cleared away the pile of loose mortar and dust covering the bottom of the niche, Ellie's hand ran over something solid in the pile of rubble. She wiped and tugged and eventually pulled out a small package covered in tattered fabric, with a thick coating of dust.

The package was about the size of an old family Bible. Ellie set it aside to finish clearing out the hollow space. It was perfect. The niche would make a wonderful focal point with a plant, some softly burning candles, or maybe a display of one of Julien's favorite photos. She cleaned out the little recessed area, wiping down the bricks with a damp cloth and clearing away as much debris as possible, eager to show Julien her unexpected find when he arrived.

After Ellie had staged the niche with one of Julien's framed pieces and a fern, she backed up to see her handiwork. It still needed something low in the center to balance it out. A book would be ideal, but Ellie wanted it to look old - like a period piece from *The Jewel's* heyday.

It was then that she remembered the dingy old package. She cleaned it off as best she could, wiping away the dust and plaster, then set it in between the fern and the frame. Perfect! It looked so authentic.

Placed there in the niche, the package seemed like an ancient gift just waiting to be opened. Maybe it was a birthday present, hidden so well that it had been forgotten. That had happened to Ellie more than once. Perhaps it was a collection of old love-letters, too precious to be discarded but too incriminating to be displayed. Could it be a journal, a Bible, a photo album?

In fact, the more she looked at the tatty package, the more intriguing it became. Ellie's imagination was in overdrive. She was torn; she wanted to open the package to see what it contained, but it looked so picture-perfect with its ragged cloth askew and the aged twine tied around it.

As she debated with herself, Ellie thought of Zyla. What would she do? Surely a history teacher would want to see if the package had any historical significance. Well, if Zyla would do it, then so would Ellie. If she opened it carefully, she could probably save the old fabric and use it to redress an empty prop box.

And that settled it. Both curiosity and reason were satisfied, so Ellie took off her gloves and removed the package from the niche. She sat down and began unwinding the layers of cloth and twine. She set aside the fabric and looked at what lay beneath.

She had been right; it was some sort of book.

For a minute, Ellie sat and stared. The book was bound in brown leather. Some of the edges were cracked, but it was not falling apart. Despite the book's wrappings, dust still obscured the cover.

Ellie swiped her hand across the cover and felt a tingling sensation run up her arm and down her back. It was not as sharp as static, but it felt electric, nonetheless. *Wow!* She thought. *If this old book is giving me chills, I wonder how Zyla would feel!*

Ellie took a breath and opened the front cover. The binding crackled with age, and she began to wonder if she should take it straight to Zyla. With her love of history, Zyla would probably know exactly how to proceed with an old book like this one.

Ellie had read somewhere that handlers wore gloves in the Vatican library. She pondered whether to put on her gloves again. But the books in the Vatican were hundreds of years older than this could possibly be. And besides, if she put her gloves on, she wouldn't have the dexterity to turn the pages one at a time like she wanted. So, Ellie continued her bare-handed exploration of the book.

The handwritten title page looked more like a list of names and initials. The authors, maybe. Some of the first entries were illegible, but as she continued skimming the list she could make out a few items.

Taken from J.J. by C.B., 1603
Taken from C.B by T.I., 1610
Taken from T.I. by A.W., 1692
Taken from A.W. by E. B. P., 1693
Released from E.B.P.R. to E.A.P., 1721

*Taken* - what did that mean? Taken down by scribes? Could the information have come from people who couldn't write for themselves? And the last entry. It said *released*. If it had to be released, what was it being released from? Prison? Could this be an old prison journal? At the end of the list, there was the cover's matching emblem, albeit much smaller and crudely hand drawn. This time Ellie could make it out better.

The emblem was a simple one that reminded Ellie of some of the indigenous art she'd seen in the Caribbean and Latin America. It looked like a cross between an hourglass and a primitive flower design. She moved on to the next page, excited to see what type of stories had been taken down over the years, deciding instantly that the book must be a collection of sorts - folk tales, planting advice, weather tips, home remedies. Perhaps she had found the original Poor Richard's Almanac!

Or maybe it was some forgotten volume like the Appalachian *FoxFire* series she had loved so much as a girl. Ellie and her cousin had spent countless hours concocting recipes in the moonlight that were supposed to do everything from removing her cousin's abundant freckles to making Ellie's flat chest develop womanly curves. Disappointingly, neither one of them got what they wanted, not through *FoxFire* recipes nor through modern technology, and both grew to love themselves as they were -- freckle-faced and flat-chested.

While old memories flooded Ellie's mind, she turned the page. It was much thicker than paper. Ellie knew that modern paper books were only expected to last about seventy-five years before decaying, but these pages didn't feel like paper and didn't crumble as she turned them. Were they vellum, or sheepskin, or papyrus? As much as Ellie loved to read, her knowledge about the assembling of books was sadly lacking. Nevertheless, she knew the text was quite old just from the entries on the title page.

The first entry was so faded and written in such curlicue handwriting that Ellie couldn't make out more than a few words. Disappointed, she continued to thumb through several more pages determined to find something she could read. Although she couldn't decipher much of the first few pages, she did notice some similarities from page to page. Each page started with a line of writing across the top, followed by a list, and ended with a section of prose in varying length.

*Oh!* It dawned on Ellie suddenly; *it must be a collection of recipes.* How interesting! She wondered if she could whip up a test batch of a few of the simpler ones in her kitchen but realized she had to find some legible writing first. She skimmed through the pages and stumbled across handwriting that was more recognizable. Elated, Ellie looked more closely at the title of the recipe.

*To Rid One's Self of Biting Bugs and Irksome Pests*

So, it wasn't a recipe book after all. This sounded more like a folk remedy for pest control. She continued reading, curious to know what their ancestors did before DEET and Raid.

Maybe she'd found an old-fashioned remedy for the gnats that loved to pester her on her porch. They definitely qualified as *irksome pests*. They circled everyone, even the animals. Julien and Ellie joked that everyone in Stusa looked like the character Pigpen from Charlie Brown.

Oddly, there was no list of ingredients as Ellie had anticipated, just some instructions and a rhyme.

*To Be Read Aloud at Dawn*

Biting bugs of bloodlust born
Fighting, failing those forsworn.
Protection provided by power plucked
Striving, starving, blood un-sucked

Ellie mumbled the words aloud as she read. She couldn't help herself. It was so *sound* worthy. She had to hear it. *So, it is an anthology of folklore,* thought Ellie, fondly remembering her cousin and the escapades of their youth. Although the *Fox-Fire* contributors had nothing on these guys when it came to rhyme and alliteration.

Ellie was about to turn the page when she heard a loud crash and the residual rumbling of falling debris. Was it Julien and the girls? When had they arrived? She hadn't heard them enter the studio. She tossed the book aside and ran toward the sound.

"Bibianne! Méline!" Her heart stopped for half a second when she reached the front right corner of the building. Where the girls' homemade fort - built with scrap material leftover from the construction crew - once stood, there was now only a pile of rubble.

Ellie's adrenaline kicked in. She raced over to the pile and started removing bricks. She called out for the girls, "Bibi! Mel! Can you hear me?" Two more people ran over to help – Julien and Tai. Ellie's mind registered annoyance that Julien had brought the babysitter along, but she filed it away for future discussion. Right then, she had to give her full attention to her girls. She heard a tiny whimper.

"Quick! Over here! I just heard one of the girls!" Ellie shouted as she tore through the debris double time. All three worked in silent unison to remove the bricks and pieces of wood. Their silence reflected their concentration and desperation as they strained to hear any sounds from the girls.

As they worked, Ellie heard Bibianne's soft crying amidst the shuffling of debris. *Thank God - she's conscious!* Ellie thought. She 'd been terrified that the girls were knocked out.

"Bibianne – are you hurt?" Ellie shouted frantically.

"N-n-nuffin," responded Bibianne between sniffles.

"What do you mean, nothing?" Ellie asked.

"Nuffin hurts except my leg," Bibianne answered. Her voice trailed off into muffled sobs at the mention of it.

"Bibi, my darling, can you see Méline? Is she beside you?" Ellie scrambled to remove enough trash to get through to her girls. Julien and Tai followed suit.

"*Maman, je suis ici*. I think I am okay." Méline responded haltingly, catching her breath. "My back hurts. The bricks are so heavy, and I don't want to smother Bibi."

"You are going to be okay, girls. We've almost broken through. Shut your eyes so trash won't fall in them." Ellie ordered.

"Y-yes, *maman*. Please hurry! Bibi is scared." Méline replied.

Ellie, Julien, and Tai kept working, but they removed bricks more carefully. As they worked, Bibianne's cries grew louder and louder. Hearing her daughter respond to questions relieved Ellie although she desperately wanted to touch her girls and comfort them. Finally, Ellie removed a brick that revealed a glimpse of Méline's golden-brown hair. What they saw when they removed more bricks made Ellie gasp.

Méline lay huddled over the top half of Bibianne, blocking her little sister's face and upper body from the avalanche. Méline must have reacted instantly to have thrown herself on top of her sister like that. Only Bibianne's legs had been exposed to the fallout.

From the looks of Méline's back, her quick reaction saved her little sister from a broken nose or worse. Ellie shuddered just thinking of it, for Méline's back was scratched and bleeding where bricks had torn through her shirt. Big, purple bruises already appeared along with large, red whelps. The back of her scalp bled into her long locks. Ellie gulped as she recognized just how serious the accident had been.

Ellie reached over and laid her hand on Méline's shoulder, the only part of her that was uninjured. "It's okay, Méline. You are both safe now. Can you move?"

Méline sat up. Dirt and tiny pieces of rubble fell from her hair and clothes. Julien lifted her from the pile. As he checked Méline's back and spine, Ellie leaned over to get Bibianne. Bibianne's face and upper body looked fine, due to her sister's sacrifice, but her left leg bled at the shin and had turned purple. *Broken or fractured*, Ellie realized.

Ellie hugged her daughter before she lifted her from the heap. "Bibianne, my love, you have been so brave. I need to get you out of here, but sweetheart, your leg is going to hurt when I move you. Hold on tight to *maman* and be brave for me once more."

Bibianne did as instructed and hugged Ellie tightly. She only let out a small cry of pain when Ellie lifted her from the floor. "*Maman*, I was so scared. I was crying. My sister hugged me, and all I remember is her telling me over and over that everything would be fine and that we would make it."

Ellie swallowed the tears that threatened to stream down her cheeks. God, her girls were everything to her. How proud she was of Méline for being such a caring big sister! How shocked she was that Méline was in that situation in the first place. Where had Julien been? Why hadn't he been there to prevent this catastrophe? Anger began to replace her anxiety.

She placed Bibianne on the counter as a makeshift hospital bed. She didn't look at Julien. "Have you called 911 yet?" She asked.

"*Non, ma vie.* I was checking out Méline's b---" Ellie didn't wait for him to finish. She whipped out her cell phone and dialed. Tai stood there, wringing her hands, looking from one to the other. Although Tai didn't apologize or explain her part in the near disaster, she did have the good sense to look chagrined.

"Well," Tai began. "Now that you've got the girls, I'm probably in the way. I'll just get out of your hair." Tai looked at Julien expectantly, waiting for his what – Permission? Approval?

Ellie, however, was the one to respond. "Yes, I think that is best. We'll let you know how they are once they've been examined." Ellie waited as Tai gathered her purse and keys and headed out to her car. She rounded on Julien as soon as Tai left.

"What on earth were you doing when the fort collapsed? I didn't even know you all had arrived! And what was Tai doing here? If she was here to look after the girls, she did a very poor job. A job, which I feel compelled to point out, was *yours* not hers. *You* are the parent."

Ellie's anger gushed out. She knew it wasn't the time or the place to have this discussion, and Julien looked horrified. Hall the color had drained from his face.

"Ellie, I never thought that this would happen. I only left the girls for a moment-," Ellie cut him off as she heard the sirens approaching.

"It doesn't matter now. Let's just get the girls to the hospital, and we'll discuss it later."

As emergency workers loaded the girls into the ambulance, Ellie returned to the niche to grab her purse. She noticed the strange anthology she had unearthed. Amidst the cave-in she'd forgotten it. The accident had left no time for her to show Julien the niche. *I'll just show him tomorrow*, Ellie thought as she picked up the book and threw it into her over-sized purse. She would need something to read; they were in for a long wait at the emergency room.

Julien and Ellie followed the EMTs outside. A large grey cloud blocked the morning light. It looked as if it would start pouring at any moment. As Julien helped Ellie into the ambulance, a chill went down her spine. "Cold, *ma chère?*" asked Julien.

"I think it's just adrenaline from the girls' accident," Ellie replied absent-mindedly as she looked back at the empty building. After Zyla's stories about the past, Ellie wondered if there really were any wandering spirits attached to the old building.

*Stop it*, Ellie told herself. *You're acting like a little girl who is afraid of the boogeyman!* She shook her head at her overactive imagination and turned to get into the ambulance. Before the EMTs could shut the door, another shiver ran down Ellie's back, but it wasn't because she was cold. Ellie had the distinct, disconcerting feeling that someone was watching her.

# CHAPTER SIXTEEN

## *THE SHADOW*

*The Shadow* remained silent and still as she watched the renovations of *The Jewel* from her perch on the roof of the neighboring building. She had already searched most of the ancient structures in town that dated from the 1600s. She had been interrupted in her systematic exploration of *The Jewel* when it suddenly and quite surprisingly sold. Real estate in Stusa moved slower than a turnip root in moonlight.

Although *The Shadow* had obtained a copy of the key to *The Jewel*, easy entrance to the building hadn't helped with her search. *The Shadow* had been forced to stop working when Julien or Ellie showed up unexpectedly. Several times, Julien had come with Tai, his new assistant, and they had worked together setting up the studio.

*The Shadow* wondered if she could use that to her advantage. A few innuendos to the right people would spark rumors that would work against Ellie and her family. It would be easy to implicate Tai; everyone suspected she was just as slutty as she looked. *The Shadow* wasn't sure if anything was going on between Tai and Julien, but that didn't matter in the least. The mere suggestion of impropriety would do more than enough damage.

As was happening far too frequently for her liking, *The Shadow's* search of *The Jewel* had been interrupted this morning; Ellie arrived much earlier than normal to work off some anger, judging by the sounds of her tools. *The Shadow* realized that Ellie and Julien were restoring the old lady to her former glory – exposing brick walls, repairing tin ceilings, and removing partitions and walls that were not in the original plans. That made it all the easier for *The Shadow*. After all, why should she expend the energy if the perky Pelletiers would do it for her?

As she watched through the warped, lead-paned windows, *The Shadow* felt a gentle, yet undeniable tug. Her vision clouded over. A scene played out in her mind; it was slightly fuzzy and shrouded with thick mist. With her vision blurred, she relied on her other senses.

She felt herself being lifted, pulled from above. She hovered for a moment and suddenly plunged downward. A shot of fear pierced her. She grasped around, desperate for something to latch onto, but she couldn't see. It was only when her hands touched the rough texture underneath her that she realized she wasn't in the air at all. She still sat on the rooftop. The sensation of flying and falling had been so real that her heart pounded, and her lungs struggled.

She held her breath and blinked her eyes. Gentle, unseen hands brushed her hair back from her face, and undressed her. As layer after layer of clothing unraveled from her body, she touched her shirt and ran her hand across the waistband of her jeans. They were still intact.

She'd been split in two; part of her sat fully clothed on the rooftop while the other part of her floated, disrobed. Strangely, the near-nakedness of her other-self left her feeling powerful and free.

A distant voice murmured a few words, and *The Shadow* saw a delicate, green cord hiss and crackle through the air. The sparking cord came closer and closer to her. When it reached her hidden position, it wound its way around her ankle and continued winding its path up her legs, her arms, her neck, and finally her head.

*The Shadow* knew she should feel alarmed; she was bound by something beyond her control, but the feeling delighted her. The warm air, the feeling of freedom – the green tendril caressed her as it traced its path over her body, searching. When she touched her ankles and throat trying to grab the cord as it travelled, there was nothing to grab.

At her movement, the cord stopped its slithering and began to tighten. As it tightened, she felt warmth spread around her left wrist. The warmth became more and more intense although never painful.

As it burned, the cord glowed. It started small, an amusement park glow-bracelet. The emerald light grew stronger. Its intensity increased until it pierced her vision; she could see nothing other than the burning light. It was too much look at. It seared her skin. The cord tightened, and her skin sizzled. It was unbearable. *The Shadow* thought she would collapse from the pain, but as she cradled the wrist in her right hand, the cord vanished. Her vision was restored.

*The Shadow* looked around. She still sat on the rooftop. Her heart still thundered against her chest. She checked her watch. Only a few minutes had passed. She felt disoriented and divided. She touched her neck and checked her ankle to see if there were any remnants of the strange, beautiful, emerald cord. She found nothing.

Jolted back to reality, *The Shadow* checked Ellie's progress. Seeing EMTs loading Ellie's daughters into an ambulance shocked her but not as much as the silver mist surrounding Ellie. roiled and undulated, blurring the edges of Ellie's silhouette. *The Shadow* remembered her own foggy vision and touched her wrist again.

At that moment, Ellie shuddered and looked up. *The Shadow* froze. Ellie frowned and continued to climb into the ambulance, and in a few seconds the Pelletiers were gone. *The Shadow* felt foolish, empty. What had just happened?

She crept through the remains of the former City Hall and made her way back to her cabin. It was only as she undressed for her shower that she saw the faint, green, scar-like mark that encircled her left wrist.

Startled, she examined the mark more closely. It resembled one of the white tattoos that had recently become popular. A thin, delicate lined swirled around her wrist, undeniably real and rather pretty. It was slightly raised and felt tender as she traced it with her finger.

With dawning comprehension, she remembered where she had seen something similar. She and her mother had been collecting milk from the dairy cows of a local farmer when the farmer had pointed out the symbol burned into each cow's hide, marking each one as his property. *The Shadow* shook her head with a jerk. The green, sparking cord from her vision - as beautiful and mesmerizing as it had been - had branded her.

# CHAPTER SEVENTEEN

## *FANTASTIC FOLKLORE*

Sunday morning found Bibianne in a cast that stretched from above her knee all the way to her tiny toes, which were left free to wriggle about. Although Méline wasn't wearing a cast, she was bruised, battered, and sore. They spent a restful morning watching television, reading, and playing board games.

After a pleasant day together, Julien volunteered to suffer through another showing of the current Disney movie-of-the-moment and then get the girls bathed and bedded for Ellie to have some time to herself before the work week started. *Obviously, he feels guilty about the accident.* She hadn't brought it up again; the sheer emotional drain of it exhausted them all. She wondered if she'd over-reacted in her fear for the girls' safety.

Ellie accepted Julien's offer. She climbed upstairs, showered, and got ready for bed. She crawled into bed planning to get a head start on her sleep for the week, but her mind kept replaying the scene of the collapsed fort. Méline's bruised back and quick thinking had certainly saved her little sister.

Where had Julien been, and what had he been doing instead of supervising the girls? She could envision Julien getting carried away with his work on the studio and not being as attentive to the girls as he might have been, but Tai had been there, too. Shouldn't she have been watching the girls? What *exactly* had he and Tai been up to? What could have been so compelling that neither of them knew what was going on until the crash startled them, as it had her?

Well, there was one *glaringly* obvious answer. Ellie sipped the idea like a drink, rolling it around her mouth, tasting it for truth. Although Tai was young, blonde, and curvy, Ellie trusted Julien. She refused to be a jealous wife. It didn't matter what the town thought of Tai and her reputation; Ellie trusted Julien, and that settled it. She had no tangible reason to doubt Tai. The drink was too bitter, so she spat it out before it could taint her.

Besides, Julien was never jealous of other men who flirted with Ellie. She never gave him reason. She remembered one time at a concert when the scoundrel next to her had flirted openly throughout the performance. Ellie had done her best to ignore him, but he hadn't gotten the hint. She would never forget when the guy leaned over and asked Julien, "Would you mind if I kissed your wife?"

Ellie's eyebrows shot up at the request, and she answered before Julien could say anything. "You'd have to get *my* permission – not my husband's!" She changed places with Julien so that he would be the one standing beside the pervert for the rest of the concert.

Ellie had been miffed with Julien for not being even a *tad* bit jealous, but she never asked Julien what his answer would have been. She was too afraid. He knew he didn't have anything to worry about. There wasn't a single atom in her that wanted to kiss the concert idiot. She didn't find other men even *mildly* attractive; Julien was her one-and-only, her world.

Similar thoughts kept running around inside her head, and Ellie couldn't fall asleep. Before she could blame Julien or doubt Tai, what had Ellie herself been doing? Why hadn't she noticed the girls' arrival?

It was then that she remembered her find. She had been perusing the anthology during the girls' accident. She'd completely forgotten about it amidst the cave-in. She grabbed her shoulder bag from the nightstand and dug through it until she found the anthology. It would be the perfect distraction from her wicked thoughts.

As she looked through the ancient book, she wondered how she could have it authenticated. If the dates on the inside cover were accurate, she could be holding a text from the late 1600s. She'd ask Zyla about it. Maybe they could send it off to the university's department of antiquities and have it examined.

First, though, Ellie wanted to study it herself. She felt exhilarated when she touched it, as if something special inside awaited her discovery. Authentication would have to wait.

Ellie scanned the pages. Her initial guess was partly correct. At the studio, she had surmised that the book was an anthology of folktales and remedies. As she continued reading, she found that to be part of what the book contained. She found some bizarre advice revolving around the phases of the moon.

-Castrate animals when the Moon is waning for less bleeding.
-Best days for fishing are between the new and full Moon.
-Set eggs to hatch on the Moon's increase, but not if a south wind blows.

She also found a recipe for switchel, more insect repellants, further planting advice, and instructions on how to make moccasins from animal hide. The farm advice amused Ellie, but another element of the book intrigued her.

Interspersed throughout the recipes and remedies, Ellie found excerpts from the diary of a young woman during precolonial times. Her writing captured Ellie's curiosity, and she found herself imagining what it would have been like to be one of the early settlers in America.

*11 April 1692*

*I am filled with equal parts fear and anger. The serving girls have all gone mad, and now my name has been dragged through their muddy lies. Today the leader of the pack guessed that I am the one who stole her slave girl's book – this very journal in which I write.*

*Although I could argue that I thought to find some means to stop her, I must confess that I also was searching for the source of her power in order to expose her for her wicked deeds.*

Ellie's pulse quickened as she read the paragraph. This sounded like a tale of intrigue, and if the dates were real, an intrigue that was hundreds of years old. Ellie flipped back to the inside cover to check the dates. All the entries started with the words "taken from" except the last inscription. It was the one Ellie was looking for, and it was unique.

Released from E.B.P.R. to E.A.P., 1721

Ellie would have to Google the dates and the initials to see if she could find further information. Could she possibly be holding a relic from the 1700s and earlier? It would be thrilling to know if the book's dates were accurate. Ellie bet Zyla would know what to do with it, but for now, Ellie just wanted to read more. She sat up straighter, no more thoughts of sleeping, and continued to read.

*I do not know what will happen to us – our village, our farmers, our children. The accusations of witchery have crazed the very people who were meant to lead us. This be a dangerous time for our town. But my prayers are more selfish. They do not intercede for the village. They beg for mine own household. I am surrounded by rumors at every turn. I am thwarted from every angle. I cannot think what I have done to earn such calumny upon mine own Christian character.*

*Nothing other than to have allowed that wretched serving girl to take shelter under my roof. She be shameless, throwing looks of desire at my 'Nathan and finding every reason to be near him. There be rumors spreading about her lust for 'Nathan among her circle. I have prayed for him to have strength to resist temptation. If he does not put her out soon, I will.*

*I have found what I believe to be an answer to my prayers in this same journal. I do not know if I should attempt to use the remedies contained herein, but I shall have to decide soon. The wickedness is very near. It knocks at mine own door and calls me out, tempting me to betray all that is sacred within me.*

*E.B.P.*

Ellie stopped reading to let her mind envision it. She might be reading the first-person account of a woman who lived in the 1700s and who maybe, just maybe, lived through the exact period she was teaching. She really ought to show it to Zyla; she would pop a vein with excitement. Zyla would probably want to donate it to the historical society, though, and Ellie wasn't ready to hand it over.

Over the following days, the personal account of life in colonial times enthralled Ellie. It made the era she was teaching more real. Digging into the anthology helped keep her mind from worrying about Julien, Tai, the studio, and the grand opening in a few weeks' time.

Julien had been gone so much lately; she'd needed somewhere to direct her energy. The anthology helped her alleviate stress. It distracted her from all the strange thoughts that played though her dreams each night.

Both Ellie and her students had been digging into

another book, *The Crucible*, and the play dominated her thoughts, even during sleep. Reading Arthur Miller's portrayal of Elizabeth Proctor, her supposed ancestor, and all the other characters in the play left Ellie feeling like there was more to the story. Where did they all end up? Could Elizabeth Proctor or her descendants really have settled in Boston and given birth to Ellie's distant ancestors?

And what happened to Abigail Williams? Had she sailed away on a cargo ship as in the movie? Or had she simply changed her name and moved to another town to start over? Wouldn't it be amazing to be able to find out what happened to the reckless young teen after Salem?

Thinking along those lines, Ellie snuggled under the covers and settled in for another good long read. What better way to research history than studying it through a primary source? She grinned; Zyla would be so proud of her, and when Ellie had it all figured out and deciphered, she'd show off her little project and see just what Zyla thought about it all. It might end up being a time-consuming, tedious task - the handwriting was hard to read and there were smudges and stains - but Ellie bet Zyla wouldn't think of Ellie as an outsider anymore. No one would.

Ellie's imagination flew into overdrive; she'd show this town something new about their past. They'd be happy to accept her then. She'd reveal the anthology at a historically themed party after having cleverly gotten it authenticated as a primary source from the 1700s. The book would be placed in the picture window of Julien's studio with a spotlight on it and a plaque.

> Discovered by the Pelletier family during renovation, this journal recounts tales of colonists' hardships when settling Stusa and the surrounding area. Entries date from the 17th and 18th centuries.

Ellie's eyelids drooped. She knew she ought to put the

book aside and go to bed, and she would - after one more entry.

A young girl was speaking to a man, and although they were dressed oddly, she recognized them. Tai and Julien looked as if they were ready for an audition at the school play; Tai wore a plain black dress with a white scarf covering her hair, and Julien wore short, brown breeches, a loose-fitting top, and brown moccasins.

They were at Bettina's bedside, a student of Ellie's who had fallen ill with something doctors hadn't yet been able to diagnose. Julien was looking down at Bettina. Tai was admiring Julien.

"I'd almost forgotten how compassionate you are, Monsieur."

Julien turned his head to look at her, "I'd almost forgotten you were here." The corners of his mouth up turned in the suggestion of a smile, "What mischief is this, Mademoiselle?"

"Oh," Tai replied, "Bettina is just playing around being overly dramatic as usual."

"Really?" Julien raised one eyebrow. "Because everyone in town is talking about drugs and parties in the woods."

Tai rolled her eyes. "That was months ago, and we were only dancing around a campfire in the forest. My uncle caught a glimpse of us and got all hot and bothered – that's all." She giggled and batted her eyelashes at Julien.

Julien laughed. "You're a little minx, aren't you? You'll be in trouble before you're eighteen, I'll wager."

Julien turned to leave, but Tai stepped into his path. "Well, it's a good thing you like trouble, then." She reached up to touch his face, but Julien slapped her hand away.

"Cut it out, Tai. There will be no more trouble between us." He pinched his eyebrows together on the word trouble.

She smirked. "Why did you come all the way over here, then? Just to see Bettina? Since when do you care about students?"

"Since your uncle started trouble for us all with his rumors. I came to find out exactly what mischief he is making." Julien retorted. There was a tapping at the door, and the scene dissolved.

Ellie found herself lying in bed looking into the bathroom as Julien shaved, tapping his razor against the sink after every few strokes. The sound must've awakened her. She'd been dreaming.

Ellie felt an immediate wave of relief followed by a clenching of her belly. Why had she dreamed that? It was some weird mash-up of the play she was teaching and her current situation.

She tried to brush off the feeling of unease as Julien crawled into bed beside her. He leaned over to kiss her good-night, but Ellie turned her head so that his kiss landed on her cheek instead of her lips.

"What is it, *mon amour*?" He looked at her in surprise.

"I don't know." She turned back to face him. "OK, maybe I do know. I just had a bad dream, and I'm still mad at you." Ellie huffed and rolled over onto her side facing away from Julien.

Julien chuckled. "You're mad at me because of a dream?" He waited. "You do realize how preposterous that is, don't you?" He laughed again.

"Well, it may be ridiculous, but it was very real, and you would have acted exactly the same way in real life. So, I'm still irritated with you. Behave better next time!"

"Ok, *ma vie*. I will make sure I behave myself in your dreams." He kissed the back of her head and laughed again as they both drifted off to sleep.

Ellie knew she was being irrational, but the idea of Tai flirting with Julien felt as real as the anger that flared upon witnessing it - even if it was just a dream. Still aggravated, Ellie closed her eyes and prayed for a dreamless night's sleep.

# CHAPTER EIGHTEEN

## RIDICULOUS RUMORS

The following week, another dream awakened Ellie. This time, a raging fury snatched her from her sleep, and she found herself sitting upright in bed, chest heaving. She threw back the covers, barely registering Julien in bed beside her. She couldn't catch her breath. The surge of anger consumed her, pounding through every nerve and fiber, pushing up her food from dinner, threatening to spew over. She was so angry that she couldn't think.

*Calm down! Breathe!* She told herself. The anger produced a burst of unwanted energy. She leapt out of bed and started pacing. She needed a way to burn off the rage. Writing wouldn't be enough; she couldn't blog or talk. It was too personal, too humiliating, too infuriating! She wasn't even sure she could make complete sentences.

She had to find a way to calm down before exploding. She threw on a pair of sneakers. She hadn't been much of a runner since high school, but that was the only way to release the pent-up fury. She barreled into the pre-dawn darkness, running down her gravel driveway, headed for the miles-long dirt road that led to the highway.

It didn't matter that it was the middle of the night. It didn't matter that she was in the middle of nowhere. The possibility of running up on snakes, wild dogs, or even escaped convicts flitted across her mind, but instead of fear, she felt eagerness.

She would *welcome* any unforeseen attacker. Her anger wanted her to fight. In her state, she could rip the claws out of any bobcat or disarm any criminal. She felt strange – invincible, powerful, reckless.

They weren't feelings Ellie was accustomed to. She needed to reign in her thoughts and emotions. She needed a deaf listener; there was no one on God's green earth she would share this with.

*Cleansing breath in. Angry breath out. Again.*

Before long, the exertion of her run took care of her breathing, and she settled into an angry, pounding rhythm. Her mind rewound and fast forwarded, clawing through the events that had spurred the anger.

The previous afternoon, the Reverintendent had summoned her to his office after school. Some teachers had approached Principal Danvers about Ellie's husband and his protégé. They didn't think it was appropriate for a high school student "like Tai" to be working with a married man twice her age. They insinuated something was going on between the two of them and asked the principal to go to the Reverintendent. The Reverintendent turned around and came to Ellie - or made her come to him.

Other rumors had made their way to administrators, too. A faculty member overheard Tai saying she had Julien "wrapped around her little finger." Instead of talking to Ellie, the teacher had gone to the principal – who had handed it over to the Reverintendent. Ellie was caught completely off guard when the Reverintendent confronted her. She'd not heard a single rumor about Tai and Julien. The news had slammed into her core and left her reeling. She'd not been able to mask her emotions. She was lucky she'd remained standing, as her insides spun out of control.

A dozen questions flooded her mind. Just how long had the stories been flying around? Why hadn't anyone approached her first before running to administration? Wouldn't it have been easier to go straight to Ellie? In addition to the knife wound to her heart, the news that everyone had gone over her head was a punch in the gut. It took her breath away and made her double over in pain.

Had Zyla known anything about the awful gossip? Surely, she would have warned Ellie if she'd had any inkling of the rumors. Ellie pushed the thoughts away and continued to pound down the dirt road.

According to the Reverintendent, the fault was entirely Julien's. A grown man shouldn't have hired a young beauty, encouraging her crush. Young girls were always taken advantage of by older, more experienced men. Somehow, Ellie doubted that Julien was more experienced than Tai – but she'd held her tongue – more out of outrage than common sense.

What really stoked her wrath was when the Reverintendent strongly suggested that Julien cut all ties with Tai – to save Julien's business, Tai's reputation, and Ellie's job. He said he couldn't afford to have teachers associated with such scuttlebutt. Teachers had to be above reproach, above suspicion. Above suspicion? Who did he think he was? Ellie put on another burst of speed.

*The people here just absolutely refuse to mind their own business! They are worse than the gnats. If it's not somebody tending to my religion, it's a whole bunch of somebodies tending to my marriage!*

What did Julien's assistant at the *studio* have to do with her job at *school*? What business did the school have nosing into her husband's career? The answer struck her forcefully, and she stumbled.

Tai was his *niece*. How could she have forgotten?

The Reverintendent would have been personally insulted, of course, due to the rumors. It was awkward for everyone. The Reverintendent, however, was determined to cast blame anywhere except on his own household. That *had* to be his motivation. He wanted to protect his niece and divert all negativity toward Julien rather than face the promiscuous problem in his own home.

That made Ellie stop short. She bent over, hands on her knees, and struggled to catch her breath as rage and doubt battled each other for control.

Even though Tai was his niece, how the devil could he believe every disgusting rumor running rampant around town and assume it was true? Was this a reverse Spanish Inquisition? Was he set against her because she was Catholic? Was Stusa now the Church of Rumors? Guilty until proven innocent?

The questions gave rise to another burst of energy, and she kicked off again. What kind of teacher would she be to condone such wantonness between her husband and a student? Exactly what kind of teacher did they think Ellie was? What kind of wife? What kind of mother?

As her feet and her thoughts raced at full speed, another idea hit Ellie. What if the Reverintendent hadn't been threatening her? What if he'd been trying to *warn* her?

If he had doubts about Tai, perhaps he wanted *Ellie* to be the one to confront Julien to keep from facing his niece. Maybe he wasn't trying to threaten Ellie. Maybe, just maybe, he thought he was helping her.

After walking the last mile home, Ellie was spent – physically and emotionally. She went straight to the shower. Ellie thought she'd prepared herself mentally for the difficulties of living in a small town, but she'd never realized that small towns could be so small-minded. What exactly was it that drove this need - this craving - for drama and gossip? Julien said that people were bored and wanted some excitement, and since there was none in Stusa, they simply created their own.

It was a narcissistic theory. Would people meddle in others' lives just to entertain themselves, cooking up stories? But that was exactly what was happening. Petty people were lighting a fire under a pot, pouring in a few facts, sprinkling in some malicious seasoning, and then stirring the pot. Intentionally. So that they could sit back and watch it boil over.

Ellie just never thought that she could be one of the ingredients of such a wicked brew.

As water rinsed the lather from her hair, Ellie couldn't deny it any longer; she admitted to herself that the rumors hurt. They made her angry. They made her anxious. They made her doubt Tai. They made her doubt Julien. After the meeting with the Reverintendent, she realized her job could be in jeopardy if they continued.

After all, teachers were public figures and were held to a higher standard of moral behavior. That constant scrutiny had never bothered Ellie before. She was a rule-follower by nature and had never been under attack. Oh, she would love to get directly to the source of the rumors and discuss the issue *tête-à-tête*, but it was hard to confront the source without knowing who it was.

Besides, the rumors mainly involved Julien. The arrows of attack weren't pointing at her, but as they glanced off Julien's broad, dark shoulders, they changed course and found the nearest target – Ellie. And while the blows were not fatal, they still pierced the skin and wounded.

Ellie didn't know how to handle it, so she buried herself in her anthology. It continued to be her favorite reading. Ellie was learning about what life was like in colonial times. Ellie found comfort there, amidst the thick pages cracked and stained with age.

Just as in *The Crucible*, whispers and accusations whirled through the journal entries, destroying some and advancing others. Everything seemed intertwined, as if sewn together by an invisible thread – the anthology, *The Crucible*, and Ellie's life in Stusa – whether stitched together by threads reality or insanity Ellie had yet to discover.

The more she read, the more similarities she found. Was she forging connections that weren't there? Or was there some relief in finding that others before her – whether fictional or real – had experienced the same?

*The Crucible* portrayed a fictionalized account of Elizabeth Proctor, and the anthology painted a very realistic portrait of EBP, whom Ellie had nicknamed Ebbie. Like Ellie, both ladies were devoted wives whose husbands had put themselves in precarious situations. Like Ellie, they defended their husbands from all sorts of rumors and accusations. Like Ellie, they believed that living a life above such base gossip would reveal innocence in the end.

And although historical records didn't show how Elizabeth Proctor dealt with her grief, Ebbie and Ellie turned to the mysterious book – both women using the pages of the anthology to escape their anger, doubts, and fears. Ellie often wondered if either of her two leading ladies ever imagined that, hundreds of years later, they would provide solace for another woman dealing with the same issues.

With all the technological progress humans had made, human nature hadn't progressed at all. Four hundred years after the Salem Witch Trials, small town gossip still thrived on the same fodder. The setting may have been more modern, but the rumors remained the same.

# CHAPTER NINETEEN

## *THE SHADOW*

A tingling from her new scar awoke *The Shadow*. She'd begun to understand the nudges and tugs it gave her; something *important* was happening. The family heirloom had begun to weave its wonders. *The Shadow* must be very close to restoring it to her family's control. No, she corrected herself – to *The Shadow's* control.

*The Shadow's* family had lost track of the beloved heirloom after its last known disciple had moved to Stusa in 1697 with an uncle and a cousin. *The Shadow* had never understood why her mother hadn't moved to Stusa herself to search for it, but her mother had stupidly believed the family connection to have been severed and for the heirloom to have been hidden somewhere else. *The Shadow*, however, had always been drawn to Stusa and firmly believed it to be the heirloom's final resting place. Now that the emerald cord had branded her, she was more convinced than ever that she'd made the right move.

The heirloom's nature, however, hadn't only called out to *The Shadow*. It had forged a connection with Ellie Pelletier, too. *The Shadow* wasn't worried. She knew Ellie would never dare to claim its power for herself. Ellie's link would have to be severed, but *The Shadow* delighted in the idea of a competition for the heirloom's allegiance. She would finally be able to release her anger and strike at an adversary, albeit a weak one. Ellie was neither worthy enough nor bold enough to control the heirloom and its power.

Gabby had spoken of the dueling powers contained within the heirloom. Every culture had a name for them - *yin* and *yang*, *egocentric* and *exocentric*, *dark* and *light*. A cunning manipulation had led to terms like *good* versus *evil*, *selfish* versus *selfless*, *instinct* versus *intellect*, but *The Shadow* inherently understood the root words that most people were mute to speak - *power* versus *weakness*.

And she'd choose power every time. Power wasn't good or bad. It was a tool, fit only for those with strength enough to wield it.

Growing up with a pathetic, neglectful mother had trained *The Shadow* to wield what power she possessed like a weapon. She was used to forcing her own way. When had things ever been easy for her? The only easy part of her childhood had been having Gabby there to tell her stories of their past. *The Shadow* smiled slightly thinking of Gabby. How different things would have been if Gabby had lived longer and had been able to guide *The Shadow* further in her quest.

As it was, Gabby had died too soon. When Gabby died after a strenuous, seven-day illness, *The Shadow* blamed her mother for not taking Gabby to the hospital and vowed to reclaim both the heirloom and its power for herself. *The Shadow* never forgave her mother for Gabby's death. They'd never been close, and when her mother died in a farming accident, *The Shadow* felt relieved, liberated.

Yes, it had been hard, but *The Shadow* had been driven by spite and anger. Her very first move was to backpack her way south, heading towards the tiny town that held an ancient family connection. She had taken her late mother's emergency cash before leaving. *The Shadow* had no intention of shunning modern living as her mother had.

In those days, *The Shadow* had found work and lodging as she traveled. She was an attractive girl, and her looks got her jobs at local diners when she needed cash. She job-hopped herself all the way to Stusa. She eventually enrolled in school to get free access to the internet. Being a sixteen-year-old girl had its advantages; it was fitting that *The Shadow* would, at the same age as her infamous ancestor, make her own indelible mark in the annals of history.

"This predilection for minding other people's business was time-honored among the people of Salem, and it undoubtedly created many of the suspicions which were to feed the coming madness."

--ARTHUR MILLER, FROM "AN OVERTURE," ACT ONE, THE CRUCIBLE

# CHAPTER TWENTY

## *CHARM TRIAL*

Ellie awoke to the burbling hiss of the cappuccino machine downstairs. She heard the clink of forks against plates and the giggles of the girls. What time was it? Was she late for work? She blinked to clear her eyes and check the clock, but Julien's footsteps coming up the stairs distracted her.

"Bonjour, ma vie," he smiled as he walked into their bedroom carrying a breakfast tray laden with fruit, croissants, and a large cappuccino. "I thought you deserved a sleep-in after homecoming week." He set the tray down over Ellie's lap as she sat up.

"Wow," she rubbed her sleepy eyes and grinned sheepishly. "Breakfast in bed. If I had known this was coming, maybe I'd have been nicer during Homecoming Week."

The previous week had been the single most disastrous of Ellie's career. Homecoming Week, called Hell Week by the faculty, was foreign to Ellie and had taken her by surprise. It had started with her supervising the float-building of the freshman class and had ended with the float falling apart in the middle of the parade. Ellie had been humiliated; parents and students had been irate.

"The girls and I are going out for a walk with the dogs. Stay in bed and relax for a while." He fluffed the pillows up against the headboard and left the room. Ellie heard the girls' enthusiastic chatter, getting ready for their walk.

She lay back against the pillows with a contented sigh.

*Aaaahhh*, she indulged in a luxurious stretch. *This almost makes everything worthwhile. Almost.* After Hell Week, she craved escapism. She turned to the bedside table and pulled out the anthology.

The more Ellie read of the folklore, the more fascinated she was. She found herself drawn to its mysterious recipes. Part of Ellie still wondered if she should turn it over to an expert, but the selfish side of her wanted to solve all its mysteries herself. She felt a bit like Nancy Drew, stumbling upon a book of secrets that would lead to some wonderful surprise. She couldn't let someone else solve the mystery; after all, no one else had known the book was hidden in the niche, so it wasn't like she was depriving anyone.

Before Hell Week, Ellie had taken to reading through the anthology before bed each night. It was her favorite part of the day. Many mornings, she found herself waking up and counting the hours until she could slink back to bed to read more.

Ebbie, her journal entries sprinkled throughout the text, felt more like a friend than a story. Ellie related to her. Ebbie was embroiled in scandal, and Ellie wholeheartedly believed Ebbie to be as innocent as she claimed. Ellie turned the pages of the anthology as if it were a novel; she couldn't wait to find out what happened next.

Since Julien had the girls and the dogs, she could afford to play catch up. It wasn't exactly easy reading; much of the anthology was smeared and splotched with what Ellie could only guess to be water damage or just plain old aging. She didn't let that hinder her reading, though. Whenever she got to a smudge or a section that was illegible, she took out her magnifying glass and tried to determine at least the first and last letter of the word. Then, she used the computer to find as many words as she could that started and ended with the same letters. She'd replace the illegible word with each trial word, testing the sentence aloud to see if it felt right. So far, she had made some progress. Smiling to herself, she settled back into bed and got to work on her guilty pleasure.

Little by little Ellie was making progress. She had become a decent researcher, something she had always abhorred in the past. After her breakfast in bed, she got down to work. The entry that greeted her wasn't one by Ebbie, though. It turned out to be some advice for getting rid of bad dreams.

### Ridding Oneself of Troubling Dreams

*Take seven heads of dried lavender blooms and crush into powder. Mix crushed lavender with one pinch each of hops, thyme and valerian root and add to a spoonful of honey. Roll mixture into the center of a beeswax candle.*

*Just before bedtime, light the candle and drink one cup of tea made from valerian root, thyme and wild lettuce. Keep the lighted candle by bedside. Let it burn until feeling drowsy, then extinguish. Repeat every night for one week and bad dreams will be expelled.*

It was just what she hadn't realized she wanted, to get rid of bad dreams, and the recipe seemed too easy not to test. She already had the lavender, thyme, and valerian root. She did a quick internet search to see if wild lettuce grew in her area. Yes! Now, what would she do about the beeswax candle and the hops?

Ellie researched candle-making supplies and hops suppliers online. When she was ready to place her order, she made a special request at the last minute for it to be delivered in an unmarked box. *If the post lady saw an order with hops marked on the outside of the package, a rumor about an illegal microbrewery would surface within minutes.* Stusa was in a dry county, after all. She was pleased with herself for thinking proactively to prevent that rumor.

What would Julien think of her latest herbal concoction? He didn't seem to mind all the time she'd been devoting to the anthology each night after tucking the girls in to bed. Well, if Ellie was honest – he hadn't noticed. She hadn't told

Julien about the anthology; a selfish part of her didn't want to share her discovery with anyone, and he hadn't seen her reading it because he had been so busy at the studio.

Ellie was reticent to tell him about the amazing anthology, knowing in advance what his sarcastic response to her sleuthing would be. He already teased her mercilessly about her herbal tendencies. He joked that she must have been married to a witch doctor in a past life.

Besides, their paths hadn't crossed much lately. This morning was the first time she'd talked to him, even briefly, in the last three days. He was either at the studio or setting up photo shoots. A lesser woman might have been jealous of his time, but Ellie knew that he was working hard to make his dream a success.

Rather than being jealous of his time away from her, Ellie had deliberately set aside all the negative rumors about him and Tai. She was proud of Julien for making a go of it. Most people were too afraid to drop everything and chase their dreams.

Most people were like Ellie. Taking the plunge to move to Stusa was risk enough for her. Amid everything else they had going on in their lives right now, Ellie would never dare make her dream shop a reality. She would just tuck that little fantasy away and use it for escapism as needed. Someone had to have steady income to pay the bills, after all, and she had her hands full with her students, the play, the girls, and their preparations for Julien's big opening night at the end of the month.

Thinking fondly of her husband and his bravery, Ellie hopped out of bed and threw on some clothes and her hiking boots. Now would be a good time to join in on the family fun and reconnect with her husband. She hadn't even thanked him for breakfast, she realized. And if she just happened to find some wild lettuce, well – that would make the morning perfect.

◆ ◆ ◆

Three days later, Ellie had everything ready. Her ship-ment had arrived unmarked as requested, and she'd found plenty of wild lettuce in the woods near their property. She even transplanted a few specimens to her herb garden to see if she could grow it herself. The beeswax candle rested by her bedside, and the ingredients for the herbal tea steeped in a mug. All she needed now was to crawl into bed, light the can-dle, and drink up.

The herbal tea, however, looked disgusting and smelled worse. She debated adding a glop of honey but decided that she'd better follow the instructions to the letter. Ellie grabbed the anthology and checked. So far, it looked like she had done everything properly.

That evening, she lit the candle, gulped the tea – it was just as bad as it smelled – and crawled under the covers. She would read a bit of the anthology until she felt drowsy, per the instructions. She gave a little snort of laughter at the tiny writing squeezed under the recipe, wondering what Julien and Zyla would say.

> Note - If any troubling dreams remain
> after treatment, they should be examined
> for prophetic insight. They could be warn-
> ings or visions.

If Julien or Zyla ever saw this, they'd laugh at her and think she was ridiculous, if not crazy. Ellie, however, found the little notes endearing. If the authors believed in visions and prophesy, who was she to argue? If she was honest with herself, a small part of her wanted to believe in them, too.

Not that she believed in visions, exactly, but some-times she felt that her dreams were messages. Pieces of infor-mation that her subconscious noticed and interpreted while she was asleep. Warnings that her waking self hadn't perceived or understood. Isn't that what sleep researchers claimed? One of the sleeping brain's jobs was to process and file memories of the day. So, if hundreds of years ago people thought they had special prophesies or visions while they were asleep, then Ellie could see why.

Ellie continued reading for at least an hour. Rather than getting sleepy, she felt energized. She was too excited to see if her remedy was going to work.

As she flipped through the anthology, she came across more pages in Ebbie's familiar handwriting. Ellie remembered last reading about the illness Ebbie had suffered after the birth of her second child. As Ellie delved back into Ebbie's storyline, she settled in for another interesting read, hoping it would help her fall asleep and test the charm she had used.

Despite the centuries separating them, Ellie found similarities to Ebbie. Both were busy mothers. Both fiercely loved their families. And both had recently moved to a small village.

After the delivery of their second son, Ebbie had been too weak to care for the child. She had nearly died in childbirth, so her husband hired a girl from the village to help.

> *April 1692*
>
> *I am afeared. I have particular reason to believe that my serving girl is a dangerous temptress sent to destroy my husband's soul. And I must choose whether to use her own evil against her. These are harsh words, but the Evil One is a harsh opponent and I know he doth wish me every harm. He dareth not confront me openly perchance I use the Good Book and the name of the Son to bind him from his wicked works. Thus, he attacks my husband, using his handmaiden to do his bidding.*
>
> *That girl. That wicked young harlot who flaunts both her vitality and her vanity without a thought for anything but her own pleasure. I rue the day she were brought into my house to touch my children and stain them with her filth. Providence protect the innocent from her, I prithee.*

*Mine own husband may well be past his innocence. I have heard noises in the night and when reaching over for him have found him absent from my bed. I dare not confront him. He hath the fury of hell when angered, and I do not want to endanger the children lest he take out his anger on them.*

*This wrath of his is a new thing. He were a gentle Christian man when I met him. The Jezebel hath brought him low with her cunning ways. I will bide my time for now as I am still in poor health, but I will rid myself of her as soon as I am able.*

*Although she be the preacher's niece, I will cast doubt upon her good name. 'Nathan must not know that I am the one to criticize his little pet. Not yet. He can naught but deny any wrongdoing in my presence. Why should he do otherwise when men have always had their pets, their intrigues?*

*I was but a naïve girl when I married. I did not know of the ways of men. I am sorely and bitterly deceived. And it grieves my heart, more so than the birthing pains that have left me physically weakened. I would suffer an 'undred more births than one more night of bitter betrayal and heartbreak.*

*It makes me question Providence, though it be a mortal sin. If men can never be trusted or faithful - why, did our Lord and Saviour take the form of a man to live amongst us? We women see how men live here on earth. They have all power, all control, and use that power to their own pleasure without regard for our being. How can we trust in that image? Would not a womanly figure have been more comforting and understanding of what we endure?*

*But that is to blaspheme and to doubt my Saviour. I will stop before I condemn mine own soul to eternal suffering. For now, life on earth is mine own damnation. I seek peace in the afterlife and will do nothing to open my soul to any damage. My body and heart may perish little by little with each betrayal, but my soul will live eternally at rest with our Lord.*

*E.B.P.*

Ellie closed the book. What a depressing read. Now she had a little more background on what Ebbie had been referring to in her earlier entry. Ellie assumed it was an earlier entry. She couldn't tell since it was marked April 1692. She turned back to find the previous entry. It was dated 11 April 1692.

Were the entries not ordered sequentially? Had Ebbie simply turned to random pages scattered throughout the anthology as she vented her thoughts? And what had happened to the mysterious remedy Ebbie had referred to in the previous entry? Ellie wanted to know what it was and why Ebbie had hesitated to use it.

More importantly, had it worked? Had the serving girl left Ebbie's husband alone? The whole situation reminded her of the play she was teaching. Elizabeth Proctor had felt the same way about Abigail Williams in Arthur Miller's version of the Salem Witch Trials. And since Ellie couldn't change the outcome of the play, she found herself desperately rooting for Ebbie, wanting the charm to work.

Instead of finding answers to her questions, Ellie only learned that 'Nathan turned out to be a selfish cheater just like nearly every other man Ellie had ever read about. Why was it so impossible for a man to be loyal to one woman? No wonder Jesus was single. Maybe that was the only way men could be faithful – by being celibate.

Ellie sighed and took off her reading glasses. Her heart cringed for poor Ebbie, and the frustration left her unsettled, conflicted about her own marriage. It would be a good night to test the tea and candle combo she had prepared. After gulping down yet another cup of the terrible tea and re-lighting the candle, Ellie rolled onto her side, curled into a ball, and closed her eyes.

She didn't feel sleepy; she felt bone-weary. As she closed her eyes, she uttered a plea for the tea to work. She didn't want to dream about any of this. She had squelched enough sparks about Julien to light a bonfire, and she didn't know how much longer she could keep them smothered.

**COREY**: Mister Hale... I have always wanted to ask a learned man—What signifies the readin' of strange books?
**HALE**: What books?
**COREY**: I cannot tell; she hides them. Martha, my wife. I have waked at night many times and found her in a corner, readin' of a book. Now what do you make of that?

--GILES COREY TO REVEREND HALE, ACT ONE, SCENE 1 THE
CRUCIBLE

# CHAPTER TWENTY-ONE

## *POSITIVE PARTICIPATION*

In the days following the tea test, Ellie noticed two things she attributed to the anthology. She was dreaming less, and fewer gnats pestered her. If only she could find a charm to keep people from pestering her. Ellie continued to pour her energy into her job and her home life. She was determined not to cater to the rumor mill. She held her head high and behaved as if nothing were amiss.

At school, she continued classes as normal. Since many of her students were struggling with the antiquated style of speaking in *The Crucible*, she had the students write a letter to one of the characters from Act I, mimicking the style and syntax of the 1600s.

About half of her students wrote to Abigail, the ringleader of the girls who accuse villagers of witchcraft to get what they want. Their letters scolded Abigail for manipulating the group of girls and for threatening them if they didn't back up her story.

The other half of Ellie's students wrote to John Proctor, the object of Abigail's desire who tries to forget about his lust for Abigail. The letters reprimanded him for acting on his feelings for Abigail in the first place.

GG, however, wrote the most perceptive letter of all. Her writing reflected real insight into both the history of the period and the position of women at that time. Her letter also displayed an excellent imitation of the speech pattern Arthur Miller used when writing the play. In short, it was an outstanding piece of work; Ellie Googled it to make sure GG hadn't plagiarized it.

GG's letter was written to Tituba, the slave from Barbados who leads the group of girls in three forbidden activities of the time - conjuring Ruth Putnam's dead sisters to "come out of the grave," helping Abigail with a "charm to kill John Proctor's wife," and dancing. Not only was it a unique idea for GG to write to Tituba, a powerless slave, but her imagination of what was happening behind the scenes in Salem Village was compelling, too. For example, GG did not assume that the girls were innocent of witchcraft, as most do.

*Poor Tituba,*

*You wretched, inexperienced little fool. It were horribly indecent of you to play at conjurin' spirits. You broke the first two rules of The Art. Twere terrible times for you, workin' as a slave and wantin' nothin' more than to fly home to Barbados, yet you should have known not to cast magick on another without her consent. Tryin' to charm Goody Proctor were not of your nature nor your ability.*

*Furthermore, The Book is clear that you cannot teach ever so small a charm to those who would not treat it respectfully. You should have known that no good could come from your meddlin' with The Art in plain view of them girls. If you had truly acknowledged The Art as a sacred gift, you would have been sure to work your magick undisturbed by others.*

*'Tis easy to understand that, when they blamed you for devil worship, you said whatever you could to prevent another bloody punishment. Although you rightly exposed Reverend Parris for his evil treatment of you, and his religious hypocrisy, you did wrongly reveal to others the nature of our Art.*

*In revealing our Art, you forgot the fourth rule -- the decree that whatever energy you send out returns to you threefold. Tis why you were punished til the end of your days. 'Tis why your Book went missin' without a trace. Your mishandlin' of the pow'r you were cravin' was your downfall.*

*Abigail Williams*

The letter lifted Ellie out of her angry fog and helped restore her belief that she was getting through to some of her students. Ellie loved how GG had taken the line about the "strange book" and turned it into an actual book of witchcraft. Ellie almost wished that GG had written more, and she considered having the students write a sequel to the play after they finished it.

All in all, it was another successful assignment, and Ellie chose to bask in the contentment of it for a few days. In November, they would be hosting the grand opening of Julien's studio. There was plenty to do to keep Ellie's mind focused on the tasks at hand rather than dwelling on the ridiculous rumors that swirled around her.

"These people had no ritual for the washing away of sins. It is another trait we inherited from them, and it has helped to discipline us as well as breed hypocrisy among us."

--ARTHUR MILLER, ACT ONE, THE CRUCIBLE

# CHAPTER TWENTY-TWO

## INESCAPABLE INSECURITY

Since Ellie's meeting with the Reverintendent, she'd purposely made an appearance each day in the faculty lounge. The others, because that's what they were to her now, sickened Ellie with the hushed silence that fell when she entered, and the quickly exchanged glances as she left.

Ellie plastered a smile on her face and acted as if no one had been poisoning her husband's good name. She sat with people who pretended to be her friend as they swapped student stories and recipes. She smiled on the outside and cringed on the inside whenever Annabelle Sarka started in on her latest gossip about student affairs and fights.

*Really*, Ellie wondered, *what would Mrs. Sarka do if she didn't have any students to meddle with*? She was a pot-stirrer and on Ellie's short list of potential rumor-starters. Mrs. Sarka rather enjoyed thinking of herself as the teacher with the best relationship with the students. She called it "being accessible," but Ellie called it being a busybody.

It was hard to maintain her façade, but the worst part was that Ellie continued to have doubts. She would find herself wondering about things that never would have crossed her mind before. She was starting to question Julien's interest in Tai.

At first, Ellie had been pleased with the idea of Julien taking an uneducated young woman under his wing and grooming her for the world of photography. It was clear that Tai had natural talent, and it was also clear that she would never be able to make a living on that creativity without guidance and exposure to the world outside of Stusa.

Ellie was proud of Julien for sharing his expertise with someone less fortunate. She was impressed that he was willing to hire someone the community looked down upon. One of the things she loved most about him was his generosity.

As Julien continued to spend more and more time at the studio, Ellie credited it to all the preparations for the grand opening at the beginning of November. When gossips questioned their relationship, Ellie ignored them; she viewed them as baseless rumors spread by the petty and the pitiful. After all, many of Ellie's female students were jealous of Tai and her ample curves – especially Jelly Sarka and Eve and Eden Matthews. They were probably the ones who started the rumors anyway - out of spite.

Lately, however, Ellie's mind had turned on her. Awful daydreams popped into her head without warning, sending icy tendrils through her veins and pricking her heart. Ellie tried to shake them off, but they struck without warning – while driving, while doing laundry, while working in the garden.

Like a lightning bolt, an image would flash in her mind then vanish. Ellie would see Tai and Julien in an embrace that lasted a moment too long, or Julien reaching over to brush the blonde hair out of Tai's face -- intimate movements that had no place in their relationship.

Twice, Ellie had to pull over to vomit on the side of the road. The thoughts sickened her and left behind a fierce rage along with dry heaves. How could her mind do this to her?

She wasn't sleeping well despite no longer having nightmares. She couldn't eat for the nausea and the stress. Her worries plagued her day and night. Why couldn't she control these images, these thoughts, these visions?

# CHAPTER TWENTY-THREE

## THE SHADOW

*The Shadow* gathered her groupies once more. She needed to invoke a scrying spell to obtain the necessary information - how to sever Ellie's connection to the heirloom, an uncoupling that would leave the heirloom's power intact yet still receptive to a new handler - one with enough willpower to direct it.

This time, they met at dawn on a small, marshy strip that jutted out into a slow-moving segment of the river. Although they were close to a cypress-filled area of swampland, the water moved enough to meet the conditions of the invocation. The ritual required running water.

*The Shadow* had not invited the shy one. Only four souls were needed to complete the task. The twins and Jelly Sarka showed up on time, once again dressed in their cloaks. While the groupies complained about wearing them, *The Shadow* knew that they secretly enjoyed the air of mystery the prescribed cloaks provided.

As she knelt by the fire watching the groupies' arrival, *The Shadow* was glad to see that Jelly had not brought her magenta cell phone. While the cloaks were no longer in pristine condition, the terrifying flight through the woods at their previous meeting having sullied them, everything looked to be in order. Eve held a small mirror. Eden brought a polished piece of black obsidian, and Jelly had a vial of holy oil. The invocation would lack nothing.

As the girls drew near, *The Shadow* put her fingers to her lips to silence them. She sat down, then motioned for them to do the same. She modeled a seated meditation pose with upward facing palms, and they obediently copied her position.

*The Shadow* withdrew a small, silver chalice, allegedly forged from a piece of the Cup of Jamshid. It had taken her mother many years to acquire the piece. It was too bad her mother had never thought to use it to scry for the heirloom.

She took a sip from it and passed it around the circle. The tincture ensured that the girls would remember nothing of the ceremony. The twins looked at each other and giggled, but Jelly drank without hesitation. For a split second, in fact, *The Shadow* feared that Jelly had consumed the entire amount, but there must have been some leftover because the twins grimaced at the bitter taste when the cup reached them.

*The Shadow* stretched out a palm and waited for the girls to hand over the items they'd brought. She placed them inside the now empty chalice. First, the tiny mirror. Then, the polished obsidian. Next, she leaned over and scooped up some of the river into the cup. Finally, she poured the oil over it all and swirled it around.

She threw a handful of ground crystals into the fire, and the flames shifted from orange to emerald green and finally to deep purple. A pungent odor arose from the flames. As the girls inhaled the fumes, their eyes glazed over, and they began to sway. *The Shadow* stared into the chalice, concentrating without blinking until her vision blurred and images began to form. Markings appeared in the chalice, floating on the oily water and Eve spoke.

"The four elements that bind the universe also bind the disciple to the script. Only by using their power can you sever the connection."

Eden continued. "Find the element that bears the strongest influence. Its opposite force will extinguish the link."

Jelly finished. "The disciple must not suspect your involvement. Otherwise the script will protect itself with powerful elemental force."

A series of three smoky lines arose from the fire. At first, they appeared as three vertical wavy lines - fire. Then, the lines rotated to hover horizontally over the fire - water. Next, the three lines of smoke straightened out into taut horizontal lines - air. Finally, the straight lines crinkled into jagged peaks and valleys - earth.

*The Shadow* smiled. She knew exactly where to start

*The Shadow* watched Ellie and Zyla walk around the county fair together. Ellie and her optimistic, happy attitude made *The Shadow* sick. She could see Ellie enjoying herself, greeting students and parents alike. Ellie was a slender, attractive woman, but no one would ever call her beautiful - not until she smiled.

Ellie's smile could light up a room, and when she chose to flash it, people immediately felt better. It was like her smile infused its recipients with a jolt of temporary, dazzling happiness. For the few seconds that they basked in the light of her smile, they got a taste of Ellie's inner joy.

And that taste was addictive. People always wanted more, so they kept coming back. Just hoping for a tiny moment in Ellie's light. Although no one would attribute Ellie's rise in popularity to her looks, people still used words like *striking* and *charming* to describe her. The townspeople of Stusa might not be able to pinpoint their attraction to Ellie, but *The Shadow* could.

*The Shadow* first suspected that Ellie had discovered her heirloom the night she'd been branded, and now she was certain. Ellie's aura reeked of electricity; it was unnatural. The enhancement to Ellie's persona was almost magical. *The*

*Shadow* attributed it to the heirloom, and she would do any-thing to get it. In a way, it was a stroke of luck that Ellie had found it for her. Now, all *The Shadow* had to do was steal it right from under Ellie's sickeningly silver glow.

She smirked as she thought of what was to come. *The Shadow* would see just how much wattage Ellie's smile held. After all, extinguishing that electric smile with the element of water was only natural.

# CHAPTER TWENTY-FOUR

## *FALL FESTIVAL*

It was mid-October, and personalities were more pleasant as the temperature finally descended below the 100-degree mark. Ellie admired Stusa's sense of community. She would have enjoyed the fair if she hadn't been coerced into sitting in the dunking booth. Mrs. Sarka had approached her a week earlier to see if, as Stusa 's newest teacher, she would be willing to submit herself to either a pie-throw or a dunking booth. It was a request far above and beyond her job requirements, but Ellie soon found out that it was a tradition. All the teachers participated in some way at the carnival. In fact, it was expected of them.

Each teacher had his or her specialty. Mrs. Sarka ran the photo booth. It suited her. She was vain, so she knew just what poses, props, and filters each model would want. It somewhat satisfied her need for being in the public eye. Mrs. Sarka craved attention in a way that made Ellie leery.

Zyla, as the history/drama teacher, oversaw the stage performance. She tried to get Ellie to perform *The Crucible*, but Ellie insisted they weren't ready. Her class had only covered Act I. Act II wouldn't be ready until spring semester was nearly done. Zyla tried to convince her to perform the first act at the fall festival and the second act at the spring fling, but Ellie didn't think she was up for that much public scrutiny yet.

Mr. Grant already had twenty years' worth of dibs on the lemonade stand, so Ellie couldn't claim a kiosk for her lavender lemonade. She thought about what other talents she could bring to the fair without subjecting herself to the bodily torture of the dunking booth, but all other posts were filled by those with a prior claim.

Being new sucked.

Ellie had eventually decided on the dunking booth when she found that she'd be replaced with a dry candidate after her first dunking. She figured one good dunking was easier than a face full of pie. Getting wet seemed a lot, well - cleaner - than getting sugary, sticky cream all over her face and hair.

As Ellie and Zyla toured the fair, Ellie grew more and more apprehensive. She felt like people were sneering at her rather than smiling. She had the unshakable feeling that someone was watching her. Several times she thought she saw someone out of the corner of her eye, but each time she turned to look, no one was there. After Ellie's third jump-and-whirl, Zyla piped up.

"OK, Ellie. You're either hyped up on sugar and caffeine, or you're training for the witness protection program. What gives?"

"What?" Ellie blushed slightly. "It's not normal to keep checking behind me? Because I think someone is following me – us" she amended.

Zyla gave an impressive eye roll and said, "I think Julien may be right. You've read too many novels. Who on earth would be following us? A student with a crush on the new teacher?"

Elli's blush deepened. "It's not like that, Zyla. I just have a strange feeling, that's all."

"No, wait," Zyla continued as if Ellie hadn't said anything. "It's probably a turnip farmer stalking us for digging up his greens in the middle of the night." Ellie chuckled. This prompted more from Zyla who loved making people laugh.

"No, hang on. I'm picking up some vibes." Zyla stretched one hand out in front of her and covered her eyes with the other one. "Yes, I am definitely getting something here. It's a weak signal, but I think I can make out – phantom, foe, fugitive – farmer! It's Farmer John! He thinks you're the one who has been cow tipping at his farm lately."

Ellie snorted, "Ha ha. Very funny. Where did you get your psychic training? Back there from old Maude the Magical?"

"Tsk, tsk," clucked Zyla. "You'll never be as smart an aleck as I am. Don't even try, missy." She turned to Ellie and grinned. "I think you've had a little too much fair food – just one funnel cake too many. You're getting mighty big for your britches." Zyla starting walking and kept her tone light and playful. "What makes you think you're being followed? Where's your evidence, Miss English Teacher?"

Ellie sighed. "I don't really have any. I just feel like someone is watching me, and I keep seeing things out of the corner of my eye. Every time I turn around, though, nothing is there. I've been feeling this way since the day the girls' fort collapsed at *The Jewel*."

To her credit, Zyla didn't laugh. "So, it's not just the fried Oreo," she held up one finger for each item on her list, "the grilled ear of corn, the cotton candy and the funnel cake talking, then? You've been feeling like this for a few weeks, now?"

"Well, when you put it like that – I guess my blood sugar is spiking about now." Ellie stopped walking. "Maybe I should go home. You know, I don't feel well now that you mention it. I think I'll just head to the car and -"

"Wait a minute, young lady." Zyla shook a finger at Ellie with a grin. "I know exactly what you're up to. You can't trick a trickster." She pointed the same finger into Ellie's chest and pushed with each word. "The. Dunking. Booth. You don't want to do it!" Zyla gave a cry of glee. "You have been manipulating me all along with your little whirls and jumps."

Zyla paused and looked Ellie up and down. "You clever

fiend. You almost had me. I repeat. Almost." Zyla cackled with delight. "Oh, you're good - too good. I'm going to be keeping an eye on you, my pretty."

Ellie sighed and smiled, "Well, you can't blame a girl for trying." Ellie grimaced at the lie that came so easily. But it was easier to pretend that she'd been kidding all along than to admit that she was actually afraid – afraid of something she couldn't explain.

A few minutes later, they reached the dunking booth. Zyla grabbed Ellie's hands and pretended to lock them behind her in a cop-and-robber stance. She escorted Ellie up to Mrs. Sarka and said, "We gotta live one, Annie! Ellie, here, was trying to shirk her civic duty and escape the clutches of the carnival." Zyla looked around to see whose attention she could rally.

"We better get her up on that there dunkin' chair afore she makes a break for it!" Zyla's southern drawl was exaggerated and cartoon-like. She was playing it up, enjoying her role as crowd-stirrer. A few people came over to see what was going on. Zyla addressed them.

"That's right, folks. Step on up. Let's watch Stusa's newcomer take one for the home team." More people were gathering, and Zyla didn't hold back. "This little lady was runnin' scared. She thought she could outsmart us all and get away clean and dry. We'd better show her what Stusa's all about." Zyla motioned to the crowd.

"Where are my pitchers? Blaize, is that you? Get on up here and show Miss Prissy Pants what a good baseball player can do!"

Zyla leaned over and whispered to Ellie, "Just go ahead and get it over with as soon as possible. After the first dunk, they'll switch you out for someone dry, and you can disappear. Toodles!" Zyla wiggled her fingers and pranced away with an exaggerated wink, wink.

Ellie mouthed, "I hate you" and tried to glare, but she was already half-smiling at Zyla's ploy. Maybe she'd only have to be here for a few minutes. Then she could sneak out and get home. Hmmm...maybe a glass of wine and a bath while waiting on Julien and the girls.

Meanwhile, Mrs. Sarka was walking Ellie up the stairs that led to the dunking seat. When they got to the top, Ellie saw a small metal seat hanging over a pool of chest high water. She could see it was attached to a lever with a saucer-sized circle on it. The target was small but hittable. Ellie was feeling better and better.

Ellie walked over to the chair and climbed into the seat. Mrs. Sarka came over and lowered a lap bar. "What's this?" Ellie asked, feeling an immediate prick of panic. "Why is there a bar to hold me down?"

Mrs. Sarka replied, "It's to keep you from flyin' outta your seat when the lever drops. As soon as you hit the water, you push it forward and stand up. The water is only four and a half feet deep. You'll barely get the top of your stylish hair wet. Remember, just push forward on the bar and stand up."

The metal lap bar clanked into place. It was snugger than she would have liked. Ellie stammered, "Let me test it. I just realized I have a deep fear of being held underwater." She was embarrassed to hear that her voice shook.

"Ha ha," Mrs. Sarka replied, "good one. You shoulda done the pie throw, hon," and walked back to the pitcher's mound, lining up Ellie's first customer. Mrs. Sarka announced, "Now, Blaize – I hear there are a few things you don't like about English class this year. Why don't you show us what you got? I'm sure Miz Paylahtay won't mind a bit. It's all for a good cause. Why don'cha show her what you think of English class? I hear you made your first "F" this semester."

Ellie realized far too late that Mrs. Sarka's job was to get people irate enough to make them want to throw something at Ellie – or throw something to dunk her, anyway. She groaned. Mrs. Sarka had hit a little too close to home.

Blaize had gotten his first "F" in Ellie's class. He'd also gotten a paddling from Principal Danvers when Ellie reported him for threatening to hit her in class. He'd been angry at Ellie for not letting him play computer games when he was supposed to be researching Colonial America. Ellie hadn't thought he'd really hit her, but she turned him in any way to set a precedent. Kids couldn't go around threatening to hit teachers without repercussion. She'd been shocked that Stusa still used corporal punishment, but she also thought he'd deserved it. Ellie was sure he would love the opportunity to get some revenge.

Blaize stepped up to the mound like he was getting ready to pitch for the World Series. He squinted his eyes at Ellie, spat once, then rubbed his shoe in the clay. He stomped twice and reared back – ping!

He had hit the target on his very first pitch. Before Ellie could take a breath, the cold water covered her. She felt a moment of fear and then remembered Mrs. Sarka's words "just push the bar forward and stand up."

Her chair yanked to a stop and her feet touched the bottom of the tank. She understood the need for a lap bar. She definitely would have gone flying if the bar hadn't held her in place. It was a herky-jerky contraption. She wondered just how old it was as she pushed against the bar.

Nothing moved.

Ellie wiggled the bar and then pushed again.

Nothing.

Maybe she was supposed to push up. She tried again. The bar didn't budge.

Ellie gripped with both feet flat on the floor of the tank and tried to heave the bar upwards. Was there a latch she was supposed to activate? She told herself to stay calm, but all her air was gone. The effort of that last push had sent her remaining breath out in little bubbles.

Ellie felt a cold sense of dread hit her like a punch to the chest. She couldn't move the bar. She was being held underwater in a tank shallow enough to stand in, and she was going to drown. She could NOT move the bar.

Ellie couldn't tell if thirty seconds had passed or thirty minutes. She remembered reading somewhere that a human could go three weeks without food, three days without water, and three minutes without air. Well, she hadn't been under for three minutes, then.

Ellie thought of Julien. What would he think? Would he sue the fair organizers? What about her girls? Who would raise them?

That thought got Ellie fighting mad. *She* would raise her daughters; there was no way she would give that job to anyone else in the world. Ellie started to thrash. Maybe if she wiggled hard enough she could twist out from underneath the bar.

She jerked and pounded her feet on the bottom of the tank, trying to get leverage all while holding her mouth tightly shut, concentrating on not gulping in water. She tried pushing herself upwards while pushing down on the bar. It was no good in her seated position.

Lungs aching, she changed strategy and tried slipping down underneath the bar. She sucked in her stomach as hard as she could and managed to get all the way down to where the bar touched her ribcage. There was no sucking in ribs.

She shoved herself down onto the bar. It hurt like the devil, and it wasn't enough. Ellie knew she was running out of time. The need to suck in air was already threatening to overpower her even though her mind knew it would be certain death. Her lungs burned and her chest throbbed from the effort of not inhaling.

It was now or never, she realized. She thrust herself down onto the metal bar again with as much strength as she could muster. She heard a crack and felt a sharp pain that made her choke out a bit more air that she didn't know she had.

Her push worked. She slipped down further in her seat, but now she was stuck with the metal bar jabbing into her bra line. Knowing she only had seconds left, Ellie grabbed the bottom of the seat with both hands and pulled with her flagging strength. The buttons popped off her shirt, and her padded bra ripped upwards, but at long last, Ellie shoved free. The sudden force made her gasp for air as she stood up as fast as possible.

Her head broke free, barely clearing the water line. The pool had to be deeper than four feet, but right then she didn't care. Her breathing was confused. She had inhaled water and her body was simultaneously trying to breathe in air and expel water. She knew one more blinding moment of panic as she gagged, unable to inhale or exhale, stuck there - drowning even though she was no longer under water.

Finally, she rammed herself into the side of the pool and knocked her body back into working order. She began coughing and retching at the same time, but blessed oxygen got through in between bouts of gagging. Her breaths came in loud, raking gulps punctuated by coughs that hurt all the way up and down her chest.

If she could just get her breathing under control. She was going to make it! She kept coughing, retching, and breathing, unable to control her body's reaction to the mix of air, water, and pain, until she felt hands on her shoulders pulling her up out of the tank.

It was Blaize's friend, Kruzer – a big, beefy football player – who hated English almost as much as Blaize did. He was strong as an ox, though, and lifted Ellie clear out of the tank and set her down on the platform beside him. Ellie was doubled over, still puking and breathing, and all she could hear Kyle say was, "Blaize, you've killed her! You've killed her! She's choking!"

Ellie couldn't respond. She wanted to tell him that no, she wasn't dead, and that the racking coughs were probably saving her lungs right now, but all she could do was crumple to her knees as her body continued to navigate its way through ridding water from her lungs. She was otherwise helpless to control her body. Tears streamed down her face although no one could see them, drenched as she was.

Someone rushed over and wrapped her in a towel which made her gasp in pain as her ribs complained. The little gasp brought on hiccups that were infinitely more painful than the gagging and retching had been. Now Ellie was crying for real. Her gagging subsided as several people started talking at once. She only heard snatches.

"She's bleedin-"

"Let the paramedics thr-"

"needs - dried off - warmed up before sho-"

And then Ellie felt a blessed warmth wrap around her. She hadn't even known she was cold until the warmth hit her. Someone gently wiped her face dry and told her she needed to get out of her wet clothes. She tried to protest but was cut off by a familiar voice.

"*Non!*" It was Julien. "Not here, and certainly not by you. I will undress and dry her. *Donnez-nous l'espace!* You -- hold up this blanket to shield her from onlookers!"

Julien sounded angry. That was rare. As soon as he reached her, she fell into his arms and cried even harder. He peeled away her wet clothes now that she was hidden from view and wrapped her in another warm blanket. He picked her up and carried her down the stairs, through the crowd to the waiting ambulance.

"You are okay, *ma vie*. Shhh. Shhh. Don't talk. You can tell me all about it later. Right now, just *breathe*."

Ellie couldn't have told him what happened if she'd wanted to. Her breathing was still interspersed with erratic hiccupping, and the pain in her ribs was starting to take center stage. She motioned to the paramedics and pointed to her ribs. "Ow, hurts."

The paramedic told Ellie that she would get an x-ray at the hospital, but that for now, she needed to concentrate on inhaling and exhaling so that he could listen to her lungs. After the initial check, he said, "You need medical attention. Near-drowning is serious and there are some complications we need to check against and try to prevent. We are taking you to the hospital. Do you understand? Nod yes if you can understand me."

Ellie nodded. Why was he talking to her like she was an idiot? The paramedic continued. "Can you tell me your name?" He was talking loudly, as if she were hard of hearing.

"Ellie Pelletier." She began coughing again.

"OK, Ellie," the paramedic responded. "I'm Ernie. I'll be monitoring you all the way to the hospital. It is normal to cough, so don't hold back. Your body is working itself out."

"Hurts," Ellie coughed, pointing to her ribs again. When would he do something about that? The pain was blinding.

"OK, I understand. We will check your ribs as soon as we arrive. I need to ask you a few questions. You can respond by a simple nod or shake of the head. Do you understand?"

Ellie nodded.

"Is your name Ebbie?" He asked.

Ellie shook her head. What was happening? How did he know about Ebbie? The world was getting blurry, and Ernie's voice sounded as if it were coming from very far away. Ellie blinked – once, twice – then heard more voices coming in and out like a radio with bad reception.

"Mental confusion - risk of hypoxemia – further testing."

Then she heard Julien's garbled voice, "permanent damage?"

*Damage?* Ellie thought. What damage? Pox? They thought she had the pox? She was drowning. Nothing about chicken pox made sense.

Her thoughts swirled along with her vision. How could she be drowning if she were in an ambulance? Her thoughts were a black current. Somehow, she was caught up in that muddled, whirling eddy. Was she underwater again? Rippling waves of blackness gathered under and around her, shutting out her vision, her hearing – and much sooner than she would like, they dragged her under.

# CHAPTER TWENTY-FIVE

## *HOSPITAL HANGOVER*

Something tugged at Ellie, forcing her whole body up from the bottom of a deep, dark lake. A grapple had been inserted right into the middle of her sternum, and it hurt. She was a fish hooked on a line, and the fisherman wouldn't lose his catch. She thrashed and wriggled, trying to get free, but the fisherman reeled her in - the pressing weight of the water smothering her. The journey left her water-logged, tired, aching, and sluggish. A fish out of water.

"Mrs. Pelletier, ma'am." She heard a male voice off in the distance. "C'mon, open those baby blues. I need to check your pupils." A finger and a thumb pulled her left eyelid open and held it for a second. A bright light flicked off and on, piercing her clouded vision and giving her an instant headache. It was worse than any hangover she'd experienced.

"I'm going to open the right eye if you won't do it. You will see a bright light." True to his word, fingers opened her right eye, and the light stabbed her again. This time the pain was enough to make her try to open her eyelids on her own. They felt heavy, swollen. She blinked.

"That's right," the voice continued. "Blink your eyes twice more and then follow my light without turning your head. Follow it with your eyes only." Ellie recognized the voice and the man behind it.

It was Dr. Patel. She followed his light with her eyes, moving them up, right, left, and down as he led. "OK," he said, clicking off the light and entering some notes on his digital tablet. "I have some questions for you, Mrs. Pelletier." He continued.

"Dr. Patel, what happened?" Ellie interrupted.

He chuckled. "Well, it's good to see you recognize me, Mrs. Pelletier. That answers the first question. You know who I am. Now, who are you?" He waited.

"I'm Ellie Pelletier. I teach your son, Parmesh, at the high school. Why does my entire chest hurt so much? Did I crack a rib?"

"Oh, more than one, Ellie. I'll tell you about your injuries in a moment. First, I need to know what you remember about the accident that landed you here in Stusa's Medical Center."

Ellie swallowed. "I was in the dunking booth. Someone dunked me, and I couldn't raise the lap bar. I pushed the bar out, in, down and up – but nothing worked. I was starting to panic. Then, I tried sliding down to wiggle out from under the bar. I got wedged in place…then I shoved as hard as I could, and I felt a crack… everything went black, and I woke up here."

"Well, Ellie," Dr. Patel continued. "You injured yourself quite severely, but in doing so, you managed to save your life. I hope that knowledge will help you deal with the pain over the next several weeks." He pulled an x-ray up on his iPad and showed it to her.

"When you heard that crack, a couple of things happened. You did, indeed, crack two ribs – here and here," he circled the fractures in red with his finger as he spoke, "but the biggest problem is this." He drew a large red circle around a tiny piece at the bottom of her sternum. When he tapped the image, it enlarged.

"This is your Xiphoid process. It's the third piece of the sternum and sits below the manubrium and the gladiolus. It snapped off during your shoving. If it had pierced your liver, you could have suffered a fatal hemorrhage. Fortunately, we were able to retrieve it during surgery without any damage to your liver or other internal organs."

"I had surgery?" Ellie asked stunned.

"Yes, it was an emergency. That is partially why you feel so groggy. I'm surprised you're not more confused." Dr. Patel smiled.

"Oh, I've been confused alright. I thought I was a hooked fish being reeled in when you called my name. It's exactly what it feels like though, like something has pierced my chest and pulled me up from the depths."

Dr. Patel chuckled again. "That's a fair depiction of the pain. I'll have to remember that. You have quite an imagination, Ellie. No wonder Parmesh enjoys your class so much."

*He'd be the only one*, Ellie thought. She kept her thoughts to herself and asked, "Dr. Patel, how long will I be here?"

"Overnight. In addition to your post-op checks, we need to keep an eye on your lungs and administer breathing treatments to prevent infection. You should be able to go home tomorrow afternoon barring any complications. Now, I believe you have some visitors awaiting you. We will get you to a room in just a bit. Julien can stay as long as he likes, and I'll allow the girls to come into the recovery area - but only for five minutes. They'll have to wait until you get a room for a longer visit." He motioned to a nurse who buzzed in Ellie's family.

"Thanks, Dr. Patel." He turned and walked away as the girls came rushing over to her bedside with Julien not far behind.

"*Maman*," Bibianne squeaked. "Does it hurt?"

Méline looked at Ellie with large eyes. She was quiet, waiting for Ellie's answer.

"Well, girls," Ellie hesitated. "Yes, it does hurt quite a bit. But it's worth it to be able to see you again!" Méline's big eyes started to water, and Ellie reached out an arm for a hug. She inhaled sharply at the pain the movement caused. "I'll heal."

Julien stepped closer and said, "*Maman* must settle for a kiss, girls." He lifted Bibianne up so she could kiss Ellie's cheek, and Méline gave her a quick peck and a pat on the arm. He leaned over and kissed her forehead gently.

"*Ma vie,* that was scary. Don't ever do that to me again." He mock-scolded her with a smile. "Dr. Patel has already spoken to us. I know the girls can't stay long. Let me get them something to eat, and we'll come back when you've got a room. I hate to leave you alone, Ellie, but we'll be back as soon as possible." He looked torn.

"It's okay. I'll be fine. You take care of the girls. I'll have plenty of people taking care of me. Plus, I've got to start those breathing treatments. Don't worry." She tried to smile.

"Well, here is your purse." Julien said as he placed it carefully on the bed beside her hips, making sure not to let it touch her chest or ribs. "Your cell phone is in there; I checked to make sure. Text me as soon as you get a room. Maybe it won't be too long." He planted another gentle kiss on her forehead and left with the girls.

Ellie drifted back to sleep after Julien and the girls left. She awoke to her bed being rolled down a long hallway. The orderly spoke to her.

"Hello, there! We wondered if you'd sleep the entire trip to your room. Looks like I won the bet, though." He leaned in and whispered. "You just earned me a drink after work with the nurse I've been trying to ask out for weeks. I owe you one! You need anything while you're here? You let Ja'Quarius know. I'll take care of you."

Ellie giggled. "Glad to be of service. Anytime you need a near drowning to secure a date, I'm your girl." She was in pain, to be sure, but giddy with relief at being out of the water and able to breathe again. Each time she woke up, she felt the thrill of not being underwater. It would have all seemed like a dream if it hadn't been for the pain in her chest and ribcage.

When they arrived at her room, Ja'Quarius docked her bed into position and left the room with a little salute in

Ellie's direction. "You remember what I told you," he said as he left the room.

The attending nurse plugged in all the tubes and cords that were monitoring Ellie's condition. The nurse was lovely, and she had the merriest dimples when she smiled. Ellie saw that her name was RayVynn. When RayVynn came around to adjust the oxygen reader on Ellie's middle finger, Ellie smiled.

"I hear you have a hot date tonight. Where will Ja'Quarius take you for drinks?" Ellie asked.

"Oh, Lord. That fool has been runnin' his mouth. He cain't keep that big flap shut." She laughed as she spoke. RayVynn continued. "Yes, thanks to you – I'll be going over to Duke's after work. We'll see if Ja'Quarius lets me get a word in before the night is over. That's how I'll decide if he gets a second date."

Ellie wanted to laugh, but it hurt too much. She smiled instead. "You two make a cute couple, if I may say so."

"He has been pesterin' me for weeks to go out with him. I swear, I don't know what came over me today to take that bet. I'll say one thing – he is persistent." RayVynn leaned over to take Ellie's purse off the bed, but Ellie interrupted her.

"No, please leave it here. I want to be able to reach my phone to text my husband." Ellie explained.

"Alright," RayVynn acquiesced. "Ja'Quarius will be back in one hour to start your breathing treatment. You take it easy until then."

Ellie opened her purse intending to call Julien. Her hands, however, landed on something other than her mobile phone - the anthology. How had it gotten into Ellie's purse? She hadn't been carrying it with her, had she? At any rate, she was glad to see it. After texting Julien her room number, she opened it and began to read.

*February 1721*
*I was widowed at 41 and I have resumed the wretched role again at the age of 69. Despite the horrors of my first mar-*

*riage and the awful Trials, my second marriage brought nothing but joy. I have often wondered if my choice in taking the journal and using it had anything to do with that.*

*When poor Daniel died last month, I knew it was time. Having no female offspring of my own, I must entrust this journal to my son's daughter Elinor. She is young – ten years old – but I must give her the chance to right the wrongs of men as I was given. It will help her in troubling times, and it will allow her to survive the coming crucible, despite the wicked ways of men.*

*This will be my last entry. I fear that my time left in the world is short. I must soon meet my Maker and face the consequences of my actions. I made my own choices and will not shrink from their results, but I am determined for my granddaughter to have the same choices available to her if needed.*

*I set off tomorrow on my journey to my son's home. I will carry few belongings, this journal being the primary reason for my visit and weighted with both authority and mystery. It will be up to Elinor to decide what to do with it. I am ready to rid myself of the burden – physical and spiritual.*
*E.B.P.R.*

Ellie stopped reading for a moment, saddened. She would never find out what happened to Ebbie other than that Ebbie had remarried and had passed the journal down to her granddaughter. Ellie sighed. She felt like she had lost a friend, an ally. Only the thought that Ebbie had been happy in her second marriage comforted Ellie.

Ebbie's note about surviving trials stirred a memory. Ellie remembered Madame Margaux and her prediction at *Le Chemise*. She could still smell the patchouli and feel Madame's breath in her ear. She could hear the clinking of Madame's many beads and bracelets.

*"When the people buzz like insects, don't lose faith; you will survive the crucible."*

Ellie hadn't thought about the strange message in a

while, but Ebbie's statement brought it to mind. The words weren't the same, but they seemed to imply the same message. *The ancient anthology would help those who needed it.*

Like the women who wrote in the journal, Ellie lived in troubling times. Besides the fact that she nearly drowned at the fall festival, there were plenty of other worries to consume her thoughts: The rumors about Julien and Tai persisted. She was teaching an entirely new subject. She had already managed to get on her boss's bad side. Julien's studio, *The Jewel*, was set to open in a month, and they weren't finished renovating it yet. Ellie had discovered that *The Jewel* had been the scene of several murders centuries ago and hadn't been able to shake the feeling that someone was watching her ever since. A student had threatened her with physical violence. The same student had been beaten because of her. And to top it all off, she had been having both nightmares and daymares about Tai and Julien.

Ellie wondered how Ebbie had handled her troubles all those years ago. If something in the anthology helped Ebbie, maybe there would be something to help Ellie, too. She found another entry and continued reading.

*Thus, I have used this book to pour out my troubles when no one else would care to listen. I would ne'er dare to speak my thoughts aloud. Daniel would say I were thinking too much and working too little. Yet I think there is power here for more than just writing. I have gained understanding as I have aged.*

*I have indeed used the book's power. I will advise my granddaughter to do the same. I will warn her, however, to hide this book if she chooses not to use it, so that no soul should stumble upon the words within in case they be a stumbling block to those of lesser faith.*

*I have burned the words of the first invocation I did ever deliver in the light of the full moon, lest the stories told by the slave girl were true. If the words were indeed a weakness*

*on my part, then let them not become a condemnation for another, for I do not regret for one moment having them uttered.*
*E.B.P.R.*

Ebbie's story so consumed Ellie's attention that she didn't hear Julien enter her hospital room until he leaned over to give her a kiss. She closed the book and jumped in surprise. He laughed.

"Did I scare you? What are you so engrossed in?" Julien asked, reaching over as if to grab the book.

"Ouch! My ribs!" Ellie interceded, stopping him mid-grasp. She shoved the book under the hospital blanket.

"You startled me! And when I jumped, it made my whole chest hurt again." That part was true, but she wasn't quite sure why she had moved the book out of his reach. "Yes, I was reading. I guess I got too involved in the story because I never heard a thing." That was true, too. Why on earth was she feeling so edgy about Julien seeing her book? Luckily, he didn't seem to notice. His concern was all for her injuries.

"Shh...shhh...take it easy, *ma belle.* Lie still. We'll get you some pain medication." He caressed her cheek and tucked one strand of hair behind her ear. Just then, Ja'Quarius came in with her first breathing treatment. As he approached her bedside, excusing himself for interrupting Ellie and Julien, Ellie spoke to him.

"I met your date. She's great! I can see why you've been trying so hard." Ja'Quarius leaned over Ellie to make some adjustments to the tubing, and Ellie whispered, "A little birdie told me that the key to tonight's date is to be a good *listener.*" Ellie winked at him.

Ja'Quarius smiled wide and said, "Girl, you got my back! You can call me JQ, and I'll be looking out for you on my shift. You can count on JQ! I owe you!" He continued about his work with a goofy grin plastered on his face.

Julien and the girls visited and talked while Ellie breathed in through the nebulizer. The girls chatted away about the prizes they had won at the fair prior to the accident. Before long, the treatment was over, and so were visiting hours. Julien gave Ellie a final kiss for the night and lifted each girl in turn so that she could do the same.

As he left the room, Julien stopped in the doorway and looked back at Ellie. "After the grand opening of the studio in November, you and I need a vacation. This move has been stressful, and after your accident – you'll need a good rest. While you're convalescing, think about places you'd like to go, and I'll start working on making travel arrangements. Let's do it over Christmas break, yes? How does that sound, *ma vie?*"

Ellie smiled and showed him a thumbs-up sign. *What a great idea*, she thought. What a great husband. Despite it all, she was a very lucky woman.

# CHAPTER TWENTY-SIX

## *THE SHADOW*

*The Shadow* crouched down low behind one of the azalea bushes that surrounded the house. The azalea didn't provide as much coverage as other plants, but the broad, sparse leaves allowed her to peek through and glimpse what was going on inside the Pelletier residence. Besides, she wasn't afraid of being seen; it was dark outside, and several interior lights were on. The Pelletiers, for all their city ways, didn't seem to be too concerned with saving energy.

The emerald cord had led her here. *The Shadow* had been furious with the failure of the dunking booth; she had scared the wits out of Ellie and Julien, but Ellie's connection had not been severed. Then last night, *The Shadow* felt the unmistakable tug at her wrist.

She had learned not to ignore its pull. Once, when she had been too slow to respond to the simultaneous pricked at her wrist and her mind, the emerald cord had expressed its displeasure. Her scar had turned a dark, fungus-green, the color of rot, and had burned what felt like all the way through her tiny wrist with excruciating pain.

So even though the scar called to her when she had just drifted off to sleep, *The Shadow* had obeyed her branded guide and made her way to the Pelletiers' yard without hesitation. She squirmed behind the azalea bush underneath the kitchen window. A conversation drifted through the open window down to the flower beds. If she held her head at just the right angle, she could see into the home from her crouched position. There was a slight breeze that moved the sheer curtains. They blew in and out of the screen-less windows.

"You what?" asked a shrill voice. "You want to take a *student* on our family vacation? Over Christmas break?"

Ellie's voice was tight and accusatory. Predictably, Julien was unruffled by Ellie's outburst. Nothing seemed to faze him. He greeted every complaint with a sardonic laugh that drove *The Shadow* mad.

"*Ma vie*," he responded and tried to pull Ellie into a hug. "She is not really a student. She is our baby-sitter, my assistant, a family friend - and if we take her along on our trip, she will be able to babysit for us whenever we want. The girls have fun with her. It will give us time to relax and reconnect. Just the two of us." *The Shadow* peered in through the window, ready to duck the second anyone began to turn in her direction.

Ellie sighed, hesitantly accepting the embrace. She winced when Julien squeezed too hard. Ellie was still recovering from her accident.

"You seriously want to bring Tai with us?" Ellie's eyebrows pinched together. "After all the rumors? Don't you think you'll just be adding fat lighter to the flame?" Ellie sounded more exasperated than angry now. She was even using local slang.

"*Mon cœur*," Julien added. "Let the small minds brood. What have we to fear? We are innocent of the rumors that surround us. I, for one, refuse to allow such nonsense to affect my life. Why are you letting such petty gossip bother you, *ma chérie*?" *The Shadow* risked another peek inside and saw Julien take Ellie's hand.

"Because it's my reputation, too, Julien!" Ellie exhaled in frustration. "The rumors at school are hurtful." She stepped back from the embrace and looked at him. "I act like I don't mind and that I'm above it all, but it takes every ounce of self-control I possess to maintain my composure. Everyone thinks she has you wrapped around her little finger and that you've cozied up in your studio taking God-knows-what-kind of photos."

The bitterness in her voice was building, and Ellie stepped away from Julien, turning her back to him. She paused to catch her breath, one hand on her side. "It's even worse; they think that I'm the unsuspecting, loyal, idiotic wife who would rather turn a blind eye than face the awful truth. I want to rail at everyone and defend you, me, the girls. It's...it's...unbearable!" She ran one hand through her hair and turned to look out the window. *The Shadow* remained perfectly still while Ellie continued.

"And what will the Reverintendent say?" Ellie asked. "You don't think he'd allow his niece to go? After all the rumors?" She stared out through the open window lost in thought. "It's not just sinning that's frowned upon; it's the mere appearance of sinning."

Ellie reached over and wiped a spider web from the window frame. *The Shadow* knew Ellie cleaned when she was anxious. *The Shadow* held her breath and hoped that Ellie wouldn't lean out the window to clean the entire sash.

Luckily, Ellie stopped wiping. "The insects here are awful! I really had no idea how annoying they would be." She gave a grunt of disapproval. "I don't know what's worse – the bugs or the busybodies."

Ellie cradled her side again. "What would we do if I were fired over this? Have you thought about that? Our savings will run out eventually, you know."

*The Shadow* smiled to herself. So, Ellie realized the precariousness of her standing in the community and its link to her employment. She'd given *The Shadow* a glimpse into her fears. Ellie felt anxious, *ungrounded*. The next element, then, would be earth.

If the water element hadn't severed Ellie's connection

to the heirloom, then an earthen element would do it. *The Shadow* took out a tiny piece of coal leftover from the fire she had made in the woods with her groupies. She drew an emblem on the side of the Pelletier's house where no one would see. It was her family insignia. Having marked the house, access would be granted.

    *The Shadow* crept back to her cottage. As she closed her eyes in satisfaction and pulled Gabby's quilt up to her chin, she decided to have a delicious rest before starting the next phase of her plan. Besides, she had to replenish her stores of herbs and essential oils. The next tisane would need time to develop to its full potential – just like her plans for Ellie.

# CHAPTER TWENTY-SEVEN

## *POLITICAL PROBLEMS*

Over the next week, Ellie kept her doubts about Tai, Julien, and their upcoming vacation bottled up. Instead, she focused on taking care of her numerous injuries and on her students' struggle with learning American Literature. For once, small-town politics kept her treading water, temporarily out of range. There were, apparently, bigger fish to hook.

Ellie discovered that small town politics were just as bad as those in big cities. They may not have involved as many people, but they seemed even worse when she knew everyone. And they affected everything that happened in Stusa.

Ellie thought the oft-quoted maxim about the only unavoidable things in life being "death and taxes" should be amended. Wealthy citizens and big corporations could probably get around taxes with accountants and lawyers, but politics? Ellie thought they were the only truly unavoidable thing besides death. Anywhere humans were involved, there would always be a power struggle.

Her glimpse into small town politics started when Ellie and her colleagues were in the teacher's lounge. The bell had just rung for lunch. As teachers were opening their lunch bags and warming up leftovers, the intercom came on. Trained as they were, they all stopped what they were doing to listen to the forthcoming announcement.

Mr. Mullis rolled his eyes and muttered under his breath, "Oh, please say that seventh period is cancelled. I can't take another hour of those hellions." A few of the other teachers chuckled. No announcement followed, however. What they heard was an apparent argument among several people who must have been crowded around the principal's desk.

"Well, *hnh hmm*, as you all know - I have already hired Remuel Hardy, retired FBI agent, to look into the matter. I don't know what else I can do. I am sick and tired of the rumors circulating about my household. I want *proof* that we are innocent, proof I can show to the public," an immediately recognizable voice said.

"That's the Superintendent." Annabelle Sarka interjected needlessly. They all recognized him from his nervous throat clearing.

*Huh*, thought Ellie. The Reverintendent was apparently as tired as she was of having his name ground through the rumor mill. *Maybe he's getting a dose of his own medicine.* Ellie still suspected the Reverintendent was largely to blame for the rumors surrounding her and Julien.

"Oh now, c'mon, Reverend." A female voice said. "There is no need for former federal investigators. No one thinks you have drugs in your house. As for your niece, I'm sure she can explain her behavior. Let's not take this outside the school grounds, I beg you. If we open it up to the local police, it will start something that can't be stopped."

"That is Allison Wesley." Mrs. Sarka narrated. Everyone was too busy concentrating on listening to shush her.

"You, sir, had no right to call in the feds without consulting the board of education!" An angry male voice proclaimed. "Board of Education policy dictates that we should have a special called meeting before any legal matters are made public!"

"That is the president of the board of education – Mr. Thomas Wellham." Mrs. Sarka was fully in charge of the narration now. Her eyes sparkled with uncontained glee at the mayhem drifting down from the intercom.

"Let's not jump to any conclusions, people." Mrs. Wesley tried to reason with the group. "What if we offer the teens of this town some good, clean fun? Then they won't have to resort to partying out in the woods. How about a dance, for instance?"

"Oh," an angry huff interrupted. "Aren't you the perfect little parent, volunteering a dance for the teenagers." Mrs. Wellham's voice dripped with sarcasm. "Well, just because we don't host parties for teenagers doesn't mean we aren't every bit as good as you are! You think you're so high and mighty because all your kids graduated with honors. You sit on your pedestal and judge me for Farrah's *one* mistake! For your information, after rehab she has been one hundred percent clean! So, don't you dare act like you're superior to us!"

"Um," Ellie interjected. "Shouldn't somebody tell the office that their conversation is being transmitted to the teachers' lounge and possibly the whole school?" Ellie had heard enough to know that this conversation should be private.

"Oh." The mood evaporated quickly, and several teachers looked abashed.

"I'll go!" Mrs. Sarka declared and left the lounge at a lively trot. The conversation over the intercom continued as she made her way to the office, and Mr. Wellham joined in to support his wife's criticism of the Wesleys before Mrs. Sarka could get to the office to warn them.

"That's right, Mr. Wesley!" Mr. Wellham said. "Reverend Peters, I have changed my mind! I fully support you in your attempt to clear your name once and for all! It's too bad we couldn't do the same! Go ahead and bring the cops." He pronounced.

"Now wait just a minute." Another voice added. It sounded like Mayor Goodwin. "We all have a say in this matter. You're not the boss here, Wellham. We don't blindly obey the BOE president, and we certainly don't cow to the wealthy

– even though you think that makes you the most important person in the room! I happen to be the mayor of th--"

*Click.* Mrs. Sarka must have finally gotten to the office. The intercom went silent. When she came back to the teacher's lounge, her enthusiasm had not diminished. She was breathless with excitement, and her eyes sparkled in a way that could only mean one thing – more gossip.

"Well, well, well." She shut the door to the lounge behind her and leaned back against it with a gleam in her eyes. "Wasn't that a right nasty piece of business!" She gloated. Ellie could tell she was just bursting with news and dying for someone to ask her for it.

"If you only knew the rest of what I overheard as I tried to get their attention. They were behind locked doors, you know." She cajoled. No one took the bait.

"I found out that our good reverend is positioning to get the parsonage signed over to him." She looked from person to person. "Well, do you want to know or not!" Mrs. Sarka stomped her foot, hands on hips.

"Go on, then. Tell us what you overheard." Mr. Grant sighed in feigned exasperation. Ellie was pretty sure he wanted to know what Mrs. Sarka had to say. Everyone must have wanted to know because nobody left the lounge. Mrs. Sarka was nearly beside herself. She trembled with excitement.

"Well, as you heard – there are several people in the principal's office. Ellie, I'll explain since you don't know all these community leaders." Mrs. Sarka geared up. She took a deep breath and lifted her shoulders as if preparing to deliver a well-rehearsed speech.

"The arguing parties include Mr. and Mrs. Thomas Wellham - Board of Education president and his wife who together own about two-thirds of the county; Mr. and Mrs. Gary Wesley - founders of the church-based home school group from First Baptist and staunch church members of the same; the superintendent - current preacher of First Baptist who has been here serving his dual roles for about three years; Principal Danvers - newly appointed principal to our school just last year; Lydia Bennet and Louella Baxter - co-presidents of the Parent Teacher Association; and Mayor Goodwin." She paused to catch her breath and revved back up again.

"You heard them arguing with the superintendent. He called in Remuel Hardy, a retired DEA agent, to investigate drug charges about his niece, Tai, and some of her friends. At first, the Wellhams were against it. I imagine Thomas felt the superintendent should have consulted him before making any decisions as he is the president of the Board of Education."

"Well, after Mrs. Wesley made Mrs. Wellham mad - she is extremely sensitive about their daughter Farrah - the Wellhams turned against the Wesleys in support of the superintendent. Then, the mayor decided to add his two cents' worth and told the Wellhams that they weren't in charge just because they are wealthy."

Ellie was just barely following the argument and its participants; she was getting a little dizzy at the tit-for-tat back and forth, trying to picture the scene in her mind. She didn't volunteer that she'd done a little eavesdropping herself and already knew about Mr. Hardy's investigation.

"So, Mr. Wellham fired back that the mayor had no business deciding what was right or wrong since he rarely attends church. Oh, that made Mayor Goodwin good and angry. He defended himself by saying that it was true – he never goes to church anymore because all the reverend preaches about is hellfire and damnation!"

This drew an audible gasp from Mrs. Sarka's audience. They hardly ever heard words like that in the teacher's lounge. "I know, right?" Mrs. Sarka continued, happy to be the bearer of such inflammatory news. "Well, you can imagine that made the reverend madder than a hornet. He rounded on Wellham and said that it was an unfounded accusation.

"So, then Mrs. Holy Roller - that's Mrs. Wesley to you, Ellie - gets on board and defends the mayor, saying it's true for many people, not just the mayor. Several people in her home-school group are afraid to take their children to church services because all he does is threaten them with hell, and it frightens the children."

Ellie squirmed in her seat. She was beginning to feel guilty about having sidestepped the principal's orders to take down the fiery adverts her students created earlier in the semester. If religion, sermons, and politics were such a hot topic in Stusa, maybe she needed to go ahead and put them away. She'd not had the faintest idea when she created the assignment. She resisted the urge to run straight to her room and take down the posters in order to hear the rest of the argument narrated so eagerly by Mrs. Sarka.

"Then the reverend mutters that it's not the *children* who need to hear his sermons. At this, Mrs. Wesley asks him pointedly if he thinks there are really so many sinners in this small town."

"Well, I guess this is just what the superintendent was waiting for," said Mrs. Sarka, "because he unloaded every complaint he must have been holding in for three years. He said that the whole town needs to hear his sermons. The church members also need to respect him and pay him what he's worth. He's not some uneducated backwoods preacher; he graduated from Harvard School of Divinity and left a thriving church near Boston to come to this podunk little town. He can't believe how difficult everyone here is. He says he can't even make one suggestion or change without starting a riot. Then he says that it must be the work of the devil!"

As a few teachers gasped again at the insinuation, Ellie tried to decipher the little alarm bells that had begun to chime in the back of her mind. Tiny and faint, they were signaling a déjà vu moment. Where had she heard this before? What did this remind her of? But Mrs. Sarka wasn't finished yet. She continued recounting what she had heard.

"That infuriated Lydia and Louella as their husbands are both preachers. The mayor stepped in and said that if the reverend is pointing out the devil's work, then why is he the first preacher who has ever wanted the deed to the parsonage?

"So, the reverend asked didn't he deserve a house of his own?"

"The mayor said, 'to live in, not to own.'"

"Then the reverend said that all he really wants is some reassurance from the town. He doesn't want to be kicked out without warning like the last two preachers. He reminded them that he's the third preacher in five years. Someone had to take on the burden of saving this godforsaken little town. Then he added that if the church doesn't get right with God, it will burn."

A third gasp emanated from Mrs. Sarka's captive audience. Ellie's alarm bells chimed madly in unison with the gasps. Mrs. Sarka picked back up, satisfied with the group's reaction.

"Well, with that comment, Lydia and Louella gathered their pocketbooks and marched out without a word. The mayor asked if the reverend could talk about anything else except Hell. He's disgusted by it all."

"The Reverend responded by saying that the mayor can't dictate the preacher's messages."

"Then the mayor said he still has freedom of speech."

"Then the Reverend responded by accusing the mayor of being the leader of the opposition against him."

"So, Mayor Goodwin asked, 'Oh, there's an opposition against you? Where can I sign up? I'll be sure and let Lydia and Louella know, too.'"

The group of teachers emitted a few chuckles this time. Ellie guessed that the mayor wasn't the only one who would like to oppose the Reverend. Mrs. Sarka continued.

"Well, after a second or two, the arguing picked back up. The mayor tells Wellham, 'Let's get out of here. I've got some trees to clear.'"

Thomas said, 'Which trees are those?'"

"The mayor responded that they're the trees on his

property *inside* his fence by the branch."

"Thomas said, 'You must be crazy. Those are my trees, fence or no fence. My grandfather left them to me in his will!'"

"The mayor said, 'Yeah, he left a lot of stuff to people in his will – stuff he didn't own in the first place.'"

"Then Mr. Wesley decided he'd held his tongue long enough and added, 'Yeah, your grandfather didn't dare do that to me because he knew I had the means to crush him. Let's go clear some land, mayor.'" Mrs. Sarka paused for a breath.

"And then I had to run to get out of the way." Mrs. Sarka added. "They came storming out of that office madder than wet hens. They didn't even see me they were so angry. But Thomas Wellham yelled, 'If you haul off one single tree of mine, I'll take you to court!' He shouted it at them as they were leaving."

"Naturally, I came straight here to tell it all before I forgot a single word." She looked proud of herself. Indeed, it was a convoluted conversation to retell.

Ellie only followed about half of it. At that moment, she was more concerned about the chiming in her head urging her to remember where she'd heard it all before. She felt like she was in a haze. She couldn't make the connection that was right there in front of her.

The lunch bell rang, breaking up the little group, and teachers headed back to classrooms. Ellie shook her head to clear the chiming in her head. Maybe she could look around in the anthology to find the nagging connection.

Once she reviewed it all in her mind and managed to decipher most of the political in-fighting, she congratulated herself. *Wheels within wheels*, she thought. Part of her was tempted to laugh at the pettiness of it all, but then again, wasn't that what always drove politics - no matter the number of constituents?

# CHAPTER TWENTY-EIGHT

## *CRUCIBLE CONNECTION*

After the overheard argument, Ellie went home and searched the anthology, convinced that it was there that she had read something similar. After hours of fruitless searching, she took a break and checked her blog. And there it was. A reader had posted a comment about the small-town politics sounding like a plot for a movie. It hit Ellie immediately with a resounding clang! Why hadn't she seen it sooner?

Because it was the plot of a movie. A movie based on a play. A play Ellie had read half a dozen times since becoming an English teacher -- The Crucible. When she realized the connection, Ellie's mind exploded with possibilities. The argument among Stusa's town leaders was eerily like the argument in Miller's play – an argument that was factual, based on historical records.

So many ideas hit Ellie at once that she felt dizzy. It wasn't a slow dawning of comprehension; it was a tsunami that came crashing down and drowned everything else.

All those little coincidences that Ellie had chuckled about - the small-town setting, the town leaders, the teenagers partying in the forest, the theocracy. The coincidences were uncanny, sinister even. They taunted Ellie, urging her to find more similarities despite the logical part of her mind denying everything.

Ellie's students had picked up on the similarities almost immediately. They had jumped in and started aligning Stusa residents to their *Crucible* counterparts. Even though she'd been proud of their analytical skills, Ellie knew she had to shut them down before they caused real trouble. The Reverintendent and the principal would be none too pleased to be compared to Reverend Parris and Judge Danforth, no matter how apt the description.

Alarm bells still sounding, Ellie ransacked her home office until she found her copy of Arthur Miller's play. Like the Reverintendent, Ellie wanted proof. Proof that she wasn't certifiably insane. This was simply too much to be a mere coincidence.

As Ellie held the play in her hands, a shudder of panic raced down her spine. If she opened the play and saw what she suspected was inside, there could be no turning back. She would somehow have crossed over into a blend of fiction and reality that no one would ever believe.

Was she ready? Was she brave enough? Was she sure she wanted to explore this possibility? She absent-mindedly rubbed her left wrist. It tingled with nerves.

She inhaled deeply and plunged into her obsession. She flipped past the note on historical accuracy, past the overture describing the characters, past the opening scene of Parris praying over Betty - and there it was.

Near the end of Act One, Reverend Hale listens to the adults describe the conditions surrounding Betty's illness. In between accusing Reverend Parris of having both a slave and a niece involved in witchcraft, they argue about land rights, ownership of the parsonage, and church attendance. It was spookily similar.

*But there are characters missing*, Ellie's rational mind argued. *Where is Rebecca Nurse? Where is Reverend Hale?*

But the essence of the argument was the same. Her intuition countered. *Who is more powerful than whom? Who has the right to call in specialists to investigate crime? Who is to blame for stirring up trouble? Who holds past grudges based on land owner-ship and the like?*

The sensation in Ellie's gut made her simultaneously want to vomit and to laugh. It wasn't just in her head. There was some connection here. Was that crazy? Yes! Could Arthur Miller have known anything about Stusa in the twenty-first century? No! *But he knew human nature*, her instinct prompted.

Part of Ellie wanted to laugh at it all and forget about her inner struggle for sanity. But another part of her wanted time to think about it, so she put her head between her knees and inhaled deeply through her nose to try to stave off the darkness clouding her peripheral vision. Bending over still made her ribcage hurt, and the pain helped her regain control.

"*Mon Dieu*, Ellie! *Qu'est qui se passe?*" Ellie heard Julien say as if from far away. She lifted her head, and he saw the play resting in Ellie's lap.

"*Mon cœur*, you are working too hard. *C'est ne pas possible!* How can you expect to maintain balance if all you do is work? It is well after midnight." He tut-tutted Ellie as he set the play on the desk.

"Let's get you to bed where you belong." He pulled Ellie up and steered her to the stairs. They were about halfway up when they heard a scream from the girls' room followed by a cry of "*Maman! Papa!*"

Both instantly alert, they scrambled up to the girls' room as fast as they could. Méline was sitting straight up, wide-eyed and crying. Ellie rushed to her side while Julien turned on the lights. Relieved that nothing visible was amiss, Ellie guessed that it was a nightmare.

"We are here. You are perfectly safe." Ellie folded Méline into her arms. "Tell *maman* what happened."

Méline's little chest heaved as she tried to explain. "I was in a dark place. It was very scary. I heard a crackling and saw an orange light. Then I was surrounded by fire, and I could not find my way out. Orange heat was burning me everywhere!" She leaned in for a hug from both her parents and buried her head in Julien's chest.

"It was *très horrible*. I could not find any of you – not my sister, not *maman*, not *papa*. Only Dedé. And she ran off before I could follow her. She squeezed through places that were too little for me. It was so hot!" She looked up at Ellie with a tear-stained face. Ellie grabbed both of her hands.

"It was just a dream, *ma petite*. You are in your own room. See your stuffed animals? And look who came to check on you." Dedé jumped in bed with Méline and licked her face.

Ellie soothed, "It is not dark or scary now. There is no fire. You probably got hot in your sleep with all these blankets, so your mind created something to wake you. See how you have kicked off all the covers? Let me get a cold bath cloth to wipe your face. It will cool you down, and you'll feel better."

Ellie went to Méline's bathroom and got a glass of tap water. She wet a bath cloth and used it to wipe Méline's tear-stained face. Méline took careful sips from the glass. Her dad stroked her hair, and they sat with her until she was calm. They read her a bedtime story, and she eventually drifted off to sleep.

"Well, *ma vie*," Julien whispered. "The girls definitely inherited their mom's creative imagination. It's unfortunate it turns so wicked at night. I fear she will have these night terrors her whole life, just as you do." Julien sighed as they walked to their bedroom, his arm draped over her shoulder. He turned to look at Ellie.

"What can we do?' He asked.

"Maybe tomorrow I'll tell her the story of the dreamcatcher and put one in her room. I can also let her sip some of my herbal tea." Ellie suggested.

"Oh, *ma chère*. Do you really believe all that hocus pocus works?" Julien asked with a roll of his eyes.

"What I think is irrelevant," Ellie replied. "It doesn't matter if it works or not. It only matters if Méline *believes* that it works. That will be the key to ridding her of the bad dreams. I'll take my dreamcatcher to her room tomorrow and explain the Native American tradition of the angels trapping the nightmares in the webbing. I think she'll like that."

"But what will that leave for your bad dreams?" He asked with a grin.

"Well, I have a man to protect me." Ellie leaned in for an embrace, and Julien lifted her off her feet and carried her to bed. With Julien at her side, Ellie forgot all about her earlier panic.

# CHAPTER TWENTY-NINE

## SPARKLING SOIREE

Before Ellie had time to catch a breath, the night of Julien's grand opening arrived. Ellie and Julien had invited a few town officials, some of the key participants in the recently-overheard argument, in fact: the mayor, the president of the board of education and his wife, the local garden club, Lydia Bennett and Louella Baxter, a few colleagues of Ellie's, and the previous owners of the property -- despite Ellie's misgivings about them having sold the place to the Pelletiers without disclosing its ominous past.

When Ellie finally told Julien of the property's history, he'd found it charming and had used the old story to his benefit. He placed old photos of Stusa throughout the studio. He staged an area for taking old fashioned 1800s-style pictures, complete with period costumes and sepia-toned printing.

Against Ellie's better judgment, the controversial but lovely Tai would be doing double duty, working at the party both as a photographer and as a back-up sitter for the girls. Ellie didn't like it, but they needed help, and Tai was the easiest solution. Julien thought it was the perfect chance to show the town that they didn't back down from the small-town blather. Ellie figured it was his way of saying "eat crow" and giving the whole town the finger, albeit elegantly.

As Ellie helped hang last-minute decorations for the

party, she paused to admire *The Jewel*. The old building looked incredible. She still had her Greek revival façade, now accompanied by an exposed-brick interior. She thought back to the hours spent chipping away at the plaster by hand and realized it had all been worth it. The uneven sizes and rough surfaces added character and provided an excellent backdrop for photos.

And more importantly, she would never have unearthed the anthology if they hadn't decided to expose the bricks. It turned out that Ellie's chance discovery had provided the solace she needed amidst the upheaval in her life. It was as if *The Jewel* had known that Ellie needed her. Ellie giggled at the thought. She was becoming obsessed with the book. It just felt like it was meant to be hers and hers alone. She scratched her tingling wrist and set about frosting her cupcakes.

Things were going well at the launch party. The guests were enjoying themselves, and the mood was celebratory and carefree. The girls charmed the adults, trying to teach everyone a few French phrases. They had just run out of smoked salmon, so Ellie went to the kitchen area to replenish the hors d'oeuvres.

When Ellie opened the fridge, she noticed a saw floral arrangement. A short, fat vase held yellow chrysanthemums and orange marigolds. There was a small card, but since the arrangement was at the rear of the fridge and her hands were full, she thought she'd get a better look at it when she returned to the kitchen for champagne refills.

As the evening progressed, Ellie forgot the flowers. The Pelletiers and their guests toasted the studio, the town, the guests, and the economy. They nibbled their way through most of the hors d'oeuvres. Tai took some shots of the party and the ribbon cutting. She was quite professional for a teenager; she flitted in and around the various conversations and clicked away without making anyone feel self-conscience or annoyed.

Tai looked the part of photographer; she had dressed in a black-knit sweater-dress, black tights, big hoop earrings, and black-rimmed glasses with her long, blonde locks pulled up in a smooth ponytail. Ellie admitted that Tai was going to be a big help to Julien. Tai knew what she was doing. If only Ellie could make herself focus on Tai's good points instead of her flaws. Maybe Julien was right about Tai.

As guests said their goodbyes and the Pelletiers started packing up the leftovers to take home, Ellie remembered the floral arrangement.

"Julien," Ellie called out to him as he entered the kitchen for the last batch of champagne. "Make sure you grab the flowers from the fridge! Someone sent you an arrangement for the grand opening! I saw it earlier but forgot to tell you. Why don't you set them out on the counter for tomorrow's clients to enjoy while I take Tai home and put the girls to bed?"

*"D'accord,"* he replied. "Drive carefully," he warned. "These dirt roads are dark, and I hear there are deer everywhere."

After dropping off Tai, Ellie and the girls headed home. As Ellie turned onto the lonely dirt road that wound its way to their farmhouse, she saw something run across the road – just beyond the scope of her headlights. There were no streetlights this far out of town, and Ellie slowed down automatically, thinking about Jules' warning of deer. She imagined how awful it would be to have a wreck with no cell service, late at night, and on a deserted rural road. She made the rest of the journey home at a snail's pace.

When they finally arrived, both Méline and Bibianne had fallen asleep. Ellie managed to get one girl in each arm and her keys in her right hand to open the door. *Wow*, Ellie thought as she climbed slowly up the stairs to the porch. *They've gotten so much bigger and heavier since the last time I did this.* She kissed

Méline on the forehead and tried to rouse her from her sleep.

"Mel, sweetheart, I need you to wake up. C'mon, sleepy-head. Stand up for me." Méline rubbed her eyes as Ellie sat her down on the porch.

"*Oui, maman. Je suis très fatiguée. Je veux mon lit.*" Ellie smiled. She adored how Mel reverted to French when she was sleepy.

"We'll get you to your bed as soon as *maman* opens the door, *ma petite.*" Ellie was digging for the key to the front door when Méline spoke up again.

"*Mais, maman.* The *porte* is already open. I am taking myself to bed." Méline pushed right through the open front door and into the foyer.

Ellie's instincts buzzed in alarm when she saw that Méline was correct. Not only had front door had been left unlocked, it was ajar. Ellie hadn't noticed it until Méline pushed through.

"*Arête*! Stop!" Ellie entered the house and turned on the lights. She scooped Méline back up in her arms again. She held onto both girls as her heart pounded in her chest. Méline looked at Ellie, startled.

"What is it, *maman*?"

"*Maman* just wants to turn on the lights and tuck you in bed." Ellie noticed that Mel and Bibi didn't feel nearly as heavy as they did just five minutes before.

*Relax*, Ellie chided herself. *It was just an oversight.* They left in such a hurry that they'd forgotten to shut the door. They were way out in the middle of nowhere. No one would think of coming out there. What was there to steal? Some lavender and mint from the garden? Besides, everybody knew everybody in Stusa, so no one would be dumb enough to break into a house. The rumors would get around town quicker than kudzu.

Ellie reasoned with herself as she wandered around downstairs, flipping on all the lights and checking inside the pantry and coat closet. Méline wriggled out of Ellie's arms, tired of waiting on Ellie to get her to bed and climbed the stairs sleepily. "Come, *Maman*. Come tuck me in, and let's snuggle."

Ellie sighed. Such a sweet invitation. Julien would be home in a few minutes, and she'd ask him about the door later. He'd probably laugh at Ellie and her instant catastrophizing of the situation. He'd blame it on too many Agatha Christie novels. Besides, the dogs weren't barking, and if there had been an intruder, they'd have been going crazy.

After getting in bed and snuggling with the girls until they fell asleep, Ellie tiptoed out of their bedroom and headed to the bathroom. A long hot shower would relax her. When she entered the bathroom, she was surprised to see a floral arrangement sitting on the counter.

"Julien?" Ellie called out. "Why'd you put the flowers in the bathroom of all places?"

As she picked up the arrangement and turned it around to read the card, Ellie saw that the vase was a vividly painted ceramic skull for Día de los Muertos. The top of the "skull" had been hollowed out to form a bowl filled with marigolds and mums – the traditional flowers for Day of the Dead, a holiday celebrated primarily in Mexico and in a handful of countries throughout Latin America and Europe.

The skull was painted with swirling designs in vivid shades of aqua, fuchsia, silver and lime green. Sequins surrounded the eye sockets, and tiny floral designs decorated each tooth. *It must be from the Spanish teacher at school.* Sra. Ribera knew about Julien's grand opening, but she hadn't been able to attend due to a prior commitment.

Ellie tried not to feel a little wary of the skull vase. It had always seemed macabre until Sra. Ribera explained it. She said that while Americans tended to fear and loathe anything that had to do with death - wrinkles, grey hair, yellowing teeth - other cultures viewed death as a natural part of life, a transition to the next world.

Death was not a Grim Reaper waiting to cut down the

next victim. Instead, she was *La Muerte*, a beautiful, vibrant lady who escorted the deceased to their next adventure. Sra. Ribera and her family celebrated death by remembering the lives of loved ones who had died and moved on to the next adventure. They cooked meals, set up memorials of the loved one's favorite foods, took flowers to the cemetery, and held vigils. It was then that Ellie began to understand and appreciate the holiday although the idea of having a skull for décor still felt a little creepy.

The sound of Julien's car pulling up in the driveway interrupted Ellie's reminiscence. *That's strange*, she thought. *How did he get these flowers home from the studio?* Maybe it was his second trip and Ellie just didn't hear him the first time. That would explain the door being open when they arrived.

Ellie heard the clink of his keys hitting the countertop and called to him as she headed downstairs, "Do you need any help unloading?"

"*Non*, I have finished. What a lovely evening, *ma belle*." Julien sighed contentedly and leaned in for a kiss. He pulled back to look Ellie in the eyes. "*Merci beaucoup pour tout, ma vie.* Are the girls asleep?" He asked as he draped his arms around Ellie's waist and pulled her into an embrace. Ellie rested her head on his shoulder and breathed in his scent. It was so comforting and familiar, like salted caramel and dark chocolate.

"Yes," she replied. "They were exhausted and fell asleep in the car. I had to carry them up the front steps! Oh, and that reminds me." She leaned back and looked at him. "When we got home, the door was ajar. You must have forgotten to close it when you dropped off the first load from the studio."

"First load?" He lifted one eyebrow. "This is my first load, *ma chérie*. I just got home and put the champagne in the fridge. I did not leave the door ajar." He hugged Ellie tighter, kissing her neck. "As I recall, you left home after I did. I think you were the one who left the door open." He nibbled her ear lobe as he chided her. Ellie pulled back a little and looked at him in concern.

"But I've never left the door open before. I can't believe I would have been so distracted." She pushed his arms down and took a step back. "What if someone had come in the house?" Ellie continued anxiously.

"Are you really worried, *ma belle*?" Julien grabbed Ellie's hands and studied her eyes. "Let's not obsess over this, sweetheart. You have been working so hard lately. I am sure you just left in a hurry to get to the party. Let's go upstairs and have a final, private toast to a perfect evening. You said the girls are asleep, *non*?" He took her hand in his and led her through the kitchen. "*Viens ici, ma poupée.*"

He grabbed two champagne flutes, a half-consumed bottle, and took Ellie to the bedroom where they did indeed share a very private, very delicious toast. All thoughts of intruders melted away into the darkness. Even after ten years together, there was still plenty to celebrate.

Ellie didn't remember the floral arrangement until the next morning. Julien woke her with a kiss on the forehead. "I'm heading to the studio early." He whispered. "And I left coffee for you downstairs." Ellie sat up.

"*Non, non, non.*" He pulled the blanket back up around her shoulders and tucked Ellie back in. "Don't get up. It's still early. Sleep in and relax. The girls aren't up yet. I'll see you at lunch."

Ellie sighed and closed her eyes. When she opened them again, she extended into a luxurious stretch and rolled over to check the time. There beside the clock was the floral arrangement.

Ellie never had gotten a good look at the card, so she reached over to read it. When she picked up the card, however, there was no name on either side. The only information on it was a little rhyme.

Marigolds & Mums
Nature's vibrant bloom
Linked to the world of spirits
Ushering in your doom

Ellie rolled her eyes. *Some silly prank*, she thought. She wondered how much Blaize had spent on this little floral arrangement. "But," a little voice inside her head pointed out, "he would've sent the flowers to school."

The more Ellie tried to forget about the note, the more the card spooked her. She tried to laugh it off, but what if Blaize was still committed to carrying out his threat? He'd have to be an idiot to do anything at school. There were cameras everywhere, even in the parking lot.

Ellie re-read the note several times. The words tasted familiar. Like a warning or a riddle that she needed to solve. No, not a riddle exactly. It felt more like a . . . conspiracy.

Despite the previous night's success, all her doubts flooded in, breaking through the mental dam she had constructed. What was Julien thinking? He was spending more time at that studio than he was with his own family, and now that the holidays were approaching, he wanted to allow Tai in on their family holiday?

Maybe all of this was connected somehow, the rumors and innuendos at school, the flowers, the feeling that she was being watched – no, directed – to live out a piece of Arthur Miller's play. Was it all part of a xenophobic attack? Or was she being paranoid?

Ellie had never felt threatened before, and now she felt like things were out of her control. It gave her chills. Her mind immediately went to the anthology. Was there anything in the book that could help? Ellie felt ungrounded; she wasn't seeing things clearly.

Ellie started to trash the flowers. At the last minute, however, she decided the ensemble was much too beautiful to discard. She'd take it to school instead and put it right up front on her desk. She might even brag on the ridiculous little rhyme. That ought to show the little punk how "afraid" she was. Ellie was peeved with herself for allowing a student to intrude on her sacred Saturday morning.

Oh! An even better idea popped into her head. First thing Monday morning, Ellie would stop by Mrs. Sarka's room and show her the flowers. Then Mrs. Sarka would do all the work for Ellie. She'd have Ellie's unfazed reaction spread before the bell rang for first period to end. Ha! That ought to show Blaize that his scare tactics didn't work.

Ellie grinned in satisfaction. She'd found another way to confront her fears – by flaunting them.

# CHAPTER THIRTY

## *THE SHADOW*

*The Shadow* plucked a few mint leaves for her morning tea. A pinch of sage would clear her mind while the mint would sharpen her senses, preparing her for her task. As she brought the kettle to a boil, she packed her rucksack.

She laughed to herself thinking of the two women she was playing against each other; they were both such easy targets. Ellie and her idealistic, optimistic view of Stusa was just too naïve an opportunity to miss. Taiteja, envied and hated by almost every girl in the school for her beautiful face and curvaceous body, was the perfect distraction for *both* Pelletiers.

Tai tended to bring trouble wherever she went. She was a walking personality disorder. While she pretended to be a victimized little angel at school – the target of bullying and harassment – her daily attire and social media clearly shouted *slut*. Her pictures on social media were so photoshopped that she didn't have a belly button. Anyone *that* desperate for attention would do anything to get it. She just needed a little push.

As *The Shadow* put on the moccasins that allowed her to slip silently through the forest, she gloated over finally figuring out how to use an earth element against Ellie. It had taken time and cleverness. Living in the marshy town of Stusa, arranging a cave-in or mining accident was impossible, and while burying Ellie alive would be quite dramatic, it was also much harder to orchestrate. Luckily, the sickly, poisonous green color of her scar inspired the idea for an elemental earth attack.

She strapped on her rucksack and took the hidden path that led from her isolated cabin to the pond behind the Pelletier's homestead. As she walked, she wondered if Ellie was close to discovering the power of *The Shadow's* heirloom. She must prevent Ellie interfering with *The Shadow's* centuries-old connection at any cost.

She scoffed to herself. The thought of someone like Ellie wielding the power of the heirloom was laughable. Ellie's naiveté and optimism were like lasers painting a target; it was impossible to resist trickery when someone absolutely begged for it.

Ellie's main problem was that she saw the good in everyone, or at least the *potential* for good. Ellie didn't see reality; instead of looking out over a class of lethargic thugs and users, Ellie saw young doctors, lawyers, and artists who had simply been waylaid on their path to success. It was disgusting - all that enthusiasm and blind faith in hollow people and empty dreams. Stusa was a void, a shadow town; it was futile to try to change it or to believe that change was even possible.

*The Shadow* peered through the trees; the Pelletier house looked empty. The cars were gone, and the dogs were on the screened-in back porch. Even so, she moved cautiously. The dogs would smell her before they saw her. If their barking didn't bring anyone out, she could be certain that no one was home.

She snorted as she entered easily through the front door. The Pelletiers had invested in structure and decoration, but not enough on the locks. They were easy to bypass for someone of *The Shadow's* talent. As she crossed the threshold, she looked to the right. On the wall, adjacent to the front door was the *bénitier*.

The *bénitier* was antique -- a French, religious, holy font. A silver figurine of Jesus Christ hanging from a wooden cross was displayed on a background of red velvet with the letters INRI on top. A small finger bowl below the crucifix held holy water. The velvet and metal showed their age, but the *bénitier's* shabby-chic condition complimented the homestead.

*The Shadow* knew that each time Ellie left the house, she dipped her right hand into the small font and crossed herself as she exited. She reached into her rucksack, withdrawing a tiny vial. She removed the dropper and squeezed three drops of amber-colored oil into the holy water. She laughed to herself and climbed the stairs to the Pelletier's bedroom.

This was almost too easy. In the master bedroom, *The Shadow* misted Ellie's pillowcase with a green-tinged liquid. Then, she went into Ellie's closet. She misted all of Ellie's blouses. She placed one drop of the amber-colored oil inside each shoe.

Her final act, however, was the cruelest of all; before exiting the closet, *The Shadow* opened Ellie's drawer of lingerie and misted it all. She waited for each lacy, flimsy piece to dry and replaced the undergarments with a smirk. This would be hard to wait for but amusing to watch unfold.

# CHAPTER THIRTY-ONE

## *UNBEARABLE URUSHIOL*

Ellie couldn't shake the sense that something was wrong. She couldn't identify the feeling. Then, it hit her. Ellie was dipping her forefinger into the *bénitier,* crossing herself as she left for work, when the word she had been searching for popped into her mind.

Ellie was feeling *persecuted.* Ellie had never played the role of victim, so she wasn't used to admitting such feelings, but there it was. She felt picked on, put upon, persecuted.

She reviewed her ever-ready mental list of what had led to those feelings. Ellie had been misled - whether intentionally or unintentionally, she wasn't sure - about her job. She had almost drowned at the fall festival due to faulty equipment. She'd been threatened by a student - twice. Rumors had spread about her husband and his assistant, and she'd faced religious scorn from those who felt themselves to be "holier."

Just that week, her students were analyzing the characters and tracing their development throughout the play. Students had been comparing the small-town settings of Salem and Stusa. They eagerly awaited Fridays so they could work on the play. They had discussed how religion played a vital role in the lives of the Salem villagers and how Salem Village was, in fact, a theocracy.

After all, Ellie's history buffs pointed out, most of the

Puritans had come over to America seeking religious freedom and a permanent escape from the English Reformation which had started with King Henry VIII and continued through the 1600s. This, naturally, led to a debate among class members as to which religious group had done more harm than the other. It became quite heated and, unfortunately, quite personal.

As students discussed the origin of the Church of England - King Henry VIII wanting to divorce himself both from his wife and the jurisdiction of the Catholic Church at the time - Ellie wondered if humanity would ever stop using religion as an excuse for hatred. In the midst of this debate, Georgianna, the daughter of a staunch Bible-thumping mother, turned the argument from a historical debate to a contemporary attack.

"Yeah, well Miz Paylaytay is a Catholic herself. She worships Mayree."

The contempt packed into those few words made Ellie sound like she sacrificed small children to Satan; Ellie's mouth dropped open as she was caught completely off-guard. The entire class inhaled a collective gasp and turned to Ellie with faces full of mistrust and disappointment.

Ellie exhaled slowly, said a quick prayer for patience, and said in her calmest teacher voice, "That is a widespread misconception among Protestants here." She clenched her jaw on that last word *here*.

Just at that moment, the tension was relieved by a tardy arrival to class. To Ellie's delight, GG entered the classroom with a late pass and took her seat as they got back to work. Ellie would have loved to hear her thoughts on the matter. GG's insight into history made her a wonderful student with an interesting perspective, but Ellie decided against it since calm had been restored.

Was the entire town's scorn directed at Ellie? Or was she being overly sensitive as Julien suggested? She supposed it was small town xenophobia, but she should have expected that, being the first new teacher in the county for over a decade. Maybe it was like some type of initiation into a fraternity; if

Ellie made the cut and withstood the crucible, they'd allow her admittance into the community and into her French classes.

Ellie put her thoughts aside as she pulled into the school parking lot and prepared for her day. Sometime during first period, Ellie began to feel a mild, tingling itch right in the middle of her forehead. *Great, a new zit popping out right here in front of my entire class.*

She tried her best not to scratch, but before too long the itch intensified. It seemed to spread all over her face. Ellie tried pinching her cheeks and tapping herself lightly to keep from giving in to the itching sensation, but soon she was full-on scratching.

Her students were beginning to stare; Geonjelo asked her if she was having a seizure. Ellie stepped into the hall, asking the teacher next door to keep an eye on her class. She headed for the teachers' lounge to put a cold, wet paper towel over her face. As Ellie was speed-walking, she felt a tingling in her toes that rapidly expanded into an intense burning-itching sensation.

As she fumbled to find the key to the lounge, she noticed red whelps on the back of her hand. She finally got the right key, opened the door, kicked off her shoes, and ran straight to the sink. To Ellie's horror, her reflection in the mirror revealed the same angry, red blotches from her hand appearing on her face. She grabbed some ice from the fridge, and held the ice where the itching was the worst. It dawned on her that she must be suffering some type of allergic reaction, so Ellie picked up the phone to call the local hospital.

As she tried to dial, she felt a strange sensation. Her face felt like a balloon being slowly inflated. She couldn't see very well. Were her eyes shrinking? No, but she could see her own cheeks puffing up like dough rising in an oven. Ellie's field of vision continued to shrink.

She began to panic. She could no longer see to make the call. Just then, Mr. Grant came into the lounge. He gave a little gasp when he realized he was not alone; the least little thing startled him. When he took a good look at Ellie, however, he absolutely shrieked. Ellie managed to croak, "911" before collapsing against the wall and sliding to the floor.

Soon, there was a flutter of activity all around Ellie as she was being lifted onto a gurney and placed inside an ambulance. Principal Danvers ordered poor Mr. Grant to ride with her to the hospital and to call him when he knew what was going on with Ellie and when she'd be back at work.

Ellie's eyes were almost swollen shut; she could only see through narrow, horizontal slits. Her forehead felt like a giant balloon waiting to pop, and her lips were so inflated that she couldn't close her mouth all the way. She thought drool might have been running down her chin, but she wasn't sure. After that, she didn't remember much.

According to the paperwork she read later, Ellie had received a Decadron shot on the way to the hospital, but it hadn't been effective. Once in the E.R, doctors hooked her up to an I.V. to administer steroids and Benadryl. Someone had called Julien, and he'd rushed to meet her at the hospital.

When Ellie eventually became aware of her surroundings, the first thing she noticed were her feet. They stuck out from under the hospital blanket at the end of her bed and looked like Hobbit feet. They were twice their normal size.

Large, red, weeping blisters seemed to cover every part of her flesh: her face, lips, mouth, toes, and even, quite embarrassingly, her most private parts. She was swollen, itchy, miserable -- unable to do anything other than lie there trying to understand what was happening to her.

Apparently, doctors explained, she had recently encountered poison ivy -- a vine that Ellie had only read about before moving to Stusa, but one that she learned grew practically everywhere in the continental United States. Ellie had suffered a rare (but not unheard of) severe allergic reaction to said vine. Henceforth, she would have to avoid poison ivy, unless she wanted to find out if the next reaction would be even worse – or fatal. The most awful part was that she wouldn't have to touch the plant itself; she could react to the oil of the plant which could be carried by the girls, the dogs, or someone's clothes. It was horribly frightening.

After the doctors left the room, Ellie looked around. She couldn't have seen her face if she wanted to; Julien had draped all the mirrors and reflective surfaces with hospital sheets from the neighboring bed. Ellie was relieved that her field of vision was increasing, but her lips were still enormous. Trying to talk was like having to form words with two gigantic, flapping butt cheeks; it was impossible. She giggled when she realized it gave a whole new meaning to the phrase "talkin' outta her ass."

Doctors eventually sent Ellie home with antibiotics, more oral steroids and creams, and orders to take Benadryl every four hours for the next three days. After she returned to normal, Ellie was under strict orders to wash every single piece of clothing in the entire house in case oil from the poison ivy was on anything. If the girls had it on their jackets, for example, Ellie could react to the lingering residue. And the worst part, the doctors informed her, was that the Urushiol - the chemical culprit within the oil that caused so much grief - could remain active for up to five years.

When they got home, Julien immediately stripped their bed and replaced all the linens before tucking Ellie in and dosing her with Benadryl. Tai had picked the girls up from school and was waiting with them when they arrived. Ellie realized she must have still looked rough because Tai gave a small gasp.

Bibianne said, "Oh! Poor *Maman*! We love you even if you are *très laide*!" Bibi rushed over to give Ellie a quick hug, and then Méline followed. Méline wasn't quite so adept at hiding the look of shock on her face upon seeing Ellie.

Fortunately, Julien took everything in stride. He was a tender care-taker and didn't complain once about waking Ellie up every four hours to give her the necessary meds. While Ellie was asleep, he washed all her clothes from the bureau. He wiped down her shoes – inside and out.

Julien turned out to be an impressive house husband. He bathed the dogs and washed all the girls' clothes. He washed their shoes, too, and threw away the ones that didn't survive the washing machine. The intense cleaning had taken two full days. Ellie wanted to help, but the medications left her woozy and thick-tongued.

Most of all, she wanted to get better so Tai wouldn't be around to help with the girls. Ellie had mixed emotions about that. She didn't like outsiders seeing her at her weakest – especially students - but she knew Julien must need the help with her being incapacitated.

Tai turned out to be thoughtful and helpful; she even brought Ellie a gift. She came upstairs and knocked gingerly on the door.

"Come in." Ellie replied groggily.

"Mrs. P? Are you okay?" Tai asked as she crossed to the bed.

"Sort of." Ellie responded with what she hoped was a sheepish grin rather than the grimace she suspected it to be.

"Well, I brought you something to cheer you up." Tai said with a smile. She pulled a painting out from behind her back and showed it to Ellie.

"Oh!" Ellie gasped. "It's lovely! My favorite artist! How did you know? How could you afford it? Even the copies are pricey." Ellie blurted without thinking.

Tai chuckled. "I didn't buy it, Mrs. P. I painted it!" A proud smile lit her face.

It was stunning. Tai had painted a replica of one of Ellie's very favorite pieces onto a thick, large canvas. It had everything Ellie loved - bright colors, abstract shapes, and just the right amount of whimsy. Ellie knew immediately where she would hang it in her classroom.

"Wow, Tai! I love it! I never knew you were so talented. I have just the spot for this in my classroom, if you don't mind me sharing it."

Tai glanced down at the floor and then back up at Ellie. "That's fine." She backed out of the room and left Ellie to enjoy her new piece of art.

As Ellie struggled not to scratch the whelps on her arms, she wondered for the dozenth time if she had misjudged Tai like the rest of Stusa. Maybe Tai was just trying to fit in with the one family who didn't seem to outright condemn her. Ellie knew that Julien would need Tai's help. Even after Ellie healed, there would still be so much left to do. For now, Ellie would have to accept Tai's assistance. She was in no condition to refuse.

**ELIZABETH**: You were alone with her?

**PROCTOR**: For a moment alone, aye.

**ELIZABETH**: Why, then, it is not as you told me.

**PROCTOR**: For a moment, I say. The others come in soon after.

**ELIZABETH**: Do as you wish, then.

**PROCTOR**: Woman. I'll not have your suspicion any more.

**ELIZABETH**: (A little loftily.) I have no...

**PROCTOR**: I'll not have it!

**ELIZABETH**: Then let you not earn it.

--ELIZABETH PROCTOR TO JOHN PROCTOR, ACT ONE, SCENE
2 THE CRUCIBLE

# CHAPTER THIRTY-TWO

## ABIDING ACCUSATIONS

As Ellie lay in bed recovering from her poison ivy reaction, she stared at her new painting to try to keep from scratching. The medicine kept her too groggy to read or watch T.V. At some point, Ellie received a phone call from the principal; he called under the pretense of checking on her health.

"Well, uh Miz Palaytay. I know you are resting and that's good." He paused. Ellie waited to see what he meant. She sensed a "but there's more" coming.

"I hate to bring up somethin' at a time like this," he continued, "but it's my Christian duty to let you know what is being said around the community. Gawd has called me to a difficult job, Miz Palatay, and I come to you with a heavy heart."

"What exactly do you mean, Principal Danvers?" Ellie asked with as much politeness as she could muster in her miasma of medicine. "People know about my rather dramatic poison ivy reaction." I don't really see how that could..."

"Well," he started. "Now, that's not really what they are talkin' about, Miz Paylaytay. I mean ever'one is worried sick about ya' I can tell ya' that right now. Yes, ma'am, we are prayin' fervently for yore recovery. You are on many a prayer-list, for more than one reason."

She waited, hoping that he would eventually reveal the

reason that everyone suddenly felt the need to pray for her. Was it because she was Catholic? That was old news. Surely the Pelletiers were not the first Catholic family in Stusa.

Principal Danvers finally intercepted the awkward pause. "Well, to be perfectly honest, there are some rumors runnin' round town about yore baby-sitter, Miz. I hate to be the one to bring it to yore attention, but Tai ain't too much of a role model. The apple don't fall far from the tree, if you know what I mean."

Ellie paused. "No, I do not know what you mean. What apple? What tree? What on earth does Tai have to do with me being on a prayer-list?" Ellie asked.

"Well, I'll just cut to the chase." Principal Danvers sighed.

"I wish you would." Ellie responded. "It's almost time for me to take another dose of medicine."

He took a deep breath and said, "The town is worried about yore children. If Tai is yore babysitter, she might have some type of detrimental influence on yore family."

"What kind of influence are you referring to, sir? Wait, is this about the drug rumor at school? We've spoken to her about that and believe her claim of innocence."

"Well, Miz – it ain't just the weed she's accused of smoking or the shady frienz she hangs out with." He paused again. "She ahhh, she ahhhh has been seen with yore husband downtown."

"Of course, she has!" Ellie rolled her eyes. "She works at Julien's studio." Ellie replied, irritated. She was so tired of hearing these baseless rumors. She had spent the better part of first semester defending both her husband and Tai from the rumor mill.

"It gets worse, Miz. They been seen hangin' out together on some of the rooftops downtown *smokin'*.

Ellie was puzzled. Julien was an adult, and smoking wasn't damning, even in Stusa. And although Ellie didn't like that Julien had resumed one of the vices she thought he had conquered, she didn't see how the activity was illicit. Was the principal implying that they were smoking pot? It just didn't add up. As she tried to digest the odd piece of information, she asked, "When was this?"

Another throat clearing. "Ever' day this week since ya' been laid up."

"What!?!" Elie choked on the water she had been sipping. She coughed and spluttered into the phone. "He has been working all week," She stammered. "It must be someone else that resembles Julien."

An awkward silence ensued.

"No, ma'am. I saw him myself on the way to our Thanksgiving luncheon. Like I say, I know you need yore rest, but I felt it was my duty to let you know. You are in our prayers. I'll let you go back to bed now." He was suddenly in a hurry to get off the phone.

Ellie ran her hands through her hair. Julien had no sense of what was appropriate and what was not! She had told him over and over that in this little town full of gnats – perception was reality and that they needed to avoid any semblance of impropriety. What on earth was he thinking?

Her thoughts began to simmer.

Could Julien and Tai be working on photo shoot prep work? The last thing Ellie needed was the whole town talking about Tai and Julien again. She thought those rumors had been squelched for good after the grand opening. But what an idiot Julien could be! Ellie had clearly expressed that she didn't want him to be alone with Tai for this very reason – rumors.

The simmering reached a slow, steady boil.

Ellie couldn't believe Julien would put her job in jeopardy over some stupid photo shoot. *Just wait until he gets home,* she thought. *He hates confrontations, but I am going to give him a piece of my mind!*

The violent roiling reached its maximum and threatened to spill over.

This was ridiculous! Ellie had worked tirelessly to

squelch the rumors swirling around them, and then Julien had to go and do something so utterly stupid! She took her dose of Benadryl and lay back on the pillow to fume. Before long, she dozed off.

*Ellie was sitting on the wooden pew of an old church. The congregation was dressed oddly; so was Ellie. They were in colonial clothing.*

*As soon as the thought came, she felt the rough-spun cloth against her skin, heavy and scratchy. She reached up to rub away the prickling on the back of her neck and felt ties fastened at the base of her neck. She was wearing a bonnet, and all her hair was tucked underneath.*

*A voice came from the front of the church. As soon as she noticed it, his muddled words cleared, and she heard his sermon - but as if from a distance. A man stood at the pulpit telling the congregation that they were all spiders dangling over the fiery pits of hell, but unlike Jonathan Edwards' calm delivery, this reverend screamed and shouted at the congregation.*

*As he ranted and raved, a sense of despair and disgust settled over Ellie. She looked around at the crowd and saw Julien across the aisle sitting with his head hanging down. He looked tired, defeated – ashamed.*

*Suddenly, the doors in the back of the church burst open. Ellie turned with the rest of the congregation. She saw a young girl enter the church carrying a basket of chrysanthemums and mari-golds in shades of yellow and orange. Her braided hair swung as she skipped down the center aisle. She looked the perfect picture of innocence. Ellie couldn't see her face clearly, so she leaned over, straining to get a better view.*

*When the young girl reached the end of the aisle just a few feet from the pulpit, she came to an abrupt halt. Her skipping stopped, and her flowers fell to the floor as she ducked, raising her hands over her head in defense. She screamed that demons were torturing her, demons that were sent by Elizabeth Proctor. Then, she pointed at Ellie.*

*Ellie gasped at the bold, unfair, and unfounded accusation.*

*Before she could even react, strong hands dragged her down the church aisle. Ellie twisted and turned trying to get away from the men who were pulling her to the pulpit. She meant to cry out for Julien, but the words that came out of her mouth were, "John – look after the boys! They'll be scared. You find a way to make it right!"*

Ellie struggled violently, thrashing and biting, but her movements were tangled in some type of restraint – a rope. When she made one last valiant attempt to break free from the unseen confinement, she jerked herself awake to find her right arm swinging as she struggled to escape the tangle of sheets that pinned the rest of her body.

Ellie was instantly and completely awake, fury coursing through her veins. Maybe she wasn't being hauled off to jail in real life, but she was desperately tired of being hauled through the rumor mill by Julien's thoughtless actions.

Ellie snatched her cell phone off the nightstand. She texted Julien fast and furious.

Where r u?
Smoking w/Tai downtown?
Whole town is talking!

No response. Ellie was so livid that even her dose of Benadryl couldn't knock her out. She flung off the bed covers and stormed downstairs figuring she might as well start some laundry to quench her anger. On her way out of the bedroom, she snatched up the useless beeswax candle and mug of herbs. They clearly had not worked. Her dreams were still bothering her, so into the trash they went. Despite her anger, she was glad she wouldn't have to swallow another drop of the disgusting tea

When Julien got home, Ellie sent the girls outside and launched her attack. "What were you thinking this past week?

Being alone with Tai in full view of the public and *smoking*? All while I'm in a fog of medication and itching!?"

Julien wasn't fazed. He shrugged. "Ma petite, we were simply taking a break from work. We went up to the roof and shared a smoke. It's not anything scandalous. Why do you let these small-town rumors bother you? Just ignore these pesky people. They have nothing better to do; they are simply bored and jealous." He reached over as if to embrace Ellie.

She stepped back and continued, "Be that as it may, I don't want you alone with Tai. You know this. And since when did you start smoking again?"

"Ellie, we shared a cigarette. That doesn't mean I've started smoking again. It was a social smoke, a stress reliever." He put one hand on each of her shoulders. "Think for a moment. I can't get everything ready by myself at the studio and at home while you are incapacitated. I need her help. Tomorrow we have our first photo shoot for the Johnsons. If I treat them well, I will get plenty of referrals. How could I prepare everything alone?"

"Well, you're a resourceful man – you'll figure something out!" Ellie snapped. "Under no circumstances will I condone you being alone with Tai!"

"What do you suggest I do?" He dropped his arms to his side, his voice dripping with sarcasm. "You want me to let my first customers arrive for their appointment unprepared? Instead of starting the photo shoot, I'll just make them wait while Tai and I set up props. I'm sure they won't mind waiting. Yes, that's brilliant, *cherie*. I'll just explain that I needed a chaperone because my wife doesn't like to face rumors" He turned away from Ellie and headed towards his office.

Ellie took a deep breath and followed him, "No, I don't like facing rumors, but that's exactly what I've been doing for four months. Stop encouraging them!" She was beginning to feel more tired than angry.

Just then, the girls ran in wanting some lavender lemonade. After Ellie took them into the kitchen and served them, she went to take a shower to cool down. She hadn't been this exasperated with Julien in a long time, since before the girls were born. How dare he refuse her in this!

Ellie entered the bathroom and did something she had never done before; she locked the door. She didn't want him to barge in on her and try to make peace. Her rage resurfaced as Ellie replayed the dialogue over again in her head. It bubbled over and spilled out as she cried hot, angry tears into the cool, steady stream of water.

It was beyond ironic; the minute they moved to their dream life in the country, her personal life started falling apart. And what had that dream been about? Hallucination was probably a better term considering all the medicine she was taking.

It was like she had been inside *The Crucible*, except it had felt real. She had been Elizabeth Proctor, and Julien had been John Proctor. They had two boys instead of two girls. Ellie had simultaneously been a participant in the dream and an observer; she saw the action from above, looking down at what was happening.

Maybe she was focusing too much on work. Maybe that was the whole problem between Julien and her. They had not resolved their argument about Tai and had never arrived at a satisfactory agreement. He had not said what he was planning to do. The issue remained unsettled. If he did continue to work with Tai, what was Ellie going to do?

# CHAPTER THIRTY-THREE

## RUMORS RESURFACE

During the next few miserable days, Ellie brooded. Not only was her entire week of Thanksgiving break being ruined by the poison ivy incident, she was pelted with rumors. Again. She wasn't safe from them in her own home anymore. They had taken on a life of their own; the rumors were a vicious, hungry predator flitting in and out of the shadows, steadily stalking Ellie.

Ellie retreated to her anthology for comfort and escape. Since she couldn't focus enough in between bouts of Benadryl to make lesson plans for school, she furiously flipped past the folk remedies, looking for the journal entries of her newfound friend - EBP.

How had Ebbie handled the ugly rumors facing her? What had she done? Had she confronted her husband in a time when husbands treated wives more like property than people? Had Ebbie looked the other way, quietly and obediently believing in her husband while the town mocked her? Or did she do as Ellie had done – pick a fight with her husband and touch on the issue without ever coming right out and asking him if he was having an affair?

As she brooded, she thumbed mindlessly through the anthology. Ellie felt ashamed of herself. What a coward she was. Why hadn't she just come right out and asked Julien if he had feelings for Tai? What was she afraid of?

If he did have a crush on Tai, at least Ellie would know the truth. The truth could be managed. If she could just get a clear diagnosis, the underlying disease could be treated.

They could get counseling. They could get away – just the two of them – and work on their marriage. They could go on one of the marriage retreats their church advertised. Ellie could finally make Julien see that he needed to banish Tai from their lives to work on their marriage and their daughters.

But part of Ellie knew why she didn't flat out ask him. If he admitted even a *platonic* crush on another woman, Ellie's world would crumble. It would destroy her. Her entire world would be rent asunder. She turned another page to redirect her thoughts.

On the other hand, if Julien didn't have a crush on Tai, he would be so very hurt. Her doubt would baffle and disappoint him. It would be better to have faith in him and let him prove himself. Making a rash decision under the influence of so much medication might bring unwanted results. She would be mature, do the right thing, and believe in her husband's fidelity. She turned another page to refocus.

Just then, she felt it – a light, tingling sensation on a page, begging for her attention. When Ellie looked down, she found another journal entry from Ebbie. Since discovering that the entries were not sequential, the only way she could keep track of Ebbie's story was to look at the dates for each entry. This one was from 4 April 1692, more than a week earlier than the very first entry Ellie had read about Ebbie and her colonial crisis.

In that entry, Ebbie's sister informed her of stories going around the village about Ebbie's husband and the preacher's niece. Now, she would get to see Ebbie's reaction.

*4 April 1692*
*After I watched my sister depart, I turned*

*to my Bible and looked for guidance. He sent a sign, for when my Bible were in my hands, the Good Book fell open to a verse that spoke to my heart at once.*

*Matthew 18:17. "If he shall neglect to hear them, then tell it to the church." Since speaking to my husband had gained me nothing but an icy hearth, I did go to find Reverend Parris to seek counsel. As it were his own niece involved in the gossip, I knew he would lead me in the path of righteousness, for his own sake if not for mine.*

So, Ebbie had talked to her husband after all. It didn't sound like she had gotten a satisfactory answer, though. *And when Ebbie was at the end of her rope, of course, she would have turned to the church.* That would be the only recourse available to her in those times. Ellie continued reading.

*The shepherd of our flock received me into his church although it were early in the day for services. I explained to him the tales that were spun by his niece's companions. I told him what shame it were bringing to my household.*

*He listened to me with a hard heart. He offered no solace but reprimanded my pride. His niece could not be involved in any such dark-ness for her soul were pure as the driven snow. My heart, then, must be searched for seeds of envy and guilt. I must pray for forgiveness and "look to the log in mine own eye before regarding the speck in the eye of my neighbor."*

*I left with a heavy heart for I knew that I had done no wrong. I have only been a faithful and loving wife. The reverend would not hear any accusations against his own kin. He would not confront his niece.*

> *Thus, I am forced to go to the darkest place of my soul. Since the Good Book holds no answers for me, I turn to another book – one I found in Abi's room under the mattress, one I suspect she stole from Parris' slave girl. This same book into which I pour out my heart.*
>
> *It has become my only comfort in this time of need. On the blank pages between family cures, I write the thoughts that I dare not speak. I keep my silence as a good Christian woman should do.*
>
> *I leave these words here in the hope that one day they will provide comfort for another. Women have a sorry lot in life. We bring life into the world - only for it to be smothered by the rule of men.*
>
> *I fear that men will never see the wisdom of women. They look to us as servants, here to keep their beds warm and their offspring healthy. I wonder if they do fear us having control of anything further than the home.      As for the Reverend, it would seem so. He doth fear the power of lust that his niece awakens in men.*

*Wow!* Ellie thought. Ebbie might have been the first woman of her time to record such feminist thoughts! She would *have* to show this to Zyla. Zyla would know if this was unusual for its time. Ellie wanted to finish reading it first, though. Ebbie's situation was beginning to sound a lot like her own. Disturbingly similar, in fact. Somehow, Ellie wasn't surprised.

> *I will end with a piece of advice perchance no one ever read, and that be a good thing, for them are not holy words of the Bible that follow. I confess that I did find a remedy in this very book, a remedy for all my suffering.*

*If it were a sin to speak the invocation, then
I pray God's mercy, for He alone knows my
works upon this earth and whether I chose
the path of the wicked or of the righteous.
E.B.P.*

A dozen questions hit Ellie as she finished the passage. What happened to Ebbie? What happened to her husband? Where did the preacher's niece go? Had Ebbie ever passed the anthology down to her granddaughter as planned?

What exactly had Ebbie meant by the invocation she delivered? Madame Margaux, spells, and charms came to mind, but Ellie cast them aside. The real question that was burning inside her, the overriding question of all -- *what was the remedy that Ebbie had used?*

A longing so fierce that it brought Ellie's knees to her chest twisted Ellie's gut. She flung the book aside and tucked her head to her knees to control the knot growing in her belly. She felt a tightening, like a bracelet being drawn too tightly around her tiny wrist, and a pounding in her chest. Her breath came in short gasps as if she'd run a race. She was too hungry for the answer, the remedy Ebbie had written about. Was Ellie being naïve, desperate, deluded?

*Too much thinking.* She sat back up. *Time for action.* Ellie grabbed the book and began searching for any possible "remedies" for a young girl tempting a married man.

Ellie started at the very beginning of the anthology and skimmed each title searching for something that Ebbie might have used. She flipped past folk cures for everything from mosquito bites to fevers. There were recipes for breathing problems, headaches, snake bites, withering crops, sick livestock, drought, and more. Some of the recipes were quite simple and only required repeating a verse, burying a coin, or snipping a lock of someone's hair. Others appeared more complex and involved candles, exotic herbs and spices, specific times of night, specific phases of the moon - and salt. There always seemed to be salt.

As she skimmed the remedies, Ellie thought of the little rhyme she had first discovered that night while working at the Jewel. The one about getting rid of "irksome pests." Should she put any stock in these simple words? Could words have power?

Of course, they could. They had so much power, in fact, that Ellie was petrified to use them against Julian, terrified that he might destroy their marriage with five little words: *I have feelings for Tai.*

Words were powerful; they could change fate, history, feelings – even life itself. Come to think of it, Ellie hadn't been bothered by the awful gnats since the night she uttered the words from the anthology, but that was due to the weather getting cooler. Her stomach squirmed, and her brain ticked.

Ellie set the book aside again. She needed time to think. Just what, exactly, had she gotten herself into? Between her bizarre dreams about the play and the small-town politics that mimicked Miller's work, she felt downright alarmed.

Maybe it wasn't time for action, after all. Before she rushed headlong into anything, maybe it would be good, for once in her life, to stop and think *before* she acted, and Ebbie's entry left her quite a bit to think about.

# CHAPTER THIRTY-FOUR

## *BACK INTO BATTLE*

Ellie's itchy, miserable Thanksgiving break finally ended, and she recovered enough to return to school. She had never dreaded going to work like she did now. She couldn't place her finger on the exact cause of her dread. It wasn't entirely based on her feelings of doubt; the feeling was more like an ocean swell of anger, anxiety, and disappointment that was building, gaining both height and momentum, growing into an enormous wave. She shivered at the thought, wondering if she'd surf that wave and ride it into the shore, or if it would crash over her and send her roiling under its weight.

Ellie was at a crossroads in her life; she could either crumble under the pressure of the rumors and her own fierce doubts, or she could continue to hold her head high and trudge through. While a large part of her wanted to give in to the frustration, another part knew that her character was being tested. It was easy to be kind, optimistic, and generous when things were going well. A woman's true nature revealed itself in times of crisis, and Ellie desperately wanted to maintain her joyful demeanor and zeal for life.

Now that December had arrived, perhaps its Christmas cheer and good-will-towards-men would lift her spirits. She would squelch her personal feelings and make Christmas a wonderful season for her girls, and - as for school - she would just have to throw herself into her lessons to bury her fears and to help regain her sense of self.

Thinking of good will, Ellie hung Tai's painting on her classroom wall. If anything could sway Ellie into believing in Tai's innocence, it was the painting. It was Tai's unsolicited measure of good will toward Ellie, and it must have taken hours to create. Every time she looked at it, the painting would remind Ellie of Tai's generosity and her potential for goodness; it would remind Ellie not to judge based on outward appearances. Tai knew just what Ellie loved; the pop art was a lively, whimsical, happy addition to her classroom that Ellie hoped would brighten her dark mood.

With only three weeks of school until the Christmas holidays, Ellie's class had to finish Act One of *The Crucible.* Some of the hardest parts of the play for the students to get through were Miller's lengthy exposition pieces and extensive psychological profiles that frequently interrupt the action, adding historical background and social commentary. As tempting as it was to skip some of the author's narrative, Ellie knew her students would benefit from the information Miller doled out in each one.

In one of Miller's commentaries, for example, Ellie's students learned that the real Putnam accused many people during the trials for retaliation and for personal gain. This brought about class discussions on manipulation and hypocrisy – topics that Ellie's students could easily understand. Touching on that teenage desire for rebellion-against-authority was one of the crucial ingredients in Ellie's recipe to hook her students. Or was it Miller's recipe? Or Salem's? Or Stusa's?

*The Crucible* had every element necessary to incite righteous indignation – intolerance, empowerment, betrayal, hypocrisy, jealousy, and hysteria - and Ellie's students could relate to most of those topics. In fact, the play hit close to home several times throughout the semester. There were plenty of verbal daggers hurled at modern day hypocrisy: the sell-outs, the haters, the bullies, the cowards, the self-righteous.

More recently, however, the students began to compare the hysteria of the witch trials to the current drug investigation going on in their own school and community, a search led by Mr. Remuel Hardy. The students were indignant about having been searched twice in the last month and were furious that the drug dogs had sniffed and slobbered all over their shoes and book bags in the process. One of the younger drug dogs had even taken a huge dump in one classroom; it took the custodians a week to get the smell out.

Ellie could sense a student rebellion coming on and hated knowing that if one occurred, she would be blamed for it. Ellie sometimes wondered about her students' intense resentment of the investigation. They were offended by the unannounced locker searches that were becoming more and more frequent, and they took every opportunity to steam about it in class. Students claimed the searches were illegal and tossed around the terms "invasion of privacy" and "unreasonable search and seizure" like budding little lawyers. They blew up social media with their rants.

Did their anger stem from having something to hide? Ellie wasn't naive enough to believe that her teenage students were saintly little martyrs, but she also had a hard time picturing them as callous criminals dealing in drugs and prostitution before they were even old enough to vote.

The underlying tension at school was building, and Ellie sensed an approaching revolt. Ellie was proud of her students for correlating the attacks in the play to an attack on their own freedom, but she hadn't intended to stir up a type of rebellion - especially not when the attack was perfectly legal and well within any school's authority.

Ellie groaned. Couldn't she at least have one tiny triumph without everything going wrong? She would have to help the students vent their anger productively rather than disruptively. She'd better think of something quickly. That teenage rebel-without-a-cause syndrome could kick in at any given moment, and Ellie didn't want to be the one on the receiving end of that kick.

# CHAPTER THIRTY-FIVE

## REDIRECTING REBELLION

Over the next few days, Ellie figured out how to channel her students' wrath into something productive. The idea came to her while reading her anthology. She was flipping through it trying to find out more about Ebbie when she felt a light, cool, pulse coming from the page, tingling her fingertips. When she looked down, a title intrigued her.

*Transferring Energy*
*Note: Since energy cannot be created or destroyed, one must learn to transfer any unwanted energy into another vessel to defeat its sting. This treatment calls for a large amount of eucalyptus leaves – at least a half a peck, a spray of vetiver, a fist-sized Schorl or electric stone, and enough white sage to encircle the object you want to protect or cleanse.*

The understanding that energy couldn't be created or destroyed surprised her. Science hadn't been very advanced in the 1600s. People still believed in witches, demons, and all sorts of supernatural forces, but the underlying principle rang true. She continued reading.

*Encircle the item you wish to cleanse in a ring of*

> *white sage. Place the Schorl inside the circle touch-*
> *ing the primary target. Light the white sage and let it*
> *burn until it emits a good, strong smoke.*

The treatment continued for several lines and involved some tricky steps the position of the sun. After she finished reading, Ellie wondered why that specific recipe had beckoned her. She didn't have any objects that needed purifying, and she had no idea what a Schorl was.

She pondered the title for a minute more, and then it hit her. Transferring energy, deflecting negativity, redirecting anger - that was it! She could use her students' energy to fuel a legitimate educational activity rather than watch that negative energy fuel a fire of rebellion. She started brainstorming ideas to capture their fire and redirect it.

Eventually, Ellie decided to have her students create promotional items for their production of Miller's play. She would give them a couple of choices and let their collective imagination run wild. It would be a perfect for two reasons: It would allow them to release their anger by creating a tangible product, and it would allow them to end the semester with a sense of accomplishment.

Ellie prefaced the project with a mini lesson on McCarthyism and how Miller had brilliantly hidden his own message within the historical setting of the Salem Witch Trials. *Wasn't it genius how he intermingled the two?* Most students thought it was cool how he flaunted his message, his rebellion really, in plain view of his opponents.

Zibby raised her hand during the lesson and asked, "But wasn't that risky? Didn't Miller know that someone would figure out what he was doing? Surely McCarthy and his cronies weren't too dumb to notice the correlation – the jibes and barbs. I mean, wasn't that their job? To track down any dissenters and investigate them? C'mon, if they pulled *Robin Hood* from the shelves, surely someone must have shut down Miller's play."

Oh, how Ellie loved Zibby. What a mature question! The girl was a wonderful student with a powerful mind and a love of learning.

"Yes, Zibby." Ellie answered. "In 1956, Miller was called before the *House of Un-American Activities Committee*, but Miller refused to testify, saying he could not 'use the name of another person and bring trouble on him.' Miller was found guilty of contempt of Congress, sentenced to a $500 fine or thirty days in prison, blacklisted, and had his passport withdrawn."

A few mumblings from the students expressed their shock at his punishment.

"Don't feel too sorry for him, though." Ellie continued. "He went on to marry Marilyn Monroe and even wrote a movie for her to star in before they divorced. Miller ended up being quite successful despite his run-in with the law. Of course, he was idolized after his refusal to snitch on his friends and colleagues."

"This brings me to my last challenge for you this semester." Ellie continued. "I want you to emulate Miller as you create your product. Can you find a way to interject your feelings on "Big Brother" looking into your own lives while masking them within the confines of the play?" She paused. "I believe you can. It's just going to take some deep thinking and careful planning. This will be your final project of the semester, so please remember that a large portion of your average will depend on this *one* assignment."

Ellie knew it wouldn't be that hard. The students wouldn't necessarily be embedding their own messages but merely echoing those of Miller himself. She was just pandering to the crowd.

"To make it a little more competitive, there is a bonus. We'll have a contest to see which product moves us the most. In summary, a large part of your task is to persuade; you're trying to persuade students to attend our play, and you're trying to persuade your classmates that your position is the most convincing, the most moving, and the most believable."

There were a few groans, but mostly there were titters of excitement. In general, her students preferred completing projects over taking traditional tests. Who wouldn't?

All in all, the project was well-received. Inwardly, Ellie breathed a huge sigh of relief. If she played her hand very carefully, maybe, just maybe she could divert their rumblings of rebellion and save both her school and herself from another calamity.

# CHAPTER THIRTY-SIX

### *STUDENT STRIFE*

As the week of final exams approached, Ellie found herself feeling hopeful. The Christmas spirit had managed to break through her anxiety. Creating a relevant final project for her students made her feel victorious. Perhaps she would survive her new role as English teacher after all.

In the past, Ellie had disliked the week of final exams. It always felt like the longest week of the school year. This year, however, Ellie was enjoying the week. Watching her students throw themselves into a project while she guided from the sidelines was gratifying. The students were motivated for perhaps the first time all semester, and Ellie was loving every minute of it.

There was only one day left before the Christmas Holidays when it all fell apart. Ellie was helping students get their videos on the interactive board when her intercom buzzed.

"Miz Payluhtay, I need to see you in my office. Now!"

"Ooooh," the students erupted into a low somebody's-in-trouble cry.

"That wat'n the secretary, Miss. That was the principal. You better hurry. He didn't sound none too pleased." TriNeika said.

"Yeah, the last time he called me to the office like that, I couldn't sit down for the rest of the day," Ja'Quan bragged.

"Shut up, fool! She a teacher. He ain't gone paddle her," TriNeika scolded.

Ellie intervened before anyone else could get a word in. "Settle down, students. Not everyone who gets called to the principal's office is in trouble. Keep working on your projects. They are due tomorrow in lieu of a final exam."

Ellie buzzed the office to tell the secretary the she had a class at the time and would go see Principal Danvers during her planning period. A few seconds later, she heard a knock at the door. Ja'Quan leapt out of his seat to open it.

Prinicipal Danvers stood in the doorway and said, "Miz Payluhtay, can I have a word with you?"

The collective cry arose again, much quieter this time since the principal was there.

Ellie was perplexed. "Mr. Danvers, I have a classroom full of students. Can this wait until next period?"

"No. It cain't." He turned his back on her and stomped down the hall, clearly expecting her to follow.

"Don't worry, Miss. I got this. I'll keep them under control while you're gone." TriNeika spoke up.

Ellie just looked around blankly and said, "Ok, class. TriNeika is in charge until I get back. Do NOT disappoint me!"

Principal Danvers flung open his office door and pointed to his desk. On his computer monitor, Ellie saw a video playing. She looked at him, puzzled. He didn't say a word. He just pointed back at the screen.

Ellie walked closer and saw the words *Modern Day Witch Hunt at Stusa High* scroll across the screen. Ellie dropped her face into her hands. Was this what she thought it was? Then she heard audio. Of course, there would be audio. She peeked through her fingers to see what followed.

The video opened with a clip from the movie version of *The Crucible*. Villagers are rounded up and hauled to jail after being implicated in witchcraft. The wagon carried Martha Corey, Rebecca Nurse, Elizabeth Proctor and more. As the bereft family members vowed to get their loved ones out of the predicament, a cutaway interrupted the scene.

The words appeared flashcard-style on an otherwise

blank screen. *On what grounds were they arrested?* Next slide. *False testimony?* Next slide. *Where was the evidence?*

The scene reverted to the prisoners being hauled away in the wagon. Scrolling script appeared beneath the rolling wagon. *How is this,* the screen changed to a shot of students being escorted to the office by Officer Hardy, *any different from this?*

The scene changed to show drug dogs sniffing at lockers, then back to students being taken to the office. *On what grounds were they accused?* Next slide. *False testimony?* Next slide. *Where was the evidence?* The video clip showed an obviously irate Principal Danvers yelling at the students.

Words appeared again at the bottom of the screen. *When will this,* the scene changed again showing clips of Japanese citizens being rounded up, *lead to this?* Ellie's jaw dropped.

This. Was. Bad.

But there was more.

A photo of Arthur Miller appeared. The words underneath his photo read, *Arthur Miller was brave enough to stand up for the rights of others.* Another shot of drug dogs, this time in classrooms. *Who will be brave enough to stand up for ours?*

The next section was a rapid-fire set of still photos – American Indians, slaves, German concentration camps, Japanese internment camps, civil rights marches – *When the rights of one group are taken away, we all lose a bit of our humanity. When will the abuse of power stop?*

The photos changed to those of Principal Danvers, Officer Hardy, and the Reverintendent.

*Who will stop it?* A photo of student sit-ins from the sixties appeared. *Join the movement. Fight for your rights.*

At this point, Ellie dared to glance at Principal Danvers. His face was contorted with rage. A bulging blood vessel in his forehead throbbed. The red on his face spread all the way down his neck. He pounded his fist on his desk, "Damn it, Ellie! Just what the hell are you teaching those kids?"

Ellie was speechless. Part of her recognized the effort

and thought that had gone into creating such a video. If she were anywhere but Stusa, she could use the video to promote discussion of civil liberties and where to draw the line for free speech. Her mind whirled. It would be a great collaborative project between American literature and U.S. history classes.

Principal Danvers's rage, however, returned Ellie to reality. "Are you deliberately tryin' to start some kinda student movement here? A sit-in? Are you one of those damn liberals tryin' to indoctrinate our children? What the hell were you thinking? This is Stusa! We are NOT known for our liberalism!"

"I had no idea," Ellie squeaked. She cleared her throat and tried again. "I never, ever intended for their project to turn into this." She said with a little more confidence. "Their assignment was to create a promotional video for our play. I was trying to turn their anger into something positive, productive."

*Well, as lame as it sounded now - that was mostly true,* she thought. Ellie had underestimated her students. She never thought they would make these types of connections, much less spend time turning those connections into such a vivid portrait of Stusa and post it on YouTube.

"I know how this must look, Mr. Danvers--"

He cut her off, "Do you, Ellie? Do you really? Those kids compared me to Hitler, for Christ's sake!" He fumed and took out a cigar from his pocket. He didn't light it; he chewed on it.

"I have reported the video and asked YouTube to take it down immediately. There are enough copyright infringements to get them to comply. It's just a matter of time. You better hope none of our parents see this. Or the superintendent. Or the board members. Or Lydia and Louella."

He gnawed on the cigar. He stood up and paced the floor of his tiny office.

"Um," Ellie decided to speak up and ask the question she dreaded. "Do I still have a job?"

"That all depends," he rounded back to face her, removing the chewed-up cigar and tossing it in the trash, "on how well you contain this mess. You have twenty-four hours." With those words, he left the office.

Ellie remained there watching the number of views tick higher and higher. It had not been a request; it had been an ultimatum. How would she fix this? Where would she even begin?

The bell for the end of class rang, prompting her to action. She'd better get to work solving this problem while she had planning time to devote to it. She would need to work fast and make some quick decisions.

By the end of her planning period, Ellie had Googled everything she could about flagged videos on You Tube. She found that its removal could take anywhere from three hours to three days; she prayed for the former. Since there was not much more she could do on that end, she decided to tackle how to handle the videos that would be turned in the following day for a grade.

Ellie had originally planned to show the videos in class and to let the kids have popcorn and soda – a homemade video extravaganza. Now, though, she wasn't sure. What if all the videos were like this? Would the students spread the news around school? That Ellie was bucking the system – or encouraging her students to buck it?

It was hard to predict their reaction. If it was something they cared about, the students would probably talk about it outside of class. But if it were seen as any other assignment, they would barely deem it worth completing - much less discuss it outside of class.

One thing she knew for certain, though, was that the quickest way to make sure everyone in the tri-county area saw the video would be to ban it.

The next day, as students filed into her room, Ellie didn't notice any unusual undercurrents, so she proceeded as if nothing had happened the day before. When the students were seated, Ellie placed a packet on each desk about copyright infringement, movie piracy, and their penalties.

"Before we get started viewing videos, I just want to make sure you guys know the rules about borrowing information from others without proper permission or citations. I know a lot of you probably used scenes from the movie, and that is fine to turn in for an assignment. You cannot, however, post said videos on YouTube or other social media without having express written consent from the movie's producer. Now, let's examine a brilliant piece of work that was submitted early."

Ellie turned on the interactive whiteboard and clicked on the link to the offending video from the day prior. While they waited for the video to load, she said, "This was a great piece. It reflects deep thinking and plenty of effort. The only problem is that it should never have been posted on YouTube – ah look – they've already taken it down. That's too bad. I wanted you to see it, but someone must have flagged it for copyright infringement. Gee, YouTube reacts quickly!"

The class moaned. Ellie smiled. "No worries, you can see it whenever the group that created it turns it in. They forgot to take credit for their amazing work. It's lucky I got to watch it last night! Anyway, just make sure none of the rest of you decide to post your videos. Besides copyright infringement, you'll have to have parental consent if anyone in your group is under eighteen." More groans.

"I know, I know." Ellie continued. "You guys are used to putting everything online. Maybe after Christmas we'll do a week-long lesson on what is legal and what is not. You need to be informed." She put on her concerned face.

TriNeika was the first to respond. "No, no, no, Miss. We won't post anything. Please, please don't make us do another Internet awareness lesson. We have been having those lessons every year since middle school. I swear we won't post anything!" TriNeika advocated for her entire class, and the rest of the class agreed.

Ellie pretended to consider it, then said, "Well, if you're sure you understand the consequences of posting copyrighted information or -"

"Omigod, yes, we know!" Students interrupted. "Let's just watch the movies!"

"Ok, if you're positive," Ellie responded with an inward smirk. "Let's get started then and see what your classmates came up with! Popcorn anyone?"

# CHAPTER THIRTY-SEVEN

## THE SHADOW

*The Shadow* sat in bed cursing the pain that started in her wrist and traveled up her forearm. She'd tried everything she could think of to stop the burning - to no avail. She resorted to submerging her forearm in a washtub of cool water spiked with lavender oil, baking soda, honey, and tea leaves.

She knew what the problem was: the pain wasn't from an external injury, so the topical remedies weren't helping; the pain was internal. It came from *inside* her wrist, radiating outward, and it was spreading.

It was the heirloom. It was calling her, punishing her for not being quick enough. Her first two elemental attacks had failed. She needed to act swiftly. The pain intensified with each failure.

The dunking booth and the poison ivy had created strife, but they had not severed Ellie's connection to the heirloom. Neither the water element nor the earth element had been Ellie's opposing force. Her link to the heirloom was dueling *The Shadow's*, and Ellie still had no idea what was going on. She hated to admit it, but the real problem hadn't been Ellie at all. The truth was that *The Shadow* had misread Ellie. How on earth could naïve little Ellie have outfoxed her? It didn't make any sense, and it infuriated *The Shadow* beyond reason.

If only she had managed to capture Julien's attention before Tai had. What did he see in Tai, the scheming little ho. *The Shadow* still couldn't believe he had hired Tai as an assistant instead of her, when she had practically thrown herself at him – hinting and flirting in ways that even an imbecile could figure out.

She'd approached him in August when the weather was swelteringly hot and humid. She had dressed carefully, completely opposite of what awaited him at home. She'd studied Ellie and had played up her own physical characteristics that Ellie lacked -- curves. *The Shadow* revealed enough of her flawless, milky-white bosom to garner attention without being entirely indecent.

The pheromones and tinctures had just been insurance. No man could resist what she'd been flaunting. She lit a cigarette just outside the studio and took a long drag. She knew Julien craved cigarettes but had given them up at Ellie's urging. She also knew that he still sneaked an occasional cigarette on the roof of his studio when Ellie wasn't around.

She'd exhaled a perfect smoke ring as she opened the door to the studio, careful to make sure he saw it as she entered. She feigned surprise at his no-smoking sign and held the door open while she crushed the cigarette under her red stiletto. She strode to the counter and leaned over, giving him an eyeful of exactly what he wasn't getting at home.

"I hear you need an assistant. I'm available, and I'm extremely skilled," she arched an eyebrow, "at giving people what they need. So, when can I start?" She licked her lips and looked him up and down.

Julien's demeanor remained impassive as he returned her stare. "I think I already have everything I need," he arched an eyebrow in return, "but *merci pour l'attention*. You flatter me." And he turned away.

She was shocked at his refusal - but not dismayed. It was part of the game. A man wanted to feel like he had won the hunt. She couldn't let him think he could win too easily.

"You *think* you have everything you need because

you've never had me. Then you'll *know* you've got it all." He turned back around to face her. *Ha! She had him!*

She continued, "I'm a wonderful assistant. I can assist in anything you like. I don't interfere with," she paused, "management." She gave a coy smile. "Here's my number. Call me when you realize how discreet I can be. Management would never have a problem with me." She threw a card onto the counter and sauntered back out, walking slowly, making sure he got as good a look at her rearview assets as he did the front ones.

When he didn't call within the week, she began to stew. Then she heard that Tai had been hired – the little slut. She'd thought Tai was too busy playing the part of innocent victim to compete. *The Shadow* fumed.

She'd burned white sage and recharged her crystals and stones by moonlight, but the results were lackluster. Somehow, she sensed that nothing would work except the heirloom itself. In fact, Gabby had warned that something like this might eventually happen if the family didn't regain control of the beloved script.

*The Shadow* grew irritable; her feminine wiles had never let her down until now. What could she do next? How would she take the heirloom? Her scar reminded her daily of her burning need to regain the heirloom.

Even more urgent was her need to expunge the wrath that built inside her. She needed to do something, anything to rid herself of the fury that blocked her prowess. She grabbed a joint and lighter. The tiny flame sparked an idea.

Marijuana. Drugs could ruin Ellie and Julien both if discovered by the right people. And *The Shadow* knew exactly where to put them to wreak the most havoc. And as for the connection to the heirloom, an elemental fire could destroy more than just Ellie's link to the heirloom.

"Long-held hatreds of neighbors could now be openly expressed, and vengeance taken, despite the Bible's charitable injunctions. Old scores could be settled on a plane of heavenly combat ... suspicions and the envy of the miserable toward the happy could and did burst out in the general revenge."

--ARTHUR MILLER, IN ACT ONE (AN OVERTURE), THE CRUCIBLE

# CHAPTER THIRTY-EIGHT

## DANGEROUS DELUSION

Ellie ended school that December afternoon feeling free, almost dizzy with relief. She had managed to squelch the video rebellion. Zibby's group had turned in a wonderful project. Her group's portrayal of the villagers' point of view was spot on. Ellie thought for sure that Zibby's group would win first place - until she saw GG's video.

GG had worked alone to create an advertisement from the accuser's point of view, specifically that of Thomas Putnam. She used still-slides and captions to show Putnam jumping at the chance, seizing the moment of chaos to work to his benefit. Her portrait of a man full of greed, malice and scheming was uncannily accurate.

GG had used images of a current money mogul to represent Putnam. Her slides showed him touring farms, then accusing owners of witchcraft when they refused to sell to him. Overall, her presentation was quiet but powerful, wicked yet wonderful. It sent a shiver down Ellie's back as she watched it with the class. GG won first place by unanimous vote and received the coveted bonus points added to her grade.

All in all, it was a good end to her first semester in Stusa. Christmas break would allow her to reconnect with her husband, too. She needed to get out of the teacher role for a while and tend to her marriage. The rumors had been stressful; maybe what Ellie needed to do was to show Julien that she believed in him. Their upcoming vacation would do a lot to help her achieve those goals.

After the final bell sounded, Ellie and Zyla toasted the end of the semester with a cup of hot tea together in the teacher's lounge. They had originally planned to go out for something a little merrier than hot tea, but Ellie had received a text message from Julien.

"Well, maybe for New Year's," Zyla laughed as they parted ways. "Send the girls my love!" she added as she hopped in her car and drove away.

Ellie agreed and unlocked her own car door. As she put the key in the ignition, she felt a wave of dizziness wash over her. She shook her head to clear her mind. Maybe it was a good thing she didn't go out for drinks after all. She was so tired from all the stress that she literally felt dizzy. She was mentally reviewing everything that had happened throughout the semester – no wonder she was exhausted - when she pulled up at the studio.

From outside *The Jewel* everything looked normal. As Ellie opened the heavy front doors, however, a tremendous wave of heat rolled out and almost knocked her down. Her hair flew back as a violent, hot wind rushed out. She saw an orange glow coming from the back of the studio. When her brain finally interpreted what was happening, Ellie rushed inside and started calling for the girls.

"Girls! Where are you?" She screamed. "I'm coming for you!" *Where were they?*

Despite her mental sluggishness in processing what was she was seeing, Ellie's maternal instincts forced her to walk directly into the heat. The fresh air she had let in upon opening the doors fed the flames, and they grew. They were alive; the flames were coming straight for her, trying to push her back outside. She wouldn't be forced out, not until she found her girls.

Regretfully, the text message she'd received hadn't

struck her as terribly urgent:

Girls at studio.
Can you pick them up?

Now that she was in the studio, however, guilt sickened her as she realized she could have hurried more and gotten there sooner. Why had she taken that last gulp of hot tea? It hadn't even been that good; it had tasted rather bitter. Why hadn't she rushed more? She should have flown right over instead of rinsing out the teacup and dawdling with Zyla. Where were her girls? How much time did she have? She yelled for them again.

"Girls! Where are you? I'm here! Let's get outside - quickly!" As Ellie searched the studio looking frantically for the girls, the heat from the fire scorched her face, singing her eyelashes and eyebrows. She grabbed one of the heavy, velvet photography drapes and wrapped it around herself like a cape as she continued searching *The Jewel.*

"Méline! Bibianne! Where are you?" She shouted, trying to control her rising panic. "It's ok, *mes petites, maman* is here. Don't be frightened. Tell me where you are!"

She took another step towards the counter. Perhaps the girls were hiding behind it. The flames were climbing up the support beams, heading for the ceiling. How much longer did she have before the wooden ceiling caught fire, too? As she made her way around the worktop, she crouched down and looked inside the open storage underneath.

She heard a whimper and rushed to the far end of the cabinetry. There, amidst the various drapes and cloths lay Dedé. Ellie grabbed her up from the nest of fabric taking one long piece with her and wrapping Dedé up like an infant, leaving only the dog's snout exposed. As she tucked the trembling dog under her left arm, she felt dizzy from the heat and smoke. She fumbled and dropped her cell phone. It shattered on the concrete floor, so she left it and continued her search.

"Mel! Bibi!" She shouted. "I found Dedé! Come out – she needs you! Tell me where you are so we can come get you!" She coaxed, trying to give the girls something to focus on other than their fear.

As she called for them, she worked her way to the back of the studio. It hit her then, Méline's dream about being in a fire and Dedé escaping without her. Was it this? Had Méline had some type of premonition?

No. It couldn't be. Ellie had Dedé safely in her arms, and the girls were together – somewhere. Hiding? In the dream Méline had been all alone. Ellie's thinking was muddled. Hadn't Julien left the girls with Tai? Why would they be here at the studio? Had Tai had some type of emergency? What had that text message said? She needed to calm down; panic and smoke clouded her thinking.

"Girls! I need to get you out of here!" She heard a creaking groan from overhead and looked up just in time to see a smoldering ceiling timber break off and fall towards her. She instinctively threw up her free hand to shield her face and sprinted backwards. As she ran, she heard glass breaking behind her and smelled burning plastic. Surely heat alone wasn't enough to crack glass.

She searched the office area and found nothing. She would have to look in the attic. She approached the wooden staircase and shouted again, "*Mes enfants*! Where are you?"

No response. She mounted the stairs cautiously. How much time did she have before the whole place burst into flame? Dizziness threatened to overwhelm her. If only she knew where the girls were! The smoke became heavier as she ascended the stairs. She coughed and gagged as she continued upward.

Ellie was about halfway up the staircase when she saw something large coming towards her. It was big, rectangular. It looked like the back of an upright piano, but they didn't have a piano. Her mind couldn't make sense of it.

When she finally processed the danger she was in, she

ducked and took a step backwards in retreat as the large object came crashing down. She forgot she was on the stairs, instinct driving her to rush backwards as quickly as possible. Her foot stepped back into nothingness. Ellie reached out grasping for something to break her fall when *thunk!*

A heavy object crashed into her upper body, pushing her into the air. She felt the air slam out of her lungs in a loud grunt. The flames and smoke around her swelled as she continued to fall backwards in slow motion. It was dizzying and graceful.

*She was flying through the air just like an acrobat. Had she missed her catch? She hoped the net below would break her fall. She didn't want to disappoint the crowd. Her velvet costume was smoking. That wasn't right. Where were the other trapeze artists? Was the net in place? Something was horribly wrong. Where were her girls? Were they in the audience?*

Her fall was broken, but not by anything nearly as nice as a net, and Ellie's head smacked against something hard. At the same time, whatever had knocked her down the stairs landed on top of her with a sickening crack. Her left arm, shoulder, and side exploded in pain. At the same time, she saw tiny pricks of light that were quickly chased away by an all-consuming darkness blocking her peripheral vision.

The darkness grew and reduced her vision to a circle that was closing in, growing ever smaller. The last thing she saw through her tiny tunnel of vision was Dedé jumping through a ring of fire. *Why was Dedé at the circus? When did she learn to do that?*

And then the blackness consumed her.

# CHAPTER THIRTY-NINE

## THE SHADOW

*The Shadow* imagined plumes of smoke climbing into the sky as she waited. Sure enough, less than five minutes later Julien's car flew past her headed towards the studio. *The Shadow* had counted on the news travelling quickly, and it had worked. Small town gossip always moved fast, but factual bad news moved even faster.

Julien didn't glance her way. His dust trail lingered longer than he did, intent as he was on getting to his precious studio. He would never know she had been there, parked off the side of the road, shielded by the trees and shrubbery of the woods.

She waited for his dust trail to clear, and then slammed her gear shift into drive, making her way down the dirt road leading to the Pelletier's house. Now that the twins had accomplished their task, she would have plenty of time to search the Pelletier home and find her heirloom. She was sure that the fire element, the strongest of the four, would burn through any connection Ellie had to it, and after a fruitless search of the studio and Ellie's classroom, *The Shadow* was convinced that Ellie kept it at home.

Ping! A text message came through on her cell phone.

EP unconscious
fire dept on the way

u have 1 hr

She smiled as she pressed delete. The tincture she had put in Ellie's tea cup had worked flawlessly, as well as the text message leading Ellie to the studio. Everything was going according to plan.

*The Shadow* threw the phone out of the window and tossed it under the car. Her back tire flattened it with a satisfying crunch. Modern technology was so useful sometimes – cheap, too. She laughed to herself wondering what her ancestors would think about how she travelled between the two worlds of modern technology and ancient casting. They probably wouldn't like it, but she was used to disapproval and, in fact, relished it. The more people disapproved, the more she enjoyed it.

The scar on her wrist started prickling, urging her to hurry. She floored it and finally reached the Pelletier homestead. She didn't bother sneaking around; she dashed right up to the front door. She knew everyone would be focused on the fire, something the town had not seen in years and feared more than anything. In fact, she probably had more than an hour before anyone would come back to the Pelletier's home. Nonetheless, she set her timer for sixty minutes.

As she opened the unlocked door, she felt disgusted with Ellie for making it so easy. Didn't Ellie realize what a prize she had? How could anyone be so stupid as to leave the heirloom unprotected and accessible?

*The Shadow* took the stairs two at a time. She felt the tug of her scar. It was pulsing with energy, and it burned with every pulse. Her first search was of Ellie's closet. She ransacked the large walk-in space, throwing items to the floor in her desperation to find the heirloom.

Nothing. She looked at her watch. She had forty-five minutes left. Plenty of time. She proceeded to the master bathroom. Was Ellie the type to read in the tub? There was, in fact, a small stack of books on a shelf above the claw-foot tub, but no heirloom. Next, she opened the door to the water closet but closed it again without looking inside. Ellie was too uptight to read on the toilet. She moved on to the next area.

*The Shadow* knelt and looked under the bed. It was empty except for a few dust bunnies that escaped Ellie's obsessive vacuuming. She dug through the drawers of Ellie's nightstand. Candles, lingerie, and pressed rose petals. *The Shadow's* repulsion was only topped by her snort of disbelief that Ellie could be so stereotypically romantic. Not much imagination there at all.

She lifted the mattress and peered underneath. A sachet of lavender blooms and five, crisp hundred-dollar bills. She pocketed the cash and continued looking. Thirty minutes remained.

Where would Ellie be most likely to read? Her office! She pushed through the door and started pillaging the desk. Papers fluttered to the ground as she slung them aside in her raid.

After all the drawers were emptied with nothing valuable found, she considered the laundry room. She pushed herself to her feet, but when she reached the door, her scar gave an intense burst of anger.

She turned back to the desk, and the pain subsided.

*A signal.* She wiggled her way underneath the desk.

Shoved at the very back was a shoe box. It was just the right size. *The Shadow* smirked. Maybe Ellie did have the foresight to hide the book.

*The Shadow* lifted the lid and cursed when she found it empty, apart from an old oilcloth and some twine. This had to be where Ellie was storing it. Where would she have taken it? *The Shadow's* stomach clenched as she thought of the studio. What if...

She checked her watch - thirty minutes remained. As she started to leave, she felt another surge from the scar. What was it this time? She was furious, both at Ellie and at her own failure to find the heirloom. She stepped over the mess she'd made and received another powerful jolt.

That was it, the evidence of her break in. The scar wanted her to clean up the mess she'd left behind. *The Shadow* guessed that she had just enough time to straighten up.

She put the drawers back and threw papers into them. She figured order didn't matter – just the semblance of order. If Ellie realized her papers were askew, she might think the girls had done it. At any rate, *The Shadow* didn't have time to over-think it. She finished rearranging the desk. If the Pelletiers didn't realize someone had been in their home, then they wouldn't call the police, and *The Shadow* would have more time to plan her next move without suspicion.

She bolted back upstairs and started cramming clothes in drawers. She straightened up the closet and returned to the bedroom. Drat! This meant she'd have to replace the money. She hated to return the cash underneath the mattress. Where else would she find such an easy stash?

A thought occurred to her. If she were going to replace the cash, then she'd leave behind another little gift as well. Who knew? Ellie might find it, or Julien might. Either way would work in her favor. She fingered the small, plastic bag filled with dried Kava leaves.

She glanced at her watch. Five minutes left. She shoved the money and the herbs in place and sprinted to her car. She felt relieved when she found the engine still running and was momentarily grateful that the old eyesore hadn't shut off. Every second counted for her get-away.

She spun out of the gravel driveway onto the dirt road. She pulled over onto the narrow shoulder of the road and into a gap in the trees. She dragged over a dried-up bramble bush to hide her rattletrap ride. She scattered forest debris to disguise any impressions her tires made on the forest floor.

She stepped back to survey her work. It would take an expert to find the teeny, overgrown path now. The surrounding forest was more of a thicket, so overgrown that a path would have to be cut with a machete for anyone to explore it.

She walked the remainder of the path, originally an animal trail before she'd widened the entrance, making her way to her cabin. When she reached a wall of briars, she bent over to uncover the end of a drainpipe. The section of pipe allowed just enough room to crawl through the thick, thorny vines unscathed. The briars had taken over the hedge that encircled her hidden copse.

Once through the opening, she stuffed a ready-made bramble into place, blocking the drainpipe. Her scar burned with the same fury as her mind, and *The Shadow* stomped into her one-room cabin.

She picked up the ceramic vase she'd crafted and smashed it as hard as she could against the wall. The sound of shattering pottery was satisfying. She threw a plate next, and then a bowl. By the time her anger was sated, *The Shadow* had destroyed every piece of pottery she'd ever made.

# CHAPTER FORTY

## *PREVENTING PREGNANCY*

Ellie woke up and blinked. Where was she? She wanted to look around but felt something strange coming out of her nose. She tried to lift a hand to her face, but pain shot from her left hand all the way up to her shoulder and collar bone. Her entire left arm was too heavy to move more than an inch. The jolt of pain that hit her when she tried to move the arm cleared the last vestiges of sleep, bringing her back to awareness.

She remembered being at the studio. There was a fire. The girls! Where were they? Were they safe?

"Méline! Bibianne!" She attempted to yell, but her voice came out as nothing more than a choked, scratchy whisper. A warm hand stroked her hair out of her face, and soft lips planted a gentle kiss on her forehead.

"It's okay, *ma vie*. The girls are safe. They are perfectly fine," Julien said.

"But...where are they? I couldn't find them. I - I'm not sure what happened to me." She had begun shifting her weight, trying to sit up but unable to. She fell back against her pillow. The effort left her breathless, wheezing.

As she tried to catch her breath and collect her thoughts, she recognized her surroundings. She was in the hospital. Again. There were tubes coming out of her nose, an IV in her left wrist, and bandages around her left ankle and neck. The heaviness she had felt earlier came from the cast covering her left arm which was also in a sling.

"Nothing happened to the girls." Julien tried to soothe her. "Calm down and rest. You are the one who has narrowly escaped death, my love."

"Escaped death? Is that why I feel so awful?" The words choked her raw throat, and she coughed. "Because it feels more like I escaped a circus elephant who mistook my chest for his stool...Hagh!" She gasped mid-sentence which led to another fit of coughing. *The circus...what was that about being an acrobat? Dedé and the ring of fire?*

She turned her head to him and croaked, "I want to know exactly what happened to me," she said very slowly. "But first, I want to know where the girls are. I need to know that they are okay." She finished with a slight shudder.

"Okay, okay, *mon cœur*. I see that you will not be dissuaded. I will explain as much as I can. As for the girls," he said with a smile and walked to the door. "You can see for yourself that they are perfectly fine. Méline, Bibianne, *venez ici*."

The girls came rushing into the room with frightened looks on their little faces. "Oh *maman*! We wanted to see you, but the doctor made us wait until you woke up! I am so glad you are awake." Méline leaned over and hugged her mother.

Bibianne was too short to reach, so Julien lifted her up to give her mom a squeeze. Bibianne crawled out of his arms and into bed with her mother, snuggling up along Ellie's right side. Ellie stifled a sob.

"Oh, girls! Thank God you are safe!" Ellie blinked back tears. "Come, Méline." Ellie reached out to hold Méline's hand, needing to touch both girls to believe that they were unharmed.

"Poor *maman*, does it hurt very much?" Bibianne asked with wide eyes taking in the cast, tubes, and sling.

"Only when you're not here," Ellie responded. "The doctors are taking good care of me. Don't fret, my pet." She managed to get it out without coughing.

Bibianne grinned. Julien lifted her up from Ellie's bed and placed her on the floor. "Let's give *maman* her rest, girls. Go sit with Madame Hughes. I will be there in a moment."

"Madame Hughes? You mean Zyla is here?" Ellie asked amidst another bout of coughing.

"*Oui, ma vie.* She has been kind enough to keep the girls for me so that I could stay with you." Julien responded.

"How long have I been here? I had the craziest ...they were more like dreams, but I was awake. I'm confused. Start at the beginning." Ellie demanded as sternly as she could with her raspy voice. She stopped to cough.

"Okay," responded Julien. "I will tell you what I know. There are some gaps that you must fill in, though." He paused wrinkling his brow, remembering.

"The girls and I were at home preparing dinner. We received a phone call saying that there was a fire at my studio. Before I could even ask if 911 had been notified, the caller hung up. I grabbed the girls and we raced over to the studio. By the time we got there, the fire truck was parked out front, getting ready to spray down the building. An ambulance was also there. Imagine my horror when I saw them loading you inside it!

"I rushed over to talk to the EMTs, and they told me to follow them to the emergency room. Zyla happened to be walking her dog across the street as we were coming in. I waved her over and asked her to watch the girls. She has been quite concerned for you, you know. She said you cancelled your plans with her because of a text message telling you to go to the studio."

Ellie interrupted, "But that text message – who sent it? Someone texted me that Tai had to leave the girls at the studio – or something like that. I don't even remember who it was from. I just went over get the girls and found the studio ablaze."

At that moment, the door to her room opened, and a physician entered. Dr. Patel's eyebrows furrowed as he studied the screen of his iPad. His expression faded into a tired smile as he nodded to Julien.

"Well, well, well." Dr. Patel addressed Ellie. "Mrs. Pelletier, you're either having a run of bad luck, or you're beginning to like it here. Isn't this the third time I've seen you in as many months?"

"Yes, but I assure you that I do not like it here." Ellie croaked.

"Isn't the old saying that bad luck comes in threes?" he asked. "Perhaps now your luck will change," he said with a grin.

"I hope so. I'm not sure my body or my wallet can handle any more accidents." Ellie rasped. "What is wrong with my body anyway? Everything hurts." She started a bout of coughing that hurt more than she ever thought possible.

"Well," he crossed his arms hugging the tablet to his chest. "There is quite a list." He took a breath. "You have some respiratory injuries due to smoke inhalation. We didn't have to intubate you, but that doesn't mean it's not serious. You will have bronchospasms and hoarseness for a few days until the lungs begin to heal. I am prescribing breathing treatments. Again.

"You also sustained injuries to your left side – your left clavicle is broken, and three more ribs are fractured due to the impact of a large piece of furniture, a dresser I am told, that fell on your left side. You are lucky it didn't land directly on your chest; it could have crushed your sternum and resulted in serious internal injuries, especially to your heart and lungs.

As it stands, your injuries will be painful and may require a lengthier recovery than you would like, but they are not life-threatening.

"Additionally, you have second degree burns on your neck and ankles – the only parts of you exposed to the flames. You may not think so now, but between the furniture that fell on you and the velvet cloth draped over you, you were remarkably well-protected from the flames. The injuries from the dresser will heal much less painfully than burns would have.

Maybe your luck isn't as bad as we first thought." He gave a brief nod to Julien.

Ellie groaned. She had barely recovered from the broken ribs on her other side, so she had an inkling as to what she was facing. How would she manage to teach and care for herself with only one arm? *Thank God*, she thought, *it was the left arm.* She would have been incapacitated again if it had been her right one.

What would happen to her family if she were out of work for several weeks? How many sick days did she have left? They were sobering thoughts.

Dr. Patel interrupted her worrying. He approached Ellie's bedside and became rather serious. "I need to ask you some questions, Mrs. Pelletier. It may take a few moments. I wonder if your husband would step outside and grab a coffee?" He left the question hanging between them.

"I can answer questions in front of Julien," Ellie rasped. "We don't keep secrets from --." She broke off in another cough.

"Well," he walked to the foot of her bed so that he could look at both of them. "All your injuries can be explained by the fire and the furniture that fell on you. What concerns me, however, is the bloodwork I was just reviewing."

He turned his attention back to his iPad. "The lab report says here that trace amounts of piper methysticum and menthe pulegium were found in your blood. These are unregulated but highly dangerous chemicals, Mrs. Pelletier, and even though there were only small amounts in your body, the effects could be devastating if you continue ingesting them." He paused and looked at Ellie. "Is there anything you'd like to tell me?"

Ellie was shocked. She furrowed her eyebrows and said, "I have no idea what you're talking about. Are you sure that's *my* lab report?" She looked at Julien. He shrugged his shoulders in bewilderment.

Dr. Patel gave Ellie a stern look and said matter-of-factly, "As you may already know, Kava, or piper methysticum, became popular for its antidepressant qualities." He looked at Julien. "What might surprise you, though, is that its use has led to liver transplants and death in as little as one to three months. Heavy use has also caused nerve damage and skin changes." He turned back to Ellie. "And as for the menthe pulegium, commonly known as Pennyroyal mint, it has been traditionally used to force abortions and can cause irreversible damage to the liver and kidneys. Now, are you sure there's nothing you want to tell me?"

He paused, reaching over and giving her arm a gentle squeeze. "We can treat any unwanted pregnancies and ensuing depression with modern medicine, Mrs. Pelletier," he said, "rather than having you resort to poisoning yourself to avoid telling your husband. I'll give you two time alone, and when I return, we can have another type of discussion." He gently closed the door behind him as he exited the room.

Ellie sputtered and coughed. "What? Is this a sick joke?" She looked at Julien. He was staring at her, through her, with widened eyes and a dazed expression.

"Julien, you know this is nonsense, right? I'm not pregnant. I'd never be able to keep such a happy secret to myself, and I would *never* terminate a pregnancy!" He remained silent.

"Secondly," Ellie's determination helped her continue without coughing, "I have never even heard of those herbs he mentioned! You've seen my garden; I have lavender, mint, basil – just your ordinary garden variety." She broke off in a cough and waited for him to respond.

"You have to believe me, Julien. I mean, we're in the hospital. I'll take a pregnancy test."

He finally spoke, looking at her quizzically, "I think the doctor believes you have already ended the pregnancy."

She asked in a small voice, "But what do you believe, Julien? Do you really think I could do something like this and hide it from you?"

He shook his head a little as if to clear his thoughts and said, "Of course not, my love. I just wonder..."

"Wonder what?" Ellie asked a little defensively.

"About your herb garden," he replied. "You grow mint, right? What if it is the wrong variety of mint? What if you have been growing this Pennyroyal mint he spoke of - by mistake? That would explain how it got into your bloodstream."

"Julien," she coughed out his name. "If that were true, then everyone who bought from the local nursery would be showing symptoms, too. I got all my herbs from them. There's no way they are selling dangerous--" A hacking cough interrupted her this time.

Julien got her a cup of cool water and helped her take a few sips. "I am sorry, *ma vie*. Obviously, it is not the time to have this conversation. You need to rest. Talking is making your cough worse, I think. Let me get the girls home. I'll come back after I get them settled with a sitter." He started towards the door. "We'll see how long the doctor thinks you'll need to stay. Is there anything you'd like me to bring you from home?"

When she caught her breath, Ellie replied, "Yes, actually. I'd like to read. Would you bring me my book bag? It might be at school, though. I can't remember if I threw it in the car or not when I headed to the studio. It's all kind of a blur."

"I will find it," Julien replied. "Before I leave, where is your cell phone? I'll put it by your bed. Call if you think of anything else you need."

"Oh," Ellie said. "I think... I dropped it in the studio. I remember hearing it shatter. Anyway, I didn't pick it up. I was frantic."

Amidst the doctor's shocking news, Ellie had temporarily forgotten all about the phone and the mysterious text message that had landed her in the hospital in the first place. *What a shame*, she thought. *Now, I'll never figure out who sent that text.*

"At least it was only a phone that was ruined. I'll leave mine with you. Call the house if you want anything." He placed his mobile phone in her right hand and turned to go. He paused at the door to look back and give her a quick smile, but Ellie couldn't help noticing that the smile didn't reach his eyes. His eyes, rather, were somewhat narrowed and pinched in an expression that she recognized could be nothing else but doubt.

Ellie lay there for a few minutes trying to imagine where the toxins could have come from. Could she have bought a mislabeled mint plant? She would have to ask at the town greenhouse. What about the other herb, though? Kava, was it? A knock at the door interrupted her thoughts.

"Come in," Ellie wheezed. A petite red head peered around the door without opening it completely.

"I only intended to drop off something for you. You sure you want me coming in?" Zyla asked. Ellie nodded her assent. Zyla stepped into the room, taking in Ellie's bandages and giving a small gasp, "Oh, Ellie! I had no idea it was this serious! Are you okay?" She approached the bedside.

"I want to hug you, but I'm afraid I'll hurt you!" Zyla cried in dismay, noting her friend's numerous injuries. "Where doesn't it hurt? Is there any place I can squeeze?"

"Here," Ellie said extending her right hand. Zyla grasped it in a gentle clasp and held it for a moment eyeing Ellie's tubes, cast, and sling. "Oh, my poor dear!" She said at last. "The last thing you'll be wanting is your school bag, and here I was thinking I would be the hero by bringing you a distraction." Zyla frowned.

"No, no. You're right," Ellie countered. I really do want my school bag. I just asked Julien to find it for me. I wanted –" she broke off in another fit of coughing.

"Oh no! Don't say another word. We'll do this the old-fashioned way. I'll ask you a yes or no question, and you simply nod or shake your head. Will that help keep you quiet?"

Ellie nodded and gave a half smile. Leave it to Zyla to figure out an easier way to communicate. Zyla started right away. "Are you going to be okay despite how awful it looks?"

Ellie nodded and cringed.

"But it hurts a lot right now, so you do actually want a distraction?" Ellie nodded again. Zyla handed her the school bag.

"I can't believe you want to work on school stuff," Zyla commented. Ellie shook her head and held up a finger, signaling Zyla to wait. Ellie dug through the bag with her one good hand and closed her eyes in relief when she pulled out the old leather anthology. She clutched it to her chest for a moment, then handed it to Zyla.

"What is this? Is it that journal you wanted me to see? The one you found at the studio?" Ellie nodded as vigorously as she could without jostling her injuries. Zyla studied the front cover and ran her fingers across the emblem embossed there.

"Well, to judge a book by its cover, it's definitely a leather one. That could place it as far back as the late 1700s. Cloth wasn't used as a binding material until the early 19th century, but that doesn't mean that leather binding was no longer in use, so it's not a certainty." She paused and ran her hand over the cover. "This symbol is rather interesting. I've seen it somewhere before...I just can't remember where. Let me look inside."

"Oh my," Zyla remarked with a gleam in her eye and in her voice. "It's written on vellum." Ellie pinched her eyebrows together. "You know - animal skin. It could be from a goat or lamb, but it's usually from a calf. I mean, technically, it must be from a calf to be called vellum instead of parchment, but that's probably more than you want to know. Anyway, see the hair follicles and the veining of the sheet? That's how we can tell it's from an animal." She leaned over to show Ellie.

Zyla continued studying the dates and the handwriting. "You know, Ellie, you could have something fairly valuable on your hands here, depending upon the content. If these dates are correct, you're looking at writings from the 1600s and earlier. Pretty much anything before 1650 is considered special. Boy, I bet the preservation society at the college would love to get their hands on this! You realize they've always dreamed of publishing a book on the local history, right?"

Ellie shook her head furiously and reached out for the book.

"Okay, I get it, Scrooge." Zyla replied with a chuckle, handing over the book. "You don't want to share it yet. I guess it does belong to you and Julien since you found it in the studio you own." She held up a professorial finger and spoke in a sing-song voice. "But you would be doing your civic duty, preserving a piece of history, if you handed it over to the local college when you're done." Ellie shook her head again with widened eyes and raised eyebrows.

"No, no. No pressure here." Zyla stepped back with both palms up. "I'm just saying that it could be interesting for the whole town if it really turns out to be a primary source from the 1600s." Zyla's wink softened the heavy hints she was dropping as she backed out of the room. "Happy reading, then!"

At Zyla's departure, Ellie got down to business. She opened the anthology, turning pages with her good hand. She didn't know if she was looking for another journal entry to distract her or another recipe to amuse her, but she'd know it when she saw it.

She glanced at each heading as she flipped past pages of notes, recipes, and journal entries. She saw the charm she had used to curtail her bad dreams. As she turned the pages, she thought about her anxiety over the rumors surrounding Julien and Tai. The look on Julien's face as he left her room reflected at least as much doubt in his mind as what she had been dealing with.

*Great*, she thought. She had been so busy doubting him that she never considered how it would feel to be on the receiving end. *He doubts me; I saw it on his face.* She closed her eyes for a moment in exasperation, but her fingers kept up their rhythm. As she continued turning pages without looking, she gave a tiny jump. She opened her eyes in surprise.

While her eyes were closed, she'd been able to sense the pages. It wasn't just the feeling of flesh to vellum. Each page emitted a physical sensation to her fingertips. Something like electricity buzzed through each entry. She studied a few pages, trying to find a reason for the feeling. There was nothing visible to the naked eye that could explain what she had felt. Had her accident jarred her brain? Was she experiencing some type of synesthesia?

Ellie shut her eyes, slowed down, and tried again. The feeling was so faint she could almost be convinced that she'd imagined it the first time, but there it was. With closed eyes, she could perceive the subtle differences of each page. This was much more than the tingling sensation she had first attributed to excitement. Some pages felt warm, some cool. Some tingled, and others prickled. Some buzzed; others burned.

Ellie opened her eyes. Could she still perceive the twinges from the pages when her eyes were open? She rubbed her forefinger and thumb across the corner of a page as she studied it. She felt a very slight sensation.

Using her right hand, she slid all five fingers down the page. This time she definitely felt sparks. So, that was the trick, to *feel* each page rather than just look at it. But what did it mean?

She shook her head to clear her thoughts. The book seemed to have *personality*. It was trying to communicate with her, and since she didn't understand via the written text, it was sending her physical cues.

Ellie suddenly felt bone weary, and it wasn't just physical. Although she hated to admit it to herself, life recently had become overwhelming- relocating her entire family, teaching a new subject, trying to fit in with the locals, remodeling the house, opening the studio, reacting to poison ivy, the video fiasco, and now a fire had ruined all their work at the studio, not to mention her body.

She closed the book and tucked it under the hospital blanket where she could reach it with her one working hand. Her mind spiraled from one worry to the next. She felt restless, trapped, exhausted.

As she lay back on the pillow and closed her eyes, Ellie tried to empty her mind of all the thoughts zooming around inside her head. She remembered a technique that suggested writing each worry on a piece of paper and then burning all the pieces. Since she couldn't access paper and pen, Ellie took each thought and imagined it fluttering in the air.

In her mind, she released one worry at a time. The wasted effort at the studio was a charcoal-colored, smoky swirl that traveled in downward spirals, hovering. An intense mustard-yellow worry zoomed out next – the fear she had felt during the fire. It was so strong that it made her jerk her eyes open.

To her complete astonishment, two translucent colors hovered over her belly at eye level. One was charcoal grey. One was mustard yellow. She blinked and rubbed her eyes with her right hand.

They were like visible, colorful ribbons of air, whirling, waiting. She reached out to touch them, but her hand passed straight through as if they were made of light. Ellie realized she hadn't imagined the scenario at all. It was playing out in front of her, and all she could do was watch.

More smoky ribbons fluttered out of her. Each one was a slightly different color. Ellie recognized the fierce magenta as her determination to protect her girls. It hovered above the other colors, nearly suffocating them, finally intertwining itself into the others.

A dingy, sickly green joined the twisting mass of emotion; it was her concern over having ingested toxic herbs.

The ribbons of light whorled and coiled in mid-air. They leaked out of Ellie's mind and flitted through the air to join their comrades. They spun and formed a sphere, like a loosely wound ball of yarn - except this ball was translucent, moving, and made entirely of light.

Dark, black anger raced out of her mind, penetrating the ball of ribbons to become its core. A frustrated, purple stream of religious hypocrisy appeared, quickly followed by a pumpkin-colored ribbon of anxiety about her mistaken expectations of rural life. A bright, scarlet-red ribbon of rage was her loss of control. Like the swirling ball of light, her life was spinning out of control.

The colors started pouring out faster: the poison ivy experience was light green; Julien's doubt of her, deep burgundy; her doubt of Julien, espresso brown; curiosity about the text message that led her to the fire, pale lilac.

The colors undulated and hovered in the air above her stomach. They had temporarily formed a ball, but now they started reshaping themselves, stretching wide at the top and narrow at the bottom - like a tornado. They revolved faster and faster with each new ribbon that joined the colorful, swirling vortex.

Snatches of thought continued to stream out of Ellie's mind - Tai and her sneaky ways, dark green; the mysterious floral arrangement, bright yellow; the work awaiting her at school, light pink; worry over Julien believing she'd aborted a baby, blood red.

The whirlwind of ribbons was twirling faster; the colors blended together as more thoughts and worries rushed out of Ellie's mind and merged to become a brilliant, painful-to-look-at, white light that wobbled indecisively for a moment.

It hovered in front of Ellie's face, just out of reach of her good hand. Ellie knew it was waiting for more worries to emerge. When the mass seemed satisfied that no more were coming, the whirling funnel stretched itself out long and thin. The bottom tip reached under Ellie's blanket and siphoned itself into the anthology, disappearing entirely into it and finally allowing Ellie to get what she needed most at that moment -- sleep.

# CHAPTER FORTY-ONE

## *RIDICULOUS REMEDY*

A distant siren was calling out to Ellie. Muffled by a blanket of haze and fog, it was an insistent sound that she knew she must mute. It was a mildly familiar, shrill chirping that she wished would go away. She tried to roll over to get away from it and gasped in pain as she dislodged her left side. The pain jolted her awake, and she realized the harsh ringing was coming from Julien's cell phone on her bedside table.

She fumbled with her right hand, slapping around blindly trying to stop the piercing noise. She managed to hit the touch screen and heard a tinny-sounding, female voice.

"Hey, Jules. I'm trying to get Mel to eat breakfast, but she is refusing. I thought maybe you could tell me what to do to get her to eat something."

Ellie bolted upright, momentarily ignoring the jarring pain that shot through her entire left side and grabbed the phone to her ear. Alarm bells were ringing, this time in her head. A thousand thoughts hit her at once, none of them pleasant.

She glanced at the time. It was 8:00am. "This is not *Julien*. This is *Mrs*. Pelletier." Ellie snapped. She didn't have the energy or the mental fortitude to pretend to be nice about it.

"Why are you calling Julien's cell phone so early this morning?" Ellie spat out. She was pleased to hear that her voice, while still a bit hoarse, was much improved from the day before and was glad that, even in her fury, she had managed to croak out the entire question without coughing.

"Oh, I thought you knew," Tai responded in a sing-song voice. "Julien asked me to watch the girls while he sorted through the damage at the studio. I was calling to get some advice on Mel and her breakfast." Tai was using that innocent-sounding, girlie voice that Ellie detested.

Ellie's blood boiled. Since when did Tai start calling Julien by his first name? When did she get his personal cell phone number? What was she doing at Ellie's house playing mommy with Ellie's kids?

"Well, Tai," Ellie responded just as sweetly. "I'm sure Julien thought you could assist, but I'll be home shortly – and I will help the girls with their breakfast. They probably just don't like your cooking. Are you trying to give them that awful pickle-flavored soda of yours?" Ellie laughed.

"Actually," Tai said, "I was trying to get them to eat leftovers. I guess they don't enjoy your cooking either." Tai replied in her sugary voice.

Without missing a beat Ellie countered, "Oh, the crepes? I guess *you* didn't know that they eat them with my home-made strawberry sauce. Don't trouble yourself, though. I'll be home shortly."

Ellie pressed the end call button before Tai could respond. She dragged her legs over the side of the bed. She had to get home. When she pulled the oxygen tubes out of her nose, an alarm started beeping. She stumbled out of bed, nearly crashing to the floor when the pain caught up with her. Before Ellie took more than a few wobbly steps, a female nurse and a male orderly rushed into her room.

"Just whut are you doin', ma'am? Ya need ta get back in bed," the orderly said while the nurse grabbed her arm and tried to steer her back to bed.

"No, I don't!" Ellie wrenched her right arm free. "I need to get home. Now!" She hobbled away from the nurse, looking at the orderly for help.

"Ma'am, it's Miz Pellahteer, right?" The nurse tried reasoning with her. "You need to calm down. The medicine may cause you to feel aggressive, but everything is fine. The doctor prescribed twenty-four hours of oxygen, and so far, you've only had sixteen hours. Now, get back into bed, and we'll get you settled."

"You don't understand!" Ellie cried out. "My girls are at home with an unreliable, sneaky, untrustworthy sitter. I must get to them! I will *not* let her mother *my* children!" Ellie was yelling now.

"Look, lady -- we got orders ta fahllah." The orderly was much sterner than the nurse had been. "I'm shore yore kids are fine. You hafta focus on taking care of yoreself right now. Get back in the bed, or we're gone hafta git the doctor."

"Fine! Go ahead and get him!" Ellie shouted. She was worked up, bordering on hysteria. How dare they keep her here when her family was threatened? "I'm sure the doctor will let me get back to my children who need me!"

Part of her couldn't believe she was making such a scene, but Ellie couldn't stop herself. She was worried and furious at the same time. She would give Julien a piece of her mind after she kicked that conniving little hussy out of her house.

Ellie continued to struggle and did not see another nurse approach from the rear until it was too late. She felt the prick of a needle at the exact moment that she realized some- one was behind her.

"Arugghh!" She groaned. She turned to face the nurse who had given her the injection. "You drugged me!" She gasped. "Don't you think I've been through enough? This is unaccept- able. Patients have rights! Call my husb-"

Ellie collapsed mid-sentence, and the orderly half-car- ried, half-dragged her back to bed. Ellie could still see them and hear them, but she could no longer put up any resistance.

When the orderly yanked back the covers, Ellie's anthology fell off the bed. When he and the nurses finally got her tucked in and reconnected to the oxygen supply, the nurse bent over to pick up the fallen book.

"This looks old. It must be what she was readi—ouch!" The nurse flung the book away from her, startled, and it landed in the window ledge beside Ellie's bed. "That book just shocked me! What in the world?" She rubbed her hand and looked at the other two. They just rolled their eyes.

The male nurse chuckled. The orderly added, "What's really shockin' is this lady. You wouldn't think it to look at'er, but she ain't no delicate flower. Handlin' her is more like handlin' a boll of cotton – soft and fluffy on the outside, but that seed will cut ya' ever'time."

"Hmph," replied the female nurse. "Prickly she may be, but that shot ought to keep her down for a while." She sighed. "I guess we have to call her husband now and explain what happened. I'll go get Dr. Patel. *He* can tell the husband. I'm not doing it. My shift ends in five minutes." She walked out and went to look for the doctor.

Ellie watched in forced silence as they all left the room. She tried to hold on to her anger but felt it ebbing away along with her energy. Finally, she could hold her eyelids up no more. Once again, she slept.

When she woke, Ellie felt groggy and cotton mouthed. She couldn't remember where she was for a second, but then it all came rushing back to her - the phone call from Tai, the fight with the nursing staff, the shot that knocked her out. She was wearing an oxygen mask, so she hadn't reached the twenty-four-hour mark on her treatment. She must have slept four to six hours, though. It couldn't be long before they would release her.

With the memory of the phone call, Ellie's anger came surging back. Her stomach clenched, and she knew suddenly what she needed to do to get rid of Tai. She reached for the anthology. It wasn't under her pillow anymore.

*Oh, no!* She thought. *What if they took it?* Now Ellie was feeling panic on top of her anger. She lifted her head to look around the room. Surely it was still here. She reached over with her right hand, flapping around the bedside table, searching. She knocked over a cup of water but felt nothing like the shape of a book.

She turned her head to the left to stare out of the window in dismay. How could they have taken her book? She *needed* it. Then, she saw it. There lay her book on the large windowsill. But how did it get there? And how would she reach it? She couldn't move her left side.

She considered calling the nurses for help, but they'd laugh in her face after the stunt she'd pulled. She imagined the looks they'd give her if she asked them for help. She groaned in frustration. Is this what it felt like to be helpless? How was she going to dress herself, care for the girls, or work? She tried to sit up but couldn't. Her limbs were still heavy from the injection.

Ellie stretched her right hand across her chest, reaching for the windowsill on her left side. She knew it was futile, but she just had to try – if for no other reason than to prove that her situation was exactly as pitiful as it felt. She would feel good and sorry for herself when this didn't work.

Ellie half-heartedly extended her right hand. She was getting worked up for a good, long pout when she saw the book quiver.

Her pulse quickened. What was this hospital visit doing to her? She had been exposed to toxic herbs and then medicated. Obviously, the drug interactions were messing with her mind. First, the tingling pages and now this. She felt another surge of exasperation; it irked her to her very core. She was spitting mad and strained further with her hand.

The book trembled. She was sure of it this time. It shuddered as if struggling to get to Ellie's hand. That only sparked her wrath. She opened her mouth and growled. "Well, c'mon! If you really wanted to help you could. Don't just sit there shaking like a scared little rabbit, do-"

*Whhhhhhhhssssssssssp!* The book landed in her outstretched hand.

Ellie gaped. Now, she was the one trembling. She sat there for a stunned moment, mouth open and eyes wide. What had just happened? Had she...had she called the book to her? Had the book heard her? No, no, no – those were crazy thoughts, yet here was the book resting in her right hand.

She lifted her knees and propped the anthology against her thighs so that she could look through it one-handed. As she nestled the anthology into place, it fell open. The page gave her exactly what she'd wished for. The title emitted a pulsing, silvery glow.

*To Banish Others from a Marriage*

Ellie inhaled sharply. The book had read her mind. Ellie had never seen this entry before. She was positive it hadn't been there when she was feeling her way through the pages earlier. The handwriting was different, and Ellie realized that Ebbie wasn't its author. But had Ebbie used it? Could it be the remedy Ebbie alluded to in a previous entry?

The charm, luckily, was a simple one. No salt or cleansing crystals involved.

*To be read aloud <u>once</u> and then destroyed*

Even though the author had underlined the word *once*, Ellie was reading ahead silently, trying to gauge the merits of the recipe.

*Power of wind I have over thee,*
*Blow this creature away from me.*
*Protect my family and all that I love,*

*Drive away evil in a cyclone from above.*
*No wickedness from tomorrow or today,*
*Can halt this wind that blows temptation away.*

It seemed too easy. All she had to do was repeat the words aloud one time and then destroy the paper. What did she have to lose? After all, they were just words in an old book. What possible harm could they do?

But then again, how had she not seen this title before? And what about the way she could *feel* the pages? The book zooming straight to her outstretched hand?

The title glowed at her steadily now, calling to her, encouraging her to get on with it. Ellie held her breath for half a second and then made her decision. She read the words aloud and ripped the page out of the book before she could change her mind.

How would she destroy the page with only one hand? She felt the ripped page growing warm in her hand and somehow knew that it wanted to be destroyed *right then*. She put one corner of the page in her mouth and held it with her teeth, using her right hand to rip the paper into small pieces. It took a few minutes, but before long, she had a small pile of shredded bits on her chest.

What now? Should she flush the paper giblets down the toilet? Should she dump them in her bag and get rid of them at home? She couldn't reach her bag, though, and if she got up to go to the toilet, the hospital buzzers would alert the nurses again.

As she looked around the room for another solution, she smelled a faint whiff of caramel. She sniffed again, and it grew stronger. Her mouth watered. When was the last time she had eaten? She didn't know, but suddenly she was hungry.

Where was the delicious smell coming from? She looked at the paper bits. No, surely not...they couldn't want her...it was too bizarre. Ellie's stomach growled.

Before she could think twice about it, she scooped up all

the bits of paper and shoved them into her mouth. She closed her eyes, chewed once or twice, then gulped down the wad of paper that somehow tasted like warm, buttery caramel. The lump slid easily down her throat as Ellie wondered if she'd lost her grip on reality.

She'd read about pregnant women craving peculiar things like clay, laundry detergent, and paper. But Ellie wasn't pregnant. Even if she had been, the doctor said that the herbs she'd ingested would've force an abortion. *What was happening to her?*

After she swallowed the paper-turned-to-caramel bits, Ellie took a deep breath and waited, half expecting a gust of wind to blow through the room or for the lights to flicker and go out. When nothing happened, she sighed and tucked the book back under her pillow.

When she reached down to pull the blankets up, she noticed an impossibly thin, shimmering, silver bracelet encircling her left wrist. When she pushed back the sling to get a better look, it vanished. Ellie almost thought she'd imagined it except for the cool, tingling sensation it left behind and the scratch-like mark in its place.

# CHAPTER FORTY-TWO

## *COUNTRY CHRISTMAS*

The hospital released Ellie several hours later. In addition to the pain of her injuries, she was disappointed when she learned Julien had cancelled their vacation plans. They were scheduled to leave in less than a week, but with Ellie's injuries and the damage at the studio, Ellie agreed that it would be foolish to go ahead with the trip.

Ellie had been given plenty of post-dismissal instructions on how to care for all her injuries, and she was admonished to rest as much as possible over the next two weeks of Christmas vacation. The only silver lining was that at least Tai would be nowhere near them.

Somehow, Ellie and Julien managed to get their home ready for Christmas despite Ellie's limited range of motion. Christmas Day arrived, and everything was in place. Ellie was glad they weren't the type of family to go over-the-top on Christmas. After the excitement of opening gifts concluded, Ellie and her family were enjoying a time of peace and harmony. The girls were playing quietly with their toys. Julien was taking a morning nap after a late-night playing Santa, not to mention a few potent mimosas served with Christmas breakfast. Ellie had no idea how long this stillness would last, so she took the time to partake in her favorite reflective hobby -- *remembering*. She studied the precious moment and tried to memorize its every detail, searing it into her mind so she would be able to recall it when future trials attacked.

The girls had arisen before dawn and ushered their parents downstairs to the Christmas tree. There were squeals of delight with each new package and even a few surprises for *maman et papa*. The girls had loved each gift and had delighted in watching Ellie and Julien open their gifts, too, although they had to help Ellie open hers. Despite her injuries, it had been a Norman Rockwell type of morning.

*Even if this were to be the last perfect moment of my life,* Ellie thought, *I have been blessed beyond measure.*

This pinnacle had been worth all the dark valleys she had traversed to get there. Thinking of dark valleys, she felt a twinge of guilt over the charm she had performed during her time in the hospital. But she smothered that thought with another mimosa, determined not to let anything ruin the perfect country Christmas she had waited for all her adult life. Everything was just as wonderful as she had let herself dream, and if she had taken drastic measures to secure that perfection, then it had been well worth it.

# CHAPTER FORTY-THREE

*NEW YEAR, NEW ATTITUDE*

Like most of Stusa, Ellie and Julien rang in the new year at Mayor Goodwin's house party. It was a chance for the adults to act like adults since no kids were allowed. Ellie could partake in the obligatory eggnog without feeling guilty, knowing that she wouldn't see any of her students. And none of their parents could judge too harshly either, since most of them were there, partaking of more than just eggnog.

Mayor Goodwin had set up an open bar, Ellie was shocked to see. Apparently dry counties could serve alcohol as long as it was in a private home. Since the chief of police was there, Ellie figured this must be the one time of year the residents of Stusa cut loose and let their hair down. There was a small *dance floor* under the back deck strung with twinkling lights and a DJ playing everything from the classics to current hits.

Ellie sipped her eggnog and watched the prim-lipped librarian cut a rug with her Buddy Holly look-alike husband. She saw the police chief ask his ex-wife for a dance. She noticed the town lawyer swaying to the beat and eyeing Jolene, the pretty young clerk at Stinson's Grocers. Even Principal Danvers and the Reverintendent looked happy and relaxed.

When their favorite song came on, Julien grabbed Ellie around the waist and tried to get Ellie to dance, but her injuries made her feel like the Bride of Frankenstein, and she asked Julien to help her to a seat at the bar. Even if her medications limited her to one eggnog, she could still enjoy the conversation.

Before long, she found herself invited to the basement game room, playing cards with a group of ladies that included Lydia and Louella. Ellie was having fun – not just pretending, but truly enjoying herself. She was playing a mean, one-handed game of poker when Julien found her.

"*Ma vie*, it is time to go get the girls. Remember, our sitter has church early tomorrow morning." Julien reminded her, smiling. Ellie looked down at her watch and gasped.

"Wow! I had no idea it was so late! Thanks for the card game and the eggnog! This was a great party, Mrs. Goodwin." She kissed the hostess on the cheek and stood as Julien helped her.

"Oh, Ellie! Just call Tai and tell her you need to finish this one last round of cards. I'm sure she won't mind." Mrs. Goodwin proclaimed.

Ellie chuckled. "I'd love to, Mrs. Goodwin, but we couldn't get in touch with Tai. Zibby is our sitter tonight, and she cleans the church each Saturday morning. I wouldn't want to make her job any more difficult. I think she's saving money for college, you know."

"Well, it was a pleasure getting to know you and your husband. I hope you'll both come back around and see us sometime when you can stay longer." Mrs. Goodwin smiled.

"And when you're healed enough to cut a rug with the rest of us." Louella said, winking at Ellie as she returned to the card game.

Ellie and Julien made their rounds and said goodbye to everyone. Most were shocked that they were leaving so soon after midnight and seemed genuinely sad to see them go. When they got into the car, Ellie turned to Julien.

"You know, Julien. I've been judging people too harshly. That was a great little shindig, and I think I made some new friends. Maybe I'll adopt a new attitude in the New Year. I need to try to understand people more and to see things from their perspective."

Julien turned to her, a look of incredulity on his face. "Is this the medicine talking or the eggnog?" He lifted one eyebrow.

"No, really," Ellie chuckled as she settled into the passenger seat. "Even Lydia and Louella have been more thoughtful than nosy. They've brought food to us after each hospital visit. At first, I thought it was part of their church membership drive, but I think they really meant the meals as gifts with no strings attached."

"How charitable of you to consider their actions as good will." Julien smirked. "Who is this woman who looks like an embattled version of my wife?" Ellie laughed.

She leaned back against the headrest and let the sensation of happiness wash over her. This was what she had wanted, what she had dreamed of when they uprooted their lives and moved out of the city. This was how life could be for her, for Julien, and for their girls – small gatherings of intimate friends, a sense of belonging and of being known and included, a healthy lifestyle far from the pressures of the urban rat race. It had been a successful evening, despite her injuries.

When they got home, Ellie and Julien went to the girls' bedroom and found Zibby snoozing in the recliner in Bibi's room. A book had slipped from Zibby's hands. Ellie picked it up and saw that Zibby had been re-reading *The Crucible*. *Wow*, Ellie thought. *What a dedicated student!*

Ellie also found the girls' favorite bedtime storybook, *The Horse and His Boy* from C.S. Lewis's tales of Narnia. Both Mel and Bibi were asleep, snuggled into Bibi's small bed, hugging their teddy bears. While Julien kissed the girls lightly on their foreheads, Ellie tapped Zibby's shoulder and whispered, "Zibby, we're back. Can I drive you home?"

Zibby opened her eyes and gave a little jump. "Oh gosh! I didn't mean to fall asleep, Mrs. P. But the girls are fine, I mean they fell asleep, so I started reading, and I guess I just drifted off. The house was so quiet-." Zibby looked embarrassed to have been discovered sleeping on the job.

Ellie smiled and put her hand on Zibby's arm. "Don't worry. They are fine, and it has happened to me more times than I can count."

Zibby stretched and yawned. "Whew! Well, I'm glad you're not angry. Hey – at least I was reading *The Crucible*. Does that earn me any brownie points?" She asked with a mischievous grin and one raised eyebrow.

Ellie chuckled softly, "Hmm. We'll see. Come downstairs, and we'll get your things together to take you home." As they headed towards the staircase, Julien asked if he should drive considering Ellie's sling.

"No, I can drive one-handed, especially since her house isn't too far. I'll be fine. And I want to talk to Zibby about the play." Ellie responded.

"Well, if it's okay with you, Mrs. P, I'd rather you drop me off at the church. It's actually closer than my house, and my mom and I are cleaning it tonight to sleep late tomorrow."

"Tonight?" Ellie asked in shock. "But it's so late, Zibby, and it's New Year's! Don't you think it would be wiser to go home?"

"No, ma'am." Zibby replied. "My mom is meeting me at the church. We'll get it clean in a jiffy. Then we'll go home, drink sparkling grape juice, and throw glitter at each other while we watch the ball drop in New York."

Ellie looked at Zibby wondering if she had been drinking more than just sparkling grape juice. "Sparkling grape juice, huh? Is that a euphemism I need to know? The ball dropped over an hour ago." Ellie remarked.

Zibby laughed. "I know. We recorded it. My mom is a recovering alcoholic, so we never have any type of alcohol in the house – not even mouth wash."

"Oh wow! I'm sorry. I didn't mean to pry." Ellie responded, chagrined.

"It's okay. I thought you knew -- everybody else does. You know how it is here, right? There aren't many secrets. Someone always blabs. It's just like Ben Franklin said, 'Three of us can keep a secret if two of us are dead.' He definitely must have visited Stusa at some point."

It pleased Ellie that Zibby remembered her lesson on Benjamin Franklin and aphorisms. No wonder Zibby was one of her favorites. She really got it.

"Well, I'll keep that in mind, Zibby. Thanks for reminding me. And, by the way, that *definitely* gets you some brownie points. Benjamin Franklin and Arthur Miller in one night? Are you buttering me up for something?" Ellie and Zibby both laughed.

"If you're going to be up half the night, let me at least make you an espresso or cappuccino for the road. What do you like?" Ellie offered.

"Yum. I'd love a cappuccino." Zibby answered.

They sipped their drinks as Ellie maneuvered the car to the First Baptist Church of Stusa. Zibby delighted in the thick foam topping and turned to Ellie with a large white mustache. She waggled her eyebrows, "Can you take me seriously like this?" I want to talk about *The Crucible*," and they both burst into giggles.

"Seriously, though," Zibby said, licking the foam from her upper lip, "I've noticed a lot of things about the play that totally fit our town. I've been wanting to talk to you about it to see if it's really there, or if I'm just over-analyzing everything." Zibby took another sip of her drink.

"I mean, am I crazy," she continued, "or can the play be understood on two different levels? On the surface, it seems to be about catching witches, but underneath it all, I think Miller is pointing out that we all tend towards hypocrisy – and the loudest accusers are often the biggest offenders." Zibby looked at Ellie to check her reaction.

"You're not crazy at all, Zibby." Ellie replied. "Great literature makes us think - and think deeply. Most stories can be understood on different levels. You'll find that when you read something for the first time, you'll view it one way, and if you read it again later in life – you'll see it from a completely different perspective." Ellie paused.

She put on an exaggerated serious face, pinching her eyebrows together and pursing her lips, then faced Zibby. "This is me - taking you seriously, by the way. Good enough?" Zibby nodded. "Then fire away, reader." Ellie said. "Ask me what you will. This is my favorite kind of conversation!"

"Well," Zibby hesitated, "I have some ideas that are pretty bizarre. And you being a teacher and such a rule-follower and all – just don't give me an F, okay? I'm going kind of anti-establishment here." She cleared her throat and started.

Ellie missed what Zibby was saying. She was thinking. *So that's how my students see me? As an uptight rule-follower?* She pondered it for a moment. *Yes, I guess I am at work. Well, at home, too. I'll have to think about this later.* She forced herself back to the present conversation.

". . . and that's why I think that Reverend Parris in the play is totally our superintendent. They both want to protect themselves no matter what, and they both get so offended when people don't just bow down to their wishes. They can't stand it when anyone dares to disagree with them. Underneath it all, I think they are just great, big" Zibby took a gulp of air, "*cowards*." Zibby, chewing on her bottom lip, turned to look at Ellie.

Ellie thought for a moment. "So, you're basically calling the superintendent a coward."

Zibby kept biting her lip and didn't say anything.

Ellie grabbed the steering wheel with both hands, leaned forward, and burst into laughter. *God, out of the mouth of babes.* She couldn't contain her laughter. Her chest shook, and her stomach tightened.

Zibby stared at first, wide-eyed. Then, she gave a little chuckle. Before long, they were both wiping their eyes and crying with glee. Zibby laughed so hard she snorted. That sent them into another fit of laughter. It felt so good to share it with someone! Ellie would never have dared to say it first - she wouldn't want to sway a student - but now that Zibby had called out the Reverintendent, her spirits lifted.

They giggled their way to the church. They were still trying to regain their composure as they entered the vestibule. They would stop laughing for a moment, and then one of them would break down again. Ellie tried to hush Zibby as they groped for the light switch.

"Shh," she laughed as she tried to be the responsible, dignified adult. "We are in a church! We must be," she coughed to cover a chuckle, "respectful."

Zibby finally flipped on the lights, and their laughter was immediately curtailed. Two girls, who had been kneeling at the altar, jumped to their feet as the lights came on. They gasped. Ellie and Zibby watched them quickly snuff out candles and shove them in their bags.

"No worries, girls." Ellie tried to calm their fears. "I'm Catholic. There is nothing shocking about lighting candles when you pray." Ellie smiled at them, but Eve and Eden Matthews were not returning her smile. They were, in fact, pale-faced and wide-eyed. They looked at each other, something unspoken passing between them. It smelled of guilt and worry.

Ellie frowned. "Is everything okay?" She amended. "What are you doing here in the middle of the night?" Ellie asked, realizing something wasn't right.

Eve spoke first. "We umm...we were praying. You were right the first time. We ... just wanted to be somewhere that felt kind of sacred, powerful...and we didn't want to be interrupted-"

Eden broke in, "Our dad wouldn't like to find us praying with candles. Please don't say anything! He'd think it was heresy or something. It's just that...well, we are worried. We've been here since sunset and were planning on staying until daybreak."

Ellie wondered where they had gotten the idea of holding a vigil. Maybe Protestants and Catholics weren't so different after all. The girls did, indeed, look quite anxious. She had not seen them like this before. She couldn't imagine what could tear them away from their precious selfies to bring them to a prayer vigil. On New Year's Eve, no less.

Something was very wrong indeed. And now that she thought about it, the girls had been using black candles. That was odd. And had she seen Eden stuff a piece of paper into her pocket?

Eve cut back in. "We tried to get Jelly to come with us, but you know how she is. She was busy putting on some kind of *Pink Party* – whatever that is."

Eden spoke up, "I think it's one of those theme parties where everyone has to wear pink or something like that but -" One glare from her sister shut her up.

"Anyway, she couldn't join us." Eden continued. "So, we were here *praying* together. You know, 'where two or three are gathered in my name' and all that business." The twins kept volleying dark looks between them.

"You won't say anything, will you, Miss? You won't tell our dad, will you?" Eve asked, eyeing her sister. "Or the Rev?" Eden added.

"Well, girls, that depends." She looked at each girl in turn. "Is anyone hurt or in danger?" Ellie asked.

The twins looked at each other. Eve gave Eden a slight nod, and Eden turned to look at Ellie. "Well, it's about Tai."

It took Ellie's entire force of will not to roll her eyes. She inhaled deeply and asked, "What has she done now?"

Eve met Ellie's question with indignation. "She hasn't *done* anything. She's missing."

Eve hurled the statement straight at Ellie with such force that Ellie felt like she was being accused of something. She brushed the thought aside and asked, "Have you talked to her uncle? I'm sure it's just a misunderstanding. I'll bet he knows where she is." Ellie paused, thinking. "Have you considered that maybe she wanted a break from the limelight and just decided to lay low for a while?" *I know I'd love to*, thought Ellie.

Eden responded, "The Reverend thought she was spending Christmas break with us, but we haven't seen her since we got out of school."

Ellie replied, "Well, I've talked to her. She babysat for us on the last day of school when the studio burned. She called me the next day, and Julien drove her home afterwards. That was a week ago. She has probably just been enjoying the break with relatives..."

Ellie's voice dropped off. Tai visiting relatives and her uncle not knowing about it? Besides, she probably didn't have any relatives if her uncle was the one rearing her. Little alarm bells were tinkling in her head again.

So, Tai had disappeared after Ellie's hospital visit, the visit in which Ellie had read a charm from her anthology. And eaten a page out of the book. A page to banish homewreckers. The ringing bells grew louder.

But that was crazy. Surely, she hadn't eaten a centuries old piece of paper? Wasn't that just a drug-induced dream? Instantly, her mouth was flooded with the same caramel, buttery goodness from that day. The alarm bells were clanging now. Ellie shook her head to rid herself of the noise.

"Well, if she has been missing for a week, has her uncle reported it to the police?" Ellie gulped, her sling suddenly weighing her down as she wondered if Julien had been the last person to see Tai before her disappearance.

"Yeah, a fat lot of good that did," Eve grumbled. "Deputy Dan said that it looked more like a case of a runaway than anything else. Her duffel bag was missing along with some clothes and her portfolio. He told the Rev to contact all their friends to see if she was holed up somewhere riding out the holidays."

"Why would he say that and not investigate further?" Ellie asked.

"Because," Eden responded gloomily, "she *has* run away

several times before. To Deputy Dan, this just looks like a repeat offense. She always turns up after a few days when she and her uncle patch things up."

"But this time," Eve butted in, "she didn't take her phone. That's how we know it's serious. She always has her phone with her – even in the bathroom. I mean, it is practically attached to her like an extra limb."

"Hmm," Ellie stalled. A shallow wave of relief washed right up to her toes but receded before it could completely cover her feet. "If she did run away, leaving her phone was deliberate. Now, no one can track her. If she wanted to get away that would be smart. Where did she leave her cell phone? At her uncle's?"

"No one knows for sure." Eden responded. "When we got online with the Rev to track it, the GPS and Bluetooth had been turned off, so we couldn't locate it. But we could see that no calls have been made from it since the Sunday after school got out."

Just then, Zibby's mom walked in with her bucket of cleaning supplies. "Well, I wondered why all the lights were blazin' this time of night. It's a regular party in here. Am I interruptin' somethin'?"

Zibby walked over to her mom, and taking the vacuum cleaner said, "No, mom. Miss P brought me here, and when we came in, we found the twins praying. Let's start in the back so they can finish up." Zibby and her mom started working in the vestibule, leaving Ellie with the twins down near the altar.

Ellie swallowed once, trying to sound braver than she felt. "It's really admirable of you girls to pray for your friend. I'm sure she'll turn up soon, but until then - keep up the prayers. Maybe Tai's uncle can pester Deputy Dan into a legitimate search. Why don't we leave and let Zibby and her mom finish their work? I'll let you know if I hear anything."

"As if," Eve grumbled as they started walking back up the aisle to leave the sanctuary.

"What do you mean by that, Eve?" Ellie cocked her head.

"Oh," Eden stuttered. "She just meant that Tai probably wouldn't call you if she were in trouble – or any *teacher* for that matter," she added quickly seeing Ellie's narrowed eyes. "She struggles with authority. C'mon, Eve, let's get out of here." Eden grabbed her twin's wrist and drug her out of the church.

Ellie hobbled back to her car without seeing her surroundings. A dozen questions were knocking around inside her head, and the alarm bells were pealing in full force now that she was outside. Was this why she and Julien hadn't been able to get Tai to babysit for them? Could Julien have been the last person to see her before she disappeared? Did he know anything about this?

A fist of anger punched her in the stomach. *If he helped her run away,* she thought, *I'll kill him!* She could just imagine Tai playing her role of innocent victim and turning to Julien for help. He would have been putty in her hands if he thought he was the only one that could save her.

But that would mean that he had deceived Ellie, and Julien would never do that. Why would he pretend he knew nothing about Tai's disappearance if he'd helped orchestrate it? He couldn't be stupid enough to help a teenager run away from home.

Ellie mulled over the questions imagining various scenes of both Julien's complicity and his innocence. Which was more likely to have happened? Ellie wasn't sure, and her stomach churned. An insistent pounding was starting behind her left eye. By the time she pulled up in the driveway, her entire body was clenched, anticipating the fight that was sure to follow.

When she entered the foyer, Julien was there waiting for her. He held two glasses of champagne aloft. He exchanged her keys for a glass before she could even say hello. It caught her off guard.

"Come, *mon amour* – let's celebrate the new year and make a resolution of our own." He pulled her close, and Ellie melted into his arms.

She couldn't help herself. He was her warmth, her comfort, her stability. How could she ever have doubted him? She didn't want to ruin the moment with accusations and fighting. Heaven forbid she allow Tai to ruin another night with her husband. No, Ellie refused to bring the wretched name into her home tonight of all nights.

She took a sip from her glass. The bubbles that raced through her weren't entirely from her drink. Breathing in the smell of him, and feeling her stomach unclench, Ellie allowed herself to be carried upstairs, where they rang in the new year with more than just champagne. And as for resolutions, Ellie resolved to be more trusting of her husband as her fears dissolved with kiss after passionate kiss.

# CHAPTER FORTY-FOUR

## THE SHADOW

January progressed, and *The Shadow* found herself in the back of the classroom watching Ellie hobble around, secretly delighting in the fact that she could take credit for every one of Ellie's injuries. She had to admit, albeit grudgingly, that Ellie was navigating them bravely. Ellie never complained in front of the students; *The Shadow* only knew she was still in pain by the winces that flickered over Ellie's face as she reached up to write on the board or grab something from overhead.

The fire's failure to sever Ellie's connection to the heirloom had stunned her. She'd been mortified when she'd failed a third time. The only remaining element was air. *The Shadow's* elemental air attack had been difficult to plan and required several steps. After all, an explosion would be very public. Several steps were involved, and blame would need to fall squarely on Pelletier shoulders.

*The Shadow* relished the thought that Ellie had no clue about what awaited her. Ellie's current suffering was nothing compared to what was coming. *The Shadow* smirked. The timing couldn't be more perfect.

They were rehearsing the scene in *The Crucible* where Mary Warren gives Elizabeth Proctor a "poppet" that she made for Elizabeth during the trials. Elizabeth doesn't know how to react to the gift, being a grown woman with two sons, but she accepts the doll as what Mary intends it to be -- a small peace offering to soothe hurt feelings after the family fight centered on Mary Warren just days before.

In the play, neither Mary nor Elizabeth realizes that Abigail Williams has hidden a needle in the poppet - a needle plunged into the stomach of the doll - that will usher in Elizabeth's imprisonment. Several lines later in the play, Abigail turns up bleeding, claiming that Elizabeth's spirit has stabbed her in the stomach, and when authorities search the Proctor's home, they find the doll and the hidden needle which seem to corroborate Abigail's story.

It was, in fact, that very scene that gave *The Shadow* her idea in the first place. Somehow it just felt like the right thing to do, and she needed to vent her anger by doing something productive. *The Shadow* had been waiting for weeks to see the results of her handiwork, and the day had finally arrived.

The drug dogs were coming. *The Shadow* just hoped that they would search Ellie's room before the end of class so she could witness Ellie's public humiliation first-hand. She settled into her part reading the role of Martha Corey and waited.

Before long, there was a knock at the door. Officer Hardy stepped in and asked everyone to clear the room and to leave all their bags, purses, coats, and shoes behind for the dogs to examine. A collective groan arose from the class along with a few mutterings of "unfair, invading my civil liberties," but in the end, everyone cleared out as instructed.

*The Shadow* watched Ellie grab her class roster and head into the hall. She watched the dogs enter the classroom and charge to the wall behind Ellie's desk. She watched Ellie's face crumple in confusion. She watched Officer Hardy come out with a little plastic baggie of pot, and a colorful, poster-sized painting.

"Is this your personal property, ma'am?"

"No, I mean yes. The painting was a gift -- just hung it a few weeks ago." Even though she was at the back of the line of students, *The Shadow* could distinguish Ellie's faint words. Ellie was shell-shocked, and so was the rest of the class, judging by their silence. *The Shadow* heard Officer Hardy tell Ellie to follow him to a more private location. The whole class heard it.

Catcalls and whistles sounded from the other students waiting in the hall. "You go, Mis Paylahtay" and "show them they ain't got no right to invade our personal property!" The students obviously knew what was going on; they were probably relieved the officer thought the marijuana belonged to Ellie instead of to one of them.

"Hey, officer! What do we do? You just arrested our teacher. Do we get the day off?" A student called out as Ellie and the officer headed down the hall.

"Go to the gym and await further instructions!" Officer Hardy barked out the order. No one moved. They were all too busy pulling out their cell phones, snapping pictures, and posting online comments. *The Shadow* stood there with them, watching. Gabby would have been so proud.

# CHAPTER FORTY-FIVE

## *ELLIE'S OUTRAGE*

Ellie drove home in shock. She'd replayed the scene over and over in her mind. How could administrators think that she would bring drugs to school? And to hide them in her own classroom? In a painting given to her by a student? She couldn't decide if it meant they thought she was stupid or arrogant. She spent the entire drive home debating that irrelevant issue – to avoid processing what had just happened.

When her thoughts caught up with her reality, Ellie felt numb; how in Hades could the administration have put her on immediate professional leave? Her mind wandered aimlessly. She turned onto the dirt road that led to their farmhouse driveway.

A deep sadness enveloped her; she'd never recover from a professional blow like this. It would be almost impossible to get another teaching job after an annotation on her professional certificate. She continued her drive under a heavy, black cloud of despair, focusing only on the twenty-foot stretch of road in front of her. She couldn't bear to look around at the beautiful, sunny day; it was too bright. January shouldn't be this bright and cheerful; it should be grey and cold, like her mood.

As she rounded the next curve and approached her gravel driveway, however, a lightning bolt of anger struck her, piercing the numbness. *That little slut!*

Ellie accelerated as she turned onto the driveway, and her tires spat gravel. *Tai gave me that painting as a distraction! She intended to stash drugs in it all along!* And Ellie had been naïve enough to accept it as a peace offering – proof that Tai wasn't really the monster Ellie had suspected.

*And to think, I let myself feel guilty for using that banishing charm on her! She's lucky I didn't find a charm to do more than just banish her.* Ellie spun up the gravel drive and screeched to a halt in front of her home.

Clouds of rage billowed inside her. She could feel them swirling, roiling, as she stormed up the walkway to the front porch. She could not wait to confront Julien and fill him in on the "innocent" little assistant he always defended. *Let's see how he explains this away.* She slammed the front door shut and pounded her way inside.

Julien sat at the kitchen table eating lunch. He stood up when he saw Ellie come into the kitchen. "*Ma chère*, what are you doing here? Is everything alright?"

Ellie walked up to him, and when he tried to embrace her, she pushed him away. She shoved hard enough to make him take a couple of steps backward.

"No, Julien! Everything is not alright. Everything is horrible, in fact. And it's all down to the conniving little hussy that you hired!"

Julien looked at her like she was speaking Greek. "What are you talking about? Why the aggressive behavior? It is beneath you. Sit down, and let's talk about this like two civilized adults, *ma chérie*."

"Aggressive? You think this is aggressive? Just wait until I get to that scheming little shrew – then you'll see aggressive." Ellie spat out the words, pacing. "And you know what else? I don't care if you think it's beneath me." She whirled to face him, pointing a finger at his chest punctuating each word. "I. Told. You. So!" She growled through clenched teeth.

Julien reached for her hand as if to soothe her, but Ellie

snatched it away and resumed her pacing.

"I have been put on professional leave because the drug dogs alerted on the painting that *Tai* gave me!" Her voice dripped with angry sarcasm. "It turns out that there was a stash of marijuana hidden inside the canvas. Now, I have an annotation on my professional certificate. I'm being investigated *by the police*! It's a miracle I wasn't *arrested* on the spot!" Her hands flew up in fury.

"Rrruhh," she snarled. "After all these years of maintaining a spotless record, just to have your little bimbo assistant ruin it in one fell swoop? I could spit *nails*! Ellie shouted. "And I'd spit them right into her chest if she were here!" She finished with venom.

She spun around to look at Julien. His face was so white with shock that it looked like guilt. His expression only fueled Ellie's anger. "I *told* you she was trouble! I *told* you not to continue to work with her. But, oh no! You had to be the *savior*, the knight in shining *armor* out to save the poor little damsel in distress."

She was on a tirade and couldn't stop. Her mouth rounded into a small "o," and she mimicked baby-talk. "You had to show the poor, misunderstood, backwoods little tramp about the world. Did it make you feel good? Did you feel like a hero?" She dropped the sickly-sweet voice. "Well, did it? Because your *noble* intentions," she raised her eyebrows and emphasized the words, "cost me my profession!"

And with that, Ellie thundered upstairs into the master bathroom and locked the door. The tears that hadn't come in the initial numbness finally broke through her angry façade and coursed down her face in a flood of hot, wet streams. Ellie sobbed. Her shoulders shook. She was furious at herself for crying. She was enraged at Julien for helping others at her expense. She was livid with Tai for being such a sneaky, manipulative hypocrite.

Mainly, though, she was disgusted with herself for not listening to her instincts.

She had felt all along that Tai was trouble, but she had listened to Julien's rationalization and somehow been suckered into believing him. She struggled to get control of herself. She looked in the mirror and wiped her eyes. As she worked to remove the mascara that ran down her cheeks, she noticed a shimmer on her wrist and immediately thought of the anthology. If anything could soothe her spirit and redirect her fierce anger, it was the anthology.

She reached down under the sink, took out the leather-bound anthology, and sat. As she thumbed through the pages, she felt the anger start to seep out of her and into the book. She remembered the funnel of light from the hospital that drained her worries into the book. The pages thrummed with energy, and her fingers flew, seeking a remedy for her tension.

Suddenly, a spark zinged through her index finger and thumb. Her fingers halted. This would be the one; it felt right. Her hungry eyes sought out the words that she had begun to rely on to bring comfort and release. Just as she started to feast on the content, she heard the door knob twist and stick.

Julien hesitated. "Why is the door locked, *ma petite*?" He asked quietly.

"Because I didn't want *you* to come in," Ellie retorted. She heard Julien's retreating footsteps a few moments later and went back to her anthology, devouring every morsel of the pages that would help her regain control.

# CHAPTER FORTY-SIX

## *WAYWARD WINTER*

During Ellie's suspension from school, the end of January faded into February. Ellie received several texts from Zyla wanting to know if Ellie was okay and if she could come over to talk. Ellie didn't respond. She withdrew into her anthology.

The ancient book called to her louder than ever, and Ellie began to answer its call amid household chores. She'd put on a load of laundry and stand there, listening to the machine run, reading her book -- telling herself that it would distract her from her worries.

She instinctively hid the anthology from Julien. Each time he entered the room, she'd slip it under whatever was available. She and Julien hadn't really gotten past their argument, but by some unspoken agreement they worked together to hide their angst from the girls.

Zyla peppered Ellie's days with encouraging text messages, telling her that no one believed the drugs were Ellie's and that the school would turn the case over to detectives who'd prove Ellie's innocence. Ellie largely ignored the texts and buried herself in household chores and her anthology.

As the days passed, Ellie grew tired of having to find new and creative ways to keep her book a secret from Julien. In the kitchen, a thought occurred to her; she had originally thought of the concoctions inside the anthology as recipes. Why not hide the recipes in plain sight?

She grabbed her beloved red-and-white-checkered

cookbook and took it to her upstairs office. First, she removed the cover and shoved the bulk of recipes in her desk. Then, she slipped the anthology inside the cover, using clear packing tape to fasten the anthology's leather cover securely inside the cookbook's red and white one. She surveyed her work. She thought it would pass inspection if there wasn't too much scrutiny.

Ellie planned the first test of her deception. She made sure she was holding the "cookbook" standing by the stovetop when Julien came in from work. He watched her from the doorway, and when she lifted her eyes to him without any malice in them, he approached her and gave her a tentative kiss on the cheek. She made herself stand without flinching. His eyes grazed over the pot and its contents without even noticing the cookbook.

"Feeling like cooking today, hmm? Isn't that one of those old cookbooks you bought when we married?" Julien asked sniffing the pot.

Ellie closed the book to her chest and faced him. "It is the *very* first cookbook I ever owned. Look at this old cover. I'm surprised it hasn't fallen apart." She continued. "I thought I'd revisit some of our favorite meals. Do you recognize this dish?" She directed his gaze from the cookbook to the simmering pot.

"Do I detect *chiquetaille de morue*?" He asked.

"Yes, it's been so long since I've made it, I thought I'd use that recipe from *Le Chemise* that I stuck in here after our honeymoon." She hesitated. Now was as good a time as any. She took a deep breath.

"You know, Julien, we need to talk about Tai before I get back to work next week. And I think I'm calm enough to discuss her now." She swallowed, waiting on Julien's reaction.

He breathed out through his nose and stepped back. "There is nothing to discuss. She won't be a problem -- for either of us."

Ellie looked at him. That sounded ominous. Was he

going to confess to being the last person to see her before she ran away? Did he even know she had run away? She hadn't exactly told him about her encounter with the twins at the church on New Year's.

"Why do you say that?" Ellie asked.

Julien rolled his eyes slightly in irritation. "Because she disappeared, that's why. I haven't seen her since before New Year's. I didn't want to upset you, but you may as well know – all the cash from the register at the studio vanished right along with her. I noticed it around the same time as her disappearance. In fact, I was going to ask her about it, but she never came in to work that day."

"How much money went missing?" Ellie asked.

Julien sighed again. "I don't know exactly but somewhere around a five hundred dollars. I hadn't really been keeping records; it was petty cash I'd been putting aside to buy props."

"Oh, Julien!" Ellie was stunned. "After investing so much time in helping her." She looked at him in dismay.

"Well, no good deed goes unpunished. I should have been more careful." He paused. "Can you ever forgive me?"

That was the closest he'd ever come to an apology where Tai was concerned, and it was enough. Ellie decided to accept the implied admission of guilt and gave him a reassuring hug. "Of course, sweetheart." Maybe now that Tai was gone, they could truly patch up their marriage.

As the chilly February days slipped by, things began to resolve. Ellie had returned to work with very little fanfare. Zyla had been right; the detectives had concluded that there wasn't enough evidence to prove who had hidden the drugs behind the painting. It could have been a crime of opportunity committed by anyone with access to Ellie's classroom.

The current working theory was that the cleaning crew

- a group of inmates from the local prison who cleaned the school as part of their *reformation* - had been caught unawares. They'd stashed illicit items wherever they could, desperate to get rid of anything incriminating, and hadn't been able to retrieve their contraband before being loaded into the prison van. It wouldn't be the first time they had been caught hiding things at school. Over the last few years, staff members had found everything from cell phones to razors hidden in the ceiling tiles and other strange places.

Ellie was relieved that her certification was no longer in jeopardy. She and Principal Danvers worked out a deal, of sorts. Ellie had originally wanted a public apology in front of the entire Board of Education. In the end, she settled for the Reverintendent's personal apology, and no annotation to her teaching certificate. She agreed to the arrangement because she knew the rumor of her innocence would spread like crazy – especially when it got out that it could have been the inmates who had committed the crime.

Doubts about Ellie would swiftly change course and target the inmates - and the whole idea of having them service the school. Parents would pitch a fit when they found out. More than likely, the Reverintendent would wind up having to hire a real custodial crew and start *paying* to have the school cleaned from there on out.

By mid-February, Ellie's injuries were healing. She hobbled less and less each day at school, and her students encouraged her when she had near-falls and setbacks. The one thing they could empathize with was *pain*. Their concern surprised her. Her teaching was back on track, and she was beginning to feel like she might have finally adjusted to her new life. Her students were progressing, her girls were growing, and her marriage was healing without constant interference from Tai.

Ellie and Julien decided to celebrate Ellie's improved health by going out to dinner on Valentine's Day. They took advantage of their church's "love offering" to parents – free babysitting services so that parents could have a night out.

Ellie supposed it was the church's way of supporting healthy marriages, and she was grateful. Even in a small town like Stusa, life could get unbelievably hectic and harried.

That night, Ellie put on Julien's favorite red dress. It was a blood-red, form-fitting wrap-dress; she never could decide if the look suited her or embarrassed her, but Julien liked it, so she wore it to remind him that she could still turn heads. She put on a pair of heels, too. It was the first time since the accident that she'd worn heels, and she hoped she wouldn't come to regret it. She simply felt the need to look attractive again and to feel appreciated, admired.

When she made her way slowly down the staircase, at a pace that she hoped looked sexy rather than sad, Julien gave a low whistle. She didn't know if he was just trying to make her feel better, but it worked. She smiled and blushed. It might be needy to think it, but it felt good to have his approval.

Even the girls got into it, clapping and cheering as she made her way downstairs. Julien gallantly offered her his arm and escorted her to the car. The girls giggled and squealed as he gave her a lingering kiss on the lips after getting her settled and buckled into place.

"Euwww," Bibianne sputtered in between giggles.

"Its's not gross, Bibi. It's how we know papa loves *maman* even when she is not at her best." Méline corrected.

Ellie smiled. *Out of the mouth of babes.* Julien looked at Ellie and winked. Ellie didn't mind the reminder that she still wasn't back to normal. She was just glad to be able to enjoy a good, old-fashioned date with her husband.

After dropping off the girls at the church social hall, Ellie and Julien drove to the nicest restaurant one town over. The restaurant was a hidden gem, a bistro and grill tucked away in a hunting lodge. The food was delicious; Ellie ordered the rack of lamb topped with sun-dried tomatoes, olives, garlic and mint, while Julien got the chestnut-dusted, pan-seared lobster ravioli. Since Ellie couldn't have wine considering her still-plentiful daily medications, she splurged and ate the house specialty for dessert – blackberry cobbler topped with homemade vanilla ice cream. It was every bit as good as she had imagined.

Throughout the meal, she and Julien reminisced about their early years. He remembered the incident with Madame Margaux. He could recite Ellie's version of her prediction almost word for word.

*When the people buzz like insects, don't lose faith. You will survive the test.*

"No, No," Ellie corrected him, laughing. "She didn't use the word *interro*, test; she used the word *creuset*, crucible." Ellie chuckled, then cocked her head to one side. "Maybe her prediction has already come true." She drew out each word slowly. "Maybe I've already survived the crucible; I've definitely been through a lot since we moved here."

Julien looked at her with a dash of condescension. "You know there is nothing to all that, Ellie." He chided.

Ellie laughed again. "But think about it -- even the first part fits. The people actually do buzz around here like insects." Ellie was getting into it. "The more I think about it, the more I think she really was predicting my time in Stusa!" It all fit. Madame Margaux might not have been a hoax after all. She reached over and grabbed Julien's wrist.

"You know, there's more to her than you think. I never told you the very first thing she said to me." She paused.

"Why not?" He looked puzzled.

"Well," Ellie blushed, "because it had to do with you. She said I'd marry you and have two kids." Ellie's blush deepened.

"You're making that up just to prove your point," Julien scoffed.

"No, no!" Ellie pleaded. "I'm not! She really did say that! Honest!"

Julien snorted. "Then why didn't you tell me? I mean, you could have told me after we were married."

"Because I didn't want you to think I'd hoodwinked you into marrying me." Ellie's face was nearly purple.

"What? Like you put a hex on me or something? Or paid Madame Margaux to do it?" He laughed.

"Exactly," Ellie whispered. Julien looked at her again, perplexed, and then burst into laughter.

"Oh, Elles, you still amuse me - even after all these years." Ellie was torn between frustration and embarrassment, but then she started laughing, too.

She knew Julien had nothing but disdain for all the island hoodoo-voodoo that tourists couldn't get enough of. She laughed with him; it felt so good to laugh together. Her laughter encouraged his, and vice versa. Before long, they were laughing so hard that other customers began to stare. Julien finally got control of himself and asked for the check before anyone complained.

On the ride home, Ellie sighed. It had been a wonderful evening, but now the dreaded sling awaited her in the glove box. She grudgingly slipped it over her shoulder and onto her arm. She and Julien were riding in comfortable silence when they saw flashing red and blue lights race around them. Julien pulled over onto the shoulder as an ambulance followed, sirens blaring. Ellie's first thought was for her girls.

"I hope nothing has happened at the church," she fretted. "Do you suppose --"

Julien interrupted, "It's not the church – look."

Ellie saw it then, a conglomeration of firetrucks, police cars, and flashing lights in the distance. Julien slowed down as they approached the area. A police officer was standing in the middle of the road with a flashlight, directing traffic. He signaled Julien to stop.

"I'm sorry, sir, but this road needs to be cleared until the first responders depart. You can either wait here or turn around to take highway 171 and skirt this area."

Ellie was shocked. That detour would add an extra forty-five minutes to their drive home. She leaned over. "Are there any short cuts that could get us to Stusa?"

"Plot it on your GPS, ma'am. We have an emergency to

deal with here. Just follow 171 and you'll make it back to Stusa by midnight." He tapped the car's hood twice as a signal for Julien to drive on.

Ellie was worried about the girls. The church only provided babysitters until eleven. She pulled out her cell phone to call ahead while Julien navigated the GPS. The church phone rang a dozen times. Ellie was about to hang up when a tearful voice answered, "Happy Valentine's Day, how may I help you?"

"Zibby? Is that you? This is Ellie – Mrs. Pelletier."

"Yes, ma'am. It's me." Zibby sniffled.

"What's wrong? Are Méline and Bibianne okay?" Ellie asked in alarm.

Sniff, sniff. "Yes, ma'am. Your girls are fine." Ellie swallowed the lump in her throat. Zibby continued. "Sacred Heart invited all local church youth groups here for a prayer vigil when they got the news."

A feeling of unease replaced the swift relief. "What has happened, Zibby?"

Zibby cleared her throat. "It's Tai. She's finally turned up, but she's had an accident. They're taking her to the hospital. After all these weeks missing...and now this."

Ellie was stunned. Was that the emergency they'd just passed? They'd been stopped near a place called "the cabin." It was a derelict, old home that had been abandoned decades ago. Teenagers used it for any number of illicit activities. It was at the very edge of the county, and the local cops didn't do much to monitor the place unless someone called to report an incident. She choked out her next question.

"Was anyone else involved in the accident?"

"No." Zibby answered. "They're saying she tried to commit suicide by swallowing an entire bottle of her anti-anxiety pills. We didn't even know she had anxiety. I feel so guilty." Another sniffle.

Ellie didn't know what to say. She managed to thank Zibby and to tell her that they might not make the curfew to pick up the girls. She felt a cold, hard lump of her own anxiety settle in the pit of her stomach.

"Don't worry, Mrs. P. There will be someone here to look after the girls. We'll all be here praying. I may not like Tai much, but I don't wish her dead."

A flicker of guilt prickled the back of Ellie's brain as she repeated the news to Julien. Something about his posture shifted. His shoulders fell back slightly, and his facial muscles unclenched. *So, he was worried about the girls after all*, she thought.

She said, "I know. My first reaction was relief that it had nothing to do with Mel or Bibi. Thank God they're okay." She paused. "And it sounds like they're doing everything they can to help Tai. We'll just have to hope for the best." She added, guiltily.

"*Oui*," Julien agreed, and they drove to the church as quickly as the detour would allow.

The following Monday, the entire school was abuzz with the story of Tai's suicide attempt. The tales ranged from her swallowing a bottle of pills to slitting her wrists, but one detail never changed – one that directly affected Ellie.

Although Ellie was unaware of the rumors circulating when she got to school, she knew right away that something was amiss as soon as she entered the building. Instead of receiving the usual sleepy greetings and slow smiles, students avoided her gaze. As she walked down the long hallway, every single student seemed to remember something needed from a locker, an untied shoe, a dropped paper, or an urge to turn around mid-stride and head in the opposite direction.

Ellie didn't have much time to ponder the circumstances of her arrival; she had an attendance committee meeting before first period. She left the meeting and hurried to class but found an empty classroom. Ellie's classroom usually had a dozen students milling about, killing time between breakfast and the bell. When the first bell rang, only three students trickled in. Another four students scooted in at the very last second before the tardy bell sounded. Where was everyone?

Ellie was counting on the class leader, Bristol, to help run lines with a small group while she worked with the rest of the class, but he wasn't there. A good fifteen minutes after class had started, Bristol breezed through the doorway and dropped a tardy pass into Ellie's open hand, nose in the air, without looking at her. He was clearly in a foul mood. Bristol could be quite the diva when irritated.

Instead of sitting in his normal desk up front, he trounced back to the very last desk, as far away from Ellie as possible, and flung his bedazzled book bag down with a flourish and a sigh. When Ellie called on him to rehearse lines with his group, he acted like he didn't hear her. He turned his back to Ellie and started working with another group of actors to avoid her gaze.

Certain that he was being defiant on purpose, not just misunderstanding Ellie's directions, she approached Bristol. She whispered, "What's wrong?"

"Oh, nothing" he answered loud enough for everyone to hear him. "I just really hate bullies." He glared at Ellie. "I'm sick of this place allowing the bullying to go unpunished." He turned to face his classmates and said "But that's okay. Because even if they never face it here on earth, I know that bullies will receive *final* judgment in the afterlife." He added a head rotation and a snap of his fingers

"Amen, Bristol. You preach it, bruthuh!" A faint echo of *Amens* and *Hallelujahs* traveled throughout the class. Ellie gave Bristol an understanding look and shook her head in disgust. It must be hard to be a religious, black, male, gay teenager in Stusa. *Someone must be pushing his buttons.*

Well, she could overlook his arrogance. Anyone would be upset in his place. Ellie continued to circulate throughout the room.

It wasn't until lunch that she cottoned on. As she was walking to the lounge, she overheard Eve and Eden. They were standing around the corner outside the girls' restrooms and didn't see her coming.

"...Tai said it was because Ellie got mad at her ... she'll be in Stony River Behavioral...all Miss P's fault...can't believe still has a job."

They nearly fell over themselves trying to get into the bathroom when they saw Ellie pass by. Ellie walked on as if she'd heard nothing, but her insides squirmed. She continued to the teacher's lounge and entered a bathroom stall as quickly as possible, her heart pounding in her ears, her stomach wadding into a tight knot.

Once inside, Ellie doubled over as everything started to click. She belatedly realized what Bristol must have been referring to earlier. Tai had blamed her suicide attempt on Ellie. *He wasn't being vague; he was calling me a bully to my face! He thinks I bullied Tai into suicide!* Everyone must have been thinking it, judging from the reactions she got when she walked into school. She imagined the gossip travelling throughout the school. A newspaper headline floated across her vision.

### Suicide Attempted Due to Teacher's Bullying

The imaginary headline made her bolt upright again. An intense wave of anger washed over her as Ellie stormed out of the teacher's lounge and back to her classroom. She turned off the lights, then shut the door and locked it. She squatted down on the floor behind her desk.

The more she thought about it, the more it started to click. She had always recognized Tai's desperate plea for male attention. Her entire demeanor shouted, "I have an absent father and would do anything to feel loved." Tai was determined to get out of Stusa, dying to get a lucky break, and craving a friend who wouldn't judge her for her smuttiness.

While Ellie had been fighting with Julien about spending too much alone time with Tai, Tai had been holed up at the cabin, scratching at her wrists, swallowing a bottle of anti-anxiety pills...and blaming it on Ellie. Little drama queen; Ellie fiercely hoped she had to have had her stomach pumped and that it was just as unpleasant as it sounded.

As soon as she thought it, she felt guilty. She couldn't believe the anger that swelled inside her. It twisted and writhed like a snake, and it was threatening to rise up and take control if Ellie wasn't careful. She swallowed, struggling to push it back down.

What exactly had Tai and Julien been up to before Christmas? What could Tai gain from blaming a suicide attempt on Ellie? Was she trying to get attention? Sympathy? Revenge?

Another emotion took Ellie's thoughts hostage as she remembered her most recent hospital stay and the charm she'd uttered and eaten. Her anger swiftly turned to a very different feeling - victory! As soon as she named it, the feeling soared up from her belly as if it had been waiting there for her to release it. It travelled upwards and flooded her limbs and extremities with a moment of pure, unadulterated glee. She was thrilled that Tai would be out of her life for even longer.

The feeling of victory was much stronger than the anger had been. It washed over her in a hot, blinding wave that nearly caused Ellie to black out. She reached over and held onto the underside of the desk to keep from falling over onto the floor as the emotions surged through her in hot waves.

Her charm had worked! *Jezebel had been banished.*

As soon as she thought it, Ellie heard someone laugh. It was a distant, eerie, wicked laugh full of gloating and devoid of joy. Where was it coming from? Who was in her classroom with her? When she shot up from behind her desk to see who had come into the room, the laughter died instantly.

Ellie gasped aloud. The laughter had come from her.

◆ ◆ ◆

At lunch, Principal Danvers and the Reverintendent announced a last-minute lunch meeting. Ellie's stomach lurched as she walked down the hall. She had a bad feeling about the impromptu meeting. Were they going to fire her in front of the entire faculty?

Ellie had no doubt that the Reverintendent would believe his niece's accusations. When had anyone here ever given her the benefit of the doubt? Rumors had sprouted the very instant she had planted herself in Stusa. Today would be no different. It would be easy for everyone to blame the outsider, the newcomer, the stranger.

Ellie stepped into the school library and joined the rest of the faculty. She refused to give in to the shame threatening to creep over her. She had done nothing wrong; she would not allow herself to look guilty or embarrassed. Ellie held her head high and waited for the meeting to start.

She glanced at her watch, glad the girls had music lessons after school with Zibby. Mondays were music days, and Zibby took the girls to the chorus room after school to give them lessons on the school's piano. Zibby would drop the girls off at home after they were done. Ellie would be able to talk to Julien before they arrived.

"Folks, we have some serious news to share." Principal Danvers interrupted her thoughts as he began the meeting. "I'll let the Rev fill you in on the details." He stepped aside and the Reverintendent cleared his throat.

"I come to you with a heavy heart." He sniffled, but Ellie noticed there were no tears in his eyes. "My niece, Tai, has been an inpatient at Stony River Behavioral Health." His voice broke, but still there were no tears. "We've not shared the information for privacy concerns, but this past weekend, as soon as she was dismissed from the center – she may have attempted suicide."

The entire faculty gasped in unison. "Oh no," someone said. "How horrible for you," another voice echoed. Someone touched his arm. Miss Sarka reached over and patted his back.

"That's not the end of it, however," the Reverintendent held up his hands to get their attention, and he stepped back a pace or two. He looked them all in the eye, one by one.

"This requires your utmost professionalism. I do not want to hear the slightest mention of this outside this room. If students get wind of this, you will all deny it vehemently."

*Finally*, Ellie thought indignantly. *He is going to squash these ridiculous rumors about me being the cause of all this!* She straightened up a little more, waiting for the explanation that was sure to follow.

The Reverintendent continued, "There is no need to besmirch our family name as Taiteja fights for her mental well-being." He paused and glanced at his feet.

"A vicious rumor has surfaced," Ellie waited with closed eyes for the oncoming vindication, "that Tai was pregnant at the time of the attempt but that she has lost the baby due to the trauma." He glared at them. Ellie's mouth dropped open. "I have no idea why anyone would want to start yet another rumor about my niece – especially at a time like this, but I assure you that it is baseless."

The silence was absolute and awkward. The entire faculty looked away from him. Some turned their heads to the side; others stared at their shoes, and some found the sudden, intense need to pick their nails. The whole room simultaneously felt the need to look away.

The Reverintendent continued. "What is there to gain from such a hurtful rumor?" His question echoed in the silence. "Unless people are attacking me through my niece, I cannot see the motivation or the gain."

At that, his eyes did fill with tears. Afraid she'd roll her eyes at how he'd managed to turn his niece's crisis into a personal attack upon himself, Ellie looked down at her shoes, too.

After a moment, the Reverintendent regained his composure. "I'm sure you understand my position. Again, I do not want *this* rumor to take root. As her closest relative, I vehemently deny any veracity to the rumor and want it stopped immediately. I will not allow my niece's character, or *mine*, to be defamed. Is that clear?"

Ellie spent the rest of the day in shock. The comments about her and Tai diminished as the day went on, but Ellie still felt the icy stares of her students and the sideways glances from the faculty. She went through the motions of teaching on autopilot. When the final bell sounded, she didn't straighten her room, collect papers, or stop by the office. She hefted her book bag over her shoulder and went straight to her car.

On her drive home, she wondered if Tai would be readmitted to the behavioral health center. If so, perhaps the rumors would die down and Ellie could regain her sense of self. How much time did she have left without Tai?

She felt a moment's twinge of guilt. Could she be the cause of Tai's accident? Not in the way people expected, by bullying, but by reading the verse aloud in the hospital? Surely not – how could reciting a simple poem aloud force another person to attempt suicide? Ellie shook her head to clear her crazy ideas. She was just feeling anxious about everything that had gone wrong.

When Ellie pulled up the long gravel drive to her home, she got instant confirmation that her ill wishes towards Tai hadn't been the least bit effective, for there in the driveway sat Tai's car.

Her anger returned full force, and Ellie fumed. Had Tai's first stop after being released been to rush over to see Julien? Ellie's tires spat gravel as she roared up the driveway and saw Tai walking down it towards her car.

As Tai approached, she didn't make eye contact with

Ellie. She simply climbed into her parked car and sat there partially blocking the driveway. Ellie spun past her, slammed the car into park, slung her heavy school bag over her shoulder, and stomped up the steps to confront Julien who stood on the front porch.

He interrupted her with a touch on the shoulder. "Oh, *ma petite*." He breathed out in relief. "I knew you would get here quickly." He wrapped his arms around her and gave a quick squeeze. "Tai has been worried sick. I thought maybe you could talk to her to calm her down."

Ellie's car keys slipped out of her hands and fell to the floor.

"What?" She sputtered. "You want *me* to console *Tai*? What on earth does *she* have to be upset about? Guilty conscience?" Ellie spun around facing away from Julien, running both hands through her hair. "What is she even doing here? I thought she was admitted into the behavioral health center."

"*Non, ma vie*." He sighed. "Think for a moment. Her character has been attacked in this fiasco. She wants a chance to explain her innocence to you." He looked into Ellie's eyes. "She cares about what you think of her."

Ellie's hands dropped to her side, and she turned back to Julien. She groaned. "I am *sick* of this!" She bent over to pick up her keys, and the red and white cookbook fell out of her book bag. She grabbed it and shoved it back inside.

"Just hear her side of the story, *ma chère*." Julien helped her pick up all the other contents that had fallen onto the porch. "You know what it is like to be falsely accused. Give her the opportunity that you never got – a chance to explain herself. It will be as good for you as it is for her."

*Fine!* Ellie thought. *I'll talk to the little slut. I'll get rid of her so that we can try to fix our glaringly broken marriage.*

"Fine," she said it aloud this time. "I'll do it." Ellie rolled her eyes.

"Perfect. I knew you'd see reason. She is waiting there in her car." Julien breezed his way back inside the house.

Ellie halted. *The nerve!* For him to insinuate that she was being unreasonable, on top of wanting Ellie to go soothe the enemy, was too much. And Tai? She was still parked in the driveway, waiting, because she knew Julien would convince Ellie to talk to her. Ellie didn't know whom she was angrier with – Tai or Julien.

She took a deep breath to quell her rising anger and turned around. Sure enough, Tai's car was still parked at the very end of their long driveway. Ellie stomped down the gravel drive, the sound of the crunching beneath her feet giving her momentary satisfaction. If only she could crush Tai as easily.

Ellie yanked open the door to Tai's car and sat in the passenger seat. "We need to talk." She turned sideways to face Tai. When Tai didn't respond, or make eye contact, Ellie waited. Finally, Ellie realized Tai wasn't about to apologize or explain herself, so she started a one-sided conversation.

"Julien says you're here to explain yourself, but since you're not talking – I will." Ellie took a long, slow breath. "You are a beautiful young woman trying to find yourself. You're only seventeen; you have plenty of time left to figure it out. I'll give you a piece of unsolicited advice. Start with friends your own age. Hanging around a forty-year-old with a wife and children isn't the way." She paused.

Tai turned her face away from Ellie to look out the driver's window. *Huh. I struck a chord there. She feels embarrassed.* Ellie decided to close the conversation as quickly as possible.

"Tai, I don't usually talk about my personal life with students, but I'm going to tell you something. Julien and I are having a hard time. Moving here has been difficult, and we need to work on our problems without any interference." She waited a beat. "And I don't think you came here to explain yourself. I think you feel guilty, and you want me to say everything is okay and that we're all friends."

Ellie swallowed. "I'm not going to say that, though. I'm

going to protect my family and my marriage." She put one leg out of the car and then turned back to say, "By the way, Julien doesn't require your assistance anymore. I'm sure you'll find another job and another family to latch onto; it just won't be ours."

Ellie finished getting out of the car. She leaned over, shut the door, and said, "Goodbye, Tai." She walked back up the long gravel drive without a glance back. She felt confident that she had done the right thing by firing Tai without telling Julien, but anger still simmered underneath her calm exterior.

Now that she'd dismissed Tai, the next step was to confront Julien. Her mind raced. Tai must have come directly from the hospital to see Julien. That didn't make sense, though. Wouldn't the Reverintendent had to have signed her out?

As she made her way back to the house, Ellie finally admitted to herself that Julien's desire to play the hero to Tai's damsel in distress had turned into an unhealthy crush. Although it hurt her to think her husband could have feelings for a student young enough to be his daughter, Ellie felt certain that they could work through it.

It wouldn't be easy. She had no illusions about that, but she knew that her love for Julien would be big enough to work through their problems. Thinking about what to say to Julien, she climbed the steps to the front porch.

A sudden realization froze Ellie mid-step, however, with one foot dangling in the air. This time, the fury was icy hot. It crashed down on her like a bucket of ice water. Ellie felt the intense iciness creep through her veins and make its way to her heart. She grabbed ahold of the railing and set her foot back down.

*That little snake!* Tai wanted Julien's attention back on her, so she'd *faked* a suicide attempt. What else could explain her quick recovery and her trip straight from the hospital to see him? Maybe she hadn't even been admitted to the behavioral health center. Maybe that had been another lie just to get

Tai out from under public scrutiny, part of her poor-little-victim act. The conniving little weasel!

She mulled over the idea, checking to see if her conscious-self agreed with what her unconscious-self had just shouted. The more Ellie thought about it, the more she believed that it had all been a sympathy ploy. Tai's pride was hurt. She wanted attention – specifically Julien's attention. What better way to get it than to appear weak and needy?

Julien always had been a sucker for that. It was a wonder he ever married Ellie; she had never been the weak, needy type. She had merely been bowled over by his good looks and charisma.

And the worst part was that Tai's ruse had worked! Instead of talking to his wife about their crumbling marriage, Julien was playing the hero, helping poor little victim feel better about herself. Ellie walked into the house and closed the door behind her. If Julien was so determined to be the knight in shining armor to Tai's damsel in distress, he could do it alone.

She entered the kitchen and set down her book bag. She took out the cookbook. Ellie had underestimated her opponent. She should have known better – teenage girls were experts in melodrama. How could Ellie have forgotten?

She took the anthology upstairs to her office and began flipping through the pages, letting her fingers feel their way to the proper recipe. She didn't rush; the chill in her veins strengthened her determination and focus. She'd seen the recipe in the hospital. Her frozen heart told her that now was the time to use it.

Why had Tai returned? What had Ellie done wrong? The charm had worked for nearly six weeks, but now Tai was right back up to her old tricks, and Julien was falling for them. No, he was snorting them like an addict.

Had Ellie's reticent belief made the spell ineffective? Because she didn't have any doubt now.

No, the problem wasn't Ellie's lack of conviction. It

was something about Julien. Ellie had intended the recipe in the hospital for Tai, but now she recognized that Julien also needed attention. The solution she needed this time would have to work on both sides of the problem – not just the Tai side.

Tai was the Delilah to Julien's Samson. Ellie had never understood why Samson kept going back to Delilah after each betrayal. Why had Samson kept giving in? Didn't he realize Delilah would have his hair in the end?

Ellie was still thinking Samson and Delilah when the book sent a jolt from her fingertips up her left arm. She glanced down and saw exactly what she needed.

*When a Man's Heart Has Turned*

*Use this remedy to restore his devotion,*
*Work quickly and surely to redirect his emotion.*
*Read this once in a voice both loud and clear,*
*Then bury it along with something you hold dear.*
*As long as your treasure remains undisturbed,*
*This charm will continue its work unperturbed.*

Without hesitation, Ellie zeroed in on "something you hold dear." She began a list of treasured items that would be small enough to be buried. It probably needed to be something valuable, too. She sensed a sacrifice on her part would strengthen the remedy. Another thought tugged at her head as if the book had reached out and pulled on her hair; the treasure needed to be something that represented Julien, too.

An idea pierced her heart like an icicle to the chest. Her diamond wedding ring. She sucked in a breath. It was her only valuable piece of jewelry. Julien had bought it on the island where they met, but not for their engagement. They hadn't had the money back then. He bought it for her on their third anniversary, the day after she had announced she was pregnant with Méline.

Ellie was not terribly vain, but she loved that sparkly diamond and the baguettes that surrounded it. She had always loved anything that glittered, shimmered, or sparkled - and Julien had chosen well. The diamond was big enough to cast mesmerizing prisms in sunlight, yet not garish.

When her heart ached at the thought of sacrificing the ring, she knew it was the right treasure for the job. Her finger throbbed in resistance; she hadn't removed the ring in years, but eventually it gave way. She took the ring off before she could change her mind. She went downstairs and grabbed her garden trowel and used it to dig a narrow, deep hole in the soft earth. She recited the poem aloud in a clear, cold voice.

When she finished, she ripped out the recipe and folded it around the ring, wrapping it like a gift. When she placed the tiny package into the hole, a light breeze caressed her. Her hair lifted slightly in the wind, and she shuddered as the draft turned from a pleasant warmth to an icy embrace. She covered her treasure with dirt, and as an afterthought, grabbed a hyacinth bulb from the garden shed and planted it on top to ensure the ring would not be accidentally unearthed.

She tamped down the soil and watered the bulb, then put away her gardening things and entered the house. She walked into the kitchen. There Julien was, sitting at the breakfast table, chin resting in his hand, eyes glazed.

Ellie cleared her throat. Julien shoved his hand into his pocket and turned to look at her. "Julien, have you figured out what Tai is doing yet? You don't seriously think she tried to commit suicide, do you?" She waited a beat. When Julien didn't respond, she continued. "It was all just a desperate plea for attention."

At that, Julien looked up at her. "Well, she swallowed half a bottle of anti-anxiety pills, so that would be about fifteen pills. Sounds pretty suicidal to me."

Ellie asked for the name of the medication and googled it for overdose information. She found what she expected

– the prescription was not fatal or even terribly dangerous. That confirmed her suspicion. Tai had orchestrated the event to get Julien's undivided attention. How could they know if she had even swallowed the pills?

Ellie told Julien about the pills not being dangerous. "Why do you think she swallowed the pills, Julien?" He didn't answer. "Do you know what everyone is saying at school? That *I* bullied her into attempting suicide!"

Julien didn't reply. Suddenly, the fury she had felt earlier rose again and burst through her glacial facade. Ellie rounded on Julien. "Did you *hear* that? Your little *petite amie* just blamed her fake suicide attempt on *me*. And what are you doing? Falling for her desperate cry for attention. You are playing right into her hands!"

Ellie whirled around with her hands in her hair and took a deep breath to calm herself. She summoned the icy chill from earlier to freeze over her anger. When heart was once again an iceberg, she started to walk out of the kitchen. At the door she turned back to say, "You two deserve each other," then went to her office.

She sat at her desk and re-opened the anthology, stunned. What was going on? Was Julien more involved with Tai than she had guessed? It certainly seemed that way. Her mind raced with possibilities – none of them happy or healthy. She didn't know what she was looking for, but she knew the book would help her regain control.

An icy gust of wind, much like the one in the garden, blew through the anthology-disguised-as-recipe-book. The pages fluttered for a few seconds then stopped. When Ellie looked down at the pages' resting place, she saw a title that read:

*Past Deeds Revealed*

*To look upon another's past*
*takes focus and resolve,*

289

*And an item of each person*
*in the memory involved.*
*Placed on this page and set aflame,*
*look deep into the glow*
*State the time, the place*
*Through time you'll race*
*And see what you want to know.*

Ellie thought for a moment. After burying the ring, she felt bound to the book. She was connected to it somehow. Should she try this next charm as well?

She scoffed. What did she have to lose? Either she believed the charms in the book worked, or she didn't. And if she didn't truly believe they worked, why had she gone to the trouble of giving up her beloved ring? *In for a dime, in for a dollar.*

Ellie glanced at the clock. She still had some time before Zibby brought the girls back from their music lessons. She looked downstairs. Julien was at his desk on the computer. His back was to her, and he didn't seem to notice her staring over the bannister at him. Wouldn't it be more mature just to flat out ask him what had happened? She hesitated.

No, he'd probably tell her more half-truths or manipulate her into feeling guilty. How he managed to turn everything into her fault infuriated her. Since when had Ellie become so pliable, so weak? Had she been a fool to trust him all these years? He had never given her reason to doubt before. Why was it so different when Tai was concerned?

Ellie made up her mind and stayed upstairs, entering the bedroom to rummage through Julien's things. What could she use of his? It needed to be something small enough to fit on the page, and it needed to be flammable. She considered going through his wallet to look for receipts, but that didn't feel personal enough. She pulled a handkerchief out of his drawer. Would it burn?

She took it to the bathroom and used a lighter to test it.

The cloth didn't flame; it was more like a smolder. She tried dousing it with Julien's cologne. That didn't produce a flame either. She kept plundering.

When she got to his bureau, she found what she needed. There, hidden among his socks, was a familiar blue, black, and white package of *Gitanes Brunes*. God knew he was a smoking snob; those French cigarettes were hard to come by now that production in France had stopped. He probably had to special order them from the Netherlands. She knew he had been lying about smoking with Tai. She removed three cigarettes in case one wasn't enough.

Next, she looked for something of Tai's. An idea bloomed; several times she had been irritated to find a strand or two of Tai's long, blonde hair in her bathroom and kitchen after Tai had watched the girls. Ellie had been irate when she found one of those same long, blonde strands sticking to one of Julien's shirts earlier in the year.

She rummaged through Julien's closet, hoping that Tai's shedding hair would be useful for once. Would hair burn? She thought she knew a way to ensure it did. She finally found one of Tai's long, blonde, wavy locks clinging to a sports coat of Julien's that was made of tweed. When had he last worn this jacket? Was it the night of the grand opening? It had been a chilly evening, and Tai had worked at the party – so Ellie couldn't be too angry that one of Tai's hairs had found a way to Julien's coat. At least she hadn't found the hair clinging to his undershirt - or worse.

Ellie lifted the strand of hair and took it back to her office. Now that she wanted to be alone with her anthology, she was glad that they had decided to put one office upstairs and the other downstairs. It had initially served to keep a better check on the girls, but now it would provide Ellie some distance from Julien. She would hear him come up the stairs long before he'd reach her office, if he even bothered to check on her. All his concern seemed to be for Tai.

And that was what bothered her the most. Why wasn't

he more concerned about Ellie? Hadn't Ellie gone through enough to merit his attention? They'd made more emergency room trips since moving to Stusa than they had in their entire courtship and marriage put together.

Why was Julien so emotionally distant? When had their troubles even started?

Ellie thought it might have been around her last hospital visit, when the doctor pretty much accused her of taking herbs to cause an abortion, or at least prevent a pregnancy. Was that what had caused their turmoil? Had Julien really thought that Ellie would end a pregnancy? Maybe that was when the mistrust seeped in.

Ellie ran her hands over her face and sat at her desk. She placed the cigarettes, the anthology, and the strand of hair on the desk top and leaned over to open the window. She opened the anthology and used Tai's hair to tie all three cigarettes together. She placed the cigarette-hair bundle on the open book page and grabbed her candle lighter. She re-read the instructions to make sure she knew what to do.

Drawing in a deep breath, she lit the cigarettes. Sure enough, they caught the small flame from the lighter and began to burn. Ellie stared at the glowing embers and imagined what she wanted to see. Feeling foolish, she said in a whisper, "Pelletier kitchen table. One hour ago." Would that be specific enough?

She waited. The hair began to burn along with the cigarettes. It smelled weird. She tried to fan the smoke out of the window. She re-read the instructions and was reminded to maintain her focus, so she gazed at the ember, trying to imagine Tai and Julien sitting at the kitchen table.

She'd stared for so long that her eyes were beginning to cross when she noticed an image in the hazy smoke. It rose slowly from the burning bundle. She blinked. Was she imagining it, or was a grey face staring at her?

She squinted her eyes. Yes, she could see an image. Tai and Julien were sitting in the kitchen, and Ellie was looking down on them. The more closely she looked, the more she saw. She could see the top of Tai's head and straight down her low-cut shirt. *Classy.*

Just when she wished she could see better, the scene started to grow. It was like being picked up out of her office and dropped into her kitchen. The smoky grey images slowly filled with color and solidified. She could see and hear everything they were saying, and it wasn't making her feel any better.

Julien had his arm around Tai and was consoling her as she cried.

Ellie rushed over to the table in a fit of anger. How dare he? She grabbed at him, but her hands passed through him, or rather he passed through her hands. It was as if she were made of air. The shock that she wasn't in the room with them brought her anger to a pause.

She looked at her arms, and they, too, were smoky, insubstantial appendages. They swirled as she tucked them back down by her side and stood back to listen. Tai and Julien were all too real; it was she, Ellie, who was made of fog, incapable of affecting the scene playing out before her.

Tai's sobs grew louder and louder. She looked up with her tear-streaked face and demanded, "Why won't you leave her? She is *nothing* to you. I am the one you want. I make you tremble with desire. I know you still want me. I see it in your eyes. I can warm you in ways that cold-hearted, skinny prude never could."

Julien interrupted. "Do not talk like that in this house! I would never leave my wife for a silly teen. What were you hoping to accomplish with your disappearing stunt? Did you think you could manipulate me?"

"Yeah," Tai choked out a sound that was half-laugh and half-sob. "I did. I still do." She stared at him. "I wonder what Ellie would think if I waited until she got home and told her exactly what we've been up to?"

Julien took a step forward and gave her a long, hard look.

Tai stifled another sob and changed tactics. "I know you love me, Jules. I know it. I remember how it was – you, sweating like a stallion – how can you have forgotten the passion that we shared?"

"You are mistaken. You are no more to me than an office assistant." He looked away from her. "We never touched."

"Oh, but we did. We touched in every way possible. And I have proof. Leave her and come with me, or I will tell the whole damn town."

"Proof? You are deluding yourself."

"Like hell, I am. I came over today to tell you something. Something important." She groaned and slammed her hand onto the table simultaneously. "You must stop living a lie with that ice queen of yours! You must choose between us. You have to choose me; I know you'll want me, especially now because . . . I'm pregnant."

Ellie's chest felt an immediate heaviness, as if her heart had solidified. It was no longer made of blood and muscle. It was stone-cold and heavy. She felt a physical pain, like someone chinking away at that stone heart with a pick axe. She doubled over, and her cloudy edges blurred and swirled in the air around her.

She tried to take in oxygen; she couldn't breathe. It was like being underwater in the dunking pool, but heavier, icier. It wasn't just her heart that had turned to stone. A heavy coldness swept through her. She'd kill him. The idiot! She wafted over to him and slapped him as hard as she could across the face.

Her palm met with no resistance. Her hand whiffled through the air without even creating a stir. She was watching images that were memories, not physical beings with whom she could interact. God, she'd kill them both!

Julien was unfazed by Tai's dramatic announcement. "Is that true, *ma belle*? Is that why you are so emotional and irrational?"

"Yes – it is true. And the baby and I need you. Come with

us! Leave Ellie here with the girls. They don't need you like we do."

Julien gazed at her silently for a moment then spoke, "How do I know the baby is even mine?" He finally asked. Tai gasped.

"You piece of-." She inhaled sharply. "Of course, the baby is yours! Whose else would it be?" She stopped crying. "What do you think? That *you* don't have to pay for *your* sins, but I do?" She pointed at her belly. "This," she pointed back at him, "is just as much *your* problem as it is mine."

"It doesn't have to be." Julien reached into his pocket and pulled out his wallet. "Take this," he shoved a wad of cash at her, "and fix the problem before it grows too *big* for us to handle."

As Tai stared, open-mouthed, Julien changed course. "Besides, would a fetus really survive the damage you've put it through? The drinking, the smoking, the pills?" He continued. "Would it be fair to bring a baby into the world knowing it would suffer for your poor choices? You don't want to live with that guilt." He didn't miss a trick. "Take the money and end it. Drive to another town. You've been gone for six weeks. Another one won't matter."

He still had the cash in his outstretched hand when there was a crunching noise. His head turned towards the front door where Sadie and Dedé were scratching to go out and greet Ellie's car – the one from an hour ago when she had returned from work. Tai snatched the cash from Julien's hand and started toward the front door.

# CHAPTER FORTY-SEVEN

## SHADOW SHOWDOWN

The images started losing their color and their substance, fading back into tones of charcoal grey. The grey wisps of smoke curled up and floated out the open window. The anthology still lay open on her desk, a tiny pile of ashes on the page. The page itself was undamaged. She held the book over the sash and blew the ashes out of the window. She wiped over the place where the ashes had been, and only a small smudge remained.

She had no doubt that what she'd seen was real. She could feel it down to her bones. It was exactly how Julien would behave if confronted with something he didn't like.

Ellie moved in a trance. She was thinking so deeply about the scene she'd watched that she didn't realize she was walking downstairs. Until she reached Julien's office. She didn't even know she was still holding the anthology. Until she launched it straight at the back of Julien's head.

It hit him with a *thunk*. "*Aïe!*" He grunted and turned to see where the projectile had come from. "*Mon Dieu*, Ellie! Did you just thr---" He stopped mid-sentence as he picked up the book. The red and white cover had come partially undone on impact. The hand that had been rubbing his sore head reached down and pulled off the rest of it.

When he finished removing the faux cover, he looked at

Ellie as if seeing her for the first time. His eyes glowed with an intensity that made them appear golden-yellow instead of their usual soft brown. Ellie thought she saw his irises flicker - like a flame.

She shook her head. Something was happening. She felt her hair stand on end as her senses went on full alert.

"Well, well, well. *Mais*, what have we here? Could it be?" He walked toward her with the book resting open in one hand while the other hand stroked his chin. "Could my silly little wife have found the object of my desires without my knowledge?" He paced as he spoke.

Ellie was confused. Why was Julien talking about *her* book like he had known about it all along? And since when did he start calling her silly?

"Ho, ho," he continued. "*Ma petite* is not as foolish as I once thought. Oh, the irony." He pulled the book to his nose and inhaled deeply. "I have searched for this for so very long. And *you* found it for me." He stopped pacing and stood directly in front of her. "I guess all these years have not been wasted, then." He turned his back to her and gave the anthology his full attention.

Ellie swallowed. Her throat was dry. Her brain had filled with cobwebs. She put a hand to her forehead.

Julien gave a brief wave without glancing back at her, as if brushing away an insect, and Ellie felt an invisible force push her hand back down. She felt an unseen cord wrap tightly around her arms, pinning them to her side. It snaked around her legs and held her frozen in place. She grunted in shock, and Julien turned to watch her.

"Oh - don't look so confused, *ma chère*. I can explain everything, and I will – even though you won't remember it." He approached her, his eyes scanning her from the feet up. He circled her once and then continued.

"I suppose I owe you an explanation after all these years," he paused and touched her hair. "Manipulating you," he said as his hand slid down from her hair to her cheek. "Seducing you," his hand caressed her face, her neck, and traced her collar bone. She thought he was going to grope her, but his hand curled into a fist with one finger pointing at her chest.

"Prodding, prying, planning," he punctuated each word with a stab of his finger. He said it all without taking his eyes off her. She wanted to flinch, but she couldn't. She squinted her eyes instead.

Julien's finger lifted off her chest and made its way to the book's cover. He studied the book. It had his undivided attention. He held it gently, reverently. He ran his palm across the cover. He raised it to his nose and sniffed it again. He closed his eyes, "Ah, the smell of ancient leather." He was talking to her, but his eyes were on the book.

"Did you know, *ma vie*, that this book is one of the *very* rare examples of anthropodermic bibliopegy? No, you don't even know what that means. And to think, you're an English teacher." His voice dripped with contempt.

"Well, let me explain. This book's author requested its pages bound together in her *skin*," he savored the word, "after her death." He paused to let that information penetrate her mental fog. Ellie felt a shiver rush down her spine. The hairs on her arms stood up, and goosebumps formed in anticipation. She dreaded what he was going to say next.

"After that original binding, each -- what word can I use? *Owner* is incorrect -- each *disciple* of the book has given a piece of skin to add to the cover. Or, rather, the book has *taken* it. A small price to pay for access to its power"

"You don't believe me?" He snatched her left arm and jerked her wrist in front of her face. "Well, look at this." He opened his mouth wide and breathed hot air over her wrist. The thin mark around her wrist that she'd largely ignored began to pulse with a cool, silver light. Her eyes grew wide as a small sliver on the cover of the book shone simultaneously, a piece that was shaped and colored exactly like the glowing band encircling her wrist. As it shone, she could feel the mark calling out for the book, or was the book calling out to the glowing scar? She didn't know, but she felt an attraction so strong that she thought she saw a thin ribbon of light linking her wrist to the anthology. She blinked.

It looked like the strand of a silver spider web floating in the air, thin and delicate. It moved, pulsing slowly, as if it were a living, corporeal extension of Ellie's body. It was frightening yet fascinating. As the silver strand tugged at her, Ellie wanted nothing more than to reach out and take the book, but her invisible bonds remained steadfast.

Julien stared at the book's cover and continued talking, delivering his speech as if it had been memorized over time. "I knew I was right. I knew the moment I set eyes on you in *Le Chemise*. I knew when Madame Margaux approached you, revealing your identity with her prophecy. Oh, yes -- I knew even then that you would be worth the trouble, and I was correct."

He hugged the book to himself and then pulled it away to examine it. He caressed it like a furry pet, stroking the cover adoringly. He continued talking, more to himself than to Ellie, as Ellie stood locked in place with no choice but to listen.

"Oh, yes. I have played my part well. You had no idea that your beloved Caribbean Crush was stalking you from the start." He glanced up at Ellie to check her reaction. She didn't disappoint; her eyes widened, her left eyebrow shot up to her hair line, and her lips mouthed one word – *what*.

Julien chuckled. "Now you are beginning to see. Our chance meeting at *Le Chemise* was no *chance* at all. It was a precision move based on years of research and study. It was coldly calculated based on your heritage, your *ancestry* to be more precise." Ellie continued to watch him, and he continued to caress the book as he talked.

"My family has looked for this book for centuries. It was harder in the past, but with the invention of the Internet, things grew easier. I knew it was a matter of time before the book revealed itself, although I confess, I thought it would reveal itself to me -- not to my gullible little *poupée*. The book always has its reasons, though, and who am I to question them? I had the foresight to attach myself to you, so in the end it doesn't matter that the book chose you.

"But I digress. Back to your ancestral line. It ties you to the pivotal moment in history when the book was lost to us. It ties you to your ancestor -- Elizabeth Proctor." He looked up at Ellie. "While your family connection has been nothing more than an amusement for you, it has been *everything* to me." His words began to pour out a little more quickly. His voice took on a hint of urgency.

"Do you remember that my grandmother was from Barbados? I am from there, too. I moved to St. Martin when I arranged your scholarship. It was so easy to lure you to the island. Did you never investigate who sponsored you? No? Well, let me fill you in. It was me.

"I found you through the Internet. You should be more careful with your online identity, *ma vie*. I found out more about you than you can imagine. Your love for French, your lineage, and your family's interesting connection to Salem. I funded your scholarship. I took a job at *Le Chemise*. I knew most of the university kids went there to blow off steam, and I thought you'd come along sooner or later.

"You were my merchandise, carefully packaged, purchased, and delivered. My patience was rewarded when you waltzed into the bar looking for a drink. Oh, how simple it was to attract your attention! You were ripe for the plucking.

"But *quelle déception*! What a disappointment to find that you knew next to nothing about your famous ancestor or the book when we married and moved back to your hometown of Boston. Anyone else living so close to the place where it happened would have connected the dots, would have wanted to know more about Elizabeth's offspring after she left Salem Village. Why your family never followed the trail -- alas, we'll never know.

"Instead, it was left to me to trace Elizabeth's path. I was the one to follow her second marriage to Daniel Richards. I was the one to discover that her son by Proctor married and moved to Stusa." He paused to take out a cigarette from his desk drawer, momentarily turning his back on Ellie.

Ellie itched to get free of her bindings. She couldn't focus on his words; she was too busy looking at him, seeing him evolve right in front of her. He'd become another person, a stranger.

It wasn't just his demeanor. His voice was different; it dripped with more than just his typical snide sarcasm. It was filled with disgust and hatred. He was no longer the indifferent French islander she had fallen in love with. His intonation had changed, and his voice had dropped about an octave.

He even looked different. His skin was darker. Instead of their usual caramel brown, his eyes were golden yellow, flickering with greed and longing. He looked at her with disdain. She was nothing more than a fleck of dirt to be swept out with the trash, or more like an insect that needed to be crushed underfoot.

"You can stop wriggling." He said with his back still towards her. He lit the cigarette and turned back to face her. "The spell that binds you cannot be broken by anyone but me. As long as I want you to remain bound, you will remain thus." He blew a perfect smoke ring over to her. "And I must confess, I have always loved a captive audience."

"You see, just as you have a connection to Elizabeth Proctor, I am linked to Tituba." He paused to chuckle at the look on Ellie's face. Ellie hated to give him the satisfaction, but his words were digging deep inside her, dredging up confusing emotions amidst her shock.

Julien continued his tale. "When Tituba was caught preparing love potions for the girls from Salem Village, she had to hide her book, *this* book. Historians tend to overlook that little nugget. They always study Salem's hysteria and persecution of villagers without understanding that the cause of it all was quite literally -- a witch." He chuckled.

"Unfortunately for Tituba, the conniving Abigail Williams found the book and wanted it for herself. Abigail, in fact, first accused Tituba of witchcraft to get her out of the way. Abigail believed that the book would then belong to her alone. Tituba would not dare risk being caught with the very book that would prove the town's accusations against her and so many others to be true.

"Reverend Parris had no idea what he brought into his home when he fetched Tituba from Barbados. His clever little niece figured it out well enough, though. She masterminded a massacre of innocents just to get her greedy hands on Tituba's book. That alone should give you a hint as to what the book is worth. Compared to Abigail, I have shown considerable restraint." He approached Ellie. "One memory lost compared to twelve lives sacrificed, a fair improvement I should think." He paused to take another drag from his cigarette. He blew the smoke right into Ellie's face.

"*Mon Dieu*, how I have longed to do that. You and your obsession with healthy living. Breathe this." He blew anther puff into her face. Ellie's eyes watered, but she kept herself from coughing. Somehow, it felt like a small victory considering her position.

"Oh! Where are my manners? Would you care to have a smoke, too? It could be your first as well as your last. At least you'd find out what you've been missing, not that you'll remember it. *Non? Mais oui, il faut vivre.* Live a little." He paused.

When she declined to answer, Julien sighed. "Well, I'll just have to smoke yours, too." He added a second cigarette to his mouth and sucked hungrily on them both. "Ahhhhh... bliss."

While he stood there enjoying his cigarettes, Ellie worked up the energy to talk. Although she still felt cotton-mouthed and befuddled, she managed to say, "Would you really leave the girls as orphans?"

"I'm not going to kill you, *ma vie*. Don't be so dramatic. I'm not a complete *salaud*." He spoke as the two cigarettes dangled from his lips. "I am going to remove these memories, however. I can't have you chasing after the book, too. There is already enough competition out there." He removed the cigarettes. "Oh, the *jalousies* that will be aroused when they find out that I have won." He chuckled. It came out like a snarl.

Ellie did not recognize the creature before her. Had she really loved this man, this monster? Had she borne his children? What was he, a warlock, a sorcerer? "Who are you?" Ellie asked in wonder.

"*Ma chère*, have you not figured it out? You poor, naïve little *poupée*. You see, I am the direct descendant of Tituba, the Barbados slave who brought the book with her to Salem so many years ago. She is, in fact, my maternal ascendant in the forty-second degree." He looked at Ellie to check her reaction.

"Oh, yes, I can trace my lineage directly back to her, her time in Salem, and beyond. I am the rightful heir to the book. It would have been in my family's possession many years ago if that cunning little fox, Abigail Williams, had not intervened. But now I am avenged. I have the book. It resides with its rightful disciple." He sighed in contentment.

Just then a clatter sounded from the front door. Someone came clomping through the house. Ellie struggled again against her invisible bonds hoping that Julien was distracted enough to let his guard down, but she only managed to wriggle her shoulders.

Julien cocked his head, listening for a moment. He didn't look even mildly concerned - merely curious. Without looking up at Ellie, Julien gave another wave of his hand, and Ellie froze mid-wriggle. One shoulder was still twisted forward while the other was stretched back. It was terribly uncomfortable, but she couldn't move to straighten herself out. She was unable to move from the neck down.

She could still move her mouth, though. Julien must have wanted her to talk to him to continue feeding his ego with her incredulity and questions. Why else would he have left her able to speak?

If words were her only defense, what she could say to convince Julien to release her? Julien sat on the edge of his desk, apparently absorbed in his double smokes, and took another long drag from the cigarettes as he waited.

Much clomping and heel-clicking preceded the door-slamming intruder. When the intruder entered the office, Ellie could only see the figure from behind. She'd expected Tai to come back for one more shot at Julien, but she never guessed that she was be at such a disadvantage – tied up like a pet dog, unable even to wipe away the tears of anger that were beginning to fall.

Restrained as she was, Ellie had nothing to do but think. And the only thinking she could do was to replay the scene she had just witnessed. Julien had betrayed her by sleeping with Tai. A seventeen-year-old! And Tai was pregnant with Julien's child. A mental image of Julien and Tai having sex stabbed her, and her tears began to flow more freely.

Her tears were hot and contained all her mixed-up emotions; they were tears of shock, tears of disbelief, tears of outrage, tears of fury. They burned her skin as they ran down her face and dripped to the floor. Their heat was so intense that Ellie watched for them to hiss and steam as they hit the hardwood planks.

The intruder had already stomped past Ellie and faced Julien. All Ellie could see was her back. That absolute whore! Ellie thought. What she would give to break free of her bonds and scratch out those big, green, simpering eyes.

Rage engulfed Ellie; it swallowed her whole. Her body burned with a fury she hadn't known she was capable of feeling; it was a physical shot to her heart, one that liquefied the stone in her chest and spread into her arms, neck, and head like lava. If only she could erupt and spew molten rocks at them both. She tried again to move forward to attack Tai.

She managed to take a step forward. Her fury fueled her on. Another step. Then another. She was sweating from the exertion. Her focus was so intense that she didn't notice the intruder until the figure turned around to face her.

"Just what do you think you're doing?" A familiar female voice asked. Ellie was confused. Where were the innocent eyes, the blonde hair, the slutty clothes? In their place, Ellie saw long brown hair, intelligent, hard eyes, and a cloak. She was dumbfounded to see that the intruder was GG.

When she recovered enough to speak, Ellie spluttered, "GG, call the police! I'm...I'm... stuck." Ellie stuttered. "I can't move. Julien is a lunatic! Don't let him –"

A snarl interrupted Ellie's outburst. "Don't let him, what? *Hurt* you? Of course, not. I'll handle that myself." GG made a slashing movement with her left hand, and Ellie's throat felt like it had been sliced open. Her hands flew to her neck and she opened her mouth in a silent shriek. No sound came out. Her voice was gone, and she was immobilized once again – this time with her hands glued to her neck.

GG walked up to Julien and stared. "Where is it?" She hissed. "Where is my heirloom? My treasure?"

Julien appeared unfazed. He continued puffing on his cigarettes and studied his nails. Ellie watched in confusion.

GG continued, "Don't think you can hide it from me, warlock. My family has the greatest claim, and we have searched for *centuries*. It is calling to me, pulling me." She showed him the green-tinged brand on her left wrist. "I know it's here. Now give it to me!"

Was GG talking about Ellie's book? Why was everyone suddenly so interested in something they hadn't even known Ellie possessed. Where was all this interest when she first discovered the book? Unless that was it. They had been waiting for her to find it so they could take it from her.

Understanding finally pierced the mental fog Ellie was under. Julien had been searching all these years - not for Ellie, not for love - for the book. But what was GG doing here? Had she been part of the scheme all along? How could that be possible since GG wasn't even born when Ellie and Julien met?

Ellie wanted answers. Unfortunately, she couldn't ask

questions. The pain in her throat had subsided, but she still had no voice. And where was her anthology? How had it vanished without Ellie realizing it? Julien had been holding it just seconds ago.

Ellie's mind reeled. Her internal lava had enveloped her brain. Her thoughts burbled in the hot, red magma, completely beyond her control. She had so many questions, too much anger, and not a small amount of fear.

GG stepped closer to Julien. She snatched the cigarettes out of his mouth and threw them on the floor, crushing them under the ball of her foot. "You can smoke your cigarettes and examine your cuticles later, you vain peacock. Right now, you'd better hand over that book while you still have a *hand* left to do it."

Julien rolled his eyes and moved away from GG. He finally spoke. "You are a bit late to the party, little one. Your *petite amie* left less than a half hour ago."

That shocked Ellie. Had it only been thirty minutes? It felt like an eternity. Had it only taken thirty minutes to watch Julien pay Tai to abort a fetus? To be bound by invisible bonds? To find out that her husband was a warlock who'd stalked her since college? To find out that both a student and her husband were after her book?

Julien continued taunting GG. "If you give that old rattletrap you drive a good, hearty push, you might be able to catch up with her." Julien's cool demeanor didn't fool Ellie. She knew underneath his bravado that he was miffed. He hated being called vain.

She could tell by the way he fiddled with the contents of his pocket that he was planning something. Ellie's first impulse was to warn GG, but on second thought, she wasn't sure she wanted to help the student who had just silenced her with a flick of the wrist. Not that Ellie could have warned her anyway, mute as she was.

"Besides," Julien spoke up. "I don't have the item you want. I wouldn't be able to give it to you, regardless." He sighed. "The book didn't choose *me*; it chose *her*." He looked at Ellie.

GG whipped around to face Ellie. "No! Not you!" She growled. She raced over to Ellie and grabbed her left wrist and stared at the glowing, silver mark. "You disgusting, hopeful, romantic little twat!" She shoved Ellie's arm away from her. "I cannot believe that the book would choose someone so positively *Pollyanna*." She took a step closer to Ellie, looking her up and down.

"Although I have to admit that I underestimated you this year. You managed to escape each one of my attacks -- the dunking booth, the poison ivy, the fire at the studio."

Ellie's eyes grew wide again, the only response she could give. Those "accidents" had been intentional! She never would have suspected GG, though.

"Maybe there's more to you than I thought." GG interrupted Ellie's thoughts. She circled Ellie as she spoke. "How fitting that Tai, the one you doubted all along, was the one who finally managed to get you out of the school and practically under house arrest." GG laughed. "And to think, she didn't even know she was helping me. She only had eyes for pretty, prissy, preening, peacock over here." GG rounded on Julien.

"I can't believe *you* let Tai suck you in like you did." She spat the words at him. "We could have been a team, you know. Remember the day I offered you a chance to hire me? If only you'd taken me up on my offer. Then we wouldn't be here with all this," she tilted her head toward Ellie, "collateral damage." She resumed her pacing. Julien sat on the edge of his desk, watching.

"What a mess you've made, Julien. Let's see, there's Ellie," she held up her fingers as she counted, "Méline, Bibianne, Tai and her baby. That makes one mistake for each *finger* of your right *hand*."

Before GG finished her statement, she made another slicing motion in the air in front of Julien, and he let out a scream. He grabbed his bloody stump of a wrist and cradled it to him as he groaned in pain.

GG talked over his cries of agony. "You can't say I didn't warn you," she sang. "Now *hand* over that book! Oh –pardon the pun." She cackled at her own joke.

Julien's face hardened. A beaded line of sweat covered his upper lip, and he managed to contain his groans. As Ellie watched, he used his left hand to make an intricate swirling motion around the bloody stump. A golden light the color of Julien's eyes burst forth from his left hand and traveled over the cut wrist, searing the skin back together. Ellie watched in horrified fascination as the skin began to grow. The flesh looked thin and pink, but it continued to expand until another tiny hand erupted from the end of the stump.

It appalled Ellie, but she stared despite herself. She couldn't look away. *Julien was re-growing his own hand.* Who was he? What had she been living with these past ten years? If he had this kind of supernatural power, why hadn't he just used it all along to get what he wanted throughout their marriage?

*Oh, my God. That is* exactly *what he did.*

Images of their courtship and marriage flooded her mind, and Ellie noticed a pattern. She'd made things easy for Julien. Hadn't she agreed to every one of his whims and relocations? Julien was the one who insisted on leaving the beautiful French island to return to her native Boston. Julien was the one who dragged her to Salem for every festival. Julien was the one who was fascinated with her lineage. Julien was the one who suggested the move to Stusa. Sure, Ellie had agreed and had been caught up in the idea of a rural childhood for the girls, but hadn't it been his idea in the first place?

A zinging streak of light whizzed just over the tip of Ellie's left ear, singeing the delicate skin and interrupting her thoughts. She felt the urgent need to move out of danger's way. She twisted against her invisible restraints and found that she could adjust her shoulders. Maybe the spell holding her in place would weaken since Julien and GG were concentrating on each other. They seemed to be aiming streams of light at each other.

She focused on her feet, realizing that she'd need them the most if she was planning on moving. As she tussled with her invisible restraints, she saw GG and Julien thrusting bolts of light at each other. As each one landed, it scorched whatever it hit. Based on their cries of rage and the scorch marks that burned and sizzled, the parries strengthened in proportion to their masters' anger.

Julien and GG growled and hissed at each other in between blows. At one point, GG's green light singed Julien's shoulder. He returned the blow with his own golden light and struck GG's ankle.

GG stumbled but didn't fall. She threw out an answering bolt as she ducked to grab her ankle. Her green streak connected with Julien's golden one, and the two lights sizzled and crackled -- each one trying to overcome the other.

Luckily for Ellie, as the attacks strengthened, her bonds weakened. Before long, she was able to lower her hands from her neck and take one small step towards the door, and then another, and another. She edged closer and closer to the door. When she could almost reach the door handle, however, she felt a tug at her back.

Something pulled her from behind. A cord had been attached behind her navel and was tugging her backwards. It was dragging her back into the room to prevent her leaving. The sensation was so real that she looked around to see if Julien or GG had lassoed her.

Instead of a rope, however, a thin, silver, glowing thread reached out from her lower back. When she turned to face the room again, the silver thread moved around with her so that the tiny line went from her belly button to a place on Julien's bookshelf.

Ellie glanced at GG and Julien. They were so busy firing spells at each other that they'd forgotten her. She inched her way over to the bookshelf, following the silver thread, trying not to call attention to herself.

The silver thread ended at a book on the left edge of the bookcase. It was a large, solid volume. It didn't look like her anthology, but the thread led straight to it. Had Julien bewitched the anthology to look like another ordinary book? Ellie reached over to pull it off the shelf.

The book was wedged in tightly. She pulled harder and heard a click. The entire section of shelving swung back revealing a small, windowless room. A *safe room*, the words formed in her mind even though she'd never seen one other than in movies. When had Julien built this? What was it even for? Why had he never- *there it was!*

The anthology lay on top of a rectangular, podium-shaped structure made of stone. There was a silver knife lying on top of the open book and a set of three black taper candles. They burned with black flames. An image of the candles the twins had in church on New Year's Eve came to mind. *Strange*, thought Ellie.

She rushed to the altar -- it could be nothing else -- but stopped before picking up the anthology. It was open. Words glowed on the page. When she squinted her eyes, she could see another, thinner, golden line that went from the anthology to Julien. If her line was a piece of yarn, Julien's was fishing line. His golden line wasn't solid. It sputtered like static on a television.

A third line, in emerald green was growing out of the book. It was a vine, trying to make its way to GG. It hadn't reached GG yet; it swayed, searching for her as it stretched its way out of the safe room.

Ellie shuddered to think of those lines becoming as solid a connection to the anthology as hers. She didn't know what would happen, but she had a feeling it would be terrible. She didn't understand why her cord had the best connection to the anthology, but she suspected it had to do with the fact that she had been the one to unearth it after all these years. Had it really been hidden away since the Salem Witch Trials?

Suddenly, Ellie knew what had to be done. Neither GG nor Julien could be allowed to possess the anthology. After what she'd seen them do, she knew that if it increased their power in any way, they'd be unstoppable. She reached out to take the book from the stone alter when an arm shot out from behind. It crooked around her neck in a wrestler's hold.

"Well, well, well. What have we here?" GG's sarcastic voice crackled. "Tsk, tsk, tsk," she clicked her tongue, scolding. "What have you been hiding from your wife, Jules? A safe room? It looks more like a *kill room*, don't you think, Ellie?"

GG frog-marched Ellie around behind the altar so that they both faced the open doorway and could see into Julien's office. "Look around, Elles. Look at all this crazy town." GG tightened her hold on Ellie's neck. She grabbed Ellie's head with her free hand and forced Ellie to face each wall in turn.

Symbols and shapes covered the walls. The writing was black and smudged, like it had been written in charcoal. Ellie's name appeared several times, and each time there was a giant brownish-red X covering it. Ellie paled in sudden understanding of what the knife had been used for.

"That can't be good, can it Elles? Looks like dear old hubby was going to get rid of you all along."

Julien was standing in the doorway watching both women. His eyes flickered back and forth from the book to GG and Ellie. He made a sudden move towards them, and GG reacted instantly. The hand that had been controlling Ellie's head reached out for the knife. Before Ellie had time to blink, the knife was at her throat, blade pressing against her skin. Ellie let out a little involuntary whimper.

"So, your voice is back, too, along with your ability to move. Huh. How'd you manage that?" GG asked. "I feel my connection to the book getting stronger. How are you able to interrupt my link?" GG laughed. "It doesn't really matter, though. I don't need *magic* to work this knife." She pressed the blade a little harder into Ellie's neck.

As soon as the blade pressed into her neck, one of the

black flames went out. GG released the pressure on the knife blade just a bit, then pressed it back into Ellie's neck making a small cut. A second black flame extinguished itself.

GG laughed in victory. "This is too easy." She laughed again in delight. "I can take the book from both of you at the same time! Ha!" She pressed the knife a little deeper and the third candle went out. Ellie could see Julien's golden line, though. It hadn't disappeared. He still had some link to the book.

Julien had been watching them from the doorway. His hands were raised as if to throw another bolt at GG, but he seemed hesitant, unsure about what would happen if he attacked GG. He finally spoke up.

"Not quite that easy, little one," he spoke to GG as if she were a child. "Yes, the book must be *taken* from each disciple, but you cannot get rid of us so easily. With a flick of his wrist, he relit all three candles. The pain in Ellie's neck vanished.

The knife clattered to the floor. GG threw a green bolt at Julien, but he ducked, and it ravaged the doorframe instead. As soon as GG's grip on Ellie loosened, Ellie reached over and grabbed the anthology. Julien and GG were battling again, and sparks were flying.

Ellie ducked down behind the stone altar to avoid getting hit. She clutched the anthology to her chest while her heart pounded in time with the blows. She knew what had to be done. She must do it quickly before Julien and GG realized what was happening.

Ellie peeked over the rim of the altar and grabbed one of the candles. Still stooped over, she held the candle to the pages. The book didn't blaze up in flames as she'd imagined, but the edges did turn black and curl a little.

Julien and GG froze mid-action and turned to look at Ellie. They gasped in unison.

"*Non*," shouted Julien, "you mustn't!"

"How dare you!" GG shrieked.

Ellie had their full attention now. They both pointed

at her, and she shoved the anthology into the two remaining flames burning on the altar. Now the book had three flames smoldering its pages. GG and Julien froze again, afraid that Ellie would damage the book.

"Both of you -- stop right now, or I swear I'll destroy this evil thing!" Ellie could see their golden and green lines still reaching out for the anthology, trying to connect to it. GG and Julien looked at each other and made some unspoken agreement. Both of their lines hovered in place and stopped growing.

"Back slowly into the office and sit down!" Ellie barked out the orders. They complied. She followed with the book in one hand and a single black candle in the other.

*Who has the power now?* She thought with a smirk. It would be so simple to keep the anthology all to herself. Her silver gossamer thread was now a shining cord, thick like a rope, and it pulsed with power as it traveled from Ellie and wrapped around the book three times.

"I have questions, and I want answers!" The anthology prompted her. "I know why Julien wants the book, but what about you?" She looked at GG. "What is your connection to this book, GG?" When GG didn't respond, Ellie felt a surge of anger course through her, and her silver rope grew an extra tentacle that lashed out at GG and struck her like a whip across the face.

GG sucked in a breath and looked at Ellie in surprise. *God, that felt good*, Ellie thought. A sense of satisfaction like none she'd ever felt wormed its way right down to her belly. How easy it was to lash out and take what she wanted. The silver rope intuited what Ellie wanted. It recoiled and poised itself, ready to strike.

A needle of panic pricked Ellie, stinging her back to her senses. *What am I doing?* Horror replaced the satisfaction she'd felt milliseconds earlier. She willed the silver cord to stop. It wanted to lash out again, but Ellie restrained, teeth clenched. "Explain yourself. Now!"

Neither GG nor Julien perceived Ellie's inner struggle. Julien watched Ellie with furrowed brow while GG's scowl of pain dissolved into resignation. She began to talk.

"Haven't you figured it out yet?" GG sneered. "You've had all year with *The Crucible*, and I've sent plenty of hints." Even in pain, GG still managed to condescend and provoke. Ellie tried not to react. She narrowed her eyes and waited for GG to continue.

"The letter I wrote from Abigail Williams' point of view? History may not know what happened to her after she left Salem, but my *family* does."

GG's smirk sent another wave of heat crashing over Ellie. She had a burning need to understand GG's connection to the anthology, and before she could think twice about it, her silver rope shot out again. It wrapped itself around GG's head three times and then slithered into her left ear. GG emitted a moan and twisted in her chair, but she was unable to escape the silver rope.

As the cord snaked its way into GG's head, Ellie saw snapshots: GG taking Ellie's cash from under her mattress, GG hitchhiking, GG setting fire to a cabin, GG as a young girl, GG with her grandmother. The memories raced through Ellie's mind like someone flipping through a photograph album. Then they stopped. A film began to play in Ellie's mind.

*A small girl kneeled in front of an elderly woman who spoke in quiet tones. "Abigale, you are the one who must find the heirloom. Your mother is not strong enough to wield its power. You are the one."*

*"You must remember this. I have seen the heirloom's future, and you will be the one who succeeds after all our family's many, many years of searching. Your mother was right to name you Abigale. Our ancestor would be proud."*

*"She started our family on this long journey. Her time in Salem led to a taste of great power. Never forget her. She will lead you to her treasure, our heirloom – and its power will become yours to brandish as you see fit."*

Ellie's thoughts interrupted the film. Abigale? GG's name was Abigale? Gale Guillaume. Of course! Gale was short for Abigale, and Guillaume was French for William. GG had changed her surname to misdirect anyone trying to poke around in her past. But could she be a descendent of *the* Abigail Williams?

Ellie tried to remember what she had read about the real Abigail Williams. Hadn't Abigail disappeared during the trials? Rumors circulated that she had moved-

*Beah, and the story of The Jewel. Could Beah have been Abigail Williams? What was it Zyla said? She had moved here with her uncle and cousin. Her uncle would've been Reverend Parris, and her cousin - Betty Parris.*

A jolt of understanding made Ellie's stomach clench. The film resumed as if she had released the pause button.

*"But how will I know, Gabby? Where can I look that mother has not already looked?"* Gabby straightened her shoulders and leaned into the back of her chair.

*"The heirloom will pull you in the right direction, child. Trust your instincts; follow them. Our family serves the only truly powerful force in this world. The One who runs free, creating havoc and tempting others to join. Our connection to His book is strong. There will come a time, however, when you must leave your mother and me behind."*

*"There are other families searching for our heirloom, child. You must take your rightful place as its disciple. Ours is still the strongest attachment. Abigail Williams, your many-times-removed maternal grandmother, was the last one to take the heirloom from Mistress Tituba. Now you must take the heirloom from its current owner. Remember, for its power to be strongest, the heirloom must be taken – not given."*

The images whirled and dissolved. Ellie watched her silver rope release GG and proceed to Julien. He gasped in pain as it wound its way into his head.

This time, the film was glitchy, as if it were missing bits, or as if it had been pieced together by an inept film editor. The

Amberley Faith

scene was blurry around the edges and had distorted audio.

*A girl in her early teens was staring out of an upstairs window. She wore a black dress and a white wimple that covered her hair. Her eyes were wide as she watched what happened below.*

*A crisp pop sounded, like the crack of linens being snapped into submission, but the sound was sharper. Ellie heard a woman cry out in pain. She looked around to find the source of the cry and saw a whip snap in her direction. Ellie lifted her arms to shield her face and saw her dark, chocolate-brown skin.*

*A man holding a Bible was standing to one side, brow wrinkled in consternation, praying aloud, while the man cracking the whip shouted at her. "Confess! Confess that you have consorted with the devil!"*

*Snap! The whip struck her back, and even though Ellie couldn't feel the pain of the blow, she could feel the fear of the slave whose memory she inhabited.*

*"Confess that you have put my dear Betty under a spell! Release her from your evil charms and this whip will stop its bite! Confess it now, Tituba, and we will deal leniently with you!"*

*The man's red face twisted in fury. Ellie could feel the confusion inside the slave's mind. Tituba wanted to confess to make the pain go away, but a confession would mean hanging. Surely death would be better than this agony.*

*A movement from the upper window caught her attention. Tituba glanced up at the young girl. The girl held something to the window for the slave to see. It was square in shape and looked about the same size as the reverend's Bible. It was a book.*

Ellie felt the anthology grow warm in her hands. This very book was the same one the girl had shown Tituba. Ellie's silver rope released Julien from its grasp. It slithered back to Ellie and wrapped itself three times around the cover of the book. Another movie reel began to play.

*A thin, pale woman tiptoed into a closet-sized bedchamber. She looked over her shoulder. When no one approached, she continued over to the cot and pulled up the straw mattress. On top of the support ropes lay the anthology.*

316

*The woman's bony, pale hand reached out and took it, stow-ing it under her white apron and tying the sash tight to hold it in place. As the woman returned to the kitchen, the same young girl from the window came in through the front door.*

*"Back so soon this morning, Abigail? Your testimony must have bored the court." Ellie could feel the icy cold of the woman's tone.*

*"Aye, I have returned from court." Abigail responded haughtily. "But only to tell you that I can no longer serve the Proc-tor household. My presence is needed, and Judge Hawthorn requires me to attend daily. You can give my room to Mary. She'll be needed at court as well, but she will still be able to work nights and early mornings so you can ... rest. You'll be needing it, Elizabeth Proctor."*

*The girl left with a toss of her head, and Ellie felt Elizabeth gasp. Ellie saw Elizabeth's hand slip under the apron to take out the book. How long before Abigail realized it had vanished, Elizabeth wondered...*

Ellie's comprehension was immediate. Neither Abigail nor Tituba had been the last to possess the book. Elizabeth Proctor had taken it from right underneath Abigail's nose, and neither Abigail nor Tituba had ever found out.

As Elizabeth's descendant, Ellie had the strongest claim to it. But how did the anthology end up in Stusa? Elizabeth Proctor had remarried a man named Daniel Richards, and they had moved away from Salem after the awful trials-.

A flash of light interrupted her thoughts. Ellie saw from the corner of her eye that GG had managed to struggle free. Ellie's focus on the memory reel had weakened the silver cord's grip on GG.

Julien, too, had escaped his bonds. Both he and GG aimed shots at Ellie. She didn't have time to think. She reacted without hesitation. As the gold and green bolts surged to-wards her, Ellie brought the anthology up in front of her face to block them.

Time slowed to a crawl. Ellie's mind processed the scene in slow succession. Ellie felt a wave of heat rolling towards her. She saw jagged lines of light reaching out for her. GG screeched, "No!"

Ellie tasted metal. She smelled burnt paper, burnt hair, and something thicker, more pungent – like animal hide.

The anthology took the brunt of the blow. It crackled and groaned under attack from the bolts of electricity that penetrated its ancient cover. The sounds were loud, and they swelled until Ellie felt her eardrums might burst. Then, a vacuum sucked away all the sound and light. Everything went silent and dark.

The book grew hot in Ellie's grasp, so hot that she snatched her hand away. The anthology did not fall. It hovered, floating in midair. A mixture of gold and green light penetrated the darkness. It came from the book.

Like the sound that swelled before, the book itself began to grow. It expanded steadily, growing ever larger. It had been the size of a Bible. Then it was a suitcase, an ottoman, an armchair.

It grew to the size of a steamer trunk. Bumps and ripples appeared - pressing and undulating against the lid and sides from the inside. Something trapped inside pushed to get out.

The growing mass had reached the size of an armoire when Ellie finally came to her senses. She glanced at GG and Julien. They didn't look horrified; they both wore narrowed eyes and slight smiles, anticipating what would emerge.

Ellie didn't know if something really was trying to climb out of the shifting shape that used to be her anthology, but she didn't want to find out. She aimed her silver whip at the growing form and lashed out with all her strength. She *must* destroy the book. She knew with absolute certainty that she *must not* let the creature out.

*Smash!* Her whip hit its target with a crashing explosion of sound, light, and heat. Debris fell from all angles. She flew through the air that had become thick, viscous. It disoriented her; she didn't know which way was up or down.

She heard the agonized scream of a woman and the deep

bellow of a man in pain. She covered her ears. The explosion rushed toward her.

Time resumed its rapid pace. Shards of glass, pieces of wood, metal, and stone exploded. Jagged flashes of color pierced her vision; a streak of bright green headed toward the now transformed anthology. A golden-yellow bolt came straight for Ellie.

Just as she felt a wave of hot, stinging energy strike her, everything went black.

# CHAPTER FORTY-EIGHT

## *ELLIE'S AFTERMATH*

Ellie blinked her eyes twice, then again. She must be dreaming. It smelled like the hospital, of all places. Since she'd spent so much time there, she understood why the hospital would appear in her dreams. But if she was dreaming, how could she be aware that she was dreaming? So, was she awake or asleep? Ellie couldn't tell.

Foggy, clouded thoughts filled her mind. She blinked her eyes again. Yep, it was the hospital. There were the tubes and the IVs and the buttons and dials and – *ow!* She felt a stinging in her scalp and right forearm. They didn't just sting, they burned, too. It was painful.

"Unh!" She moaned and tried to turn over on her side.

A nurse came in. "Try to remain calm, Mrs. Pelletier. This will help in five, four, three, two..."

Another darkness. Another painful awakening. This time, Ellie heard voices, but that couldn't be right. She was underwater, struggling to make her way through a gel-like substance, fighting to breathe.

*"No. Patient... no condition... questioning. Notify... when stable."*

The next time Ellie opened her eyes, she was still in the hospital. The stinging and burning told her she wasn't dreaming. This time, however, there was someone in the room with her, calling her name.

"Mrs. Pelletier? Ellie?" A male voice asked. "Can you hear me?"

A female voice added in hushed tones, "Ellie? The nurse said you would be aware of your surroundings this time - enough to talk to us. Or for us to talk to you, rather. Can you hear me? This is important, sweetie."

Ellie knew that voice. She blinked her eyes and saw Zyla sitting by her bedside along with a uniformed cop. They both looked at her with concern as they hesitated, waiting for her to respond.

"Uhhn, thith can't be good." Ellie's tongue felt like a swollen log of dry wood. "A cop and a colleague."

"Detective, actually." The male voice responded.

"Do you know where you are, sugar?" Zyla asked.

Ellie nodded. "But why? What happened? Where are girlth? Why doth everything hurt?" She couldn't work up the energy to panic. She simply asked the questions that were running through her mind and waited.

Zyla looked at the detective. He nodded, so she started to explain. "You've been in an accident, Ellie. Tell me the last thing you remember, and I'll get you up to speed."

"I member...I remember..." She groped through her foggy memories. "Drug dogth alerted on painting in my clathroom...I wath... at home... arguing. Where ith he? Why ithn't he here?" Ellie's heart began to thud in her chest at that question, and her monitor corresponded with a series of fast beeps.

Zyla took Ellie's good hand in her own. "You *were* at home, Ellie. I don't know about arguing, but you and Julien were both at home. The girls were at music lessons with Zibby; they're staying with me until you are released from the hospital." Zyla gulped.

"What I must tell you is very painful, Ellie." Zyla looked at the detective. "Are you sure they think she is able to deal with this?" He nodded.

Ellie interrupted. "Juth tell me, Thyla."

Zyla swallowed hard again. "There was an explosion, Ellie. From what the cops can tell, it was caused by," she hesitated, "something in the garage."

"What?" Ellie snorted. "Houthes don't just exthplode."

The detective cleared his throat. "Houses with meth labs do." Ellie turned to look at him.

"Not funny. What are you talking about? I do NOT have a meth lab. And I need thome water!"

Zyla looked at the detective again, and he stepped closer. "We don't think it was you, Mrs. Pelletier. We think it was your husband. We've found certain evidence..."

Ellie turned from the detective to Zyla as Zyla offered her the flexible straw from a Styrofoam cup of water. Ellie took a sip and flopped back against her pillow. "Thith ith ridiculouth." The monitor at Ellie's side registered her rising heartbeat with a series of beeps.

Zyla squeezed her hand. "It gets worse, honey. Have another sip or two." Ellie did as instructed. Zyla gulped again.

"There is no easy way to say this. Julien is not here, Ellie, because he ...didn't make it. He didn't survive the explosion. It's a miracle you did."

The beeps grew faster and louder. Ellie's heart thudded. Something inside her chest felt like a swelling balloon. She thought it might burst. This had to be a nightmare. This could not be happening.

A nurse rushed in and administered another dose of meds into her IV bag. A second nurse, RayVynn, ushered Zyla and the detective out of the room, scolding them loudly. "We told you ... her health ... out!"

Ellie couldn't stop her heart from racing. It physically hurt as it pounded inside her chest. She couldn't breathe. She gasped for air. Just when she thought she couldn't take it any longer, she felt something like a shot of tequila. Her heartrate subsided almost instantly, and she drifted into another troubled sleep.

When Ellie next opened her eyes, she felt numb. Had it all been a dream? She looked over at the person next to her. Zyla was watching her intently with wrinkled brow. Ellie croaked, "Is it true, Zyla?" Her words were less garbled than before. "Is the father of my children really...dead?"

Zyla cringed at the word. "Yes, sweetheart. I'm so sorry! I thought you'd rather hear it from me than from the police." Zyla swallowed, then rushed to add, "I know it's too much to handle. The girls are staying with me, and they are doing as well as can be expected." Zyla paused.

Ellie was too numb to react. She simply asked, "Do they know, Zyla? Has anyone told them that their father is gone – forever?"

Zyla took a long, deep breath. "Yes, they do. They knew that you were in the hospital and asked why their dad couldn't keep them." Her voice broke. "They have been so brave, Ellie, bless them." Zyla wiped the tears from her cheeks. "They have prayed for you every morning and every evening since the accident. They drew some - "

"Every evening? How long have I been here?" Ellie interrupted in alarm.

"The explosion was Monday. Today is Wednesday, so two nights and two days."

"Oh my God!" Ellie tried to sit up. "My girls have been without their parents for two days! Oh, my poor babies!"

The tears wouldn't come. She was too devastated – too empty, too burnt to cry. She couldn't process the loss of her husband. It didn't seem real. Her girls needed her. How horrible to lose a parent so early!

"Bring them to me right away! I need to see them!" Ellie was frantic, and her pulse quickened. The machines started to beep again.

Zyla reacted quickly. "Ellie, take a deep breath. Try to

breathe. If you don't calm down, the nurses will kick me out, and you won't get to see your girls. Hurry! Breathe in deeply – now exhale. Again. You must regain control if you want to see Mel and Bibi. Focus on *them*."

That got Ellie's attention. She breathed in through her nose and out through her mouth. Zyla was right. She must get control of herself or the hospital wouldn't allow her daughters in, and she *had* to see her girls. They needed their mother, and truth be told, she needed them.

She managed to calm down and looked at Zyla. "Okay, you're right. I need to get myself together. The girls need me. I want to see them as soon as possible. Where are they?"

At this, Zyla managed to smile. "They're in the waiting room."

"Well, what are you waiting for? Bring them to me!"

Zyla gave Ellie's hand a little squeeze, and she got up to fetch the girls. In the meantime, Ellie told herself to be brave. She forced herself to take long, steady breaths. She didn't want to scare the girls any more than necessary. What must they be going through?

She prepared herself mentally. She rehearsed what to say. She pressed the button that raised her bed to a seated position. She looked at her hands; they were unmarked, but her wedding ring was gone. Had it been lost in the blast? She couldn't remember. A dry sob escaped her as she realized she'd lost both the ring and the man that bought it for her. She ran her fingers through her hair.

She gasped when her fingertips touched short, prickly fringe and bandages covering her forehead. She understood immediately; her hair had been singed in the explosion.

Tears still refused to come, and she wondered what she'd look like with a pixie cut. Maybe RayVynn could bring scissors before the girls arrived, but then she heard voices. A new haircut would have to wait.

"Now, girls – your mom doesn't look like herself. She has bandages on her head and arms, and there is a tube giving her the medicine she needs. She might look a little scary, but she is going to be right as rain in just a few weeks. Be gentle with her, okay?" She added in a conspiratorial whisper that Ellie could hear, "And don't say anything about her hair. It will grow back. But we don't want to make her feel worse."

Ellie tensed for the girls to come through the door way. When they did, she gave her best smile and reached out for them. They rushed straight to her and fell into her embrace.

The tears finally came. She hugged them tightly and offered up a silent prayer of thanks that they hadn't been home when the accident happened. They all three cried together for a moment, then Bibianne pulled back and kissed Ellie's hand. Both girls covered Ellie with gentle kisses.

"Thank God you're okay!" Ellie took one hand each and squeezed. "Those kisses are just what the doctor ordered. I feel better already!"

Bibianne pulled back and said, "But there is one terrible thing, *Maman*, that our kisses won't fix – do you know about papa? It is very, very sad." Bibianne looked down in chagrin.

Ellie pulled both girls back into her chest and said, "Yes, *mes belles*, I know about papa. You're right. It is very sad." She stroked their hair. "We will miss him for a very long time, but," she pulled away to look them in the eyes, "we will feel better one day. Until then, I will take care of you." Ellie paused to swallow and push down her tears. "I have enough love for all of us. You'll see."

This time, Méline was the one to ask. "Is it wrong to feel happy, *maman*? I am *très triste* about papa, but I'm so happy that you are still here. Is that bad?"

"Oh, my sweet girl! It isn't wrong; it's normal. I feel mixed up inside, too. I'm sad about papa, but more than anything I am mainly happy that you and your sister are okay. I think *papa* would agree. You have done nothing wrong."

They all cried a little longer as they hugged each other. Bibianne eventually climbed into bed with Ellie, and Méline sat on the edge with them. Ellie asked, "Tell me, what you have done with Aunt Zy? Tell me all that has happened to you while I've been here."

The girls launched into tales of bedtime games and ice cream for breakfast and caring for Sadie. "Was she hurt in the accident?" Ellie asked.

"Yes," Mel replied, "but Auntie Zy took her to the vet, and we learned how to care for her. She will be okay in a few weeks – just like you. I will take care of both of you, *maman*." She added, "I like being a nurse. It makes me feel good inside."

Zyla piped up at this comment. "Mel is a good little nurse, Elles. She changes Sadie's bandages and everything. You'll be so proud of her when you see." Zyla smiled at the girls, and Mel blushed at the compliment.

"But she is not Sadie's *nurse*." Bibianne interrupted. "She is Sadie's *doctor*." At that, Mel and Ellie laughed.

Zyla turned scarlet. "I didn't mean to... to...underestimate," she stuttered.

"Out of the mouth of babes," Ellie said with a weak smile.

After a few more minutes, the nurse came in and told them visiting hours were over and that Ellie needed her rest. She assured the girls they could see their mother the next day and that Ellie would be going home soon.

At those words, Ellie's gut clenched. What home was there for her to go to? She made a mental note to ask the detective as soon as he returned. She had a feeling it wouldn't be too long before she saw him again.

Ellie's intuition had been right. The next time she awoke, she found the detective at her side making notes. She opened one eye and looked over at him. "Ever heard of knocking first?"

He didn't even have the decency to look embarrassed, Ellie noticed. "RayVynn, said it was okay. She is very protective of you, you know. You motioned me in but dozed off while I was talking, so I waited." He cocked his head to one side. "You don't remember?"

Ellie opened the other eye and frowned, trying to remember if what he said was true. "I'm having trouble remembering things, actually." She gave a long sigh. "Maybe it's the medication, but I can't remember anything at all about the explosion, and I have lots of questions." She raised her bed to a seated position as she spoke.

"Perhaps we can help each other then, Mrs. Pelletier. I have some questions for you, too, Let's start at the beginning."

He waited for her assent. She nodded, so he started asking questions, typing into his iPad. "Were you aware of your husband's drug activity?" He asked.

"No," Ellie sputtered, "and I he was not involved in something like that. What *evidence* did you find?" Ellie asked.

The detective shifted in his chair. "Are you sure you're ready to hear this?" He asked.

"No," Ellie sighed. "But I need you to tell me anyway." She laid her head back against the pillow.

Detective Stephens looked from one eye to the other. "The explosion decimated more than half of your home, Mrs. Pelletier. Although there wasn't anything salvageable, we did find you – wedged under an overturned sofa – and," he paused and set his iPad aside.

"I need to warn you, Mrs. Pelletier, that this is rather gruesome. The fire burned at an exceedingly high temperature. The only discernible remains of your husband was," he winced, "his right hand." The detective looked at his hands.

Alarm bells sounded in Ellie's mind, and the detective's words faded to the distance. *His hand, his hand.* Something about that seemed familiar -- like a piece of a dream remembered. God, was she losing her mind? The detective's words seemed far away.

"-- pattern of the explosion is consistent with that of a meth lab, as well as the high burn temperature. We calculate that, to have been entirely consumed by the fire, your husband must have been at its epicenter. Somehow the blast pushed you out before the fire could consume you. Your friend wasn't exaggerating when she said it was a miracle you survived." He was looking at his iPad again.

As the full impact of the detective's words hit her, Ellie's mind began to spin through a list of what she'd lost. Not only was Julien gone, her home had been destroyed. Family photos that had decorated the walls, her sunny kitchen with dried herbs hanging over the sink, her coveted front porch with its fans and swing -- too many images to process -- all rushed through her mind like snapshots in a scrapbook.

It would have to be a mental scrapbook; there was nothing left to put in a real one.

"What about our other dog, Dedé?" She blurted suddenly, unable to remember if Zyla had mentioned them both.

The detective took a breath. Ellie's eyes began to tear up. The detective replied, "The little, white one managed to escape somehow. We don't know if she was outside or inside when it happened. The fire department turned her over to Doctor Griffin to get her checked out. Zyla and the girls picked her up and have been caring for her at home. We haven't seen any other dogs. I'm sorry."

Zyla and the girls had already told her that Sadie had managed to survive, but somehow the thought of losing Dedé, her first real pet, devastated Ellie. After losing her home and her husband, it was too much. She crumpled into herself, and the detective reached out awkwardly to touch her shoulder. "Ma'am? Why don't I give you a moment to process all of this? I'll get you something to drink." Her stepped out of the room.

Ellie was too distraught to respond. She found herself crying over the dog instead of the home and husband she had loved so dearly. She knew it was irrational. Her thoughts were still so fuzzy; she had forgotten something important. She cried uncontrollably without registering what was wrong; she only knew that her world had come apart even though she couldn't feel it or remember how it had happened.

The detective waited outside, and when her cries subsided, he had Ellie sipping cool water before she could begin to feel awkward. Some part of her knew she should be embarrassed, losing control like that in front of a stranger, but she couldn't summon the emotion. The only thing she felt was emptiness and loss.

When she trusted herself to speak, she asked, "How long will it be before I can get out there? I want to see the house for myself."

The detective turned to look at her. He gave her a once-over. Finally, he breathed in through his nose. "You can explore the yard and surrounding area when you're released from the hospital, but the homestead has been cordoned off. Anytime there is an explosion like this, we have to investigate. I'm afraid you won't be able to go through the remains for a few days. The forensics team has to verify the cause was definitely a meth lab."

She started struggling to untangle herself from the tubes and blankets keeping her in place in the hospital bed. "Let's go, then."

The detective stuttered, "Now? The doctors haven't released you yet. You need to stay in bed, Mrs. Pelletier. Mrs. Pelletier -- stop!" He leaned in to the hallway and called for a nurse.

RayVynn stepped in between Ellie and the detective. "Surely this can wait, Detective Stephens. Obviously, she is in shock. It's written all over her face." RayVynn smiled sadly and patted Ellie on the back.

Detective Stephens regarded the nurse and replied, "You do your job, and I'll do mine. Stay in here, if you'd like, while I finish questioning the *only remaining eyewitness*."

Ellie's bewilderment was slowly giving way. She stopped struggling to get out of bed and sat back with a heavy *thunk*. "You can't possibly think I had anything to do with this? My God, what would possess me to blow up my house – the very one that I just spent six months renovating? And I know what you're going to ask, but no one has reason to sabotage me or my home. I mean, I don't think people here particularly like me, but no one wants to kill me."

"Okay, people. Let's be clear. I'll be taking Mrs. Pelletier's official statement now. There will be no interruptions other than what is deemed medically necessary." Detective Stephens glanced pointedly at RayVynn. Two orderlies who were cleaning promptly vacated the room.

Detective Stephens took out the ever-ready iPad and pulled up a chair across from Ellie so that he was facing her. "I just have a few more questions for you, Mrs. Pelletier, and then we can leave you to finish recuperating."

From somewhere, the detective managed to scrounge up a cup of strong, black coffee. He offered it to Ellie, "Here. Drink this. It will help clear your mind. I understand you're in a bit of shock," he glanced at RayVynn placatingly, "but I need you to focus."

Ellie took a sip and spluttered, "Hot!" The steaming coffee had scalded her tongue, but it had also startled her into awareness. Was that what the detective had intended?

He took the coffee from her. "I know how to cool it down." He took out a small flask out from an inner pocket of his jacket and poured a generous splash of something amber-colored into the cup. RayVynn tut-tutted but didn't interfere. "This should be cooler now" he said as he offered her the cup again.

He sat back in his chair and resumed taking notes on the iPad. "I already know the answer, but I need to get an official statement from you. Where were you at 3:34 on Monday afternoon?"

Ellie tested the coffee and then took a giant gulp. "I was at home. I remember being at home."

"Okay," he muttered as he tapped on his tablet. "And do you know of any flammable substances that were in the home? Did you routinely store battery acid, drain cleaner, lantern fuel or antifreeze? Were you working with paint thinner or other chemicals?" He waited for her to answer.

Ellie thought for a moment. "I'm sure we had drain

cleaner and lantern fuel. I'm not sure about antifreeze...we did just refinish the house, so maybe there were leftover paint cans. Nothing I would consider dangerous or explosive. I cannot imagine what caused it. I mean, did it start as a *fire* that "blew up" or are you talking literally about an explosion like a bomb?"

"We'll go over all that later. I just have a few more questions. Did anyone else have keys to your house besides you and your husband?"

"No, why? Has someone else been in the house? That would explain it! My husband is *not* cooking up drugs." Ellie replied, wincing when she realized she spoke of him in the present tense.

Instead of answering her, Detective Stephens asked another question, "When was the last time you remember communicating with your husband?"

"Like I said before, I'm having trouble remembering anything specific. I remember mundane things like cleaning, cooking that afternoon. I was angry about something. Maybe Julien and I were arguing? I remember something about a cook book - but that's irrelevant."

She didn't want to voice her doubts about Julien and Tai – especially now. Would she ever learn the truth? Had Julien betrayed their wedding vows? Was her ring missing because she'd taken it off in anger? Why couldn't she remember anything after being blamed for Tai's suicide attempt?

The detective cleared his throat and said, "I have one last question, Mrs. Pelletier." He paused. "When was the last time you had contact with Taiteja Jenssen?"

Ellie rolled her eyes before she could stop herself. *That little witch! God, she was tired of thinking about her! If she had anything to do with the explosion...*

Ellie felt murderous. She tried to tame her emotions, but she was sure the detective had seen the anger that had crossed her face. She took another large gulp of the liquor-laced coffee to stall. As she set the cup down, her anger erupted.

"Look, I know everyone in this hyper-critical town thinks she and my husband are having an affair, and I am SICK to death of having to defend them. There is NOTHING going on between Julien and Tai!"

"Just answer the question, ma'am." The detective continued typing. "When was the last time you saw or spoke to Taiteja Jenssen?"

Ellie groaned in frustration. "Well, at school, I guess." She thought for a moment. "No, it would have been before her suicide attempt. I guess it was when she was helping Julien with a photoshoot several weeks ago. The girls and I stopped by to watch them work for a few minutes."

"You were keeping an eye on the two of them." It wasn't a question. He continued entering his notes.

"Don't put words in my mouth!" Ellie snapped. Her animosity surprised herself.

Suddenly, her anger evaporated and was replaced by utter weariness. She leaned back against the pillow and wondered if the detective was writing comments about her. *Witness extremely defensive, hostile.*

"I'm sorry," she mumbled. "That came out wrong. I'm just...tired of my marriage being attacked, not that it matters now. I'll never know -" Her voice cracked, and she closed her eyes, pulling the blanket up as far as she could, defeated.

The detective's tone remained neutral. "Well, that's it for now. If I have any further information, I'll stop by and let you know." He paused. "I'm very sorry for your loss, Mrs. Pelletier. You seem like a nice lady, and what you're experiencing is tough. You'll get through it. Chin up!"

Ellie gave a joyless smile at his remark and let herself drift back into sleep.

# CHAPTER FORTY-NINE

### FACING FEARS

A day later, Detective Stephens had better news for Ellie. He brought the girls with him into her room. "Look who came with me to get you outta here!" He glanced at the curtains pulled tight, shutting out the sun. Her room was dark, and her mood was darker.

"Oh, really? Just where will we go?" She asked, her voice flat, emotionless. Méline, always the hopeful, optimistic child replied.

"We have a surprise for you...you'd better get ready!" Méline grinned at Bibianne.

Bibianne giggled and looked at the detective. "It is true, *maman*. And we get to ride in a police car, too! Let's go!"

Twenty minutes later, Detective Stephens rolled Ellie out of the hospital in her mandatory wheelchair. Bibianne sat in her lap and kept yelling, "faster, faster," while Méline walked beside them and shushed Bibianne.

Both girls, however, squealed as they caught sight of the patrol car. When Detective Stephens opened the door for them, they began pestering him in unison. "Can we use the sirens? And the lights? Please? Please?" The girls begged shamelessly.

Detective Stephens gave a half grin. "Well, I don't see why not. Especially since you asked so nicely." He looked at

Ellie and winked. True to his word, he blared the sirens and flashed his lights, and the girls giggled and pretended to be in pursuit of criminals. Fortunately for Ellie, the piercing sounds and lights only lasted a few minutes before they'd had enough.

Ellie was surprised at her normally shy Méline who peppered the detective with questions. Had he ever arrested anyone? Had he ever been shot? Had he ever had a high-speed car chase? Had he ever stopped a robbery? *Where did she even hear of these things?* Ellie wondered.

Detective Stephens indulged the girls and kept them entertained with tales of police bravery. Before Ellie knew it, they were driving up the gravel driveway to their home. Méline looked at her with big eyes and said, "This is not the surprise, *maman*. This is the hard part."

From a distance, Ellie couldn't tell anything was wrong. The house wasn't levelled, as she'd imagined, but as they drove closer, she could see the scorch marks on the porch. The front door was crooked and dangling from one hinge half open.

As they rounded the bend, she could see that the entire right exterior wall was missing. Burned debris was hanging out of the end of the house like stuffing on an old couch. There was, in fact, a green loveseat now resting in her side yard that was half blackened with its innards protruding. It looked like the garage had vomited the home's contents into the yard. A doll was lying face down in the burned grass along with several pairs of the girls' shoes.

Realizing the explosion had originated in the garage, directly below the girls' bedroom, Ellie gagged. The entire area was scorched. Shelves were lying scattered all over the yard with their contents -- papers, bottles, Christmas decorations, tools -- blown around the entrance extending into the side yard.

As the detective parked the car, he explained, "You can look around outside, but you are not allowed inside any part of the home. We haven't determined if it is structurally sound, and the chemical residue from a fire can be toxic, so you're only allowed ten minutes to see what you can." He paused and gave Ellie's arm a light squeeze. "I know this is tough, but you may be right to look at it. It might provide closure. And it might jog your memories. Good luck."

She looked at him and mumbled a thank you as she and the girls stumbled out of the car. The girls ran straight to their toys that were scattered about while Ellie circled the house trying to figure out if any rooms were undamaged. Looking in through the garage, she could see straight to the kitchen. The walls that had been there now had huge, gaping holes.

No wonder the detective had said it could be structurally unsound. She shivered, imagining herself or the girls going inside and being crushed by the upper floor crashing down on them. She turned around quickly to find them. "Méline, Bibianne!"

Suddenly, it didn't matter what remained of their home. Any thoughts of retrieving toys or personal items vanished. She and the girls were safe; she didn't need to see anymore.

Just then, the girls came running to her side. "*Maman,* look who we found!" Méline was struggling to carry Dedé who was quivering with her ears laid back but her tail thumping against Méline's side.

"Oh, Dedé!" Ellie gently took the dog from Méline and set her on the ground. "Are you hurt?" She and the girls examined the dog but found no visible injuries. "Girls," Ellie started, "I think our ten minutes are up. Let's get Dedé to the car, and we'll ask the detective to take her to the vet for us."

In the joy of finding the missing dog and in the resiliency of childhood, the girls seemed unfazed by the destruction that surrounded them. Ellie decided to be brave and follow their example; they seemed to have their priorities in perfect order.

On the way to the vet, Ellie voiced her concerns again about not having anywhere to spend the night. "Detective, we can't all crowd in with Zyla. Her one-bedroom cottage would never survive us and Dedé. Do you think the local motel would allow Dedé to stay overnight with us? We have no-where else to go, and I hate to leave her with the vet. She's too scared. Plus, I think it would help comfort us to be together tonight. Do you think you could pull any strings?

"Already taken care of, Mrs. Pelletier. That's part of the surprise. Right, girls?" Méline and Bibianne giggled again and looked at Ellie with big smiles. "Well, here we are ladies," the detective said as he pulled into the driveway of a small, tidy-looking brick house. He parked the car in the carport and turned to look back at Ellie.

"The First Baptist Church has offered you their parson-age which is empty at the moment. The church ladies have been here, getting everything spic and span for you and your girls. There's a small fenced-in back yard for the dogs, too. Sadie is there waiting for you. They say you can stay as long as needed. They don't expect it to be used since their preacher owns his own home."

Ellie was stunned into silence. She thought the ladies at First Baptist pretty much hated her. Wasn't that where much of the gossip originated? "I-I d-don't know what to say," Ellie stammered.

He smiled. "A simple thank you will suffice." They got out of the car and the detective escorted them to the front door. He opened it with a key and then handed it to Ellie. "You can thank them later when things aren't so fresh and pain-ful. If I know them like I think I do, you'll have supper wait-ing on you tonight and casseroles for the next week. Cooking shouldn't be a problem amidst everything else you're going to have to deal with."

That reminded Ellie of all the decisions and calls she would have to make. She groaned and sat down in the swing that hung on the front porch. She slid her hand down her face and asked, "Were any of our clothes recovered? I'm pretty sure some survived the accident."

"I'm sorry, no. The Department of Health ruled in

2013 that all low-value, high-contact materials must be destroyed."

"OK," Ellie responded, trying to be logical. "Since food and lodging are covered, the first order of business will be to find something to sleep in tonight and something to wear for tomorrow. Or at least to get some laundry detergent and wash what we're wearing now." Ellie was verbalizing her to-do list and entering full-steam-ahead into provider mode. Maybe that would help her forget about Julien. The girls walked over to her and grabbed her hands, practically dragging her inside.

"Come in and look, *maman!*" They prompted.

Instead of accompanying them inside, the detective left with Dedé, promising to take her straight to the vet. He left his card with Ellie in case she needed anything. He also told her that he would be checking in with her daily to provide updates about the investigation.

When the detective and Dedé had driven off, Ellie and the girls entered the parsonage and started looking around. It was a small, one-bathroom house from the 1950s. There was one largish bedroom that looked like it must have been the master, and then a smaller one that had been turned into a study. That was fine with Ellie. She would feel better with the girls in her bedroom anyway.

The detective had been right about the church ladies. The house smelled clean rather than musty. There was food in the refrigerator, detergent in the laundry closet, and basic toiletries in the bathroom. When she opened the closet in her bedroom, she even found an oversized sleep shirt for herself and pajamas for the girls, all with the tags still on them. *Wow! When had they had time to do all this?* She wondered. *Those First Baptist ladies must be more efficient than FEMA.* The realization hit her that she owed them a debt greater than she could ever repay.

After their brief tour, they all three collapsed on the living room sofa. Ellie turned on the TV and she and the girls watched cartoons until it was time to eat. After a wonderful chicken casserole, everyone showered and piled into the King-sized bed. Exhaustion finally took over as they fell asleep to the sounds of the Sadie's contented, light snoring.

A ping that sounded like an incoming text woke Ellie in the night. She grabbed her phone, thinking that it was Julien. Her heart dropped into her stomach when she remembered that he wouldn't be texting her – ever again. She looked at the empty spot on her ring finger.

The text message turned out to be a reminder that tomorrow the girls had dentist appointments. What was she going to do? It was overwhelming. She instinctively grabbed her phone and sent a text.

> Girls and I are fine. House is not.
> Please help – we need you!

She waited for a few seconds. Nothing. What was she doing texting her dead husband? Had she crossed the line between sanity and insanity? What could it hurt, though? No one would ever read the message. She added another few lines.

> What happened to you?
> What were you involved in?
> Why did you leave us?

Another five minutes ticked by slowly with no response. A sick feeling that had been building all day hit Ellie forcefully in the gut and rose to her throat. She jumped out of bed and ran to the toilet where she vomited up the chicken casserole in great heaving streams that left her breathless and teary-eyed. As she leaned over the toilet making sure nothing more was coming up, she began to cry.

Why had this happened? Why couldn't she remember

the accident? Why did she feel angry at Julien? Why couldn't she remember what they'd argued about?

She heaved the remaining contents of her stomach into the toilet and wondered if she'd have to live the rest of her life with the guilt, both of having argued with him before his death and of not having the chance to make amends. Try as she might, she couldn't remember what had happened, and she knew she was forgetting something important.

No! She shook her head. She could not let that worrisome seed take root on top of everything else she was feeling. Ellie would just have to move on. Eventually, time would heal this crippling wound, but until then, she'd have to do the hardest thing in the world -- *wait.*

# CHAPTER FIFTY

## *BOLD BEGINNINGS*

One Saturday morning, several weeks after the accident, Ellie and the girls were having breakfast at the tiny kitchen table in the parsonage when they heard a knock on the door. Bibianne rushed to let the visitors in before Ellie could remind her they were all still in their pajamas.

Bibianne returned to the kitchen escorting Mrs. Lydia Bennett and Mrs. Louella Baxter. Ellie wondered what could bring them over so early. The two preachers' wives quivered and smiled with what could only be enthusiasm.

Mrs. Bennet spoke first. "Good morning, Ellie, girls. I know it's early, but we were too eager to wait any longer. We have something to show you." She beamed.

Mrs. Baxter chimed in. "Let us clean up your breakfast dishes while you go get dressed. We want to take you somewhere."

Ellie tried to protest, but the ladies shushed her with their efficiency. Mrs. Bennet was already wrist deep in dishwater, and Mrs. Baxter was taking the girls to the bedroom before Ellie had processed what was happening. She let herself be guided to the bedroom where she and the girls dutifully dressed for the day.

Ellie wondered how the dynamic duo had taken over so effortlessly. She felt like a small tornado had just bustled through. The girls picked up on the atmosphere of excitement that pervaded the parsonage. They chatted to each other, "I wonder where we're going?" Bibianne asked.

"On an adventure, silly!" giggled Méline. "Let's go, *maman! Vite, vite!*"

Ellie wondered how her kids could bounce back so quickly. They had lost their home and their dad in the last six weeks, yet they seemed perfectly content to go on an adventure this early Saturday morning without a moment's hesitation and with good cheer to boot.

Ellie decided she'd follow their lead. She put on a happy face and said, "Well, okay! I'm ready if you are! Race you to the bathroom to see who can brush her teeth first!"

Moments later, they were in the church van and heading towards downtown Stusa. Mrs. Baxter was driving, and Mrs. Bennet was explaining. "Now, we know you have been through a lot over the course of this year. Being new to our community is hard enough, but you have also had more than your share of tragic events. We couldn't let you get the wrong idea about Stusa. We wanted to show you how wonderful it can be if you give us a chance."

Mrs. Baxter added, "I think today you will find that Stusa is full of people who care about you and your girls. We are willing to help if you'll let us." She cocked an eyebrow at Ellie in the rearview mirror.

Ellie was puzzled; she couldn't decide if she was being reprimanded or rewarded. The mood in the van was far too cheerful to be a scolding, so she figured maybe it was both at once. That's how these church ladies worked – all compliment-and-correct simultaneously. Their intentions were good, though, and Ellie knew they had a point. She hadn't been very open to accepting help from anyone until she had been forced by horrible events to move into the parsonage. She opened her mouth to thank them again for their generosity.

"Ladies, we are so grateful for your help at the parsonage. We couldn't have made it without you! Thanks so-"

"Oh, dearie," Mrs. Bennett cut her off. "It's not about that. We were thrilled someone could make use of that empty old house. No, no, don't thank us yet. We want to show you something else entirely." Mrs. Bennett and Mrs. Baxter beamed.

As they went under the town's one traffic light, Ellie figured out their destination - *The Jewel* - although it seemed a little grandiose to call it that anymore. After the fire at Julien's studio, Ellie had meticulously avoided passing by it, and had been careful to take another route home that didn't wind through downtown. She simply hadn't wanted another reminder of everything that had gone wrong in her life.

She saw what looked like a new sign on the front, covered with a tarp, and groaned inwardly. She didn't want to disappoint the church ladies, but if they expected her to be glad that they cleaned up Julien's studio, she would have a hard time faking it. She hadn't even begun to recover from Julien's death or the incomprehensible anger she felt at him. She didn't want to see another photography studio for the rest of her life. She leaned back against the head rest and shut her eyes.

Maybe if she just sat here, it would all go away. Or maybe she would wake up and it would have all been an awful nightmare. She and the girls would be in bed snuggled together at the comfortable, restored farmhouse. Julien would be downstairs making crepes and cappuccino. The dogs would be whining for crumbs. Ellie's life would be exactly what she had planned.

Tears collected in her closed eyes, and she stopped herself angrily. Daydreaming would not help. It would only make her pine for something that was unattainable and unhealthy. She had to be brave; she had to face her fears.

This was her life now. She had to accept it. She was a widow, a single mom, currently living on the charity of others. Her deceased husband was suspected of foul-play. There was a missing student, a destroyed farmhouse, and a job teaching kids who thought she'd bullied a girl into suicide. There really was no way to *hope* her way around the facts.

This was her reality, a waking nightmare. She couldn't see a bright side at all. Her present and her future looked entirely black.

As she'd suspected, the van pulled up in front of *The Jewel*. Mrs. Bennet and Mrs. Baxter made Ellie and the girls close their eyes as they led them to the front entrance. Ellie peeked. She felt, rather than saw, a crowd gather behind her.

"Okay! Open your eyes!" Mrs. Bennet shouted gleefully. The tarp covering the sign was being pulled down by two men with cords.

Ellie gasped.

Méline and Bibianne squealed and looked up at their mom. The crowd behind them clapped and cheered. Where there had once been a sign for Julien's photography, now hung a sign in emerald-green calligraphy.

*Tea and Tomes*

Ellie's face froze. How had they known? Just then Zyla stepped out from behind one of the columns, nervously checking Ellie's reaction. She was literally wringing her hands.

"Well, what do you think? I couldn't decide between purple and green for the sign. I thought green looked earthier. Plus, it shows up better against the color of the bricks."

Ellie couldn't think of anything to say. She swallowed. "I like the sign. I don't understand, exactly. But I like the sign. Green is perfect."

Zyla heaved a sigh of relief and grabbed Ellie's hand. "C'mon girls, Mrs. Bennet, Mrs. Baxter. Let's show her the rest! You guys," she shouted to the small crowd, "fall in behind us and wait downstairs. There are refreshments for everyone!" Another small cheer erupted, and Ellie was swept into the building.

The sight that met her made her stop in her tracks, and a few people bumped right into her from behind.

Where there once had been smoky, charred timbers and scorched brick walls, now stood a cozy café replete with small tables, a couple of over-stuffed chairs, lamps, and bookshelf-lined walls. White lights twinkled from the ceiling, giving the place a cheerful look. It was almost exactly what Ellie had pictured in her head when she'd described it to Zyla nearly nine months earlier.

At the back, Ellie could see a small galley kitchen. On the countertop sat two large mason jars - one filled with lemons and another filled with dried lavender blooms. A small chalkboard announced the house specialties – lavender lemonade and vanilla cupcakes. Ellie couldn't believe what she was seeing. She blinked her eyes several times and turned to face the crowd behind her.

"You guys!" She gulped. "How? When? This is...*perfect.*"

A round of applause exploded as soon as the word left her mouth. People started clapping her on the back, and everyone was talking at once. Mrs. Dennis pointed out the doilies she'd crocheted for each table. Mr. Evans pointed at the wrought iron staircase he had welded for her in the back. Mrs. Juniper showed Ellie the curtains she had sewn for the front windows. Mrs. Towns had donated the small lamps at each table, wonderfully eclectic and charmingly mismatched. Mr. Bruce had painted the café chairs donated from various families to give them coherence despite their differing styles.

The girls had run into the café's kitchen and were pointing out the industrial grade lemon squeezer. "*Maman,* look! It's for your lavender lemonade!" Bibianne squealed. Ellie looked over the counter area where she could make and serve drinks. Mrs. Bennett and Mrs. Baxter - *Do call us Lydia and Louella* - showed her into the kitchen behind swinging doors. It was tiny, but it was just exactly what Ellie would need to whip up cupcakes and sandwiches – *nothing extravagant* - she found herself thinking.

She hadn't realized she was getting caught up in the excitement until she found herself planning menus and ticking off a mental list of ingredients she would need. With summer holidays right around the corner, she thought she'd have enough time to get it up and running by Memorial Day. For the first time in over six weeks, she smiled.

She could do this. Stusa had given her every reason to try and no reason to doubt her little dream café any longer. There were no barriers, no excuses. Tea and Tomes was a reality. She stopped dead in her tracks and turned to give Zyla, Lydia, and Louella a ferocious hug.

"Thank you! Thank you! A thousand times thank you!" she whispered as tears ran down her cheeks. "I don't know if I'll ever be able to repay you for your kindness!"

"Oh, now. There's no need for that." Said Louella, clearly embarrassed by the outpouring of affection from Ellie.

"We'll just expect you to host all our book club meetings into perpetuity," laughed Lydia.

"With pleasure!" cried Ellie. At that moment, Mr. Evans came back to the group rocking back and forth on his heels while the rest of the crowd munched on the refreshments set out on the tables in the café.

"Ummm...Mrs. Pelletier? I'd love to show you upstairs if you're ready." He said nervously.

"What, you mean there's more?" Ellie asked in disbelief. Lydia and Louella grabbed her hands and dragged her up the beautiful staircase Mr. Evans had constructed. The black spiral staircase was a work of art itself. She oohed and ahhhed, and Mr. Evans blushed.

"You know; I think I'll leave the swinging doors open so everyone can see this gorgeous staircase!" Ellie said.

"Well, I don't know about all that, but I'm glad you like it." Mr. Evans smiled. "Me and my fellow deacons worked on this upstairs part." He paused as Ellie looked around. They had reached the top of the staircase which opened into a small sitting room in what used to be Julien's attic.

There was a cushy loveseat and a side chair with a reading lamp. A colorful, crocheted afghan covered the back of the sofa. It was just the right size for Ellie and her two girls.

"How could you afford all this?" The question popped out before she thought about how it sounded.

"Well, it's all used furniture that people no longer needed. Except the lemon squeezer. That is brand new." Lydia replied.

"And one or two things in your kitchen." Louella added.

Ellie was speechless. Seeing her astonishment, the ladies and Mr. Evans led her down a short hall. There was a bedroom on the left and a bedroom on the right. The hall ended in a tiny bathroom that Ellie realized must be right over the one downstairs. The one for customers.

The layout was perfect. Ellie's room was over the café section. Her bedroom had a large spacious window that let light in from the street side of the café. It was high enough that no one would be able to see inside, and big enough to let in the copious amounts of light that Ellie craved. She chuckled to herself. There would be no danger of oversleeping in this bedroom. She'd be up every morning with the sun, bright-eyed and bushy-tailed.

It was the girls' room that pushed Ellie over the edge and made her break into her ugly cry. The girls' room was above the kitchen area and faced the back of the lot. It overlooked a tiny fenced-in yard for the dogs. Ellie saw that there was a little balcony accessible via their window. When the girls and Ellie crowded together on the tiny balcony, Ellie looked down to see a small herb garden, already blooming with lavender, mint, and basil.

She burst into tears. "You...you've thought of everything!" She wailed, unable to hold back the sobs. "I...I can't believe it. I th-thought... you didn't even like me." She broke off due to more sobbing.

Zyla helped her back through the window. "See, Ellie?" She whispered. "I told you to give us a chance. We care. We just weren't sure how to show it until the fires wiped out everything you had."

"No," replied Ellie. "Not everything. I have my girls, my dogs," she paused, "and my *friends*." This brought on tears from everyone. Ellie thought she even heard Mr. Evans sniffling as they went downstairs to rejoin the crowd.

Ellie knew she needed to let people know how much their work meant to her. She walked over to the serving counter and climbed on top. When Méline and Bibianne saw her climbing up to stand on the brand-new counter, they stared at her.

"*Maman, mais - qu'est-ce que tu fais?*" Méline asked, wide-eyed.

"Can we come, too, *maman*? Please, please, please?" begged Bibianne.

"*Bien sûr, mes enfants.*" She lifted Bibianne up as Méline climbed on one of the barstools to reach the counter. People began to notice the Pelletier ladies climbing up on their brand-new serving counter.

The sheriff figured out what they were doing and started the call, "speech, speech, speech!" By the time they had taken their places facing the crowd, everyone was encouraging them to speak.

Ellie grabbed both girls' hands and started. "Hi, everyone! I'd like to say a few words if you can hear me over this crowd." She laughed, and people began shushing each other until there was silence. Ellie started again.

"I hardly know what to say. I am overwhelmed with feelings right now. Let's see if I can get through this without crying." Ellie smiled and swallowed. She turned to the girls and said in an exaggerated whisper, "If they only knew how much I *loathe* crying."

Ellie continued. "My girls and I are so amazed and, well - humbled, - by the unimaginable effort and generosity you have shown us. We have been through some hard times lately, but everyone here has been through hard times, too. We know our case is not unique." She cleared her throat.

"What is unique is how your community – our community – has worked to help us through our trouble. I'll confess, I did spend some time feeling sorry for myself, but from the very start, you all have been here for us – offering us food and shelter and now this – well, it's just..." She bit her bottom lip to keep from crying. "It's a gorgeous gesture. I know we'll never be able to repay you, but maybe we can at least pay it forward. You have inspired us -- right, girls?"

Méline nodded shyly, but Bibianne piped right up without hesitation, "Oh, yes! I love our new room! I can't wait to bring Sadie and Dedé and watch them play from our balcony! And then when *maman* goes to bed, Mellie and I can sneak downstairs and have tea parties and –"

Ellie cut her off, as did the laughter of the crowd. "Umm...you've kind of ruined your secret plan by announcing it." More laughter erupted as Bibianne smacked herself in the forehead and let her palm slide down over her squinted eyes and big grin. *What a ham.*

"We just have one last thing to say, everyone! Girls, in three, two, one – *merci beaucoup!*" Ellie and the girls shouted amidst more cheering.

As they hopped down from the counter, Ellie marveled at how wrong she'd been about Stusa. People hadn't avoided her out of xenophobia; they simply hadn't known how to help, or if she would accept their help. They hadn't known how to react which was understandable considering the series of troubles that had plagued them since moving to Stusa.

Starting over was never easy, but Ellie knew that with the love and support she had received from her community, she would able to face all the trials to come. She looked around at her new business-residence. She could picture the girls growing up here, working tables and learning her recipe for lavender lemonade. It wasn't how she had pictured her life, but this cafe was her present and her future. She could and would accept it.

Ellie's story wasn't ending; she was beginning a new chapter. She and the girls would endure; they might even flourish. A thought struck her. Madame Margeaux had been correct; Ellie had survived the crucible.

# CHAPTER FIFTY-ONE

## *THE SHADOW*

*The Shadow* smirked as she made her way to the Big Easy. Now that she had her beloved heirloom, nothing would stop her, and New Orleans would be the perfect place to set up shop. A tourist-stop front to hide her backdoor dealing would do nicely. Yes, she'd fit in well with the local culture.

Since Julien was out of the way, she would no longer have to compete for the heirloom's attention. His reach had gone farther than she'd known. He had been after the tome all along, chasing it through his ancestral line to Tituba's family in Barbados. She hadn't suspected his connection to the heirloom until the very end. He had played his part well, but *The Shadow* had done even better.

What she'd thought had been bad luck turned out to be good fortune. When Julien had rejected her, she'd begun an invisible war with him. By placing an infatuation spell on Julien and Tai, he had been distracted enough to miss the tome. *The Shadow* shuddered to think what could have happened if he had gotten to the tome first.

Ellie finding it was an unexpected turn. Of course, she'd had no idea what she'd really found, and her connection to the heirloom was insignificant. After all, *The Shadow's* ancestor, Abigail Williams, had been the final one to possess the tome. The fact that Ellie was a descendant of Elizabeth Proctor was irrelevant. From all accounts, Elizabeth had been a sniveling, sickly woman with no idea about the struggle for the heirloom between Tituba and Abigail.

No matter, all that was done. *The Shadow* had ended the war between the two ancient, feuding families; Abigail Williams' side had finally won. With Ellie's missing memory and Julien's death, her elemental attacks had prevailed. It had taken nothing short of an explosion, but she had broken all other connections.

*The Shadow* smirked as she thought of Julien's final act. His ultimate spell had been powerful; *The Shadow* had underestimated him. In the end, he'd chosen sacrifice over victory. When he'd cast his last spell, one to erase Ellie's memories, he'd relinquished his hold on the tome.

Erasing specific pieces of someone's memory was incredibly difficult. She'd felt the surge of power pound past her, racing toward Ellie. *The Shadow* realized what Julien was doing and had used the last milliseconds to save herself and the heirloom.

She had successfully *taken* it from both its previous disciples. Its loyalty now lay with her, and her alone. With no one to challenge her connection to the heirloom, *The Shadow* was free to reign as she wished. Gabby would be proud.

Both Tituba and Julien had made the one mistake she never would; they'd *given up* on the tome when they thought they'd lost. Tituba confessed to stop Parris's beatings, and Julien sacrificed himself to protect Ellie.

*The Shadow* wouldn't be so foolish. Just like Abigail Williams had taken Tituba's idea and perfected it, *The Shadow* had taken Julien's game and bested not only him, but Tituba's entire line. *The Shadow* wouldn't allow herself to die for anyone. The only thing she'd bury would be her old name. Gale Guillaume would be erased along with all traces of her prior life.

Henceforth, she'd be known by her true name. Under the influence of the heirloom, with no competition or prior claims on its power, *The Shadow* would live forever.

As *The Shadow* drove to New Orleans, another car wound its way to a new start on life, driven by a young, buxom blonde. When she'd learned her unborn baby was a boy, Tai had decided to make a run for it. She could never kill the baby inside of her, a boy she was going to name Barbados - Bade for short - after Julien's exotic stories. It would be a unique name, even if her child would be just another statistic. Tai would be singlehandedly raising a racially mixed child.

They needed a new life, a place to divorce themselves from the judgment of Stusa. Tai had an idea about how she could make money after the baby was born, and she had stolen enough cash to live for a few months if she was careful with her money. Tai had always wanted to live in New Orleans.

# EPILOGUE

Although six years had passed since the horrible accident that robbed Ellie of both her memories and her husband, she still came to the old home site once a month. She replenished her herb supply by picking over the ones that had sprouted up amongst the ruins, leftovers from her former garden. She especially loved the fragrant, purple hyacinth blossoms that beckoned her each spring.

Today, she'd decided to dig up some of the bulbs and transplant them to her tiny back yard. Méline and Bibianne, now fifteen and thirteen, were tending the shop, so Ellie had time to spare. She depended on the girls as much as they depended on her. They were a tight-knit trio, working hard to protect each other and their beloved tea shop.

Ellie tugged gently and used her trowel to nudge the bulbs apart. She didn't remember planting hyacinth, but her memory had been stolen by the explosion. She'd never recovered those last hours with Julien before the accident. Since his death, she'd been drawn to the hyacinths, especially after reading that the purple variety traditionally represented feelings of deep sorrow and apology. Maybe that was why she felt nostalgic each time she gathered their heady blooms.

As she prodded the dirt aside, her trowel nudged something. She brushed aside the dirt with her hands, unwilling to damage the paper-colored bulbs, when her fingers unearthed a tiny package. It looked like a dirty, old piece of folded parchment, but it felt *important*.

Made in the USA
Columbia, SC
27 August 2019